Indigo Island

Indigo Island

Books 1–4

Kaira Rouda

TULE
PUBLISHING

Table of Contents

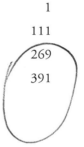

Weekend with the Tycoon

An Indigo Island Romance

Kaira Rouda

Dedication

To Jane Porter.
You rock.
Thank you.
xo

Note to Readers

Dear Reader!

Thank you for taking a chance on my first true romance! I'm a long-time women's fiction author who just knew someday she'd find herself swept away to a romantic island. And now, the dream has come true with Tule Publishing's backing of my Indigo Island series of romances. I hope you'll come to love this low country island, just off the coast of South Carolina, and the people who live and visit there. I know I do. The stories are based on a wonderful time in my life, when my children were young and we'd load up the mini van and head from Ohio down to Hilton Head, and from there take a ferry to Daufuskie Island, a very magical place much like my imagined Indigo Island. I love the Southeast – I'm a Vanderbilt graduate – and I love the Sea Islands. Join me there, won't you?

Chapter One

S AMANTHA PUNCHED THE elevator button for the top floor. She'd never been to Mr. Putnam's office but of course, she'd heard rumors about it, the starkness, the vast size. To be summoned for a meeting first thing Thursday morning made her heart race. After all, he was the boss, CEO of Blake Genetics, a genetics testing firm he'd founded after his college graduation that had become, in just 10 years, a dominant player worldwide. Blake Putnam was the man. Tall, built like Tom Brady with an athletic body that still looked good in the European suits he wore to the office every day. He was sexy, assertive, rich and very, very distant.

By contrast, Samantha felt plain, boring and unaccomplished. She'd just graduated college a year and a half before, and had worked for Blake Genetics since then. She examined her anxious expression in the reflection of the elevator walls and adjusted her simple black shift dress. Then she checked her long blonde hair anchored in a loose knot behind her back. Even though the offices were overly cool, she was perspiring and fanned herself with the white notepad in her hand as the elevator shot up to the top floor.

The doors parted revealing an expansive white marble floor, with an impressively large white desk placed in the exact middle of the space. A severe, elegantly coiffed woman sat behind the desk and seemed to float in the room of white. Samantha shivered as sweat trickled down her back.

She stepped off the elevator, which closed soundlessly behind her. The woman never looked up. This was the infamous Marlene, Mr. Putnam's personal assistant, who had summoned her. Samantha waited to be acknowledged. Rumors about Marlene's power were whispered throughout the building. Samantha felt another spurt of panic shoot down her spine.

Am I being fired?

She stared at Marlene mutely. She couldn't think of anything she'd done to warrant being fired, and she was almost certain they wouldn't handle such things on the executive floor. Would they? Samantha tried to distract herself by noticing details—Marlene's timeless face without a single wrinkle, her short, dark, edgy bob, her elegant, black pantsuit and tall stiletto heels that Samantha could barely look at without wincing. No way would she ever be able to walk in those. They looked more like weapons than shoes.

"Have a seat, Ms. Jones," Marlene said without looking up. Samantha chose one of two white leather chairs with cold metal arms. She shivered, her bare arms exposed. Her feet began to feel numb inside her sensible black pumps. She wished they'd just fire her. The waiting was more torture than she'd imagined. *Breathe*, she told herself, and started doodling a daisy on her notepad.

I'm drowning in a sea of quiet white, Samantha thought. No art. No plants. No sound. No smell. Nothing. After a ten-minute wait, spent staring at the wall in front of her while Marlene worked intently at her massive desk, Samantha was about to ask why she was here when Marlene finally spoke.

"Mr. Putnam will see you now."

Without moving from her seat, Marlene pushed a button and the stainless steel door to his office swung open. Samantha could almost hear the drum beat of doom, and she felt Marlene's eyes on her back as she entered Mr. Putnam's office.

Mr. Putnam was seated behind a glass desk, and beyond him, was a glass wall with a commanding view of the city. As she entered, he remained seated and swiveled his chair, turning his back to her. Along the far wall of his office to her left was a large fish tank with spectacularly colored fish. The other two walls were floor to ceiling glass. The air smelled of success and ocean.

Blake Putnam was on the phone. She turned around to leave, but the door had closed tightly behind her. Unsure what to do, Samantha stopped, frozen about five feet from his desk. *Breathe*, she reminded herself, even as she started to get angry about the situation. Sure, he was the boss but ordering her to what she privately thought of as his lair and then turning his back on her without so much as a nod in her direction? She tried to keep the irritation off her face.

He finished the call, swiveled his chair in her direction and waved her to the white leather chair in front of his desk. He wore a crisp white dress shirt and a black and navy striped tie, the blue matching the color of his deep blue eyes. His black suit jacket hung from the back of his black leather chair. Samantha hurried to the seat.

"Ms. Jones," Mr. Putnam tilted back in his black leather chair, steepling his hands below his chin. Samantha could see his biceps push against his shirt, but forced her attention back on his words. She waited for him to explain why she was here, but he stared at her. Samantha tried not to fidget. He continued to stare, and she wondered wildly what game was this? He could win tournaments in poker. World championships. What could he possibly be thinking? Maybe she should speak, but the longer the silence stretched, the fewer words jangled around in her brain.

"I'm impressed by how you handled the preliminary Daycon meetings. Even with all the friction over the increased rates and government regulation, you walked through all of the reasoning better than some of my more senior executives could have done, frankly," Putnam said.

Whatever she'd been expecting, it hadn't been praise. Samantha sagged in relief.

"You think well on your feet," he said.

Samantha smiled. He liked her work. He had noticed her during the meeting. And he had the bluest eyes she'd ever seen.

"You're smart, and you have a great grasp of Blake Genetics' future."

He leaned forward. "I like your presentation skills. Exactly what I need for this upcoming weekend."

Basking in his praise, Samantha almost missed the last line. She leaned forward and pursed her lips in the shape of a W, but for once managed to still her question.

"I need an associate to attend a business meeting with me. We will finalize Monday's Daycon pitch and review every aspect of the presentation."

"Me? You?"

"There will be others there. Meetings could run day and night," he continued as if she hadn't spoken. "More formal wear," he looked at her dress, "Will be required for the evening. We leave this afternoon."

She didn't know what to say. She wasn't sure what had just happened. Could she say no to the boss? Why would she?

"Samantha?" Mr. Putnam asked.

"Oh, yes, sure I'd love to work on the presentation with you. I have so many ideas. This is exciting," Samantha said, her words tumbled out of her mouth too quickly. She had dreamed of pitching her new idea to him. This could be her big break.

"Good," Mr. Putnam said, standing up. At 6'3" he towered over her. He leaned forward, both palms on his glass desk, his blue eyes bore into hers. Samantha felt small, and nervous, she stumbled to her feet when he extended his hand.

Samantha felt a shock of electricity as their palms touched, and she caught her breath. She must have imagined it. This was a business deal. Period. As she stood there awkwardly, the handshake long over, she noticed a stack of folders on the corner of his desk, her name written on the top folder.

What did that mean? Were others coming? If she'd said no, who would have been up next? Her curiosity burned.

"I will pay for your wardrobe for the weekend," Blake said. "Elegant, sophisticated attire. No short skirts, no midriff bearing dresses some girls your age are wearing. You will go to Andrea's with Marlene. It is all set up."

Samantha crossed her arms in front of her insulted. She'd never been anything but professionally attired. "I have good taste, sir," she said, taking a step back away from him.

"You will go to Andrea's with Marlene. She's set up an appointment."

"I have plenty of clothes," Samantha insisted. "Appropriate business attire," she stressed.

"Yes, but this is a bit...exceptional. That's why I selected you," Mr. Putnam said and gestured toward the stack of folders on this desk.

He picked up Samantha's and shuffled through the papers inside.

"Marlene did the research," he said, answering a question she hadn't asked. "I needed to be certain you would feel comfortable in a more...intimate, and important setting."

It was the first time he seemed less than comfortable, and Samantha practically heard the alarm bells going off. Intimate could have different meanings, but Mr. Iceman Putnam as everyone called him. And her? Ridiculous.

"I needed to be familiar with how you spend your leisure time."

That was none of his business, Samantha thought.

"You enjoy yoga, scrapbooking – whatever that is – your family had money for most of your life, you had a stable, upper middle class upbringing, and you excelled in college. Here, your work and your compartment has been nothing but the best, and aside from your relationship with Ryan Brody in sales, you've been a perfect employee."

Samantha dropped her head at the mention of Ryan's name. What a stupid mistake, she thought for the millionth time. "Yes, well, obviously Ryan was a mistake. I should not have recommended him for a job," she said quickly. "And I should have been up front about our relationship – our past relationship. I was lonely when I moved to Charlotte and I guess I let my guard down," Samantha trailed off, embarrassed.

"Don't repeat that mistake. Mr. Brody won't be at Blake Genetics much longer. I cannot retain sales associates who don't meet their performance metrics."

Samantha started to speak, to defend Ryan, but caught herself. Mr. Putnam could do whatever he wanted with his company, his employees. And Ryan was a jerk.

Mr. Putnam dropped her file folder on top of the pile on his desk and sat back down as she stood awkwardly in front of him. She could feel herself get hot.

"Here's a credit card," he said, sliding the black card across the glass desk.

"Your stylist will have outfits pulled to choose from."

"My what?"

"Make sure the labels are something to brag about," he waved his hand dismissively towards the door.

Who would have ever thought they'd hear a man say that, Samantha thought dimly as she stared at the black card? Her father had complained about her mother's trips to Costco and Target, and that had been before their financial difficulties. She didn't even know American Express offered a Black Card. Stunned, she tried to convince her feet to move.

"I expect you back to the office by three this afternoon. Shopped and packed." Mr. Putnam said. "Naturally I expect your complete discretion about our work meetings this weekend."

He picked up the telephone, another signal for her to leave.

Samantha nodded, but still she stood rooted, staring at the

card, trying to figure out what this work weekend really meant. It couldn't mean what she feared it might mean. That was impossible, right? She was being paranoid. She'd only even seen Mr. Putnam once at a meeting, and that had been at a long table with more than a dozen other people. This was an opportunity. A business opportunity. He picked her out of a stack of folders.

"This way, Ms. Jones," Marlene said.

Samantha startled out of her daze. She hadn't realized the office door was open, nor that Marlene stood waiting—poised, sleek, elegant and detached.

"Right," she said, even though nothing seemed right about this situation. She turned and hurried after Marlene not even hearing his office door swing shut behind her.

Chapter Two

SAMANTHA SAT ENVELOPED in luxury in the back of the Blake Genetics limo in a state of shock. Monday of this week she'd been dumped by her college boyfriend Ryan via text message. She'd helped get him the sales job at Blake Genetics and now he'd repaid her by hooking up with an administrative assistant in sales. She'd been focusing on her career and dreaming of their wedding while he'd been playing around.

And now just three days later, this, whatever this was. She ran her finger along a seam in the black leather seat. She wasn't completely sure what **this** entailed, but wherever they were going, she intended to prove just how valuable she was to Blake Genetics. Samantha knew she could help him nail the Daycon presentation. He viewed her as an asset to his company. This weekend could be her chance to tell him about her special project.

Marlene never looked up from whatever she was typing on her tablet.

"Oh, my purse," Samantha remembered in dismay. "My phone."

"Not necessary," Marlene's cool voice washed over her, and made her feel about ten again. "And don't even think about posting anything about this weekend on Facebook. I'm sure you know that."

"Of course," Samantha said indignantly, although she had been thinking that she would post pictures of scenery if they were going anywhere beautiful. "I would never compromise anything of a work related nature."

Marlene did look up then, eyeing Samantha with a blank expression. "Of course you won't post anything dear. That would ruin your future here."

What was the deal? Was Marlene threatening her? Did everyone who hung around Blake Putnam lose their humanity, their emotions? Or did they just hide everything better than she did?

"This is all work related, right?" She asked anxiously.

"Of course," Marlene finally said, and though her expression didn't change, Samantha felt a strong vibe of frustration. "Why would you even think anything else?"

Marlene slid out of the limo as soon as the driver opened the door. Samantha hadn't even realized the limo had stopped.

"This is the most exclusive boutique in the city. Raymond and I will tell you what you need. Remember, enjoy yourself, dear."

The bright May sunshine briefly blinded Samantha as she followed Marlene out of the car, still clutching the credit card and the note pad in her hands. The uniformed driver tipped his hat to her closing the door behind her. She would have pinched herself if her hands weren't full. She was standing in front of the clothing boutique featured in every fashion magazine in the city, probably the East Coast. Every wealthy woman in the city tried to get photographed wearing something from Andrea's. It was guaranteed to make the society pages. And she was about to go inside, and even own an outfit from there.

"We will have lunch here," Marlene said, finally pausing long enough for Samantha to catch up. "I've arranged a duplicate of all your toiletries and have purchased a luggage set. The Andrea's team has selected some ensembles for you to choose from, based on your measurements and hair and skin coloring."

Samantha had to force herself not to say something sarcastic about the beauty of freedom of choice. She was still stuck on the 'duplicate toiletries.'

"Welcome to Andrea's Miss Jones!" said a man and woman who held the double doors open and hurried her inside.

"Samantha, you're even lovelier than the photos," the man said, hugging her around the shoulders. "I'm Raymond, dear, here to help you select everything you need for your weekend."

Despite her dismay that somehow he'd seen photos of her, Samantha liked Raymond immediately. His eyes sparkled, and his smile lit up the room. He wore all black, as if on the Putnam payroll, but on him, it seemed friendly.

The woman who had opened the door for her wore a red baseball cap and gray sweatpants and sweatshirt. She didn't seem like someone who would work in a sophisticated, expensive boutique, but really, Samantha mentally shrugged, what did she know? Marlene immediately drew the baseball-capped woman aside and they were deep in conversation in the corner of the boutique.

Samantha took a moment to look around the sophisticated store. The walls were all white, the floors gray cement and the ceilings two stories high. Clothing racks and metal and glass display cases were sprinkled throughout the large room, as were elegant sitting areas of white and brown leather. Lighting hung on metal cords, perfectly illuminating each area, presenting the clothing items as art, which she supposed they were. Glass vases were filled with yellow orchids, adding the only color to the environment aside from the clothing. The shop reminded Samantha of Mr. Putnam's office, and she wondered if he owned the place.

"Walk with me," Raymond said, wrapping an arm through Samantha's and guiding her to a seating area. "You need some champagne, it will take the shock off, my darling. You were only just told about this trip this morning, right?"

Raymond returned with a flute of champagne and a crystal glass filled with ice water. "Drink up, my dear, and I'll begin showing you all the goodies."

Samantha gulped the champagne. She didn't realize she was so thirsty. As Raymond refilled the flute, he whispered, "Pace yourself, dear."

She leaned back in the couch, and finally, took a deep breath.

"Outfit One, is for this afternoon. A traveling ensemble. Simple black linen dress from Herve Leger – much more breathable than that work shift dear, although I like your thinking – paired with these sexy Michael Kors black sandals. We'll pull your hair back in a low pony, tie it with this black Chanel scarf, pop these perfect pearl studs in your ears and voila, my little Audrey Hepburn is born!"

Samantha laughed, for the first time all day. "I love it all," she said, and realized as she tried to stand up to hug him that the champagne had gone straight to her head. "Whoa," she said, sitting down quickly.

"You just stay seated dear. I only need you to try the evening options. I've narrowed it down to three, but you will need only two," Raymond said, his black eyes twinkling.

"Why do I need evening wear?" Samantha asked, startled. "And let's not go crazy. A couple pieces I can mix and match and one night outfit is more than enough for a weekend. I'm really simple."

"Yes, dear, I see you have the whole J. Crew vibe going," Raymond said. "But it's time to step up your game. You're going to be surrounded by very wealthy people. You will have twelve different 'looks', dear."

"Twelve?"

Samantha banged down her champagne flute.

"Naturally, dear. Boss' orders. Just say 'thank you, Sir' and enjoy, know what I mean?"

"Well, yes, I guess," Samantha said, feeling more uncomfortable with this situation every time Raymond opened his mouth.

"Do you know where I am going?"

"Nope," Raymond said and turned back toward his assistant who was taking another set of clothes off a wheeled in rack. "Outfit Two."

"This is so overwhelming," Samantha interrupted. "So *Pretty Woman* –ish. I mean, I have my own clothes. I'm sort of on trend, right?" she asked pointing to herself.

"Girl, you're 23. Gorgeous. Fit. Perfect little body. But, you're working hard for the money. Mr. Putnam, he's got more than he needs. If he'd like to buy you some 'business' clothes, let him," Raymond said, using the air quotes around business and making Samantha blush. "Outfit Three."

Samantha wasn't a fool. Did they all think she was? When men buy younger women things there usually are strings attached, especially when the older man is the boss. What had she gotten herself into? Who wears evening clothes at a business conference? How had she gotten herself into this mess? She'd never even spoken to Mr. Putnam before this morning, much less let him think she was interested. Or available. She stamped down the memory of the shot of electricity when they'd shaken hands. She needed to call this whole thing off. Could she and still keep her job? Samantha picked at her fingernail polish and ignored Raymond's rhapsodies about Outfits Two and Three.

"Samantha, this is Judy, your stylist," Marlene said, waving Raymond off. "She'll be doing hair and makeup, photographing you in each outfit so you'll know how to accomplish the looks on your own this weekend. Expect a lot of humidity, Judy," Marlene added.

"I packed her a lot of hairspray," Judy answered, grinning down at Samantha, a smile so broad her gums showed top and bottom, the red of her mouth matching her red baseball cap.

"I know how to fix my hair," Samantha said, annoyed that they were treating her like a doll.

Judy looked amused.

"Ta da!" Raymond said, reappearing from behind the curtain holding a wonderful and simple outfit. Samantha smiled.

"White AG jeans, tight to show off that perfect little body, a James Pearse fitted light blue shirt. Big bangle jewelry. These great gray booties from Stuart Weitzman. These gorgeous diamond and rose gold A Link small cloud diamond earrings – to die for, am I right?"

Raymond handed her the gorgeous earrings and Samantha saw the price tag – $4,450 for the earrings alone.

"No, Marlene, I can't," Samantha said, standing up, finally able to walk to where Marlene and Judy stood packing a travel bag full of brand new makeup. "No, this is too much."

She held out the earrings as if they were an explosive.

"Judy, excuse us," Marlene said and pulled Samantha over to the far wall of the store. "Look young lady. This," her sweeping gesture included the entire room. "Is what Mr. Putnam wants. What he expects. It's what you agreed to. You are living every woman's dream, you are living my dream, and boosting your career. I suggest you pull yourself together and enjoy the moment."

She stared into Samantha's eyes, her tone softened. "I know this is overwhelming dear, but truly, you should try to relax. It's business, Mr. Putnam's way. Don't disappoint him. Be thankful. Lunch will be served in an hour."

Marlene patted Samantha on the shoulder and walked away. Samantha stood alone, humiliated and confused. This is what I signed up for she reasoned. But she still wasn't clear on what "this" entailed. It was so over the top. Samantha leaned against the wall and closed her eyes. She had to get a grip.

Something Raymond had said, burbled into her consciousness. There were going to be a lot of wealthy people there. But he didn't know where or who.

"There must be a reason Mr. Putnam wants me to look a certain way, to dress a certain way," Sam said under her breath.

A sudden thought struck her. *Maybe this is actually the deal negotiation he is bringing me to, not just the practice,* she realized. Yes, that was it. Nothing inappropriate. It was business. She was representing Blake Genetics. She would need to look her best, to dress like a top executive on a weekend business conference. She could do this, accept these gifts because it would help seal the deal. And she could wear them during other work events. Mr. Putman was making an investment in her.

"Ok Raymond," Samantha said, strutting across the room in an attempt to channel an inner diva she never thought she'd need. "Bring it on. Outfit Four I think. I can't wait to see what I get next!"

"That a girl!" Raymond said, kissing her on both cheeks. "Let's do evening wear, since you're in the mood. Follow me to the dressing room. We've been instructed to photograph you in each look! This will be so fun!"

Samantha tried on a strapless bias ruffle Oscar de la Renta floor length gown – light blue to match her eyes, according to Raymond – price $7,000 according to tag – that fit her perfectly. She'd never felt like a princess before. The diamond studs and simple diamond choker complimented the dress perfectly. And she now owned her first pair of Christian Louboutin heels, thank you Mr. Putnam.

Samantha gave her practical side the rest of the morning off as she approved, if that were the word for it, a wonderful Tadashi Shoji sleeveless scallop-neck and hem cocktail dress in a vibrant blue – to make her eyes more intense, according to Raymond – price $500, according to tag – that also fit perfectly.

By the time the Monique Lhuilier Cap-Sleeve lace cocktail dress in a floral white and azalea pattern, was brought out for a Sunday brunch, Samantha had given up looking at price tags. Entire outfits along with the accessories were carefully placed in black garment bags or were placed into the new Louis Vuitton suitcases Marlene had delivered. Each item had been tagged with its corresponding number so that she would know what to wear when.

"More detailed than my first time away at camp when I was eight," Samantha joked.

Raymond's assistants smiled politely. Marlene supervised everything with the attention to detail of a surgical team nurse. She had even smiled at Samantha when she modeled the blue Oscar de la Renta gown. She knew it was silly, but it made Samantha feel better when Marlene was happy with her.

What about me makes them think I have no idea how to dress myself?

But she let it go. Samantha reminded herself to stay focused on the fun and on not disappointing Mr. Putnam. She would help him close this deal with efficiency and skill. And she'd be able to pitch him her new ideas for ancestry testing that she thought would be cutting edge and allow Blake Genetics to capitalize on the market. Samantha was on her third glass of champagne and anything seemed possible.

"Lunch is served, Samantha," Marlene said.

Before Samantha followed Marlene, she grabbed Raymond.

"I know you didn't select them so it's probably against the rules, but I love those boyfriend jeans over there. With a simple white blouse? Could we throw that in?" she asked.

"He wanted all fitted clothing, dear," Raymond said. "But you know what they say about rules," he winked. "Who doesn't take a pair of jeans for the weekend? You'll look adorable. Wear them with the gray booties, ok? Our little secret!"

After lunch of a fancy green leaf salad with chilled shrimp, avocado and artichokes, Marlene announced it was time for her hair and makeup lesson. Samantha, still a bit tipsy from the champagne and lack of bread during the meal dreaded the thought of spending time with Judy. She'd been doing her own make up since high school.

"Really? Still frowning?" Marlene said. "If you don't want to attend this business meeting with Mr. Putnam, I can still get someone else," Marlene looked at her watch. "There were five other women I had selected as candidates for this assignment. You weren't even on my radar. For some reason Mr. Putnam wanted your name added."

Mr. Putnam wanted me added, Samantha thought, a small smile crossing her face as Marlene confirmed what Mr. Putnam had said in his office. "No, I want to attend the negotiations. It's just a makeup lesson seems over the top, but I'm sure Judy can teach me a few tricks of the trade. This will be great."

Marlene stood up from the table. "Good. I don't want to have to call candidate number two, even though she is your same size and coloring. I'm glad we have an understanding. You did look simply smashing in that blue Oscar de la Renta ball gown."

Samantha stood up slowly. She briefly wondered what other woman from the office they had considered, but heard Marlene's message loud and clear: she was replaceable.

"I understand everything. I will make you proud," she said.

She didn't need Marlene changing her mind, calling Mr. Putnam and sending for her replacement. Somehow the thought of Raymond plying some unknown woman with her figure, coloring and career aspiration with champagne and an encouraging "dear," was almost as irritating as losing out this career opportunity.

"Judy," she said. "What do you suggest for my day makeup?"

Samantha climbed up onto the barstool seat Marlene indicated.

"You aren't wearing very much," Judy said, wiping at Samantha's face after she'd climbed up onto the barstool.

"No, I don't like a lot of makeup and what I do wear is organic, is that what you use?" Samantha asked.

"No, I use what works. It's all about improving your appearance, not hugging trees," Judy said, grinning widely.

Samantha bit her tongue, hoping her makeup transformation

would be quick, and knowing she could scrub it all off once she was out of here, and away from Marlene, of course.

Then a thought stopped her cold. What if Marlene were coming on this business trip? That would make sense. She was Mr. Putnam's PA. Perfectly normal for her to come. That thought made her lunch swirl uncomfortably in her stomach along with her champagne. Somehow Mr. Putnam seemed less intimidating than Marlene, but now she could be suffering their aloof superiority in stereo.

She wondered how to ask the question without appearing to care about the answer while Judy created her "daytime look," took a photo, and then scrubbed Samantha's face. Next she created the "evening look" and then the "Main Event" look. Each time she took a photo, she'd show it to Marlene who would approve it or not. Samantha realized they were forwarding the photos to someone.

"Where are you sending those photos?" Samantha asked.

"Mr. Putnam needs to approve each transformation," Marlene said evenly, not even looking at her.

Good thing because her mouth was hanging open. She snapped it shut. She was his employee, not his Barbie.

Control freak, she thought, annoyed. *He's actually trying to turn me into someone else. Her newly manicured nails curled into her palms. Well, you can change the outside, Mr. Putnam, but not the inside.*

"Another champagne, please," she said, handing Marlene her empty glass.

"You've had enough. You can hardly arrive staggering about," she said, and nodded at the reply that came through on the tablet. "We are cleared," she told Judy. "It's 2:15. The car's due back soon, and we are on a tight schedule."

"Of course," Judy murmured as she scrubbed Samantha's face one last time, applied the "travel day look" snapped a photo and smiled.

"Time to get changed!" Raymond said clapping his hands together and smiling.

Samantha jumped out of the makeup chair and hurried over to his side of the store.

"Calling Audrey Hepburn," Raymond sang out. "Try not to get any makeup on the black dress dear."

As Samantha changed into the new linen dress, new shoes and slipped the pearl earrings into her ears she looked at herself in the mirror. A stranger stared back at her.

Be strong, she told her reflection.

This is an odd way to begin a working weekend, but then again, it would be a great story to tell her friends. And she loved all the clothes, all of them. Even the dresses. She wondered when would be the best time to pitch her idea about new ancestry testing protocols to Mr. Putman. In the car? After dinner? Maybe she should wait until Saturday afternoon after he had seen more of her knowledge and negotiating skills.

"Hurry up, Samantha, I need to do your hair," Judy said, breaking the spell.

Samantha hurried out of the dressing room, with Raymond encouraging her along the way, and popped back into the makeup chair. Judy brushed her hair and secured it in a long ponytail, tied with her new Chanel scarf. Next came a furious blast of hairspray, leaving Samantha coughing in the chair.

"Effortless beauty," Raymond said, without a trace of sarcasm. "You're perfect now! I've placed all of your old things in a bag and Marlene will have them dry cleaned and waiting for you upon your return. You'll find some beautiful Hanky Panky underwear in your suitcase and some other fun underlings I picked out for you. Do have a fabulous time, hope to see you again dear," Raymond added, kissing her on both cheeks before helping her from the barstool as Judy, Marlene, Raymond and the driver all helped carry Samantha's new luggage to the car.

Samantha followed behind, still dazed, a little drunk, but all in all, happy. She'd go on this business trip, help her boss, enjoy her new clothes and maybe not hate the makeup and pitch her ancestry ideas to Mr. Putnam. It would all work out, perfectly she thought, waving at Raymond.

She slipped inside the already cool town car. Instantly they were speeding back to Blake Genetics. Samantha still didn't know where the business meeting was being held, but she was quite confident she'd be the best-dressed woman in the room.

Chapter Three

CROSSING THROUGH THE lobby behind Marlene, Samantha wondered what would happen next. She knew she had to be in Mr. Putnam's office at 3 p.m. sharp. It was 2:45 p.m., so she'd have time to grab her purse and her phone.

At the elevator bank, Marlene pushed the express button up to the suite.

"I need to go to my desk, grab my purse and my phone," Samantha said. "I'll meet you up there."

"I've taken the liberty of replacing your purse with a black Gucci tote, just to fit in with the rest of the weekend's attire. All of your belongings as well as your telephone are inside of the bag, up in the suite," Marlene said as the executive suite elevator doors opened.

The silence in the elevator made Samantha's skin crawl. What kind of cold, control freaks were these people? Samantha thought again, but since her first designer bag awaited her as the elevator doors opened, she would let it go. Just think of the day as being full of surprises, she sternly told herself. Each moment required a smile and leap of faith. And, she wished, more champagne.

The women stepped into the stark white executive floor, both of them wearing black, a perfect, and probably planned, contrast to the environment, Samantha realized. She stifled a grin remembering how her colleagues all joked that the only colors Blake Genetics acknowledged were white, black and khaki. All new employees picked up on the uniform the day they finally made it as far as their first face-to-face interview.

"Do you need to use the ladies' room?" Marlene asked, crossing the lobby briskly and then stationing herself behind her pristine white command center. She handed Samantha her new designer bag.

"Thank you. This is lovely. And I will use the restroom."

Samantha cringed at how she was starting to sound as formal and cool as they were. Marlene pushed a button at her desk and a white door opened to the right of the elevators. "Through there," Marlene said and Samantha hurried inside.

This is business *Pretty Woman*, Samantha told herself, smiling at her own reflection. Sure, she had more makeup on than usual, but she had to admit, she looked good. She didn't look like a hooker and she never had been a hooker like Julia Roberts' character, and she wasn't going to let Mr. Putnam get any ideas like that. She was just a right-out-of-college over-achiever who happened to catch the eye of the boss with her presentation skills. She should be proud of herself, she thought. So why did she feel so on edge, so uncomfortable?

She opened her new purse and found brand new Valentino sunglasses, black, with tiny V's made of diamonds. Now accustomed to all of this outlandish gifting, she just shrugged, put the sunglasses back inside the purse and told herself she was ready to face Mr. Putnam. Maybe this was when she could ask the important questions, questions such as where were they headed and who were they meeting with, for starters.

As she crossed back to Marlene's desk, Samantha realized she'd left her laptop at her desk. She'd need it for the weekend.

"I...."

"Here, dear," Marlene said, pointing to what appeared to be a laptop, in a new black leather Coach satchel.

"Thank you," Samantha said.

"He will see you now," Marlene said, pushing the button

that caused Mr. Putnam's door to swing open. Samantha glanced at her new Platinum Cartier watch: precisely three o'clock.

"Are you coming too?" Samantha asked.

"No dear. Remember, this is your time to shine. You have everything you need," Marlene said.

Samantha smiled at Marlene and noticed a slight smile back before she walked back into the sterile whiteness of Mr. Putnam's office. The door closed behind her. But, she was alone in the large office. He was nowhere to be seen. Could Marlene have made an error? Samantha checked her watch and sighed with relief. She was on time. And suddenly, there he was, appearing as if by magic from a concealed door on the opposite wall.

Samantha felt her mouth completely dry up. Quite a feat after all the champagne she'd downed as well as the water and coffee hoping to sober her up to handle any meetings this afternoon. He glanced at his watch.

"Good. Right on time," he said. "I like that outfit. Nice choice."

"Um, thanks," Samantha said, unsure of the correct answer in such a situation. There had been no 'choice' about any of it. He'd approved all of the outfits before Raymond could even show them to her.

Control freak.

"Ready?" he asked.

"Yes, sir," she said.

"Samantha, since we are spending the weekend together, it would be appropriate for you to call me Blake."

She stared into his blue eyes. He was gorgeous. Really gorgeous. She felt dizzy. She was drowning in blue.

"That is what business associates do," he said.

"Of course, Blake," she said feeling bold and far older than twenty three.

They were business associates.

"Come," he said, opening the door he'd just emerged from

and she followed him out the door.

Blinding sunlight. They were outside. The top of the Blake Genetics building. It was terrifying and unexpected, and Samantha fumbled around in her new purse, trying to find her new sunglasses as she hurried to keep up with Blake, who had just turned a corner in front of her. She broke out in cold sweat and could barely catch her breath. Samantha's fear of heights was well known – why wasn't that in his precious file on her? What was he trying to do? Kill her after dressing her like she was a cover model for *Town and Country*?

Trying not to look at the horizon and only the glare off the ground under her feet, Samantha rounded the corner. She heard the whoosh of something mechanical. She looked up and spotted Blake already climbing into a white helicopter, emblazoned with Blake Genetics on the side.

Samantha froze against the wall and squeezed her eyes shut. They were traveling in a helicopter? A tiny, white tin can with a propeller on top? She didn't even know the company had a helicopter. No way was she getting in that thing. She'd take a cab. She'd drive herself and meet him there. Her luggage alone wouldn't allow that hunk of metal to get off the ground.

"What the hell is wrong with you?"

She didn't realize he'd come back for her and could barely hear him over the thump of the rotors.

"I'm not getting on that thing," Samantha said. "I can't."

"Yes, you can and you will. We have an agreement."

"You said nothing about a helicopter," she said, her voice jerky with panic. "I'll drive and meet you there."

She braced herself because he looked angry. Not even her father had glared at her like that when she'd backed into a wall when she was sixteen.

"I have a Prius," she said shakily and waited for him to fire her or…

He laughed.

"A Prius."

"Yes," she said cautiously.

"Does it float?"

"What?" She was starting to hyperventilate. She could feel it. Her vision was black around the edges. This had happened on a school trip to New York on the Empire State Building.

"We're going to an island."

She swallowed hard. Island. It was as if her life flashed in front of her eyes. No chance to show off her knowledge. Her skills. No promotion. No chance to pitch her ancestry idea.

"I…you'll have to take the second girl," she whispered, trying to back away but unable to move, fear keeping her frozen, and the wall blocking escape.

"Too late."

"I'm afraid of heights," she confessed as if that weren't totally obvious.

"Close your eyes."

"They are closed," she whispered, too scared to even feel stupid.

"Keep them closed. Do you like swimming?"

"Yes," she was puzzled about the last question.

"Think of swimming," he told her and then picked her up.

"What are you…?" She struggled against him, but then she saw the edge of the building and sky and scrunched her eyes shut again.

He strode easily with her across the roof of the building, and Samantha was too scared to move. What if he tripped? Dropped her off the building?

Then she was seated, and she felt the back of his hands brush across her shoulders and breasts, the she heard the click of a seatbelt. Then the door slammed, and it was a lot quieter. She sat upright and fumbled with the seatbelt.

"You can have all the clothes back," she said. "I don't want to ride in a helicopter," she finished on a squeak as the helicopter lifted off from the building.

She scrunched her eyes shut again, and wished she knew a prayer or something. Then she felt his fingers brush her cheeks. Something was placed over her ears, and then she could hear him.

"Keep your eyes closed if you need to. It's not a long trip."

She could still feel them moving, flying through the air, and she was trapped, scared and alone.

"I just don't understand what you want from me, Mr. Putnam," Samantha said, tears welling up in her eyes. She knew she shouldn't cry, she'd ruin her daytime travel makeup. She just couldn't help it, she was so scared, so confused. The sun was hot, and they were up so high.

"Calling me Blake would be great for starters," he said, the irritation plain in his voice. "Here, Samantha, focus on some reading material. This should explain things better. Take some deep breaths, we will be there soon."

A thick paper card dropped in her lap. Samantha breathed in and out and counted to ten. Counting was good to calm down wasn't it? Cautiously she opened her eyes and touched the thick cream paper stock. The words were engraved in simple gold script, but Samantha's fear kept her from reading. All she could feel was luxury.

"I still don't understand," she said. It looked like a formal invitation, a wedding invitation. "I thought this was business."

"It is business," he said. "Business first. My sister's wedding is this weekend. She's my only sister."

Samantha forced herself to keep her eyes open, to focus on the letters, at least a few of them.

"Obviously I have to attend. And I definitely need to work."

The pieces began to fall into place, but Samantha couldn't quite believe the picture they made.

"If I didn't bring a date, my mother would have set me up again. I cannot deal with any more stupid conversations or artificial set-ups or playing nice with some entitled, vapid society woman," his voice rang with distaste. "I'm focused on the Daycon deal and as you know, it's supposed to close next week," he said. "So you are my date, but really my work assistant for the weekend."

"We're going to your sister's wedding," she repeated slowly.

"And finishing up the details of the Daycon deal."

He emphasized the last part to make it sound more reasonable, she supposed.

"Don't look so shocked. It is business. You'll have your own room. We're going to my family's plantation on Indigo Island. They'll be some social events of course, which you'll attend with me as my date, but we will have plenty of time to work."

"Date? What exactly does being your date mean?" Samantha asked.

She found if she focused on the little details, the faint line in his suit fabric as it stretched across his back, she could ward off motion sickness. But everything he said made her feel more anxious.

"A date. Like we're dating. But nothing…," he paused. "I'm not physically demonstrative in public. My family knows that so," he spread his hands out, fingers wide as if that somehow gave her the answer to her question.

He turned around in his seat so he could face her. Samantha could see her pinched pale features reflected in his Aviators.

"I know it's a bit different from what you agreed to," he smiled, but it looked strained. "But it's really the same deal. Just business. We'll knock out the presentation. You can swim in the ocean, walk on the beach, have some fun and we'll have some…meals together. With my family."

He didn't sound excited about that part.

"I have no expectations of you other than being pleasant to my family, acting friendly towards me in public, making intelligent conversation and being willing to work on the presentation with me when time permits."

She nodded. That sounded like business, but she could feel the anger bubble up and surround her. The clothes made more sense now, but that made it worse. He should have been upfront. Why hadn't he been? There must be more, she thought, heart thumping unevenly even though she wasn't allowing herself to look beyond the weave in his fabric.

She had to do this now, though. This was her career. She loved her work at Blake Genetics. She'd already been given more responsibility than many of the team members who'd been there longer than she had. But he was a control freak. And manipulative. He hadn't told her it was a family wedding. That she was a date.

"Are we supposed to have been dating long?" She finally asked after he'd turned around and a long silence stretched between them where he'd spoken exclusively to the pilot on a different channel.

He didn't answer. She took a deep breath. He was her boss, but he needed her. She wasn't going to let him push her totally around. She tapped him on the shoulder and he turned around.

"Aren't you worried at all about the no – um – relationship clause in the employment agreement?" Samantha asked. "I mean, I know this is pretend, but if Betty in HR hears..."

"I'll handle Betty," he said, his jaw clenched. "Besides this is a working relationship. I'm not opening myself up for a lawsuit. Samantha, I do really hope you enjoy yourself. My family is great and the island is amazing. We'll get the presentation done and the rest is just dress up." His eyes sparkled a bit, before he turned around and started talking to the pilot again.

She did have plenty of options for dress up, she realized, feeling a spurt of relief. And she'd never been to this Indigo Island before, although she had spent some time in Hilton Head. She focused on the invitation in her hand, trying to learn more about all the activities she would be expected to attend as the pretend date. Why couldn't he have just been honest, she thought again, angry enough she could scream, so afraid she would be sick.

Focus on the invitation, she told herself.

There were three different events planned by Avery Putnam and her husband to be – beach barbeque, rehearsal dinner and the wedding itself. Now she realized why she had all the outfits, the depth of everyone's deceit, even Raymond's, and now, her own as she showed up at his family home as his date for a wedding. Weddings were sacred events, Samantha thought. She was crashing Avery's wedding, lying to his family.

Her heart plummeted into her chest as they shot out over the city, out over the roads, over the buildings and above the rest of her normal life heading east toward the ocean. Looking down she saw golf courses, and the carefully manicured homes and shops and restaurants of Charlotte. Looking into the front seat of the helicopter, all she saw was a controlling man who had tricked her into being his date with the promise of sparkly clothes and access to him to advance her career.

No way they'd be able to keep this quiet. She'd heard all the speculation about others in the office. She'd be the topic of all the office gossips again, that was for sure, as she had suddenly and quite accidentally become Blake Putnam's paid arm candy for his sister's wedding weekend. Samantha rummaged in her new purse and found a tissue, using it to wipe below her eyes as the tears softly flowed. She was thankful for the huge sunglasses.

No, she told herself, the roar of the helicopter blades undermining her resolve, this wasn't a time for sadness. This was a time to be angry. She'd been tricked. Easily tricked, but she was not the person who was wrong. Blake was tricking his family. And once they got to the island, he would need her cooperation to make the trick come off. The realization made the tears finally stop. She dared to open her eyes again, and looked down. She spotted the signature red and white striped lighthouse of Hilton Head and tried to take a deep breath and enjoy the view just as the helicopter shot out over open water.

She closed her eyes again.

Chapter Four

I F SHE ALLOWED herself to look down, she would have seen the sparkling blue water of Calibogue Sound. But she couldn't. The roar of the helicopter propellers filled her ears and her mind was just as loud, wondering what she would do once they landed. What did she want to do? She wanted to scream. Or be sick, as her stomach was dangerously close to it. But neither of those were good options, especially wearing her new outfit, so she decided once they landed, if they landed, she'd never talk to Blake again.

Well, after this weekend. She had to keep her word, to keep her job. And it was better to have a job when looking for one. She felt another burst of anger. She loved her career. The long hours and intellection stimulation energized her. She had great ideas. She didn't want Blake and his fake date idea to affect her career. But maybe it wouldn't.

After this weekend, he'd owe her. She wasn't powerless. If she pulled this off, he'd have to listen to her ideas about the new ancestry testing. And then with her ideas and drive, she'd be promoted. It was just a weekend. She could fake friendliness. She'd pretended confidence in job interviews. She'd projected expertise during negotiations when nerves had fluttered in her stomach. She would just pretend friendliness towards Blake.

She'd always wanted to see how the one percent lived. This weekend would be an education she decided, once she got off this horrible helicopter. Life required attitude, and once she stopped feeling so sick and panicky she was going to charm everyone, including Mr. Too Busy To Find A Real Date.

Really it was a win-win, Samantha told herself as she fingered the wedding invitation. Career win for her. Ego win for her because Ryan would hear about this weekend. And Blake would win because he would have a hard working, smart and ambitious team member who would help him close this Daycon deal with ease.

Promotion here I come.

She needed the promotion. And more money. Since her father had fallen victim to the real estate bubble and lost everything including Samantha's college funds, he'd eventually succumbed to despair and depression and killed himself. Samantha had been left with grief and then a staggering college loan amount she was barely putting a dent in. She needed to move up the career ladder so she could start saving for other things—a house for starters. She'd prove her value to Mr. Putnam.

"Blake," she reminded herself. A girlfriend would call him Blake.

She wondered what he would do if she touched him, held his hand in front of his family. The idea gave her a thrill of fear. Would serve him right. Date.

"Still with us?" Blake asked into the mouthpiece, filling her ears with his mumbled voice and reigniting her anger.

"Yes," Samantha lied, keeping her eyes tightly closed as Blake's deep laughter filled her ears.

Maybe she'd kiss him in front of Avery or his mother. What would he do then? She almost laughed at the thought of kissing the block of ice. He could hardly push her away without giving up his secret. She'd never have the nerve to do it, but still, she gazed at the back of his head where his dark hair lay so thick and springy and wondered what it felt like. Silky. If she were kissing him, she'd spear her fingers through his hair and let it slide through her fingers. Her palm tingled. Sometimes, her imagination was too vivid.

Chapter Five

BLAKE AND CHARLIE, the pilot, were old friends from boarding school, so they'd been catching up most of the flight. Charlie tried to get Blake to talk about his new girl in the backseat, but Blake deflected the conversation. He could imagine Charlie's curiosity as he hadn't brought another woman to the island since.... He stopped that train of thought.

Every time Blake glanced behind him, Samantha looked miserable, the color drained from her face, eyes closed, head resting against the inside of the helicopter. He hoped she wouldn't throw up. His sister, Avery, threw up in the family helicopter one year, on the way from Atlanta to Indigo Island. She had been young, but still. They'd all had to endure the rest of the flight with that nauseating smell permeating the helicopter's cabin. This weekend was going to be challenging enough without starting it off all wrong.

He hoped he'd made a good choice. This had all been Marlene's idea. She'd pulled the files on all the attractive single women who worked for the company and ran background checks on them all. Samantha hadn't been included in the original batch, but after he'd seen her performance under fire at a meeting, he'd told Marlene to pull her file.

"I don't really care which one it is, Marlene," he remembered telling her. "I just need someone discreet, polite and capable of handling my family. No drama. I just want to fly to the island, make it through these blasted events, and leave in one piece with all my energy intact for the big merger talks."

He'd barely looked at the headshots, well, not entirely true. He had lingered a bit over Samantha's, but then he'd closed the file, determined to let Marlene handle the task. Only really, she hadn't, not the way he'd initially planned. He hoped he didn't regret his impulse. He still didn't fully understand what had come over him, and why he had let, putting Samantha Jones' file back on top.

He had promised himself he would be completely logical with relationships with women after the disaster that had been Jane, his long-term college girlfriend, who had nearly become his wife. She had been wrong for him in so many ways, yet how she'd wrapped him around her finger was still a mystery. None of his friends had liked Jane, in fact, they all urged him to break up with her all during college, but somehow she'd held him enthralled for five long years, until she'd broken his heart. No woman would ever be allowed that close to him again.

So Samantha had made first cut, and he'd then casually put her folder on top and said something about starting with her. He'd pretended to ignore Marlene's piercing, questioning look. Blake now mulled over what he knew about her other than the obvious physical charms, which were proving to be more of a distraction than he had expected, but so far he knew she was prompt, and efficient. Her work reviews raved about her diligence, initiative and intellect. Her upbringing would make her fairly comfortable with his family's old Southern money elegance. Yes, he'd chosen well. His mom would love Samantha's blonde Audrey Hepburn look. His dad liked anybody his boys brought home so he wasn't worried about fooling his old man.

Blake thought back to the moment Samantha froze on the rooftop near the helipad. Even with the oversized black-rimmed sunglasses covering half of her face, Blake had seen the terror wash over her. He'd been irritated by her fear, but there hadn't been time to pick someone else. He just hoped she didn't have any other phobias. At least she hadn't made a fuss once he'd buckled her in the helicopter.

Now, he'd wished he had asked her about motion sickness. Maybe he'd send her back on the ferry after the weekend was over. *Yes, that was a perfect idea*, he thought. She didn't need to be back as quickly as he did, and by Sunday afternoon, their act would be over. Everything would go according to his plan. Things always did for Blake Putnam. He made sure of it.

SAMANTHA FELT HER stomach lurch into her throat, and she opened her eyes to search for a barf bag but realized the helicopter was dropping and before she knew it, they'd landed on an orange helipad. *Thank God*, she thought.

The roar of the propellers faded away quickly and Blake hopped out of the front seat, climbed down and disappeared. The pilot climbed out and opened the door for her. Samantha sat frozen, not trusting her legs to be able to walk down even a couple steps.

"Wasn't that a blast, Samantha?" the pilot asked, expertly unbuckling the safety harness while Sam sat motionless. "Did you see that huge pod of dolphins? Hey, you Ok?"

"No," she answered, trying not to cry.

"Oh, no, here, let me help you," the pilot said, climbing backwards down the stairs and half-carrying Samantha behind him.

Once back on solid ground, Samantha felt better. The helicopter pilot handed her a cold water bottle and Samantha gulped it hoping to settle her nerves and stomach. A white golf cart with a script P painted on the side in orange waited and their luggage had been loaded in the back.

"Ready to meet the family?" Blake said, impatiently looking at his watch.

"Oh, yes, I've never felt better. Thanks for asking," Samantha said, glaring at him before finishing the water bottle.

"Maybe you should take something for your stomach before you travel," Blake said.

"Maybe I will if I know how and when I'm going to travel," she snapped before she could stop herself.

He stiffened.

"Next time you pick a file, you might want to mention the helipad."

"Are you planning to snipe at me all weekend?"

"Nope," she screwed the cap back on the bottle.

"Good," Blake said, and turned away.

He walked to the golf cart, greeted the driver and climbed into the front seat, of course, leaving Samantha to walk over on shaky legs by herself. She made it, smiled at the driver and climbed into the back seat alone. She realized now how she'd underestimated the power of the weekend. She'd be miserable all weekend, not knowing what was coming next and expected to follow behind Blake like an obedient dog. She wouldn't be able to handle his aloof and condescending personality through cocktails much less dinner. She'd mess up and be out of a job by Monday.

Chapter Six

B LAKE WISHED THERE was more than water in the bottle he was chugging as he sat next to the driver, with Samantha in the back seat of the golf cart. Soon he'd be dealing with his entire family, something he tried to avoid whenever possible. He loved them all, individually. In groups, well, they were overwhelming. Especially his two brothers, who were, by their choices, proving themselves to be as weak as his own father.

James already worked for Putnam Industries and was the heir apparent. Putnam Industries was one of the largest paper companies in the U.S. His family was responsible for more deforestation than he could swallow – and they continued to be despite the grave environmental warnings. Nearly four billion trees worldwide are cut down each year for paper. Those numbers disgusted Blake in a digital world, even as it made his family even wealthier. World consumption of paper had grown 400 percent in the last 40 years. Every board meeting Blake attended left him in despair.

"People still need paper, son," his father Richard would tell him whenever he mentioned the trees. "Don't be a tree hugger. You know we have a massive reforestation program. And Putnam Industries employs thousands. Without us, what would those people do for a living?"

Blah, blah, blah was all Blake heard. His grandfather had started the business back in 1898, and today it had grown to more than 60,000 employees, headquartered in Atlanta where everyone in his family still lived, except Blake. The company prided itself on being the largest producer of plastic lids and paper cups, manufacturing for fast-food giants like McDonald's, Wendy's, Subway and the rest. All Blake envisioned was the ever-expanding plastic garbage dump in the middle of the ocean, a dump with his family's logo floating on top, choking everything in the seas.

As much as Blake was angry with his father and with how James was steering the business, Blake had loved his grandfather. He was such a visionary. Blake was certain his grandfather would have rolled the entire business into a model for the future, renewable paper or something, instead of the past. That's what Blake would do with his genetics company. He would help people, help decode disease, provide individuals with answers. Save things, people, animals and plants, instead of killing trees and all that depended on them. His short-sighted and selfish family chose money over the earth, the familiar over innovation.

Blake also wished he could just drive himself somewhere, but no, he was back with his family and that meant being driven. And it meant being polite to the drivers like John who was driving the golf cart now. All the Putnam kids were grown and capable of driving themselves, but his family insisted on being driven around the estate. Some of the people who worked here had actually worked for Blake's grandfather, too, and probably had a stronger backbone than any of the Putnam men, he thought.

"Thanks John," Blake said as he pulled the golf cart up in front of the main entrance of the Putnam's Indigo Island Plantation estate. Blake hoped Samantha would get over her motion sickness soon. He needed her making a good impression from the start, so he wouldn't have any worries this weekend. And she looked much better when she smiled. A smile he hadn't seen since they'd lifted off from the flight pad on top of his office building.

"We're here, Samantha," Blake said, and after hesitating, he stretched out his hand to help her from the cart. Her touch felt stirring. Her hand was small, and soft but the electricity was powerful, a current between them, even more intense than in his office. He found himself trying to see her eyes, her expression behind her sunglasses. Why had he let Marlene pick such a big pair? He had held her hand too long, he realized, and dropped it, breaking the connection.

"Welcome to the Putnam's," he said, realizing he had to be smoother than this.

He would have to touch her to appear normal, but when he touched her, he felt…. He stopped that train of thought.

"This is a house?" Samantha asked. "Your house?"

She gazed up at what was a replica of an original plantation house built at the turn of the century for one of the wealthy indigo farming families. At one point, the indigo plant grown to make dye had been a bigger crop on the island than oysters, Blake knew. But now, of course, Indigo Island's biggest crop was its wealthy southern families and their second, or third, homes.

"It's a replica of the plantation home that used to be here, one that was wiped out by a hurricane decades ago."

She listened to him intently, and Blake, who loved history, continued.

"Mom researched the history and while it has all the finest of everything modern, she tried to make it seem like it has always been here. Of course the two wings on either side are contemporary," Blake added.

"Of course," Samantha said, and somehow, that two-word response left him feeling both spoiled and clueless. Two things he despised.

"Are you mocking me?" Blake asked, his voice hushed to a whisper, anger flowing through his veins replacing whatever positive energy had been there a moment before.

They were climbing the brick stairs up to the main wrap

around porch. Samantha stopped and took off her sunglasses.

"Why would you think that?" She asked.

Blake stared down into her guileless eyes and had no idea what he'd been about to say.

"Blake," his mother flung open the door. "You are finally here."

She enveloped him in a hug, but he could see her attention immediately fixated on Samantha.

Even though his mom had never been the cuddly, play-on-the-floor-with-you type of mom, Blake respected her. Evalyn was elegant, refined and strong. The one in the family most like himself, Blake thought.

He kissed her on both cheeks.

"Now the family is all together," she pulled away from him slightly and ran her slim fingers through her blonde hair, cut in a stylish bob.

"Are you going to introduce me?" She teased and smoothed the skirt of her floral cocktail dress and pink shoes. "We've all been taking bets on who would be skilled and intriguing enough to pull you out of a board meeting for a date, much less a second date or maybe even a third."

Her eyes scanned Samantha intently.

"Mother, this is Samantha Jones," he said, and exhaled as Sam's face lit up with her signature smile, and she stepped forward to shake his mother's hand.

"None of that," she said, and quickly hugged Samantha. "So nice to meet you dear," Evalyn said. "Please come inside you two. This afternoon heat is intolerable."

SAMANTHA GAVE MRS. Putnam her best fake smile and then felt guilty. She seemed so warm and nice. How did she end up with a son as cool as Blake? Samantha still wanted to give him a piece of her mind for not telling her about the wedding and the helicopter but, seeing how happy his mom was to see him made Samantha remember her role in this whole set-up. She was to be seen, to smile, and not to be heard. She didn't matter aside from being a quiet, manageable presence so Blake didn't have to answer uncomfortable questions.

She was not going to let this business opportunity pass, though. She was going to charm his family so much that he'd be begging to hear about her ancestry testing. If he'd just keep his hands off her so she could concentrate. Twice now he'd touched her, and she'd felt like a live wire. What was up with that? He was hot, but so not her type. Controlling and aloof.

He'd felt the chemistry too, she thought with a stab of smugness. He couldn't let go of her fast enough. Good. She wanted to make him uncomfortable.

They followed his mother through the house. Samantha felt as if she were in a museum. She wanted to stop and look at everything, but Evalyn set a brisk pace, clearly with a destination in mind. Focus, Samantha reminded herself. Show Blake what she was made of.

They entered an opulent room where quite a few people were sitting in small groups or standing about in front of the floor to ceiling windows that looked out over the green, rolling lawn and the Atlantic beyond. Immediately Samantha could feel the hot stare of a man, who stood up when she entered. She quickly broke eye contact and without thinking, stepped closer to Blake.

While Blake introduced her to each of his siblings—the oldest James, his sister Avery and finally the baby, Denton – Samantha smiled and shook hands. They were all gorgeous just like Blake, tall, blonde with sparkling blue eyes. The boys all had what must be the Putnam build. Broad shoulders tapering to a thin waist.

Avery, the sister, was glowing from a hint of a suntan and

also because it was her big weekend. But even as she chatted with Avery, oohing and aahing over her gigantic engagement ring, Samantha felt tingles on the back of her neck, and when she looked past Blake, to her left, she saw the man staring again. This time, he flashed her a big smile.

He stood alone, leaning against a white wall, at the edge of the circular entry area, taking in all of the introductions, but not participating. He was incredibly sexy, with dark brown hair, dark brown eyes and he was tall enough to be seen over the heads of all the Putnams. But who was he? And why was he staring at her?

"You are doing well," Blake said, appearing next to her. "You've met almost all of my family. Just missing the old man."

"They are all very nice, but none of them have dates." Samantha said.

"Not true. James and Denton's dates are walking the beach and Avery's fiancé is over there, next to his brother Max," he said, pointing to the man who had been staring at her.

Avery's fiancé, and his brother, began heading toward them.

"We're all not so sure about him, but Avery is, so what are you going to do?" Blake said. "Mom's tried to break them up for years, but it just made them closer. Let's go get a drink."

"Hey Blake, good to see you. I'm Mark, Avery's fiancé," the man said to Samantha reaching out to shake her hand.

"Nice to meet you," Samantha said.

"And I'm Max," he said, winking at Samantha and kissing the top of her hand. "You are gorgeous."

Samantha blushed uncomfortably. Blake placed his hand on the small of her back. "We were just going for a walk," he said. "See you both later," he added, gently guiding Samantha away from the two men. His touch had made her stomach flip, and Samantha thought she saw Blake shoot a warning glance at Max, but she wasn't sure. She did know she loved the feel of Blake's hand on her back, it made her feel safe and protected. And his possessiveness gave her a bit of a thrill, which she shouldn't even admit to she admonished herself sternly. She was his fake date. He was her boss. Hot but unattainable. And she didn't want to attain him.

The minute they left the room, his hand dropped from her back, and Samantha wondered if she were imagining the chemistry, the possessiveness, but maybe he was thinking of her as his intellectual property for the weekend. No different than his laptop. That was deflating, but he could hardly let Max flirt with his date, Samantha realized. And she didn't want him to flirt with her. Max had made her uncomfortable. She better avoid him.

Samantha nearly stumbled into Blake as she followed him through the house. She'd expected the house or hotel where the wedding was to be beautiful, but this was over the top amazing. They had entered a home beyond her wildest dreams, where dark wood floors, crystal chandeliers, and stark white walls were accented by huge arrangements of red and white roses in glass vases everywhere Samantha could see, in every room beyond the grand staircase in front of her.

They entered a room off the foyer that appeared to be a replica of a men's drinking club from the turn of the century. Big leather chairs were arranged around oversized tables and a large wooden bar lined the back wall. The views out the front windows were directly to the ocean.

"This is gorgeous," Samantha said. "The room, the view. I can't wait to explore the island. We, I mean, I will have time, right?"

"Of course," Blake said. "When we are not working."

"Of course," she echoed feeling like he was reminding her of her purpose, as if she could forget the whole reason she'd agreed to come on this crazy scheme.

"What can I get you?" Blake asked and headed behind the bar. "Bloody Point Bloody Mary?"

"What's a Bloody Point?" Samantha asked.

"Son, you haven't told her the family secret," Blake's father

Richard said, as he walked into the room and wrapped Samantha up in a big hug. "Nice to meet you young lady. You are sure a beauty. Come here Blake. Give your old man a hug!"

Samantha watched as Blake's dad hurried to hug his son. It was like foreshadowing, Samantha realized. Blake would look just like this man, 30 years from now, and it was an impressive sight. Blake's father was slim with the same Putnam blue eyes but with gray hair instead of blonde. He was wearing white golf shorts and a bright orange golf shirt, the Putnam Industries colors. He looked fit, and happy and in the prime of his life.

"So my dear, have a seat and tell me all about yourself," Richard said, settling into the oversized leather arm chair across from her while Blake finished making the drinks. "I hope you're making me one, too, son."

"Of course, dad," Blake answered, "Tell her about Bloody Point."

"Right. The history of this island is actually quite tragic," Richard said as Blake placed a Bloody Mary glass in front of each of them and took a seat next to Samantha, sharing her chair. He was really putting on a show now, Samantha smiled but found it difficult to concentrate because she was distracted by Blake's proximity. She felt the heat of his thigh through his khaki pants, and she felt a warm sensation deep inside. She took a big sip of her Bloody Mary, wondering if she could handle this at all.

"Bloody Point, the piece of land where we're sitting but also the tip of the island right out there was named for the bloody ambush that took place back in 1781," Richard said. "It was just after the Revolution and of course, as always, this island still kept her secrets, and her secret residents. In this case it was the Tory Loyalists – those folks loyal to the British and in most cases related to the first British Land Grantee Thomas Cowte back in 1707. For some reason these Tories got together and attacked Hilton Head's Skull Creek Plantations in 1781."

"What is with all these names, creepy," Samantha blurted before she could stop herself, trying to focus on the story, and not on Blake.

"I know, it's very rugged here on Indigo Island," Richard said and took a big drink. "Well after the Tories attacked them, the Revolutionary War Patriots of Hilton Head formed the Bloody Legion and retaliated by attacking the homes on this island. Apparently these row boat skirmishes, as they were called, happened all during the Revolutionary War. Only that sound out there separated the Indigo Island Royal Militia from the Blood Legion of South Carolina over there on Hilton Head."

"Ok dad, I'm sure Samantha's not the history buff you and I are," Blake said, his dimpled smile busting out.

"Actually, I am," Samantha answered, noticing the approving nod sent her way by the elder Putnam. "I was a history major at Vanderbilt."

"Beautiful and smart, too," Richard said. "So how long have you two been an item?"

"About six months," Blake said, smiling down at her and pressing his thigh more closely against hers. "Right Sam?"

"Right," Samantha said, as her stomach fluttered. She didn't have to fake her embarrassed giggle.

She took another drink of her Bloody Mary.

"Are you a tree hugger, too?" Richard asked, and Samantha felt Blake stiffen next to her.

"What do you mean, Mr. Putnam?" Samantha asked.

"My middle son here thinks our family business is killing the environment. He doesn't believe our new policies are making any difference. That's why he started his own thing," Richard said.

Interesting, Samantha thought, but said, "Yes, I am concerned about the environment and all the toxins in our food and water and even in cosmetics. I guess I would consider myself a tree hugger, but I don't want to imply anything against your business. I don't know enough. I do know what Blake has started with the genetic testing business will be revolutionary, hopefully saving lives and improving the environment for future generations."

"Well, young lady, you are very impressive for a tree hugger," Richard said, his eyes twinkling. "You two seem well suited, and you know, Blake, your mother and I didn't date for more than six months, if you can believe that! Now, 37 years later we're still going strong," Richard said. "When you know, you know. It just doesn't work any other way. You two seem to know. I best go clean up or your mother will kill me. She's been planning these wedding festivities for a year. Can't say I'm sorry it's finally here, it's about to kill me. You two have my permission to elope."

"Dad," Blake said, but the older man just laughed and walked out of the room.

Samantha sank back into the cool, comfortable chair and stared out at the sparkling ocean just beyond the front porch, across the sandy beach. Blake stood up and carried their glasses over to the bar. She hadn't really thought about the Putnam's reaction to her, just about her not messing up.

"Sorry, my dad's a romantic. You did great. Thanks for sticking up for me. You really don't need to," Blake said. His hands were stuffed into the pockets of his khakis, his white button down shirt wrinkled but sexy in an island life sort of way.

"Oh, I thought the battle info was very entertaining," Samantha said, stretching her arms up above her head, before bursting into laughter. The Bloody Mary had gone straight to her head.

"You know what I'm talking about!" Blake said, a small smile escaping. "All of his conversations with me revolve around joining the family business or getting married. He does it every time. Any time I have a date, he tells me she's the one."

Samantha stood and walked to the window. She should be relieved that Blake's dad wasn't taking her seriously but for some reason, his words stung. She had believed his father when he said he noticed the chemistry between them. She felt it. Blake must be completely emotionless. How many other women had come here just like her? How many others did he use as dates so he could continue to feel nothing?

"Well, you don't have to worry about me pressing the topic, right? That's why I'm here. I'm here to do my job," Samantha said. "I'm going to go walk on the beach if that's ok, sir?"

"Alone?" Blake asked, but she had already left the room.

BLAKE WAS RELIEVED when Samantha left to walk the beach on her own. He cherished the opportunity to be alone in his favorite room in the home, but Samantha had seemed upset even though he had sat by her, made her a drink, even talked with her like a real date. Maybe he should walk with her though. His family would expect that.

He grabbed his suitcase from the foyer, quickly changed into his running gear. He jogged to the right, the direction he'd seen Samantha walk as she left the plantation. As he ran, he marveled at how she affected him. She was smart and kind, but she definitely had a confidence that wouldn't allow people to walk on her. He admired that, but it made him a little uncomfortable. He needed her to follow the plan. Already his body was ignoring the plan. She was beautiful, but it was more than that. And whenever he touched her, his body kept ignoring that she was off limits. If she hadn't been an employee….

She was, though. And he had to remember that at all times. Having separate bedrooms would definitely keep his libido at bay. He ran a little faster, surprised he hadn't caught up to her yet. Maybe she was doing a little running of her own.

When he spotted Max and Samantha together on the beach, he was irritated. Max was wasting no time, typical. But when he saw Max touch Samantha's face, he felt a burn of anger that was foreign to him. He saw Samantha pull away from Max, but Max leaned closer. Blake put on a burst of speed.

Chapter Seven

SAMANTHA WALKED QUICKLY down the beach, her shoes in her hand. The fresh air felt wonderful and the ability to walk along the deserted beach was heaven. Blake Putnam, however, was hell. How dare he be so dismissive to everything she said? He didn't have all the answers. He couldn't even hang out with his family and enjoy himself. He had a father and a mother who loved him. And siblings. All she had was her mother, still grieving and trying to make ends meet working as a receptionist for their local vet. Blake Putnam was definitely brilliant, and her boss, but he needed a lesson in humanity.

"Hey gorgeous," someone jogged up behind her.

"Hello Max," Samantha said, wishing she could be alone.

"At your service. And please tell me, what's a catch like you doing with a cold bastard like Blake?" Max said matching her pace as they neared the tip of the island.

"What's your problem with Blake?" Samantha asked, even though she'd been wondering the same thing.

"I asked you first, honey," Max said, reaching over and brushing a stray hair from Samantha's face.

Samantha smiled, realizing Judy's ultra-hold hairspray had finally met its match in this hot humid island air. "Well, Blake and I –"

"There you are Samantha," Blake said, appearing behind them, wearing jogging shorts and a tight T-shirt. He was amazingly fit, and Samantha's heart raced to see him sweaty. He smelled amazing. It was all she could do to not bury her nose in his shirt like a laundry commercial. She laughed at the image, and her anger evaporated.

"Hey Blake. Jogging?" Samantha said. "What about your reputation as a desk jockey," she teased, hoping to needle him. "I didn't know you were one for jogging or fresh air."

Challenging him was exciting.

"Oh sure you do sweetie," he matched her mood, and she nearly bounced in excitement. "Sam's just teasing Max. We jog most nights after work, don't we?"

"Religiously," she said. "Unless we have tantric yoga class. Have you tried that Max?" She had to bite her inner cheek to not laugh Blake's face was so shocked. "It's couple's yoga, Max," she sighed and stood closer to Blake.

Daringly she traced a finger down his arm. Solid muscle. A thrill shot through her. "It's so magical. Almost like we're circus performers, the way Blake holds me in the downward dog position."

"For real?" Max laughed. "Blake's as flexible as a steel beam. Yoga?"

"You'd be surprised what Blake can do," Samantha leaned her whole body into him, and snaked her arm around his waist. "He can be amazingly flexible, but actually, our favorite thing to do is take long walks together, alone. See you around, Max."

She turned around and laced her fingers through Blake's and started to walk. Part of her was terrified of her audacity. Another part was entertained. She felt so alive baiting him like that. Throwing their non-existent relationship in Max's face. And really what could Blake do? Still she held her breath, waiting for his reaction.

He didn't say anything but walked with her. When she saw that Max had rounded a corner as he headed back to the house, Samantha dropped Blake's hand and crossed her arms in front of her.

"Was he bothering you?" Blake asked.

"No, but you are," Samantha said, taking a deep breath. She had to be careful, but this had to be said. "All I ask is that you treat me with kindness, ok? Nothing over the top, just common courtesy. Hold doors for me, be kind even when no one is watching, listen when I'm talking, be honest, tell me what's going on, and in return I'll make this weekend and the Daycon presentation a total success. And, what's more, I will share my idea I've been working on for a while for a project that could blow Daycon away, and make Blake Genetics a lot of money. I'm ambitious Blake. You are too. I want you to respect me as a person."

Blake turned away from Samantha, kicking sand with the toe of his running shoe.

"That's quite a list," he said, his voice tight. "Totally reasonable. Sure, I can do that, of course I can."

He walked a few steps away from her, then circled back. His features were stiff as he faced her.

"I'm sorry, Samantha. I'm sorry. I'm tense here," he smiled bitterly, and his expression was tighter than his voice, and Samantha felt like his obvious pain was stabbing her. "Tenser than I usually am. I don't mean to be such an ass. But really? Tantric yoga?"

Samantha laughed but didn't say anything. If he thought about it he would realize there were a lot worse things she could say this weekend to reveal the lie he was living.

"I have a hard enough time remembering our agreement, and you bring up tantric."

It was as if he'd lit a flare and was waving it in front of her. There it was, the attraction right out in the open. He was being honest, just as she'd asked, but was she ready for that? Samantha smiled to herself and continued to walk, not wanting to reveal her excitement or to make things harder for him. But he had noticed her as a woman. He did find her attractive. And now she was imagining him doing tantric yoga, and it was as absurd an image as it should have been.

"I'm glad you're into saving the environment," Blake said, breaking the silence as they walked side by side along the shore. "It's important. To say that my family of origin's business is part of the problem is an understatement. Do you understand why it's so uncomfortable for me to be around them? They're so unconscious about it."

"Maybe, but I know if you stick to your beliefs and tell them what you know, with kindness, they'll be a lot more receptive," Samantha said. "Your dad is bristling because you're shoving all the wrong in his face. Maybe you should give him some positive feedback too. I'm just saying, from experience, it's a lot easier to trust you when you're open and friendly."

BLAKE LOOKED OVER at the beautiful blonde, who was his pretend date. She was smart, kind, and had shown him she wasn't going to play dependent variable in his science experiment. She wasn't proving to be as easily manipulated as he'd predicted. He needed her on his side this weekend. But what did she need from him now that they were here?

The realization shook Blake to the core. Samantha was in charge of how this weekend would turn out. She could choose to blow his cover at any moment. The reality caused him to stop.

"Blake? Something wrong?" Samantha said. "You have a weird look on your face."

"No, no, everything is fine," he said.

She was too perceptive. "By the way, I got a call from Bob Morrison with Daycon, and they are now expecting to have you in the meeting Monday," Blake said, measuring his words, thoughts and ideas colliding in his brain.

"Wow, that's great!" Samantha said. "I can't believe they

liked my ideas as much as you did."

"They did. In fact, I was thinking if you are that adverse to helicopter rides, I could get you on the ferry tomorrow and fly you out of Hilton Head. You'd be back in Charlotte Saturday night with plenty of time to rest and prepare for the meeting."

An egret flew above them as the sun sparkled on the sound. Blake had many fond memories of this island, and many fond memories of getting himself out of bad situations. This could be one of his best plays ever, he realized. Samantha was hard to keep at arm's length, and they hadn't even spent a day together.

"No, actually, I think it is good for me to experience everything here, with you. It will help me understand you better, represent you better when we do meet with Daycon. We haven't even reviewed the presentation," Samantha said. Blake noticed her blue eyes sparkling and a hint of a smile crossed her face.

"What about the helicopter ride? I know you hated that," Blake said, frustrated she wasn't agreeing to his new plan.

"Well, Charlie, your pilot, handed me a packet of motion sickness medicine to take before we head back, so I'm all set," Samantha said. "Isn't that great?"

"Great," Blake said, trying to sound enthusiastic. "I guess we better get back to the plantation."

"Yes, we'd better," Samantha agreed, walking ahead of him along the shore.

They walked back in silence. Blake was happy that way, in silence, deep inside his own head. His heart sealed deep inside. She'd be staying, and he was glad about that, especially since he'd regained control. She knew now that he could ask her to leave the island at any moment.

SAMANTHA HAD ENJOYED her walk on the beach, with and without Blake. She was surprised he was trying to get her to leave the island. It was like he'd been spooked by the teasing and the lack of control he had over her now that they'd arrived, and that made her feel a whole lot better. Samantha had even spotted a pod of dolphins and considered them a good luck sign. All in all, things were a lot better now than they had been this morning and afternoon.

Evalyn Putnam greeted them at the front door.

"Well there you two are. I've been looking for you. I thought you'd like to see your room for the weekend," Mrs. Putnam said, ushering them inside.

"You mean rooms," Blake said.

She smiled. "That heat just drives me crazy, but I guess it doesn't bother you young people."

Samantha followed Blake's mother up the wide spiral stairway to the second floor, with Blake trailing behind. Samantha would have to talk to him about keeping up with her, she thought with a smile.

"Weddings always bring out the worst in folks," Blake's mom said as they neared the end of a long grand hall. "It's an emotional time. Just keep your head down and let me know if you need anything, dear. Blake, why are you following so far behind, son? Your manners have become slack since you've moved up north."

"Mother, I'm in Charlotte, I'm not even north of the Mason-Dixon line," Blake said, catching up to them. "I'm just tired that's all. Business, getting here, well, you know."

"What I know is this is your sister's most important life choice so you best be happy and supportive. I want to see you at your best, son," Evalyn said, grabbing Blake by the arm and giving him a hug.

"Well kids, here's your room," Evalyn said as they reached the end of the long hall. "Blake is so old fashioned, I'll declare. He wanted to make sure I gave you each your own room. But we're all full. Last to arrive gets the last choice, I'm afraid. I thought you two would be OK sharing," Evalyn added a conspiratorial wink to the end of her sentence and Samantha blushed. Blake's face was drained of color.

While Samantha tried to figure out what to say, Mrs. Putnam had opened the door to the most luxurious bedroom Samantha had ever seen. Everything was white – white area rug, white comforter, white pillows, two white chairs facing toward the ocean in the corner by the window. Contrasted with the dark oak floors and the dark wood ceiling fan, the look was breathtaking.

Samantha had turned to tell Evalyn the room was beautiful, but she was gone. So was Blake.

Samantha noticed her suitcase had been unpacked and all of her clothes were hanging up, wrinkle free, in an elegant dark mahogany armoire. And, she noticed Blake's clothes were hung next to hers.

"What's this?" She stared at his clothes in dismay, but comforted herself with the knowledge that Blake would fix the room problem.

BLAKE CAUGHT UP with his mother before she made the stairs.

"Mom, I always have my own room."

"Not this time."

She'd never been so curt with him.

"I need my own room. I like privacy."

"There are no other options Blake, period, every room is taken," Evalyn said, her blue eyes icy with impatience. "I have enough to worry about this weekend without you acting like a reclusive baby. Privacy. Don't tell me you and this Samantha haven't fooled around. I'm not stupid. Women don't attend weddings with men unless they are special, and unless they want to fool around. You said you've been dating for a while. I'm busy.

Go get ready for the barbeque."

"I just want my own room so I can work this weekend. I have an...."

"It's your sister's wedding, Blake, not a work retreat. And if you're such a prude, find a couch to sleep on this weekend."

"It's not that," he said, but his mom shook her head and walked away.

His hand gripped the banister. He could hardly tell his mom he needed his own room because Samantha could sue him for sexual harassment. He'd promised her separate rooms. He barely knew her. He felt the beginnings of a headache setting in and consciously tried to unclench his jaw. This weekend was getting out of control. He had to talk to Samantha, to explain, but he didn't have an explanation.

"Hey Blake why aren't you getting ready?" His younger brother, Denton, asked.

"Ah, well, Samantha's using our room, and well, we're running late, and I didn't want to bother her, so could I use yours or is your date in there?" Blake asked.

"Sure man, go ahead," Denton said. "Shelby has her own room. Make yourself at home. We're the same size so just grab whatever you want to wear and come on down. Can't wait to catch up!"

Denton was Blake's favorite brother. While James always treated Blake as a second fiddle – another reason Blake would never join Putnam Industries, he'd always be second in line— Denton was full of respect for Blake and everything he'd accomplished. Blake hurried into his brother's room. Maybe he could share Denton's room for the weekend. No, he cut that thought short. His mom would discover his lie, not to mention his brothers. They'd mock him until they were all old enough to have entirely lost their memories.

❧

BLAKE HURRIED DOWN the front stairs of the plantation, crossed the grass and found himself at the beach barbeque about fifteen minutes late. He hated being late and he could feel his jaw tense. He'd done his best, but this weekend was getting away from him.

He spotted his younger brother walking toward him and donned his happy family mask. It was the smile he put on for family and business.

"Hey Denton, thanks," Blake said to his little brother who handed him an ice-cold beer from one of the white buckets filled with ice and beverages. Blake had showered and changed quickly, picking one of Denton's light blue polo shirts, a navy blazer and a pair of khaki pants. He popped the cap off his beer, took a deep swallow and tried to relax. He owed Denton a genuine smile, he knew that much, and some conversation.

"Your Samantha sure is a looker," Denton said, smiling at his big brother. He was a junior in college, still enjoying the fun, freedom and lack of pressure that college was. His big plans were to graduate and roll into the family business. Blake grimaced at the thought. Maybe he could change his mind, Blake thought but then shook his head. That was ridiculous. He'd never change his brother's loyalty or brainwashing, or their grasp on the golden ticket. They'd never take the leap of faith Blake had.

"Thanks! Ah, yes, she is a nice girl," Blake said.

"Nice? Really? You talk like you're 80. She's hot. And it's great to see you bring your own date instead of ending up with one of those awful society girls from Atlanta that mom always sets you up with," Denton said.

"Yes, much better than that," Blake said. "Who's your date?"

"Oh, Shelby, she's a friend, a friend with benefits if you know what I mean," Denton said, giving his brother an elbow to the side.

"Ah, yes, the good old days," Blake said, remembering college. It seemed so long ago that he was carefree and enjoying life like his little brother. Had there ever been a time he'd been completely carefree, he wondered. He doubted it. He'd blocked out college since the breakup. College to Blake would always equate to a broken heart, a heart he'd never allow to be broken again. A heart buried so deep inside his businessman demeanor, Blake wasn't sure if it was there anymore.

"Hey Sam!" Denton said as Samantha walked up to them. Denton gave her a kiss on the cheek while Blake held up his beer. "Cheers," Blake said.

Denton looked at his older brother and shook his head. "Dude, give her a kiss at least."

Blake leaned forward and planted an awkward kiss on Samantha's cheek, her cheek was so soft. Something stirred inside him, almost uncurled as if it were alive, and the feeling was something he wanted to keep buried. Samantha looked beautiful. She'd curled her hair, the blonde waves fell softly over her shoulders. Her lips glistened a soft pink, and she was smiling.

"Outfit Two," she whispered. "Admire the grey booties."

He couldn't believe she was joking with him. She should be yelling, glaring, something.

"Admired," he said.

"Get a room you two," Denton called out. "Oh wait, you have one," he emphasized the last word and then laughed.

Blake winced at the reminder.

"What would you like to drink?" Blake said, hoping to have an excuse to put some distance between them.

"Beer is great, thanks," Samantha said.

"I'll get it, Blake. I've gotta grab Shelby, too," Denton said.

Once he'd left them alone, Blake leaned forward and, before he could stop himself, whispered in her ear: "You look beautiful."

HER STOMACH FLIPPED at the compliment, and an unexpected longing washed over her. She turned away from him just in time to see Denton and Shelby working their way over to them. She breathed in deeply and looked back at Blake. He was smiling down at her, his face glowing softly in the sunset-pink perfect light. She realized their shirts were the same color of baby blue, and she wondered if he had planned that. Around her, everything seemed to be perfection, but inside of her she felt in turmoil. He was getting to her, and he wasn't even trying. Was she getting to him, too?

"Where did you go? Did you resolve the room?" Samantha asked needing to talk about it.

"I talked to my mother, but it seems the house really is full because of the wedding," Blake said, finishing his beer before adding, "Don't worry. I'll figure it out. The room is yours."

Samantha smiled. "I'm not worried Blake."

She heard Blake release a big breath, a sigh of relief she supposed. She wouldn't make the room situation tougher on him. It wasn't his fault. And he was so handsome when he worried about her. She wondered what he would say if she just shrugged it off and said they could share? Relief or more distance? He was so hard for her to read.

"Shelby, what a lovely dress," Samantha said, breaking the tension and electricity that had surrounded her and Blake. Shelby reminded Samantha of herself just a few short years ago, before her dad died. Eager to please, comfortable knowing that she was usually the cutest and maybe even the smartest girl at the picnic. Enjoying the attention of every man – and boy – in the room. Samantha wished she could regain that confidence, get a piece back of what she'd lost because of her dad's decisions and Ryan. Perhaps this weekend would provide the spark.

"Thank you Samantha," Shelby answered, spinning around in a twirl as the full skirt of her dress flared out and up around her tanned legs, almost high enough to show her underwear, or lack thereof, Samantha thought. "My mamma said I needed to do a lot of shopping to attend a Putnam wedding, and so we did.

We tore up Atlanta."

One of the wait staff rang a silver bell and called everyone to dinner.

"I hope I'm seated by you," Shelby whispered in Samantha's ear as they followed the Putnam brothers to the dinner table, "Not by her, James' girlfriend."

Samantha laughed. James' girlfriend and Shelby had gone on a beach walk together, but it had been short-lived. Shelby told Samantha that Melissa was a snob.

"Thank god," Shelby said, noting her placement on the other side of Blake from Samantha. "Blake, you don't mind switching, do you?"

"I do mind, actually, and mom will be upset, so you just stay put," Blake said.

The sun had set and the table was aglow with hundreds of white tea lights in glass holders. The bride and groom to be were seated at the other picnic table, with both sets of parents and a couple grandparents, leaving the other picnic table to the Putnam kids, their dates and a couple cousins.

"You smell good," Blake said, leaning close to Samantha.

"You do too," Samantha answered. "I think it's the soap your mom has, it's lavender and I love it."

"Are you cold?" Blake asked, noticing the goose bumps covering Samantha's arm.

"No, I'm fine," Samantha said, still reeling from sitting this close to him.

"Here, allow me," Blake said, standing as he removed his navy blazer and placed it tenderly around her shoulders. As she reached up to her shoulder to help, their hands touched. Samantha quickly pulled her hand away from his, but his touch felt magical, natural and special, all at the same time. He is just doing this, giving me his jacket, to make it look like we are dating. It's ok, Samantha told herself. Calm down.

She also declined a second beer. Drinking could lower her

guard, and she didn't want to say something she shouldn't in front of Blake's family. She was determined to play her role well.

"Better?" Blake asked, taking his seat next to her again, sitting close enough their thighs were touching under the picnic table. Samantha wondered if he felt the current between them, or if he was trying to stay away from Shelby on the other side of him. That was probably all it was, she realized. But still. Even if Blake were a great actor, Samantha's cheeks flushed because they were touching, and a wonderful warmth spread through her body.

"Thank you for being here," Blake said.

Samantha's stomach flipped again. She couldn't believe the feelings rushing through her body, her instant attraction to her boss. She was panicked. This wasn't supposed to be happening. Blake would be so angry with her. He was being polite and she was acting like a schoolgirl with a crush. She felt so ashamed. He was acting, being the perfect date in front of his family, and his brother who sat across the table from her. She was ridiculous.

"Blake," Samantha said, breathless. "It's my pleasure." She was aware of the irony of her words, even as they tumbled out. Samantha tried to move her leg away from his under the table, but she couldn't. Sitting on the end, she had nowhere to move, nowhere to go. And she wondered, why was he being this nice, this sexy? Was he over doing what she'd asked him to do earlier or deliberately trying to throw her off balance?

"Um, you guys, the toast?" Shelby said loudly enough the entire table turned to stare at the two of them. Samantha jumped.

"Who's toasting?" Blake asked.

"We are, brother," James said from the opposite end of the picnic table, grinning like a maniac in Blake's direction.

"Dude, you got the emails? James sent them to you, right?" Denton asked from across the table.

"No, I don't know what you're talking about, James never

sent me an email," Blake said as James stood and began to recite a poem/rap to his sister.

"Your part's next," Denton said.

Blake looked at Samantha, his jaw tight. She realized he'd been set up by his older brother. Sibling rivalry. Maybe it was good she was an only. Blake could handle it though. She pulled him to her, holding his head close to hers.

"You've got this," she said, her lips so close to his ear she could almost imagine they were brushing. "Just like a presentation at the office, only more fun. Remember when the meeting went way off topic and you just started telling the story behind your company? Your vision for what it could be and what it was becoming. You had the room in the palm of your hand. Imagine you're closing the Daycon deal. Only this time, tell your sister the story behind the two of you. Tell her how special she is to you. Don't worry about James' script or the fact he didn't copy you on an email. Give a speech your only sister deserves, straight from your heart," she said, squeezing his hand for encouragement.

And that was all he needed. Something deep inside opened up and he expressed the deep love for his only sister, a love that had been there all along. Not only did Blake jump into the toast/rap, he added movement, regaling the audience with stories of when they were young, picking Avery up in his arms and spinning her around before turning the last of the toast over to his little brother. There wasn't a dry eye on the beach.

Samantha beamed as he returned to the table. She loved seeing this side of Blake, a light-hearted brother who loved his sister. Genuine and unguarded, a type of man she would love to love. The exact man she would love to love, if he wasn't so off limits. Her heart squeezed in disappointment.

"That was wonderful," she said, leaning in close to him, their shoulders were touching now, and Samantha felt a connection to him like she'd never experienced before. It was like they were a team. She'd never felt that with Ryan. He'd been so competitive with her, always trying to do better than her on everything. Samantha couldn't stop smiling.

"Yeah, thanks for the tips. It really helped, but don't tell anyone at work about that little show," Blake said, his eyes narrowing, a darkness crossed his face. He was serious. His mask was back.

Samantha leaned away from him, and said, "Of course not."

"Bon appetite," the waiter said, stepping in between them to place her dinner in front of her, breaking the awkward moment. "Please enjoy this low country boil."

"It looks so yummy, don't you think Blake?" Shelby declared and Blake turned to talk to her.

Samantha and Denton struck up their own friendly banter across the table, and the conversation was light and fun. The live oak trees with their hanging moss danced among the stars. The sky was among the most brilliantly starlite Samantha had ever seen. The taste of the low country sausage, shrimp and okra melted in her mouth. The candlelight twinkled and the gentle breeze blew off the sound. Frequent toasts and roasts interrupted the flow of the night while Mrs. Putnam kept reminding everyone the real rehearsal dinner would be the following evening at the club. And that rehearsal was mandatory, in front of the gazebo at Melrose Plantation at noon sharp tomorrow. No matter the hangovers.

For Samantha, even though the setting was magical, the dinner was the longest in her life, or so it seemed. As much as she enjoyed talking to his little brother, all she wanted to do was grab Blake and kiss him, to feel him kiss her, to have him to herself. To tell him it was ok to have fun, to be silly, to enjoy life. She couldn't help but wonder why he reacted the way he did about his performance, what his dark side was all about. Finally, after desert was served and cleared, Mr. Putnam made one last toast and they were free.

"Come with me," Blake said, pulling her from the table before either of them could say goodbye. Samantha worried that she had done something else to upset him, but all she did was talk with Denton through most of dinner. Nothing important, all surface chatter, just like he'd asked her to do with his family. She needed to remember she was OK here; it was her stage to set. Blake had brought her here under false pretenses, but now that she was here, she'd make him proud. Holding his hand as he led her toward the ocean made her both nervous and excited. She hoped she'd done everything right. She knew she'd find out as soon as they got to wherever Blake was taking her.

Blake held her hand and led her down the beach, far away from the glowing lights of their beach picnic to a dark area of the beach, where white crabs with one arm popped out at them in an eerie stance under the light of the glowing moon.

The tide was calm, waves gently rolling onto shore.

Blake slowed his pace, and Samantha let out a deep breath. She felt certain he was happy with her tonight, at least at this moment.

"It's so beautiful on this island," Samantha said as they walked the moonlit shore. "Thank you for bringing me here."

"It's especially beautiful with you here," he said.

Samantha's heart skipped a beat, the warmth of his words combined with his hand around hers made her dizzy. She wanted to please this man, she wanted to kiss this man. "Don't worry about your performance with your brothers, nobody will hear a thing about it, I promise," she said, the words tumbling out before she realized it.

Blake dropped her hand and stood silently by her side, she could see the muscles in his jaw tighten.

Now she'd ruined everything, Samantha thought. Why did she bring that up? Ugh. She was sure he was going to send her home, put her on that stupid ferry he'd mentioned.

"I know," he said finally. "I don't really trust, but I'm starting to trust you," he ran his fingers through his hair. "This weekend's not going the way I planned." Blake said, turning to face Samantha, a small smile working its way across his model-gorgeous face.

Samantha let out a breath she didn't even know she was holding.

"That's the beauty of it," she said softly. "You need to not get your way more often."

"That might be true," he said, a hint of a smile touching his masculine lips. "It's definitely best that I don't get what I want now."

"What's that?" She asked breathlessly.

His hands loosely gripped her shoulders.

"I want to kiss you," Blake answered in a low, deep voice, his eyes dark in the moonlight.

"I feel the same way," Samantha said impulsively, even though she knew it couldn't work between them.

Blake leaned down and gently pressed his lips against hers. The heat exploded from the center of her body, and she swayed backwards until Blake wrapped a strong arm around her waist.

He pulled away then, but still kept his arm around her. "You could really mess up my life."

"I'm sorry," she answered, breathless, aching for another kiss and letting his words wash over her, devoid of meaning.

When his mouth found hers this time it was with an intensity she felt throughout her body as his tongue parted her lips and began to explore, thrusting deeply, adding to her desire. He tasted spicy and salty, and Samantha gripped his broad shoulders, pulling him to her, feeling all of his hard body pressed close.

Blake wrapped Samantha's long blonde hair around his hand, gently pulling her head backwards, moving his kiss to her neck as she moaned. He pulled her closer, sealing his mouth over hers once again, thrusting his tongue inside her as she felt him harden.

"Wait," Blake said, ending the kiss but pulling Samantha to him, enveloping her in a strong embrace.

Samantha stepped back, rubbed her swollen lips, and looked up into his eyes, wanting him with every ounce of her being, but knowing this should never happen. This shouldn't be happening. "Don't worry, nobody will know about this either. I promise," she said.

Samantha saw Blake take a deep breath, he seemed torn, but then she saw the control return to his face, his jaw tighten.

"I apologize. Kissing you, putting you in this situation was not my intention," he said stiffly.

Back to the reason she was here, Samantha thought with a burst of resentment. He saw her as nothing more than a prop he could manipulate. She was a mannequin to dress, an assistant to help type his presentation, a hooker to kiss when he was lonely at night. All he wanted was an uncomplicated weekend. All she wanted was to get out of here, with some dignity left.

"You're a good kisser," she said, striving to keep her voice light. "But don't worry. I won't turn into a stalker."

"Samantha," he reached out for her, but she backed out of range.

"I'm tired," she said. "Think I'll turn in."

Then she remembered about the bedroom situation, and slapped her hand over her mouth.

"Yes, we should get back to the house," he said. "Thank you for all your efforts today, but you're right. Tomorrow's another long day of wedding stuff. And, we need to work on the Daycon presentation. After you."

Well, that was awkward, Samantha thought, walking ahead of Blake back towards the beach picnic where candles were still glowing on the tables as the waiters worked to clean up, and back to the plantation house beyond.

One moment Blake was in the moment, the next, he became the unemotional, calculating boss everyone knew him to be at

Blake Genetics. She was tired of it. She tried to remind herself to stay focus on the fact she would have the chance to present her project to him, that she still had his ear for another two days.

Right, Samantha thought, realizing how wrong she'd been about this whole situation. One touch, and she melted. How ridiculous. She was smarter than this. She needed to use her brains to get through the weekend. But now they were walking back to the plantation where they were assigned the same bedroom. That's the worst thing that could have happened. What would they do?

"I'm going to sleep in the library. I should be able to wake up before anybody else, but I may need to come into the bedroom to get a change of clothes, if that's ok," Blake said as they walked up the steps of the porch.

"Of course, it's your room, too," Samantha said. "Why don't you go get your things now and I'll wait out here."

"Good idea. I'll knock on your door tomorrow around 9? Let's try to get some work done in the morning," Blake added, opening the door to the plantation. "Good night," he said before disappearing inside.

Samantha let out a deep sigh and looked up into the cloudless sky. All she wanted to do was follow Blake up to their room.

70

Chapter Eight

B LAKE'S ALARM BEEPED and he woke up with sunlight streaming into the library, still tired after a restless night's sleep. The problem wasn't the couch in the library. The problem was Samantha. His heart beat just a little faster every time he was near her. And last night, with the drinking and the champagne and the perfect moonlit sky, the moment he held her hand he couldn't stop himself. Even though it hadn't been in the plan, he'd had to taste her. Her lips had been as soft as he imagined, and breathing in the smell of her hair, letting his fingers slide through her silky tresses, had made him dizzy. The heat between them was intense. He's been immediately aroused. Samantha made him feel alive.

He sat up, not wanting any of his family to find him sleeping on the couch. He had to stop thinking about her like that. She was a fake date. He was her boss. She had seemed more comfortable with the awkwardness of yesterday, and yet he had planned the whole weekend date idea, thinking a new wardrobe would be ample compensation for putting up with his family. Plus he'd seen she was ambitious at the meeting they'd attended. Ambitious, smart, quick to problem solve without the complications of a big ego. He'd known she'd jump at the chance to be a bigger part of the Daycon merger team. He was lucky to have her.

Now it was like he was caught up in her sexual spell, and even though she was nothing like Jane, he couldn't let that happen. Instead of sleeping so he'd have a clear head to review the final details of the biggest deal of his life today, he'd continued to remember how she'd felt in his arms, warm and supple. Even the way she'd hummed under her breath when they'd been walking back to the house after their kiss had charmed him. He had wanted…what? He didn't even know. He just felt different with her. Relaxed, letting his guard down. He wanted to not play his boss role. Not be in charge. Just be a man, only he didn't remember who that man was anymore.

He stood up and stared out of the window. He'd missed the sunrise. When was the last time that had happened? He had to get himself under control, and shake off these unfamiliar feelings and this almost consuming desire to spend more time with Samantha. He even had the idiotic idea of trying to say things to make her laugh, just so that he could see her smile. He was lucky Samantha wasn't falling under his spell, not that he had one to fall under. She was ambitious and smart enough to want to keep this whole fake date weekend to herself so she didn't fall under the scrutiny of office gossips.

Deliberately Blake walked over to an oil portrait of his grandfather, Howard Putnam. While Blake viewed his own father as weak, because he'd given up his dreams of becoming a doctor so that he could step into the much larger shoes of his father and blindingly continuing to build a business that was killing the planet, he had the utmost respect for the founder of Putnam Industries. He tried to model himself after his grandfather. Howard Putnam had grown a business from nothing to one of the biggest in the Southeast. It was the right business for the right time, just like Blake's genetic testing firm was now. What Blake liked the best was that when Howard Putnam spoke, everyone had listened. Blake learned everything he knew about discipline, control, management and keeping his emotions in check.

Howard Putnam hadn't hired fools. He'd fired people who followed blindly. His grandfather had always reinvested in his business, been interested in the latest technologies. Blake's own father Richard's eyes and ears were closed to innovation and the reality of the damage Putnam Industries was doing. He had no long-term plans, besides handing over the keys to James. He ignored Blake's pleas to invest in recycling efforts, and mocked his presentation about agri-pulp, a stand in for wood made from wheat, oat, barley and other crop stalks. Blake knew converting a paper mill to process wood pulp alternatives would cost tens of millions of dollars – but still, in the long run, it would be a win-win. Blake's pleas fell on deaf ears. His brothers and now probably Avery's husband would work for the company and collect an enormous bonus and salary each year for doing essentially nothing.

Blake was used to being on his own, making it on his own. He wasn't tapping into his family wealth and settling like his brothers. His eldest brother James had gone off to college—Tulane, earned his degree and then immediately came back home and taken a job at Putnam Industries that had he not been a Putnam, he never would have qualified for. Where was the self-respect in that?

Chapter Nine

SAMANTHA GAZED OUT the bedroom window. She had never stayed in such a luxurious room, nor had such a spectacular view, but all she could think about was Blake. She ached for Blake with a need so raw, so primal she didn't know how to deal with it. She was so confused. One moment Blake was the most engaging, most wonderful date in the world. A sexy, loving man with a sense of humor and their chemistry, oh my god. But then, he'd switch off, becoming the heartless, cold businessman who asked her here as a fake date to impress his parents. And she didn't think he was doing it on purpose. It was almost as if he were as lost as she felt, and that made her heart ache even more for him.

Maybe because she was doing such a great job as his fake girlfriend she was losing her way. She was falling for the man she wanted him to be. She'd smiled and been charming all through dinner. She'd encouraged his toast, and entertained his younger brother all through the meal. She'd felt like she was really part of this event. She felt invested.

It had all started when they touched. Just thinking about his arm around her made her head swim again, and remembering their kiss made her stomach flip.

Here she was wrapped in a cocoon of luxury, in her own room of white comfort and dark wood, and yet all she could think of, all she wanted to think about, was the kiss she shared with Blake – and how he'd stopped it.

He felt the chemistry, he had to it was so strong the air around them became electric. And she felt his response during their kiss, she knew it. Why had he switched back into boss mode?

Stop daydreaming.

Samantha was a woman of action. She just wished she knew what action to take.

Samantha finished in the bathroom. She had just slipped on her grey booties when she heard a light tap on the door. Catching her breath in excitement, she opened the door.

"Great you're awake," Blake said. "And ready to work," he said, noticing the laptop in her hand.

"Reporting for duty, Sir," Samantha grinned and mock saluted.

His eyes opened in surprise, but she thought she saw a hint of a smile touch his lips. She had to fight not to lean in close.

"Is this Outfit Three I should be noticing?"

"Oops, caught," Samantha felt herself blush a little, but she brazened it out. "These are boyfriend jeans. A bit of a bonus, Raymond slipped in as a favor, but I doubt it was gratis."

"Boyfriend jeans," he repeated as if he'd never heard the phrase. "I should give you more of my jeans. They look much better on you."

He froze.

Samantha caught her breath.

"Why don't you ah…," she broke off then tried again. "Get ready. I'll go get us some coffee, and we can get to work. Where do you want to work?"

"Up here's great. By the window."

"On the floor?"

"I am a circus yogi."

Samantha laughed. "I'll leave you to it then. Remember. Be one with your breath."

She left her laptop on the bed and lightly ran down the stairs.

BLAKE COULDN'T HELP himself. He walked out into the hall so he could watch her leave. He loved the way she moved, so light and quick. Graceful.

Fake date. Not real. Employee. He reminded himself, stripping off his clothes so he could take a shower. A very cold shower, but a quick one. He had work to do. He rushed, but even he had to admit to himself that it was because he wanted to see Samantha again. She had smelled of flowers and sea air, and it had pierced him on a level he didn't even know he had. And the simple jeans and T-shirt. Why had he ordered such formal clothes from Andrea's? He wished he could just say to hell with the wedding and....

He turned off the shower and realized he hadn't brought his clothes in with him. Awkward. She really made him lose his head. He quickly shaved and brushed his teeth, hoping to beat her back, but imaging how he would feel if the situation were reversed, and she walked into the room with just a towel, made it difficult to leave the room as quickly as he'd planned as his anatomy was not cooperating.

When he opened the door, she was sitting on the floor at the foot of the bed. Her long legs were stretched out in front of her. She was gorgeous.

"Ready to get to work?" she asked. "Oh," she spotted him with just the towel wrapped around his lean waist. "Not quite."

"The staff is efficient as ever," he said drily. "You are back more quickly than I anticipated."

Blake went to the armoire, quickly picked some clothes and hurried back to the bathroom to get dressed.

"How do you take your coffee?" She asked as he reemerged. *With you.*

"Black."

All he could think about was grabbing her and throwing her

on the bed, kissing her everywhere. "What are you working on?"

"My secret project. Can I tell you about it? I've figured out how we can utilize our DNA testing protocols direct to consumer. It's the new hottest thing, Blake, and I really think we could be at the forefront," Samantha said, her enthusiasm sparkling all over her face.

"Tell me more," Blake said and perched on the corner of the bed. He was certain if he sat down next to her on the floor, he wouldn't be able to keep his mind on her presentation.

"Well, Mr. Putnam, here's how it would work. You, Mr. Consumer, would start by ordering your DNA kit from our online portal," Samantha said. She turned her computer to face him and revealed a slide that showed him the branding she'd developed as well as a simple, consumer-friendly interface. Blake was accustomed to the scientific, business applications of his model – he'd never considered direct to consumer.

"Then, we'd ship them a really cool DNA collection kit. They spit into it, return it to us in the prepaid package and we reveal the results online. We can have pages of enlightening information about where the individual came from, all the different ancestry found. It could be revolutionary. The next step will be the medical side of DNA testing. Giving consumers access to their risk of diseases like cancer, diabetes, Parkinson's and the like. Right now, it looks like the FDA is blocking that application from happening, unfortunately. Shouldn't each person have the right to know their genetically programmed future and maybe be able to do something about it?"

Blake was stunned. Yes, of course. This was the way to close the Daycon deal, and much, much more. He'd been so focused on the business to business aspects of genetics, within the scientific community. He'd been blind to the true empowerment opportunities. Samantha was brilliant, and beautiful. It took every ounce of control to stay perched on the side of the bed. He wanted to reach down and pull her to him.

"How long have you been working on this, Samantha?" Blake asked. He spoke slowly, trying to keep control.

"Well, don't worry, it was during weekends and weekdays after work. I didn't slack on any of my other projects. It's just that I think this could be transformative for us," Samantha said. "I've always been into ancestry. I told you, I'm a history buff."

Blake allowed a smile to cross his face, and Samantha smiled in return.

"So?" she said.

"Samantha, I love it. Can we share the new direction of Blake Genetics with Daycon?" Blake asked.

"Of course, oh my gosh!" Samantha said, jumping up and giving Blake a high-five. "You like it!"

"Like it? I think I'm beginning to love it!" Blake said as someone knocked on the door.

Samantha hurried over to open it, revealing Evalyn.

"Just making sure you are both awake. How was your night?" she asked, winking again.

Samantha blushed, so Blake answered, "Fine Mother. We'll see you down at breakfast."

"Sorry, she throws me off with those winks," Samantha said, once Blake had closed the door.

You throw me off, Blake thought. "Can I see the deck again before we go down for breakfast? I loved that presentation Samantha. Everything about it is perfect."

Just like you.

SAMANTHA GLOWED. BLAKE loved the DNA project. During breakfast they'd sat next to each other at the kitchen table, talking about her project, Blake added ideas and expanded on the presentation even more. As far as work was concerned, they were clicking. And that was the most important thing, Samantha reminded herself. But Blake sure did look amazing in his navy shorts and white polo. The current between them pulsed stronger than ever, and she wondered how they'd be able to keep their relationship business only. She wanted that, right?

EVALYN HAD SCHEDULED the rehearsal for noon, to beat the afternoon heat, and to assure her sons would not stay up too late partying the night before as she'd told them all during the beach barbeque. But it was still hot and muggy. So there they were, assembled in the front row of white folding chairs, in the too-bright sunshine, grumpy, just trying to make it through and onto the next event. Blake included. He was pretending to listen to what Denton was saying, but was actually tuning everything out.

"Everyone, please, I just need your attention for a brief moment," screamed the tiny brunette woman standing just outside the gazebo. Between the wind, the waves, and the Putnams, nobody could hear a word she was saying. The Putnams and the wedding party had gathered on the lawn in front of the Melrose Inn, another gorgeous replica of a southern plantation home complete with a rose garden and the white ocean-front gazebo where Avery would be married the next day.

Suddenly a man pulled up in a golf cart. He jumped out of the cart and held a bullhorn up to his lips.

"Hey, y'all listen up. My name is Steve and I'm the general manager of the club. If you need anything, come see me. But not until you give this lady the attention she deserves," Steve said, finishing his bullhorn aided speech.

"Really, a bullhorn?" Blake said loudly, but was quickly shushed by the rest of the wedding party.

"Let's just get through this," Denton mumbled. "My hangover needs to get this whole thing we're doing now over with."

Blake smiled, noting his little brother had no idea what he

was saying, and then resumed searching the crowd again for Samantha. *Sure, she doesn't have a role in this,* he reasoned, *but she should at least show up.*

She'd excused herself after breakfast, and told him she'd see him at the rehearsal. Once the wedding party had finally settled into the folding chairs arranged on the lawn, Blake could finally see Samantha standing to the side of the gazebo. She looked beautiful, yet all she was wearing were khaki shorts, sandals and a white cotton top. She looked better than any woman here.

Control, he reminded himself, and tried to focus on the wedding planner's directions. But he couldn't hear a word the woman was saying. The wind was howling off the sound, carrying her words away with it.

This was torture. All of it. He just needed to get over Samantha. He was thinking about her too much. Last night was a mistake, an alcohol fueled moment that would never happen again. They were a perfect business team. That was all. Well, it wasn't all, but it needed to be enough.

SAMANTHA STOOD NEXT to the gazebo and she could hear everything, Amy, the wedding planner, was saying. *Why didn't the Putnams just stand up from their seats on the lawn and move closer?* she wondered. Spoiled, that's what they were, all of them.

"Do you need help?" Samantha asked Amy.

Amy was Samantha's age or younger, a beautiful thin brunette with impossibly large breasts. Trying to garner the attention of all the Putnams seemed to be impossible. They were standing outside, at the edge of a huge seawall, facing the majestic Melrose Plantation, a traditional Southern-style yellow beauty now an Inn and Club for Indigo Island members and guests. The white lattice gazebo would be the backdrop for Avery and Mark's vows. It was a gorgeous setting, and would be perfect as long as the wind stopped by tomorrow afternoon, Samantha thought.

"I wish they would all come closer," Amy said.

"Y'all listen up, now!" Steve yelled into the bullhorn. "We're going to move this rehearsal inside the Inn. Head into the owner's club and we'll take it from there."

Now we decide to move inside, Samantha thought, after every last strand of her hair had been whipped around and tangled by the wind. It had felt good though, being out in this tempest, unable to talk to him. She was so confused. One minute they were brainstorming business, the next staring hungrily at each other, almost unable to speak. She'd nearly kissed him this morning. When he'd walked out of the bathroom with just the towel, she hadn't been able to breathe.

How was she going to be able to work with all this desire swirling around? It was more than desire, she admitted to herself for the first time. Their kisses last night had been magical, leaving her breathless and wanting more. She had felt things inside, deep inside, sensations that she'd never felt before. She closed her eyes for a moment and turned away from the wedding party who had begun walking across the lawn towards the inn. She needed to keep to the agreement for both of them. She needed her job far more than she needed a man.

But still, if she closed her eyes and ran her tongue over her lips, she could taste him, feel his breath on her cheek. She needed to stop daydreaming. He was her boss. She wasn't allowed to think anything more about him, no matter how handsome he was.

Chapter Ten

SAMANTHA WAS EXCITED about the rehearsal dinner, mostly because of the dress she'd selected – or rather Blake had selected with Raymond for her – to wear. She loved the way the bright blue silk cocktail dress made her eyes look a more intense, Pacific Ocean blue. The lace and silk gown fit her perfectly, like an extra layer of skin. Raymond had exclaimed that it was made for her. Samantha had never worn a dress this expensive, this stunning before. This dress will give me the confidence to play my role, Samantha told herself.

Standing in front of the full-length mirror in the bathroom of her suite, she spun around and admired the back of the dress, cut to show much of her back. She was checking herself out in the mirror as Blake barged through the door.

"Oh God, sorry," he stammered, backing up quickly. "The door was open. I thought you were downstairs already."

"My fault," Samantha said, quickly. "I was just finishing up."

Blake had returned from a round of golf, Samantha realized. He smelled like sweat and grass and ocean spray. She felt her heart leap, despite her lectures to herself. If he were really her boyfriend, she could walk across the room and press her body against him.

"You look gorgeous," Blake said, his eyes locked with hers.

"Thank you," Samantha said, a blush working its way up her neck.

"About last night –" they both said, in unison, and started laughing.

"Blake, listen, that kiss, I can't stop thinking about it," Samantha said. "But I know this is for work. I'm ok faking it, it's just that, well, I feel something, I feel a lot of things when I'm with you."

"I can't stop thinking about it either," Blake said and entered the room and closed the door behind him.

Samantha walked toward him slowly. This was crazy, wasn't it? He couldn't possibly be interested in her more than an employee or maybe someone to mess around with for a convenient weekend. He was Blake Putnam and she was Samantha Jones.

Blake stepped closer to her, close enough she could feel his breath down the back of her neck, giving her chills. "You make me feel things, no matter how much I try not to," Blake said, reaching up and brushing a strand of hair away from her face. "I was not expecting this. This was not part of the plan."

"I know. I don't think you tried to trick me about this."

He had tricked her about the wedding though, but his confusion about the attraction between them seemed real. He seemed as unable to stop his reaction as she was.

"I know you're worried because I'm your boss, but I would never, ever use this against you, no matter what happens or doesn't happen between us."

His hand reached up to cup her cheek.

"Look, I'm shaking. I can't stop thinking about you, about touching all of you. God, I bought you all these clothes and now all I want to do is undress you."

Samantha's nipples hardened beneath the silk dress and her breath caught in her throat. Blake leaned down and gently pressed his lips against hers, and she could smell his manliness, smell his sweat and desire. Blake's hand gently brushed against each nipple and Samantha shuddered. When Blake's tongue began to push against her lips, Samantha opened her mouth, welcoming him in, teasing him with her tongue, too.

Blake wrapped both arms around her waist and, as they remained locked in a kiss, he propelled her backwards and up against the bathroom counter.

"Oh Blake," Samantha said, as Blake pressed his erection against her.

"I really, really want you," he said in a low deep voice.

Samantha leaned forward, her breathing heavy, a moan escaping her lips before Blake wrapped his arms around her again and bit her lower lip.

"Oh my god," she said, a shudder overtaking her.

All she wanted was him, to take off the dress and have him insider her.

But Blake pulled away from their kiss, gently pressing her cheek against his strong, hard chest. Holding her close to him, where she could hear his heart beating loudly in his chest.

"Not like this," he murmured against her hair. "Not rushed. We have to get to the rehearsal dinner," he said, his voice tight. "I want our time together to be special. You go on down for cocktails."

Samantha wanted to object, to wait for him, but maybe it would be easier to make small talk with his family instead of walking into the room with him and pretending that she had any control over her body or her reaction to him. Her center clenched with desire, remembering how he'd touched her, and kissed her, bringing her to the brink of orgasm even though both of them still had their clothes on.

Imagine how he could make her feel later. She went to reapply her lipstick and smiled at her red, puffy lips, knowing they didn't really need any lipstick to give them the "just-kissed" look.

Oh, Sam, she asked herself, *what have you gotten yourself into?*

BLAKE NEEDED A long, cold shower. Somehow he'd managed to pull himself away from Samantha just in time. What he'd wanted to do was rip the gorgeous dress off her body, pick her up and put her on top of the bathroom counter, palm her perfect breasts in his hands and watch her blue eyes darken as he thrust inside her, deep inside her. But he knew his being her boss complicated things, and that he had to stick to his promise of a platonic weekend if she wanted. He wouldn't push her. He shouldn't be wanting her at all, but Blake realized it was too late to ignore his desire.

He splashed aftershave on his face, and smiled as he looked down at the white marble countertop. He imagined Samantha sitting there just a few moments before, naked after he pulled the blue silk dress from her body – shaking his head, he walked into his bedroom, closing the bathroom door behind him.

They'd reconnect tonight, and he could hardly wait. Checking his tie in the bedroom mirror, he nodded at his reflection and steeled himself for the festivities of the evening. As he reached the bottom of the main staircase, he scanned the crowd for Samantha. There were only 30 people invited to the rehearsal dinner, he remembered, so it shouldn't be hard to spot Samantha. He looked again, taking in the crowd, but she was nowhere.

"A martini sir?" asked a waiter carrying a silver tray.

"Yes, thank you," Blake answered, surprised when the waiter handed him his favorite drink, the exact way he liked it: double stuffed blue cheese olives, dirty and up.

And then he spotted his sister, grinning at him from the corner of the grand foyer.

Avery hurried across the room to hug him.

"You look gorgeous big sis," Blake said, kissing Avery on the cheek and stepping back to admire her yellow silk dress. Her cheeks were flushed and Blake realized, just then, how happy she was.

"Thanks little brother," she answered. "I ordered you a

drink, I hope I got it right. I really like Samantha, by the way. I hope Mark is growing on you."

Blake took a big sip of his martini, allowing the searing liquid to coat his throat, giving him time to answer. "Sis, if you're happy, I'm happy. And Mark seems to make you happy so he's welcome, just another part of the family," Blake answered, measuring his words.

"He's joining Putnam Enterprises!" Avery confided. "He's so excited. He'll be right under James!"

Of course he would, Blake thought, taking another big drink of his martini. Mark would be married to his sister tomorrow, and then, he'd have a job for life. Not because he was the smartest, or the most skilled, or the most qualified – no it would be simply because he was family. Blake wanted to change the subject before he said something he'd regret.

"Avery, have you seen Samantha? I haven't spotted her since I came down," Blake said.

"Oh, last I saw she was in the library," Avery answered. "I'm so glad you're happy for me, Blake! Your opinion means a lot."

"Cheers," Blake said, kissing his sister on the cheek and happy that for once he hadn't shared his opinion.

He placed his empty glass on a passing waiter's tray. "Another please. I'll be in the library."

"Yes, sir," the waiter said.

Blake walked in the door of the library, and froze.

Samantha, wearing the elegant blue dress, that he hoped to peel off her delectable body later tonight was backed into the corner of his father's library, talking intimately with Mark's brother, Max, the same guy who had tried to flirt with her before on the beach. Blake didn't care if they were about to be family, all he cared about was Sam, and she looked uncomfortable.

Max had her pinned against the bookcase, and she had to crane her neck to look up at him. She was leaning away from him, and he was talking to her intensely.

"Blake," she said, and he caught the note of relief in her voice. "I thought women were supposed to take ages to get ready, not men."

Max had backed off enough so that she could slip past him. She linked her fingers with his, and when the waiter joined them and handed Blake the drink he'd ordered, she stole it, took a sip, her eyes smiling into his.

"I'm glad you're here."

Blake pulled her close and gave her a soft kiss on the lips.

"Was he bothering you?" Blake asked, narrowing his eyes at Max, who leaned against the books and smiled at them.

"It's nothing," she handed his drink back.

"Do you want one?"

"Exactly like that," Samantha told the waiter.

"Have mine," he whispered in her ear. "Let's go outside. I want to be alone with you."

Blake looked into her beautiful blue eyes, and softened. He looked away from Max and focused on Samantha. "You do look beautiful. I just, I don't trust Mark's brother or his family."

"Blake, you do trust me though," she led him back into the larger room. "I was just having a conversation with him. He flirts, but not my type."

"What's your type?" He asked curiously.

"Evolving," Samantha said, relaxing enough to tease him.

She took the martini off the waiter's tray as he paused in front of her.

"Olive?" She asked him, as she put one in her mouth and stood on tip toe so he could eat the other one on the stick.

Blake never did public displays of affection. Ever. He'd even told her that, but he caught the olive between his lips and with his free hand pulled her in tight to his body so that she could feel what she did to him. Samantha sighed into his mouth, and moved against him, so that his erection pressed into her belly.

"Things have changed, Sam," Blake said. "Forget the business deal. I want to be together."

She pulled away. "What do you mean forget the…?" She whispered.

"Dinner is served," the waiter hovered by his elbow.

Blake bit back a curse. "Samantha, wait," he called out.

She was already crossing the room following the others into the grand dining room. He practically had to run to catch up to her. He looked down at her. Her expression was unreadable, but she bit down on her full bottom lip. Even that was sexy, Blake thought. She looked tense, but he didn't know why. He debated what to do. There was distance between them. He traced a finger down her bare arm and covered her small hand with his. She smiled up at him and flipped her wrist so that they were holding hands.

"We could just make a run for it," he whispered in her ear.

"You wouldn't dare."

He stopped walking right on the threshold. "Try me."

Samantha looked at his expression, and he could tell she was uncertain.

"Blake, it's your sister's wedding weekend. It's why we're here."

She squeezed his hand and then let him go.

AS THEY WALKED into the grand dining room – and it was grand, bigger than any room Samantha had ever had dined in before, including restaurants – all she could feel, all she could sense was the pressure of Blake's hand on the small of her back. It made her feel cared for, a part of something, and she hadn't felt like that in a long time, but what did he mean, forget the business deal. Did he expect her to quit her job now and date him? Is that what he thought?

She squared her shoulders. She wanted to whirl around and

demand an answer right now, but Avery smiled and waved at her, and then said something to her fiancé, who then looked at them.

She smiled back. She'd get through the dinner somehow and then before she'd get lost in his kisses, she wanted to know exactly what Blake was thinking.

She didn't trust herself with words, so she simply smiled at his entire family as they entered the room. The warmth of his hand, which had now settled on her waist, seemed to ignite a fire that flared through her blood stream. He was touching her in front of his entire family and the wedding party. That must mean something, but Samantha couldn't analyze anything anymore as her attention was focused on imagining Blake's chest without his dress shirt. She was fueled by lust and longing. She turned to look at Blake, wearing a perfectly fitted European cut suit, navy blue, white shirt, navy tie with tiny light blue dots – she realized suddenly, his tie perfectly matched her dress. She imagined his broad shoulders, his perfect six-pack—

"Hello you two," Blake's dad said, interrupting her fantasy.

"Hello Mr. Putnam," Samantha said, giving Blake's dad a kiss on the cheek.

"Tonight you two are split up, I'm afraid. But no worries, this evening should be over in a couple of hours," Mr. Putnam said, extending his arm. "Samantha, allow me to escort you to your table."

Blake shot a look at Samantha, and she could tell he was about to say something, but she jumped in.

"That's fine. That's how it should be. I'm sure there is a table for family, Blake," Samantha said, squeezing his hand. She felt him relax, just by reassuring him that she would be ok.

"Yes, of course," Blake said. "Thank you, Dad." Blake motioned for his dad and Samantha to go ahead of him, and he shot Samantha a knowing grin.

Samantha was sure Blake's dad could tell how attracted she was to his son, that her excitement, and anticipation, was obvious to everybody in the room. But she focused on small talk as Richard Putnam escorted her to a table filled with "the others", non-family members including, unfortunately, Mark's brother, Max, whom Samantha was seated beside.

"Here you are dear," Richard Putnam said, pulling out her chair for her. The dining room was gorgeous, filled with red and white roses, exquisite candelabras, china place settings ringed with silver and white, crystal stemware and silver flatware all sparkling in the dim light. Everything was perfect, except for the fact that she would have to endure Max with his caustic comments about Blake coupled with his intense flirting.

"Thank you so much, Richard," Samantha said giving Blake's dad a hug as he deposited her at her seat while subtly moving her chair away from Max. She knew Blake would be furious about who she was sitting next to, but would he hold it against her again?

"Well, look who's here," Max said, his speech already slurred by the cocktails at the reception. "Miss Icy Hot, that's who."

Samantha couldn't decide what to say to him, realizing the best response would be to ignore him. Instead she looked around the large circular table and smiled at all the other "others". Unfortunately, Shelby was seated at the next table over, another table of others. She'd hoped the younger girl would carry the conversation. From the looks of her own table, Samantha looked to be the one who was expected to carry the conversation at this one.

First, she'd need to put Max in his place.

"Look Max, you're a great guy, I'm sure," Samantha said, as soon as Max and his entire body began to lean toward her. "But I'm here with Blake. I know you want to respect that. Blake is Avery's brother, soon to be your in-law."

"Look Sam," Max said, still slurring his words. "I'm nothing to the Putnams and neither are you. You might think Blake likes you, but he's just using you. That guy doesn't "like" anybody, not even his own family. Ask them."

The room rang out with the clinking of forks on crystal, and the words "toast" "a toast".

Samantha tried to turn in her chair, to face the front of the room where Avery and her wedding party were seated, trying to turn her back on Max, trying to block out the words ringing in her ears. She knew how Blake felt, she'd experienced the passion of their embrace. She knew Blake wanted to end up in bed with her, and she wanted the same thing and more. The more part, well, that's what Max was trying to make her doubt. Even as she could feel him leaning towards her, even as she felt his breath on her back, she forced herself to ignore him and listened to the toast.

"To Avery and Mark, may they enjoy the best of everything!" Denton said, his broad smile lighting up the front of the room. Samantha glanced over to the table next to her and watched as Shelby beamed. Those two were cute together, she thought. She wondered what people thought of her and Blake. They all knew she was seven years his junior, and that she worked for him. She hoped they didn't hold it against her.

She realized she was thinking about Blake as if they were in a relationship, not on a make-believe weekend.

Blake stood to offer a toast, and Samantha felt his eyes connect with hers from across the room. "A toast, to my favorite sister, Avery. I hope you find happiness and a lifelong connection. Some relationships, no matter how they begin, are simply meant to be."

Samantha felt his words inside her body, as if he was whispering into her ear, not projecting his toast across three tables.

"Mark, you know our family had our early doubts about you." Blake said, pausing as uncomfortable laughter erupted in the room. "But you make Avery happy and as long as you continue to do that, the Putnams welcome you into our family. Cheers."

"Asshole," Max said, loud enough for Samantha's entire table, and the adjoining table to hear.

"Max," Samantha said, turning to glare at him. "That was a wonderful toast."

Before she knew what was happening, Max was clinging his wine glass with his desert spoon.

"I'd like to follow that warm toast with one of my own," Max slurred, standing up, almost spilling his half-empty glass of red wine on Samantha's head. "When my brother started getting serious about a Putnam, I told him he was crazy. That family will eat you alive, I said. But Avery's a nice enough girl, so what's a guy to do? It's hard to find that, right Samantha? A real man who isn't just using you for a date? Well, cheers and good luck to the couple or couples!"

Samantha dropped her head, staring at her food. This was humiliating, she thought, unsure of what to say or do. She was sure of one thing, "You're awful, Max," she said in a low voice.

"What did you say Miss Icy Hot?" Max leered at her. "At least I'm not an asshole, I'm the only non-asshole here. In fact, you are an asshole, too. A gold digging asshole."

The ugliness of Max's words were sinking in, her humiliation deepened. She wanted to leave, but wasn't sure she could make her legs do it. Blake bore down on the table. Samantha sighed in relief that he wasn't just abandoning her.

Blake grabbed Max by both lapels, holding his face close to his own.

"You don't talk to Sam that way. You don't know her. You never will. You don't know me or my family."

Max struggled, then Blake released him. Max threw an awkward punch, but Blake countered and sent Max soaring backwards, where he sprawled on the plush dining room carpet. Blake leaned over him.

"Don't insult Samantha and don't try to strike at me with an insulting toast at my sister's wedding. Get out or I'll throw you out."

Max sat up and sneered.

"You think you're so...,"

Blake reached down to grab Max again, but both Denton and James were at his side, restraining him. "That's enough Blake," Denton said. "You made your point."

"Get out of here, Max," Denton said. "For good, or you'll be dealing with all three of us." And the three brothers stood together as Max, holding his face, hurried out of the room.

At the front table, Richard Putnam clinked his glass and said, "Please, everyone, this is my daughter and Mark's evening. Let's not allow this incident to ruin anything. Carry on."

James and Denton walked back to the front as Blake took Max's seat next to Samantha. Her head was in her hands, shame and shock mingled together. She noticed the sound of dinner party chatter was returning to the room. And then she felt him next to her, her body responded immediately, feeling better simply by his nearness.

"Sam, it's ok," Blake said in a low voice, his head next to hers.

His hand smoothed over her back.

"Please, Sam look at me."

She dropped her hands from her face and stared into his blue eyes. She could see his jaw was tense with worry. He ran his thumbs along her cheekbone.

"Max has always disliked me. We knew each other in school. I'm sorry it spilled over to you."

She caught his right hand and kissed his knuckles.

"Do they hurt?"

"A little," he said ruefully. "Out of practice."

Her eyes filled with tears, tears she didn't want to spill in public, not during Avery's special night.

"Come on," Blake said, pulling her to standing and then tucking her into him, folding her tightly into his side. She could feel his powerful bicep holding them together.

Together they walked through the impressive foyer and out into the beautiful Low Country night, full moon twinkling off the calm waters of the sound, the red and white striped lighthouse of Hilton Head Island visible in the distance.

Samantha had dried her tears with Blake's handkerchief. They stood side by side on the wrap around porch, simply breathing in the night air, each of them lost in thought. There were words, possibly hard words to hear, but words that had to be said.

Chapter Eleven

"BLAKE," SAMANTHA SPOKE, knowing the words had to be said. "What did you mean the deal's off?"

"What?" He sounded far away.

"In the library. You said the deal was off. Did you mean that if you and I have a…," Samantha broke off because he hadn't offered a relationship had he?

"If we," she took a deep breath. She was an adult. She wanted to try for a relationship with Blake and keep her career at Blake Genetics. She had to be able to stand up for herself.

"You said you wanted me. Is that for just tonight on the island, or did you want to date, see where it goes?"

She had his attention now.

"Why would you think I would sleep with you only once?"

His hands were on her shoulders. He smiled.

"You have seriously underestimated your power over me."

"But what about the merger talks and my job? If we date, you don't expect me to leave Blake Genetics."

"No."

"But?"

"But nothing. It might be awkward sometimes, but we'll deal with anything like that together. I knew I was right to pull your file. I picked you over Marlene's first choice. I knew I shouldn't give in to my impulse, but there was something about you," he shook his head and smiled, self-deprecating. "There is something about you. I couldn't…I can't resist."

Samantha stood on her tip toes.
"Then don't."

BLAKE STARED DOWN into her gorgeous, expressive eyes. Next to him on the porch, stood a woman different from any woman he'd ever known. She was smart, independent, an asset to his business, a history buff, and gorgeous. Everything he'd given up trying to find. He could even imagine letting her into his tightly guarded, very controlled life. He wanted that, he realized. He wanted her to change his life.

He pulled her close to him and briefly kissed her. Then he closed his eyes, and let his forehead rest against hers. He could feel emotion wash over him, every time she was close to him, and he no longer was sure he wanted to fight it.

"Well," Samantha said, pressing kisses down his face until her lips were millimeters from his. "I guess we need to go back inside and join the festivities."

"I'd rather stay here next to you," Blake said, breathing her in. "I'm sorry for what Max said. It's not true."

"Which part?" Samantha asked, looking up into his eyes, loving the man she saw there, the crinkles next to his eyes, his slight smile he saved only for special moments, like this.

"The part when he said you were just a date. That's what you were supposed to be. We were supposed to be faking it, but I can't. Not with you. It's probably the reason I pulled your file in the first place. I had planned on using you to just get through the weekend as quickly and easily as possible, and now I can't stop thinking about you. I've been attracted to you since the moment I saw you in that meeting. I want you. I want to protect you. I don't want us to end."

"Oh Blake," Samantha said, as Blake leaned down to kiss her, placing a firm hand behind her neck and gently brushing her lips with his. Samantha pushed her lips into his, wanting him, all of him.

Blake struggled to break off the kiss. "But you're right, Sam, we have to go back inside. God this is hard."

"Yes, it is," Samantha said, smiling while placing her hand on his erection, visible through his suit pants.

"That's what you do to me," Blake said.

Her fingers traced his length, and he groaned against her lips.

"You are supposed to be helping me."

"I am very helpful. Do you want to see what you do to me?" She asked playfully.

The front door opened and Blake's mother appeared. "Dear, I hope I'm not intruding but we really need you back at the family table Blake. It isn't right without you, son," Evalyn said, firmly, more of a directive than a request, as she returned inside.

"You heard the woman," Blake said, holding the door open for Sam. "After you. And, I'll be after you later."

SHELBY HURRIED TO Samantha's side as soon as she rejoined her table. Max's place setting had been cleared, as had his chair. All traces of him, and the incident had been removed by the efficient staff.

"Are you ok?" Shelby asked, hugging Samantha around the shoulders.

"Yes, I'm fine, just embarrassed," Samantha said.

"Don't be. Everyone thought he was a jerk, and now we all know he is a jerk," Shelby said. "He's just jealous of you and Blake. You two are so perfect together. Oopsie, I've gotta go eat."

The rest of the rehearsal dinner seemed to last forever, at least for Samantha, who could not wait to be in Blake's arms again. She barely touched the prime rib and potatoes, even though the meal tasted fabulous. Her stomach clenched at the thought of his hands on her body.

Finally, when the last toast was delivered and the bride and groom thanked everyone again, the dinner was over. Blake appeared as Samantha was standing up, wishing her table mates a good evening.

"Hello, gorgeous," he whispered in her ear. "Come with me."

Blake maneuvered the two of them through the dinner crowd and out the front door, making impressive time. Samantha noticed the bruise forming on his right hand, the spot where he made contact with Max's face, but she didn't mention it. She wanted tonight to be about just the two of them. Once they were outside, Blake hurried them down the stairs, leading her to a golf cart parked in the circular drive.

"For once, no driver," he said, looking as happy as Samantha had ever seen him. He looked carefree and completely irresistible. "Climb in."

Samantha slid into the passenger seat, and Blake hopped into the driver's seat, and quickly, they were driving along a cart path bordering the ocean. It was another perfect moonlit evening, with a bit of a chill in the air.

Blake noticed her goose bumps. He stopped the cart, took off his dinner jacket and wrapped it around Samantha. The coat was huge, warm and smelled just like his cologne.

"Where are we headed?" Samantha asked.

"To a place where we can have a little privacy. Trust me, do you?" Blake asked.

"Yes," Samantha answered, swallowing hard, anticipation and desire were building inside her, consuming her thoughts and words.

Blake shot her a devious grin as they rounded a corner and the Melrose Inn came into sight. Samantha looked at him, but didn't say a word, not trusting herself. This was where the wedding would take place tomorrow, outside near the gazebo. But why were they here now?

Pulling the golf cart into a parking spot, Blake walked around to her side of the cart and offered his hand. She took it, and instantly, the connection zinged through her. They climbed the stairs to the grand inn, and walked inside to the front desk. Samantha admired the wide hardwood floors, the huge floral arrangement greeting visitors. The Melrose Inn felt at the once steeped in history, and very modern.

"Enjoy your stay, Mr. and Mrs. Putnam," the hotel clerk said, handing Blake a key with a wink. Samantha blushed and looked away, as Blake took her hand and led her to the main staircase.

"We don't even have luggage," Samantha whispered, embarrassed. She was excited to be here, to be with Blake, but at the same time, she felt a bit like a hooker, walking into a hotel late at night, grabbing a room for a hookup.

"Relax," Blake said as the reached the top of the stairs. Samantha followed him down a long hallway, and stopped when they reached the room at the end. He put the key in the door, and then stepped aside to allow Samantha to walk in first.

The room was a suite, with a direct view of the ocean, the moon framed in the center of the sliding glass doors that led out to their private terrace. Candles were lit throughout the sitting area and a dozen long-stemmed roses in a crystal vase adorned the coffee table.

"Oh, Blake, this is beautiful," Samantha said, shrugging off his suit jacket and hanging it on the back of the desk chair. She crossed the room and slid open the door to the outdoor porch, noticing the gazebo below and then the ocean beyond. Blake came up behind her and pulled her into him. Samantha could feel his need, and she trembled with desire.

Blake began kissing her neck, gently, and then, quickly spun her around to face him. His lips found hers, pressing hard, parting her lips with his tongue, his need as apparent as her own. She wrapped her arms around his neck, lost in him, in this moment, feeling dizzy and excited, smelling Blake's masculine scent and feeling his strong arms around her.

Samantha's lips parted allowing Blake's tongue inside. She heard Blake moan, as he held their kiss but bent down and scooped her up into his arms.

She'd never been carried literally by a man or carried away with desire, he could have taken her anywhere and she would have gone. Where he took her was to the bedroom of their suite, to a bed covered with red rose petals. He gently placed her in the center of the bed, her blue dress a beautiful contrast to the red rose petals surrounding her.

"Samantha," Blake said, standing and staring down at her with an intensity, a longing that made her crazy.

Samantha needed him on top of her, needed to feel him inside her. She writhed on the bed of rose petals, feeling the silky softness under her arms and back while reaching towards Blake. "Please," she moaned.

Finally, Blake climbed onto the bed, lying on his side next to her. Samantha reached for him, trying to pull him on top of her, but he resisted. "Shh, let's take this slowly," he said, his eyes dark and wanting.

She sucked in a big gulp of air as Blake reached over and slid one strap of her dress off her shoulder followed by the other. He trailed his fingers lightly across the top of her collarbone, up her neck and up to her lips. Samantha wanted to scream, she reached down, reaching for his belt, but Blake grabbed her hand and placed it flat on the bed.

"No," Blake commanded. "I want to touch all of you first."

Samantha's head swam, but she did as Blake instructed keeping her hands pressed against the rose petals as he slowly unzipped the side of her dress, pushing the fabric aside to reveal her left breast, as her nipples hardened.

"Gorgeous," he murmured, cupping her breast, rolling her nipple between his fingers.

Samantha arched her back, reaching for him, but Blake said, "No," grabbing both of her wrists in his left hand, holding them together above her head.

"If you don't behave, I'm going to need to tie you up," Blake said, kissing her ear, her neck and her exposed breasts while holding her arms tight.

"Oh my God," Samantha cried, squirming in place, trying to control the growing urge inside, the need, wetness flowed soaking her underwear. She was losing control and she didn't care.

Blake released her arms and in a quick movement, slid her dress down her body and all the way off. She was naked, exposed except for her underwear. And he was fully dressed, except for his suit coat. She couldn't find a way to ask him to undress, she couldn't form a thought. She'd become a ball of need.

"I dreamed you would be this beautiful, this sexy," he said, climbing back on the bed, slipping a finger under the lace of her underwear. "And now I'm going to taste you." Blake pulled her panties off quickly. Samantha gasped, her hips bucking as Blake's expertise took her over the edge, his lips sucked on her nipples, and moved down to her sex. She pulled his hair, reached for his shoulders and grabbed bunches of his shirt, until he inserted one finger inside her and she screamed, her orgasm rolling through her body.

Samantha shuddered, and writhed on the bed, having just experienced the best orgasm of her life, rose petals attaching to parts of her body now slick with sweat. "Blake, please, I want you inside me," she moaned, it was something she'd never desired more in her life.

BLAKE COULDN'T BELIEVE how turned on Samantha made him.

She was so hot, with perfect breasts and tiny waist. He rose and stood at the side of the bed, still watching her writhe with pleasure. Her eyes were closed, a small smile formed over her heart-shaped lips.

Blake yanked off his tie, tossing it to the ground, removed his belt, and grabbed the condom out of his pocket, tossing it on the bed. His shirt and pants were joined by his boxers and socks in a heap on the floor. He tried to calm his breathing, to regain control of himself, of his emotions. He wanted Samantha with a fervor he'd never felt before, a desire so strong he wondered if it could ever be satisfied.

Finally, she opened her eyes and looked up at him. "Please," she said again.

"Since you asked so nicely," Blake said, climbing onto the bed, and finally laying on top of her, their naked bodies fitting perfectly together, the heat between them a fire.

"I knew you'd have an eight-pack," Samantha murmured, lying beneath him, but moving her hand appreciatively across his chest. "You are the perfect man, Mr. Putnam."

"No, not perfect, but hopefully just right for you," Blake answered, beginning to move his hips, his erection growing even harder, his need almost overwhelming. He began to glide his member over her sensitive sex, and she reached out and grabbed his shoulders, bringing her legs up and wrapping them around his waist.

"Please," she begged, but Blake wanted to tease her, to push her over the edge again, so he controlled himself, rubbing against her with his hips and his erection, leaving her whimpering.

"Come again," Blake said, "Do you feel me? Let yourself go." Blake could feel her shaking beneath him, he could feel her pelvis thrusting upward, wanting him inside, and even though he wasn't, it was enough to send her over the edge and she screamed.

"Oh my god," she said, "I can't take anymore."

Blake reached for the condom and quickly pulled it on.

"Shh, baby, I'm here," Blake said, rubbing her cheek, pushing her hair off of her face until she looked up at him, her pupils huge with desire. "Let's do this together."

Blake stared down into Samantha's eyes as he thrust inside her, slowly pushing into her, thrusting again, her tightness forcing him to moan. "God Sam you feel so good."

"You're so big," Samantha said and Blake swelled with pride. Nobody had made him feel like this in bed. This was what it was about, he realized, lowering his head and kissing one of her nipples, teasing her again. She writhed and moaned beneath him as he thrust deeper inside.

Blake pulled out halfway, causing Samantha to wrap her legs around him, trying to pull him back in. "Ok, I'll give you it all," Blake growled, pushing and thrusting completely inside her, as deep as he could go, rocking his hips, causing his erection to fill her fully, completely.

They climaxed together, with Samantha shouting his name as he exploded inside her, and then collapsed on top of her, drenched in sweat, his muscles beginning to relax as he regained control.

Finally, when his breathing had almost returned to normal, Blake wanted to make sure Samantha was ok. She had a folded rose petal crushed against her stomach. Her long blonde hair was wild, and tangled, and she looked like a dream, a dream he never imagined he'd live.

Blake pulled her close to him, and they spooned, each of them breathing a bit easier as time went by. He couldn't believe how great it made him feel, to hold her this way. Sure the sex was amazing, but this, this was something more. This was something he'd never felt before. Usually, he'd want to get out as soon as sex was over. He didn't want to lose control to anyone, he didn't need complications in his life.

But Samantha was more than a complication. She could become a permanent part of his life, his real life, he realized. He wouldn't lose his edge if he cared for this woman. No, he could still be a strong man, a successful entrepreneur, and have someone by his side, as long as that someone was Samantha.

But did she feel the same way?

"Samantha?"

"Hmm," she said, rolling over to face him, a rose petal stuck to her cheek.

"How was it?" Blake asked, worry, an unfamiliar emotion, flooded his brain.

"That was the best thing that ever happened to me," Samantha said, staring intently into his eyes. "You are the best thing that has ever happened to me Blake."

Samantha sat up next to him, pulling a throw around herself, a shy move Blake found adorable after all they'd just done together.

"How about some champagne?" Blake asked, sliding off the bed and returning from the other room with an iced bucket with Veuve Cliquot.

"Sounds great, just let me go freshen up," Samantha said.

"You'll find some clothes to put on in the closet," Blake said as Samantha made her way towards the bathroom and the walk-in closet. "I had them sent over from the house, just in case."

"Wow, you're amazing," Samantha said, turning to give him her signature smile.

Blake felt a lightness, a carefree feeling, he hadn't felt since he was a child.

Chapter Twelve

AFTER SHARING HALF a bottle of champagne on the balcony, enjoying the moonlight, Samantha had suggested they'd need to get some sleep for the wedding the following afternoon. How they'd managed to have sex again, before turning in, she wasn't sure, because she didn't think it was possible for her to have that many orgasms in one night. But she did.

Blake was an amazing lover, and he had such a strong, hard body, she loved the feel of all of him. This morning, they'd had breakfast brought to their suite. She'd changed into the jogging clothes he'd brought over from her room and had decided to run back to the plantation, hoping she could have an enjoyable morning run, and that it would give them a chance to each return to the Putnam Plantation alone. Maybe nobody had noticed they'd spent the night out, she hoped. By the time she returned from her jog, nobody was milling around the first floor so she was able to make it up to their room without talking to anyone.

With a couple hours before she needed to get ready for the wedding, she decided to take a shower and a quick nap. She opened the door to the bathroom and walked in on a naked Blake, just out of the shower.

"Oh good, it's you," he said, his eyes narrowing as he walked towards her, locking the bathroom door behind her. "I was hoping you'd join me for a shower."

THE WEATHER WAS perfect for an early evening wedding. Samantha, dressed in her baby blue Oscar de la Renta and dripping in diamonds, as Shelby noted, sat next to Shelby in the back of the Putnam family section and beamed at Blake, handsome in his tux, standing between his two brothers as the groomsmen. Max had left the island, so only Avery's brothers stood up for Mark. He seemed fine with it, though. Maybe Max was a jerk to him, too, Samantha realized.

Avery glided down the aisle escorted by both her mom and dad. She looked beautiful in a simple white gown, with a thin diamond studded tiara holding her delicate veil. The string quartet played the wedding march, and Samantha and Shelby stood and held hands as Avery walked by.

"I can't wait to be a bride," Shelby said, leaning in close to Samantha.

Samantha, who had dreamed of all the details of becoming a bride in her scrapbooks and on Pintrest, suddenly realized her dreams might come true. She turned to look at Blake. He was smiling at her, his blue eyes communicating the secrets and the passion they shared.

"Me too," Samantha said to Shelby.

The wedding reception took place on the lawn of the Melrose Inn, and Samantha and Blake were inseparable. At one point, Blake suggested they make a break for the suite, visible from where they were standing, but Samantha knew that would be wrong.

"I just want to rip that gown off of your body," Blake whispered, sending shivers down her spine.

"Behave, Mr. Putnam. Do you know how much you spent on this little gown?" Samantha teased. "Besides, your family needs you here today. We have plenty of time for that once we get back to Charlotte. Don't we?" Samantha asked. Worry had crept into her voice, she knew, as she thought about how everything could change once they were away from this island.

"We do. You'll help me close the Daycon deal next week, we'll pitch them on the direct to consumer DNA testing which will of course close the deal. We'll celebrate by taking a trip somewhere fabulous, getting to know each other even better," Blake answered, pulling her into an embrace. "And I can't wait for that."

"Hello you two," Richard Putnam said walking up to them.

Samantha gave him a kiss on the cheek as his son clapped him on the back. "How's it going Dad?" Blake asked.

"It's great Son. Beautiful wedding. Life is as it should be but I still wish you were down here, with us, in the business. I miss you, that's all," Richard said.

"That's the best thing I've ever heard a dad say to his son," Samantha said, while Blake smiled.

"He's just sentimental. Besides, you've got James, Dad. And Denton soon enough. I'd just be in the way," Blake said.

"Son, there will always be room for you. We could make you and James co-presidents eventually," Richard said.

Samantha realized there might be a stronger sibling rivalry between Blake and James than she'd thought. She knew Blake would never be number two to anyone. Maybe that was the real reason he'd started his own company, Samantha thought.

"Dad, I love you, but I'm happy making my own way," Blake said, and Samantha's heart warmed as he expressed love to his dad.

"I know Son. And I know I'm loyal. Loyal to a fault, as your mom would say. But there isn't anything weak about that. It's a character trait that's served me well. Blake thinks I'm soft, Samantha. You see, I was raised by an egotistical, distant, control freak who for some reason, Blake decided to emulate."

"Dad, Grandfather was amazing, look what he built," Blake said, crossing his arms. Samantha saw him as a boy, stubborn, confident.

"Yes, he did create Putnam Industries and grew it through his cold, ruthless management style. That worked for him, but not for me. I've quadrupled the size of the business, and continue to do so with heart, Blake, and hard work, and loyalty to family. They can go together quite well," Richard said, taking a big sip of his martini. "There are many different ways to operate in life, and in business. Some ways enhance your life and the people you care about, some make you seem cold and detached. Life's too short, Son. Excuse me."

Samantha was puzzled by Blake's seeming resistance to his dad's way of living, of being. When in fact, Samantha knew if Blake allowed himself, he could be just like his father. She'd begun to see glimpses of that kindness, that loyalty already.

"Conversations with him always end that way," Blake said, taking a sip of his drink. "I just don't agree with my family's business, about what they're doing to the environment. And I don't agree about the nepotism, that will continue now again with Avery's husband. It's not merit based, it's embarrassing." Blake didn't mention it, but now she knew he never would be comfortable reporting to James.

"Well, it's good you are out of that business then. You shouldn't be there if you don't believe in it. But they do. Maybe they'll change, but maybe they won't. All you can do is live your truth. Your dad is right, you have all of those wonderful traits inside you. You are a warm, caring man. Just like your dad. Let everybody at Blake Genetics see that side of you. You'll be even more successful, you'll help even more people and maybe you'll be able to change the family business someday."

Blake stared out at the sound. Samantha was afraid she'd upset him, but she knew his true nature was in there. He was funny, and warm, he could connect emotionally with people. She'd help him, if he'd let her.

"Well, alright then, I guess I need your help," he said, and turned and pulled her close to him, breathing in her sweet lavender scent. Blake leaned forward, pressing his lips against hers, a brief tender kiss with a promise of much more to come.

"Glad to be of service, boss," Samantha said with a smile.

The End

Her Forbidden Love

An Indigo Island Romance

Kaira Rouda

Dedication

To the people of Daufuskie Island, South Carolina, for sharing your island and inspiring my stories. And to my puppy love, Oreo, for always being at my feet and sharing my love for the beach.

Note to Readers

Thank you for choosing an Indigo Island Romance!

I'm thrilled to be writing a series of books that share a setting on a beautiful South Carolina Sea Island. *Her Forbidden Love* is the story of Dorsey and Jack, two young people trying to figure out their futures, individually and perhaps, together. I attempted to weave some Gullah culture into the story, because it's an important part of our shared history and in my opinion, needs to be preserved and treasured. I hope you enjoy your glimpses of Gullah via Barbara in the story. Happy reading!

Chapter One

Dorsey

DORSEY'S STRAWBERRY BLONDE hair had expanded from curly to frizz in the short forty-five minutes it took the ferry to cross the Calibogue Sound, the body of water separating Hilton Head Island from Indigo Island. Before the ferry, her hair had reached the middle of her back, but was now circling her head in a clown-like poof. She searched in her duffle bag to find a hair tie, attempting to tame her life-long nemesis.

At twenty-five, she had tried every product known to Sephora to straighten or even simply manage her mane. After a couple Brazilian straightening treatments gone wrong, during which time she discovered that the chemicals used were the same as embalming fluid – she'd decided to just set her hair free. She smiled at her reflection in the mirror. It was time to start a new life, let the past, and her hair, go.

As the ferry continued to chug through the warm, still water at the backside of the island, Dorsey imagined how great it would feel to jump into the water to cool off. Sure, she could just go inside the main cabin and freeze in the air conditioning. But she wanted to stay out on deck. She was excited to experience everything about her new home and workplace, to see it for the first time. She couldn't wait to swim in the warm waters of the sound even though she knew it contained horseshoe crabs and other creatures. There were even sand sharks, she'd read, so maybe she'd swim close to shore. But after living in Ohio most of her life, she was excited to get to know all about what was in the ocean and everything else about the Sea Islands. She'd focus on her future, build a new life and hopefully replace her bad dreams with new memories.

Dorsey had felt the healing beginning the moment she had stepped on the ferry, even as she was running away from everything she had ever known. She stretched, contemplating a Kate Winslet Titanic pose at the bow when –

"Miss, we're pulling into the dock, please take your seat," the captain said over the loudspeaker.

Dorsey hurried inside the empty, brightly lit and frigid cabin, goose bumps immediately covering her body with the dramatic change in temperature. Dorsey's white blouse was drenched in sweat and sticking to her everywhere, becoming translucent. She covered her chest with her arms, and hoped to dry soon. Before she knew it, the clanking sound of a metal ramp being attached to the boat announced she'd arrived.

"Watch youself, little landlubber, it's slippery," said a tall, skinny, blond man with oversized Ray Ban sunglasses. He walked toward Dorsey down the gangway. "Let me give you a hand."

"Ah, sure," she said, as the man grabbed her under her right arm and hauled her up the ramp. *Well, I guess I've arrived.*

"Okay, well, here we are," the man said, dropping her arm once they had reached the top. "That's how I like to see us greet any guest who may be a little sea-sick. Don't want them falling in here, it's really shallow and murky. Not a quality experience," he said. "You're Dorsey, right?"

"Yes, right, but I'm not sea-sick, just hot," Dorsey said, noticing his gleaming Top Club name badge said Steve.

"Just noticing from your size that you'll need to eat some of our good ol Low Country cooking. Fatten you up a bit. I do like the freckles though, and your greenish-blue eyes. The kids will love you, I suspect," Steve said. They stood staring at each other at the top of the ramp, sweating in the late afternoon heat.

"Thanks, and what do you do here besides greet the ferry?" Dorsey said. *And manhandle employees?* She was getting irritated that he was sizing her up and seemed to know all about her when all she knew about him was what was written on his shirt badge. He reminded her of a turtle, his long neck poking out of his preppy polo shirt.

"Steve Fordham. I am Club Manager. I oversee everything on this plantation. All of the recreational activities for the club, the golf, tennis, swimming complex, and all forty guest cottages and the inn. And, of course, the staff. And that's what you are, so I oversee you. You're mine, for the duration of your contract," he said. His laugh was too high-pitched for such a tall man. "I've been with Top Club for four years now, and I've been here on Indigo Island for two. Been in the hospitality business all my career. So far, this is my favorite spot. I like the isolation, the peace. I call it home now, like it's my island. I'm the driver of all this success," Steve added, with a grand sweeping gesture.

Success? she wondered, following the arc of his arm and seeing only a dirt road and an old, beat-up pink school bus behind him. *Godforsaken*—that was the word that suddenly popped into Dorsey's head. There must be more to this place than this, she realized, standing in the middle of the sand/dirt parking lot/ferry landing. She'd checked it out online, and it looked beautiful.

"Well, are you my boss then?" she asked, hoping that he was her boss's boss or something more removed.

"Yes I am. I take pride in directly managing most of the staff. I like to know what everybody is up to, at all times," Steve answered, his round, mirrored sunglasses glinting in the orange-pink sunset light. "To become the best club in the Top Club chain we're going to have to step it up a notch. You're part of my master plan. Come along. Employees ride in the old bus. The air-conditioned shuttle is for our club guests. Suppose this will be your first taste of roughing it, huh, city girl? Come this way."

"Right," she answered, realizing he probably knew everything about her – well everything she put on her application. Hometown: Grandville, Ohio. College degree: Early childhood education with a minor in hospitality from the Ohio State University. Work experience: Live-in nanny for the Rogers family for the last four years.

What Dorsey wanted to know was how a six-foot-tall man sporting Popeye-like biceps ended up with a squeaky-high voice? Genetic freak of nature, she decided. She couldn't tell if he was looking at her or past her from behind his 1980's sunglasses. Oh well, she didn't care. She was excited to get to work, and as long as the Kids Cottage looked like the photos she'd seen online, everything would work out fine.

She followed him through the dusty, sand-covered parking area to the bubble-gum pink school bus.

She climbed up the stairs to the bus ahead of Steve and nodded to the hat-clad driver who looked seventy years old but could be fifty, she simply couldn't tell. She took a seat three rows back in the empty bus, behind the driver who made eye contact through the large mirror suspended above his head. The driver shook his head back and forth, slowly, almost imperceptibly, as his dark brown eyes darted toward Steve who was climbing onto the bus. Dorsey could taste the driver's dislike of Steve in her mouth, as if she'd just taken a big gulp from a spoiled carton of milk. A chill ran down her spine and she nodded at him.

The bumpy drive to her new job and new life wasn't any more reassuring than the ferry arrival area had been. Through the open window she saw desolate, shadowy forests of hanging-moss-covered trees and dirt roads peeling off from the main road in many directions. The huge, bent trees hoisted tangles of moss, looking like witches. Thick groves of pines obscured the light in several places as they bumped along. Every pond they drove past was covered with green ooze, pollen, and swarms of insects as large as her hand. Dorsey shifted in her seat, leaving a slick trail of sweat where her legs had just been. She wiped her forehead with the back of her hand, praying the employee housing had air conditioning.

"Under that water are some huge gators," Steve said. "This is the backside of the island. You don't want to find yourself out here, especially not alone, and especially not at night. It's primitive, you know what I mean? Ol' Jim lives out there, don't you, son?"

"Yes, sir," the driver answered quickly, eyes fixed on the road.

Steve lowered his voice. "If it wasn't for the club, I don't know how Jim there would make it. There's a one-room schoolhouse down that way. Some of 'em don't even have plumbing. Primitive, that's all I'll say. It's different inside the plantation. Night and day. You'll like it better there. Girls like you shouldn't venture out to where you don't understand things." Steve had taken the seat across the aisle from Dorsey, but he moved closer to her with each sentence. He leaned over her seat now, resting one arm on the back of Dorsey's seat and one on the seat in front of her, caging her in.

"You should say women. I'm not a girl. I'm a woman, and could you stop crowding me?" Dorsey said.

"Right. Spoiled. College-educated. Skinny," Steve said, not changing his position. "You think you know everything, don't cha?"

"No, not at all. Just that men like Jim are men, not boys, and women like me are women, not girls. I'm not trying to be disrespectful, just saying," Dorsey said; it was fun having her spunk back. She wasn't sure Steve was enjoying it quite as much, though.

Steve dropped his voice lower, his jaw clenched and she could see a small river of sweat working its way down the side of his face. "It really doesn't matter what we call each other. I expect Excellence, Team Work and Quality. ETQ, at all times. That's how we treat the guests and each other at Top Club. You'll have orientation tomorrow, eight a.m. sharp. You have a lot to learn."

"I'm sure I do, sir," Dorsey said, sliding over to the window, pretending to peer outside. Probably, the first lesson was to keep her mouth shut, she realized.

"Do you know how many people applied for your position? Just want to make sure you know how lucky you are to be here. Oh, look, we're home. Welcome to Melrose Plantation," Steve said.

Suddenly the road was paved and the bus stopped jumping around. White wood fences sprung up on Dorsey's side of the bus, and brilliant emerald-green grass stretched beyond the fence as far as she could see. They turned left and a guard appeared and opened the gate. Next thing she knew, they were inside an oasis of manicured grass and bright tropical flowers. The world had turned from sepia to Technicolor, a *Wizard of Oz*–like experience. A large pond glistened, ooze-free, next to horse stables on her left, and in front of Dorsey, the water of the sound and beyond it, the Atlantic Ocean, sparkled. Across the sound she spotted the red-and-white-striped lighthouse of Hilton Head Island. *Paradise found,* she thought, and took a deep breath.

"This is beautiful," she said, smiling at Jim, who met her gaze.

For the first time in ten long years, Dorsey felt the tension in her neck releasing, just a little. Steve was right about one thing: she liked the manicured version of the island inside the gates of the plantation the best. This was what she'd seen online, the place she'd dreamed about.

The bus stopped in front of a bright blue wood cottage. Pulling the door open, Jim said, "You're in cottage twenty-four, miss. It's unlocked." He delivered the speech without ever once making eye contact. Quietly he added, "Miss, keep ya tongue een ya teet an put fire een ya feet. E tuh wicket."

Dorsey leaned down to try to hear him. "What? I don't understand."

Jim turned his head, his dark eyes locked with hers, and again, slowly, he shook his head. He was telling her to stay away from Steve, she was sure of it.

She turned to look at Steve, but he remained seated in the middle of the bus. "Let me know if you need anything, girl. See ya later," he said.

Every man for himself, she thought, and realized she'd probably made Steve mad with the women not girls comment. *It's fine,* she reminded herself. *This is what I wanted. A fresh start. Independence. To prove to myself I can make it on my own. I probably won't even see Steve very often.* Dorsey continued giving herself this pep talk as she dragged her suitcase and duffle bag out of the bus and then pulled them across the wood-plank steps of the cottage. When she finally got the suitcases inside, she realized she'd entered the land of giant bugs.

"This is the price of paradise," she said, covering her mouth with her hand, stifling a scream.

Love bugs, mushy and plentiful, covered the front door of the cottage and littered the floor just inside—victims of pest control, she assumed. Unfortunately, the spiders adorning the ceiling were quite alive, as was the cockroach the size of a tube of toothpaste that skittered brazenly across the floor in front of her. She looked around what was otherwise a nice room, complete with a checkered couch, a round dining-room table, and a kitchenette with bright white appliances.

The only item in the kitchenette mini-refrigerator was a beetle cruising the bottom shelf, and she bravely used the often-copied "Welcome to the team!" note to squish it, leaving bug and note inside the icebox.

Wandering over to an open door with her name taped to it, Dorsey discovered her bedroom and loved it: two queen beds, a smaller television, and her own bathroom. But when she pulled the cream comforter from the bed she had decided to call her own, a black cricket jumped out. Stifling a scream, she decided to sleep in the other bed.

Breathe. Dorsey walked into the kitchen and grabbed ice, and some water from the sink, ignoring all of the bug remnants from her killing spree. She reminded herself this was where she'd start over, bugs, and all. *A firm line between my past and future. Nobody needs to know anything about me except for who I am right now.*

"Cheers," Dorsey said to the beetle crawling under the coffee table before heading back to her bedroom to unpack. Orientation was early in the morning, and she was excited to see how her new life would begin.

Chapter Two

Jack

JACK LEANED AGAINST the wall outside the conference room and eyed with disinterest the crop of new summer employees filing into the mandatory orientation meeting. It was the same types every summer and some of the same actual people – college co-eds, a few retirees, some jock guys to fill in the recreation staff, seasoned waiters recruited for summer work, golf and tennis pros who travelled to clubs all year round. This was Jack's fifth summer on Indigo Island as an employee and his tenth summer visiting the island. This year was different though. When all the summer tourists departed on Labor Day, he'd still be here. It was too late to apply anywhere else.

He'd arrived two weeks before Memorial Day, a week after graduating with honors from University of Central Florida's Rosen College of Hospitality Management in Orlando. Jack had a blast his senior year, knowing he'd landed a management position with Top Club on Indigo Island as soon as he graduated. He had the offer in-hand at Christmas, with Steve Fordham's signature across the bottom welcoming him to the team, welcoming him to management. He'd be the first person promoted from lifeguard to the front office, and the youngest in management ever.

His mom had been so proud, her eyes were glistening at the dinner table as he told her the news. Since he was the only child now, he knew it would be especially hard when he moved away. But he'd always take care of his mom. He was all she had.

Jack's ambitions were huge. He knew he'd own his own chain of hotels someday. At least that was the plan. He'd learned a lot at college – tourism and guest services management, hospitality industry finance, information systems management and even techniques of food preparation. He'd loved classes in culture and cuisine, facilities management and even enjoyed the revenue management courses. When he'd told his mom he took an elective in Yacht, Country and City Club management she had laughed hysterically over the telephone. He didn't mention any of the other classes after that, especially not the history and culture of wine. Jack wasn't laughing, not about any of this. It was his future. He'd make her proud, and, with his success, he'd try to make his mom happy again.

A group of five newly hired college co-eds walked noisily down the hall headed for orientation. When they spotted Jack, they all started to hit each other and whisper, a situation Jack was more than accustomed to. He flashed them his dimpled smile as they walked past. He'd always be friendly to them, but he wasn't available, not more than a one-night stand. Not to them, not to anyone.

"Oh my God, he's so hot," the short blonde said as they passed him and strutted into the conference room.

"Aren't you joining us, Jack?" Steve said, punching him in the arm. Steve was drenched, as always, in aftershave, a scent so strong it must double as bug repellent. Jack sneezed.

"Sure, if you need me to. I feel like I already know this stuff."

"This stuff, as you call it, is important, son. Especially if you want to be in management," Steve said, lowering his voice.

"I have an offer in hand from you. I am in management. I should have started two weeks ago," Jack said, his brown eyes narrowing as he stared at his boss.

"I told you, I'll honor it. I paid you for the summer, upfront, like you demanded as I recall. So now you just need to wait until the season is over. Three months and the position is yours, as long as you maintain a stellar employment record. You can do that, can't you?" Steve said, patting Jack on the shoulder.

Jack wanted to pull away, or punch him, but said, "Sure, Steve. ETQ all the way."

"Good," Steve said, and walked into the conference room.

Jack hated being lied to more than anything. He was a man of his word. Knowing he'd turned down three other job offers, one with a company rivaling the size of Top Club pissed him off. He had been offered a job, he'd accepted it and then, when he arrived on the island he was told he'd be a lifeguard again for the summer. Now he had no choice. He had to make it work. He'd checked. The other three positions he'd been offered already were filled.

He balled his hands into fists, took a deep breath and followed Steve inside.

Jack looked around the ballroom, the setting for corporate retreats and indoor weddings in case of bad weather, and the scene of Steve's power trip meetings. He saw some familiar faces, repeats from the summer before. Rebecca was back, and trying to catch his eye. They'd had some fun, especially in bed, but that's all it was. Fun. Most girls got that, and he'd tell them that up front. No strings, no relationship. He'd had trouble shaking Rebecca last summer, though. He found an empty seat in the second-to-last row and sat down, dreading hearing Steve and his pompous squeaky voice drone on about how great the summer would be. Jack knew it would be the longest in his life, because of Steve.

Jack's attention was drawn to a pretty strawberry blonde who walked down the center aisle like a deer in the headlights. Her hair was crazy curly, nothing like the rest of the girls who flattened and primped so much their hair all looked the same.

She had freckles on her nose and gorgeous green eyes. He wanted to jump up and help her find a seat.

What's wrong with me? Sure she's adorable, but you aren't looking for anyone this summer. Just work and get promoted, Jack reminded himself.

"Don't we have a fabulous-looking group of new Top Club team members?" Steve said enthusiastically, using his stupid bullhorn as usual. "I know a couple of you are on long-term contracts. Dorsey, where are you?"

"Here," said the girl Jack had just been watching. He could see her face blush a deep red. He could tell she hated to be singled out. Jack knew that would make Steve draw even more attention to her.

"Stand up, honey," Steve said, bounding down the aisle and reaching her row, pulling Dorsey up by her hand.

"Dorsey's our new Kids Club leader. Better her than me, if you know what I mean," Steve said, and a few employees laughed.

"Where's Jack?"

Oh shit, really? Two can play this game, Steve.

"Hey, I'm Jack. So happy to be here for my fifth season," Jack said, standing up before Steve could reach his row, taking charge of the room. Jack knew the smile on his face was forced. Usually because of his dimples, people believed it anyway. His smiles never had reached his eyes, not since his brother's accident. "Steve here hired me in management, but then changed his mind. So I get to be a lifeguard for the summer. Again."

"Jack, let's tell them the whole story," Steve said to him without his handy bullhorn. Then he held the thing back up to his lying lips and said, "Jack here is going to be head lifeguard and in charge of all pool staff for the summer. After Labor Day, he is joining management. The youngest person we've ever hired to management, something which he should be grateful for," Steve said. "Let's give him a round of applause."

Steve walked back up to the front of the room, basking in Jack's applause. Jack caught Dorsey looking at him, clapping vigorously. He gave her a quick smile. She blushed and lowered her eyes. She was a babe, he decided. He dropped back into his seat, prepared for a two-hour lecture from Steve about the rules he already knew, about a system he helped create over the past five years. Steve himself had only been here for two seasons.

Jack put his head down on the table in front of him and settled in for a nap.

"Jack, wake up," Rebecca said.

Disoriented, Jack sat up, realizing he'd slept through orientation and employees were filing out of the ballroom. He stood up quickly, wiping drool from the side of his mouth.

"Uh, thanks," he said, looking past her, trying to figure out an escape route.

"Look, I know you said we were over last summer, but I'm here, you're here as well," she said, smiling up at Jack hopefully.

"No, we're over," he said, too loudly he realized as he looked up and saw Dorsey standing in the aisle in front of him. He pushed past Rebecca and Dorsey and walked quickly out of the ballroom.

"Jerk!" Rebecca yelled in his wake.

Chapter Three

Dorsey

DORSEY FOUND THE young woman Jack had been talking to outside the ballroom. She was leaning against the wall, alone, crying.

"Are you OK?" she asked, worried about her and wondering what was going on with her and Jack.

"I'm fine," she sniffed. "I just shouldn't have gone out with him. They all warned me what he was like. I thought I'd change him, that he'd actually like me, not just want sex."

"Oh, well," Dorsey said, stepping back. She didn't want to know any more. Didn't need to know any more. She'd seen the way all the women here looked at Jack, like he was a piece of meat, a prize to be won.

"I'd stay away from him if I were you," Rebecca said. "He's bad news, but I miss him."

Dorsey walked away, not sure she could be of any help, and she had work to do. By the end of the second day on the island, Dorsey had the Kids Club cleaned up and ready for the new crop of vacationers arriving the next morning. Memorial Day Weekend started tomorrow and kicked off the season. Dorsey couldn't wait for the kids to arrive. Laughter and fun would fill the now-quiet air. The Kids Club was housed in a bright white cottage, closest to the swimming pool facilities and adjacent to a wonderful play area with swings and climbing structures, and plenty of shade from the giant pine trees. Steve had shown her the supply closet and the order form if she needed more crayons or the like. She'd scrubbed the black-and-white-checked linoleum floor until it shined, and she'd ordered a new bright blue area rug for the kids to sit on. The windows shone. Everything was ready.

Dorsey headed for the beach after locking the Kids Club behind her for the day. She was feeling more settled, more at home on the island each moment. All the new staff were nice and friendly, even if she didn't have anything to talk to them about. At least they said hello and good morning. They were all, she had realized, freakishly good looking – bright white teeth, big smiles, perfect skin. All the guys were built like lifeguards and body builders. All the girls were in shape and model-looking.

Jack was especially in shape and looked like a model. She'd watched him stand up to Steve in front of the whole staff, but she'd also watched his incredible dimples. She had noticed that, like her, his smile didn't reach his eyes, not when Steve was around at least. Jack was the epitome of a lifeguard – broad shoulders, dark wavy hair and muscles like she'd never seen. He could be a movie star. He was that gorgeous. And he was closer to her age, older than the rest of the staff. Whenever she thought about him her heart beat a little faster.

But that was silly. Dorsey heard how rude he had been to the young woman during orientation. Rebecca had burst into tears. Dorsey watched all the young, cute women flirting with him during staff meetings or whenever she walked through the pool complex. She knew she didn't have a chance of catching his eye. Even so, it was nice to realize she could get a little crush again. She hadn't had the butterfly feeling in her stomach since the early days with Chad. It was a fun feeling, even if it wouldn't amount to anything.

She walked along the wide warm sandy beach alone, getting her feet wet at the edge of the warm water. She looked across

Calibogue Sound to Hilton Head Island and suddenly felt envious of the throngs of people lining the beach. She was aware of how very alone she was here and in the world. She swallowed hard and kept walking.

Behind Dorsey, huge egret nests were perched on the tops of the trees at the edge of the sand. Beyond the egret homes was a vast forest that the club planned to develop someday. It was early evening and only the end of May, but five minutes into her walk, she was drenched in sweat. Out in the ocean, shrimp boats bobbed in the flat water, just as they did every day. The lazy arms of the boats worked all summer and continued long into the fall in a quest to find the popcornball-sized delicacies as they hopped by in schools called swarms.

Feeling uncharacteristically brave and particularly hot, Dorsey decided to wade farther out into the water. She was careful to shuffle her feet to avoid stepping on a horseshoe crab. She'd made it out to just about her shorts line when a loud clicking sound erupted on the water, like a bunch of people snapping their fingers. She turned in time to see a swarm of shrimp lurching toward her. She didn't know what was chasing them, but she didn't wait to find out. Her heart racing, she hurried out of the water, tripping over a rock or a large shell on her way out.

"Ack!" she hopped to the dry-sand line and plopped down to examine the bottom of her foot. A big gash on the pad of her foot below her big toe was blooming with blood, dripping down her foot and onto the sand.

"Hey, can I help?"

Dorsey looked up and realized it was the god of lifeguards. Shirtless, sweaty, sexy.

"Hi, I'm Jack," he said, extending his hand.

"Dorsey," she said, fighting to remain calm. She realized she was a clumsy mess, her hair frizzy, her foot dripping with blood. But still, his touch had been electric, at least to Dorsey.

Jack kneeled down next to her. "What happened?" he asked, his huge brown eyes kind and caring. He smelled like sea air and sweat, a surprisingly intoxicating mixture.

Dorsey's heart thumped in her chest.

"I tripped on something. I'll be fine, I think," she answered, although the blood was still flowing from her cut and her foot was beginning to throb.

Jack gently held her foot in his hand, assessing the wound. "Wait here, I'll be right back with a medical kit from the pool," he said, giving her shoulder a squeeze before jogging off in the direction of the main clubhouse.

Dorsey leaned back into the warm sand. Her foot throbbed but Jack's touch still lingered on her shoulder. She couldn't believe how his touch made her feel, and as she thought about it, her stomach flipped again. Stop it, she told herself. He was just being nice and she was acting like a schoolgirl with a crush.

Jack came jogging back, sweating muscles glistening, carrying a fully stocked first aid kit under his left arm, two water bottles in his right.

"Drink this. I'm glad I decided to go for a beach run today. I usually just run on the cart paths," Jack said, bending down to examine her foot. "Sorry I took so long. It's at least a mile back to the plantation."

"Thanks so much," she said, pouring the cool water into her mouth, trying not to wince as he doused her foot with antiseptic. Dorsey didn't trust herself to say anything else, she simply leaned back on the sand, enjoying his care, his skilled touch.

"This is too deep for a shell cut," Jack said.

He bandaged her foot and then rose, standing over Dorsey and looking out at the calm ocean. "Where'd you go in? Right here?" Without waiting for an answer, he walked slowly into the ocean and then dove in right where the shrimp swarm had been. She watched as he swam slowly around in the shallow water, popping underneath the waves in the spot where she'd cut her foot.

"Eureka!" he said, walking back to shore, soaking wet. He looked like he'd just stepped out of the pages of a magazine, abs defined and hard, his arms strong and powerful. *Stop it,* she told herself. He handed her an arrowhead, carved of pink quartz. The tip—the obvious culprit—was still as sharp as it must have been when it was crafted by one of the first residents of the island.

"Wow!" she said as he dropped it into her hand. The arrowhead, more of a spearhead, was longer than her hand and beautiful, with different gradations of pink. The tip was sharp. Very sharp. She shivered.

"I'm sorry I didn't bring a towel or anything. But the golf cart should be here any minute." Jack sat down on the sand next to her. "You'll need some stitches. It's a great find, though. I've found six arrowheads so far, but nothing like this. These Savannah River points, as they're called, can be eight thousand years old."

"How do you know all of this?" she asked, playing with the spearhead in her hands. Her heart was beating faster just because he was sitting next to her; she could feel the heat from his body, and it was making her dizzy.

"I like to know all about the place I'm going to live," he said. "It's amazing what you find when you know what you should be looking for. Now that you know you might find an arrowhead, you might find one every time you're out walking. Just wait. I can't walk the beach without finding one."

"So you're here past the summer, too, right? I saw you at orientation." Dorsey blushed, and looked away. She tried not to stare at his six-pack.

"I saw you, too," Jack said, nudging Dorsey's shoulder with his. Electricity shot through her body. "I am making my career here, I hope. I was promised a management position but when I arrived, Steve told me I had to lifeguard again through the summer. Asshole. He better keep his word when Labor Day rolls around."

"I heard. Sorry about that," she said. "I'm head of the Kids Club. I'm excited to get working with the kids. I hope it's the start of a new career. All I've done so far is clean. It was a mess."

"Yeah, Lila left in a hurry. Anyway, you'll be bringing the kids to the pool, so we'll see a lot of each other," Jack said. "So, um, want to go to the employee bonfire with me tonight? You're going to need help with that foot of yours, I mean if you want to go."

Dorsey was shocked. She swallowed. Was Jack asking her on a date? "Sure. Great."

"Cell phones don't work here, as you know, so call my cottage if you change your mind. Otherwise, I'll swing by about seven?"

"Perfect," Dorsey said, as Steve pulled up in an all-terrain golf cart.

Dorsey tried to stand up, but fell back on the sand. Jack reached for her hands as Steve said, "Here, Dorsey, let me help you," scooping her up off the sand as Jack turned away. "You're good to walk back, right, Means?" Steve asked Jack. Steve dropped her into the back of the cart and they drove away, leaving Jack behind on the hot sand.

"Why didn't we give Jack a ride back?" she asked. "He really helped me a lot back there."

"I'm sure he did. You know my policy, right? No dating among employees. I enforce it very strictly," Steve said. "Summer staff is one thing, but you are an employee, like Jack is now. Will be quite a change for the lad from last summer."

"Right," Dorsey said, getting the chills. Her foot was throbbing, the sun was hot and Steve was, well, Steve.

"Quite the playboy, that one, but now he is in management. Rules change. I learned that the hard way on my first management job. I was quite the ladies' man back in my day," he said. "Yup, but now I'm a career man. Career first, pleasure second.

Excellence in everything."

As she held on to the golf cart, Dorsey realized she'd sort of agreed to go on a date, a date with the hottest guy on the island. Hopefully, though, Steve would just think Jack was helping her out by taking her to the bonfire because of her injured foot. And really, that's all they could ever be anyway, even without Steve's strict rules. Friends. She knew she wasn't ready for more. She'd made a promise to herself after Chad broke up with her that she'd spend this time, this chapter of her life alone. It only made sense.

Dorsey looked at her foot, at the blood seeping through the bandage Jack had applied, and shuddered, remembering years ago the blood that had splattered all over her face and pink t-shirt, and all over the flowers they had been planting in the garden. The police said the killer must not have seen Dorsey, as she was kneeling down, planting a row of seeds. They also told her she must have seen the shooter, just before he turned to run away.

She'd been fourteen years old, old enough to remember, her mom kept saying.

Dorsey wrapped her hand tightly around the arrowhead as tears flooded her eyes.

Five stitches later, and with orders to use crutches for the next three days to allow the cut to heal, Dorsey was released from the resort's clinic. Steve hadn't left her side, insisting on being there as the doctor cleaned the cut and then stitched her foot, an excruciatingly painful process. She didn't understand why he had to be with her, watching her suffer, his beady eyes glinting under the fluorescent clinic lights.

"I'll drive you back, Dorsey," Steve said, holding the door for her as she learned to walk with the crutches. "Tomorrow is a busy day. You should stay in and rest tonight. It's OK for you to skip the bonfire."

"Um, right," Dorsey said, swallowing. He couldn't know

about her plans with Jack, she realized. But it was almost like he did. She shook her head. The pain pills were making her loopy.

As soon as she walked awkwardly out the clinic door, sweat formed on her forehead and dripped into her eyes. The cart ride provided a brief respite until Steve stopped and parked near the ocean, just below the swimming pool, where a group of happy day-trip vacationers stood waiting for their "nature walk and history talk."

"I hope you don't mind but I've got to do a little talk for these good folks before I run you home," he said. He climbed out of the cart and approached the group.

Really? More time in the sun was the last thing she needed, but she had no choice. She reached for her water bottle and swallowed another pain pill.

"This is what it was like over in Hilton Head forty years ago," Steve explained. "It'll take a while for us to get this old island into Top Club shape. But it'll happen. We'll embrace the past of the place. There were bloody Indian battles here, grand Southern plantations with fields of cotton, famous oyster-canning companies, and flourishing Indigo fields. We'll bring it all back around, fix up what we can. That's Top Club's com-mitment."

Nothing would ever fix the summer weather. It was only May and stepping outside felt like walking into a steam shower, but she supposed with air conditioning and swimming pools, tourists would still come. And she was getting accustomed to her new look, she thought, reaching up and touching her hair, an uncontrollable frizz shooting out all around her head. She'd have to give up. Back home in Grandville, it had taken an unusually fiery and damp August day to cause the kind of havoc each day brought on the island. Here every day would be a big hair day, but nobody would notice. She would simply be one of many blue-shirted employees there to serve wealthy vacationers' kids.

As she strained to listen to Steve's history talk, her foot started throbbing. She still couldn't believe she had been attacked by an inanimate object in thigh-deep water. *I'm feeling sorry for myself,* she thought.

But if she hadn't stepped on the arrowhead, Jack wouldn't have come to her rescue, and they wouldn't have a date tonight for the bonfire. She knew he'd only asked her because he felt sorry for her, her clumsiness, her lack of friends, her chaotic hair. But she had felt the electricity between them, even if the current had only run one way. She'd enjoy every minute around his perfect muscular body, even if it was a pity date.

Chapter Four

Jack

FROM HIS LIFEGUARD chair, Jack saw Dorsey trapped on Steve's golf cart – her bandaged foot propped up on the dashboard – as Steve performed his show for the day-trippers. She must be hot and uncomfortable. He knew she should be taken to her cottage, she needed air conditioning and rest. What was the jerk doing? Trying to make her suffer or trying to impress her with his king-like knowledge of the island? Either way, Jack was disgusted.

Jack was stuck in the chair, even though there were only two 30-something sunbathers at the entire pool complex and the two women hadn't gone in the water past their ankles so far. Most of the time, they just smiled at Jack and whispered as they flipped through their gossip magazines.

The two college girls working the snack shack and pool hut looked equally bored. He knew they should all be appreciating this relaxing day as tomorrow was a full house, with every room and cottage booked. But he hated being bored, and he hated that he couldn't go rescue Dorsey.

What was it about her that immediately attracted him, he wondered? He'd noticed her at orientation, of course. She had looked like a deer in the headlights when Steve had called her out. He'd wanted to protect her from that moment on. She had crazy curly strawberry blonde hair and gorgeous green eyes, and now that he'd been close to her on the beach, he couldn't stop thinking about her. About the freckles dotting her small nose, about her full lips, about the heat that sparked between them.

He'd spontaneously asked her to the bonfire, a move he hadn't thought through at all. Steve would be there, and Jack knew how Steve felt about staff relationships. They were strictly prohibited. ETQ left no room for romance, Steve was fond of saying at staff meetings.

They'd have to be careful. For some reason, Jack knew Dorsey was worth it. He gazed at her stuck in the golf cart in the blazing sun and shook his head, anger making him too antsy to sit any longer.

Steve was such a jerk, he thought, as he climbed down from the chair and dove into the cool blue swimming pool. Underwater, he imagined that he didn't need this job so badly. He saw himself running over to the group lecture, grabbing Steve, punching him in the nose, and hopping in the golf cart and driving Dorsey to her cottage where she belonged.

As he surfaced for air he reminded himself again that this was the only job he had. His mom, long deserted by his father, expected the best from him. And, he'd promised to pay off her mortgage so she wouldn't lose the house. He was her only child now, her only hope. Before, she had been a strong person who wore the pants in his family, teaching her sons that women were their equals. After the accident, she'd lost her passion for life. All her hopes and dreams rested on Jack's shoulders, and he felt the weight every day.

No matter how much he hated that liar, Steve, he needed to stay calm and play the game. He'd already mailed his mom the check Steve had advanced him and she'd taken it to the bank just in time to save the home from foreclosure. That meant Jack would bide his time, play the lifeguard until Labor Day. Once he was a member of the management team, nothing and nobody would stand in his way. One of his first missions would be to write up Steve for everything he did wrong. His weird control methods, his overt sexual harassment of the summer staff. Jack had seen enough last summer to fill a book of complaints, even if everyone else just let Steve get away with it all.

Jack wouldn't. Once he had the position he'd been promised he'd fix everything. He would do almost anything to get what he wanted – to make his mother proud, to help heal her heart. And now he had another reason to succeed on Indigo Island, he thought as he climbed back into the lifeguard chair, and she was sitting in a golf cart just out of his reach.

He pounded his right fist into his left hand, imagining it was Steve's face. It felt good. Jack smiled, and the two women at the pool smiled back, not realizing the smile was not meant for them.

Chapter Five

Dorsey

DORSEY AWOKE SUDDENLY, unsure where she was, with damp hair stuck to her forehead. *It was just another bad dream.* She took a breath, trying to calm her thumping heart. Of course her nightmares would follow her here to Indigo Island. She'd never be able to be free of them.

She was on the couch in the living room of her cottage, where she must have fallen asleep after Steve finally dropped her off. He'd told her to rest, take it easy and to stay home tonight. It was dark outside, and inside her cottage. She wondered what time it was. Sitting up slowly she blinked at the clock in the kitchen. It was nine o'clock.

Jack, we had a date.

Dorsey reached for the telephone on the side table next to the couch.

"Jack Means's room please," Dorsey said into the phone. She listened through four rings before voicemail answered. "Hi Jack, it's me, Dorsey. I fell asleep, and I'm so sorry." She hung up.

Frustrated, Dorsey slowly stood up, shoved a crutch under each arm, and made her way to her bedroom, slamming the door behind her. She tossed and turned all night, hoping Jack would call. But he didn't. Once the sun finally rose, she decided she needed to get to work. Fortunately, Steve had arranged for a golf cart to be dropped off for her use until her foot healed, so Dorsey zipped over to the Kids Club. The first kids wouldn't arrive until nine a.m. She had an hour to kill and decided to drive over to the pool, hoping to find Jack. A group of the college girls were busy setting up the pool hut.

"Hey Dorsey, heard about your foot. Sounds ouchy," said one.

Dorsey couldn't remember anybody's names yet, so she just smiled.

"Great way to get the hunk's attention," said another. "He's all about saving people. Did you know he saved a little kid who was drowning just last summer? I watched the whole thing."

"No, I didn't know about that."

"Did he pick you up and carry you out of the water? Did he ask you out? He doesn't give anybody here the time of day and then you show up. It's just not fair," the third girl said, giggling.

Dorsey didn't see Jack anywhere around, the pool wasn't officially open yet so there weren't any lifeguards in the chairs. Dorsey was about to ask the pool staff if they'd seen him when a blood-piercing scream rang out.

Grabbing her crutches, she headed toward the kids' pool, where she found a family in panic.

"Oh my God, what is it? What got her?" The distraught mother cradled a screaming girl of about three.

"What happened?" she asked as the mother carried the child to Dorsey.

"A huge bug bit her. Look," the mother said, pointing at the middle of the child's forehead, where blood seeped from a bite.

"Horsefly," Dorsey said. "They're awful this year, we were told. They hang out by the swimming pools. Let's go get some ice for you, OK?"

Suddenly, Jack appeared but instead of stopping where they were gathered by the toddler pool he ran past them and dove into the deep end of the main pool.

"My God, there's a child under there," somebody screamed,

and as quickly, Jack appeared on the surface of the water, cradling a small boy. He hurried to the edge of the pool, handing the limp body to the other lifeguard and then jumping out himself and beginning CPR.

"No, Tommy," the woman next to Dorsey wailed before shoving the little girl into Dorsey's arms and running to where Jack was at work.

Dorsey grabbed the little girl's hand and hopped on her good foot to the pool hut.

"Call 9-1-1," she said to the two pool hut staffers who were frozen in place. "Put ice on her forehead. Call now."

As quickly as she could she hopped to the side of the pool where, thankfully, the young boy was coughing and throwing up water. His mother held the child and was crying as Jack glared down at her.

"What the hell were you thinking?" he said to the woman, quietly. His anger was palpable, coursing through the air as if tangible. Dorsey could feel it as she stood next to him.

"Jack, go get the kit, and be sure the squad is coming," the other lifeguard instructed. "Now."

"He almost died," Jack said to the mother, his eyes tearing up, his face contorted into a grimace with what was both anger and grief mixed, before walking away, causing the mother to wail again.

Dorsey hurried after him, forgetting the crutches.

"Jack, what is it? How can I help?" she said, but he was in too much of a hurry, outpacing her every step.

As she reached the pool hut, Jack was escorting the paramedics to the pool, filling them in on everything that happened. The little girl who had been bitten had calmed down and was playing peek-a-boo with the pool hut staffers.

"Dorsey, what happened?" asked Sabrina, one of the pool hut staff. Finally they'd put on name badges.

"That little boy, he, he was drowning," Dorsey said, realizing tears had sprung to her eyes. "It was awful, he was so white and limp when Jack pulled him out."

The paramedics wheeled the boy past in a stretcher, his small face covered with an oxygen mask, followed by his distraught mother.

"Mommy!" cried the little girl as she saw her mom pass by.

"Oh baby," the mom said, grabbing the toddler from Sabrina's arms and hurrying to the waiting emergency squad.

Dorsey turned to look back at the pool and saw Jack, his head hanging, leaning against the side of the lifeguard chair. The female lifeguard was talking to him and he was shaking his head. She climbed into the chair, but Jack remained where he was.

He saved a life, in front of her eyes.

Dorsey crutched slowly to where Jack was standing, his back to her.

"Jack, you were amazing," she said. She reached out and touched his shoulder, his tan skin was warm and firm. Her fingers were still trembling from the events while he had been so brave, so in control.

"I was just doing my job," he said, his back to her. "I just can't believe parents don't watch their kids. Drownings happen all the time. It's such a silent, awful death."

"But you weren't even on duty, you weren't even here when I got here to look for you." Dorsey blushed, realizing her slip, hoping he hadn't heard it.

Clearly, he had. Jack turned then and faced her. He smiled his dimpled smile. His eyes were still shiny, hinting at his previous emotion. "I'm glad you were looking for me. You'll always find me here, all summer. Remember, Steve made it so. I'm in charge so it is my job. I've got to go write up my report, so I'll, um, see you around."

As Jack grabbed a white pool towel and rubbed it through his still wet dark hair, Dorsey remembered she hadn't apologized for sleeping through the bonfire. Then again, he hadn't returned her call, so clearly it had been a pity date after all. She decided not to say anything, and sighed as she watched him walk away. She knew she should stay away from him. There was something guarded and distant about him and that was just fine with her. She knew she had that quality herself. She wasn't looking for anything but to start a career on Indigo Island. That's all.

Dorsey made it back to the Kids Club just in time to welcome her first camper, a towheaded ten-year-old boy by the name of Tade, pronounced like Tate with a D he explained. He was dressed like a little preppy in a pink polo shirt and blue golf shorts.

"I'll be the only one here most days," he said after his parents had left in a swirl of hellos and goodbyes. "I liked the other girl who was here before you. I sort of miss her. She was really pretty. Did you know Miss Lila?"

"No, I didn't," Dorsey said. "But I hope you'll like me, too."

"I will, I think. Miss Lila didn't like Mr. Steve. She thought he was icky," Tade said. "What happened to your foot?"

"Arrowhead," she answered, wondering if she should press Tade for more information about Miss Lila and her problems with Steve. Maybe later. He was her boss, so any information could be useful as she worked her way up the Top Club ladder. First things first, she reminded herself. Make the Kids Club a model all the clubs would want to copy.

"Can I see it?"

"What? My stitches. No!"

"No, the arrowhead, silly!" Tade said.

"Sure, I'll bring it tomorrow. What do you want to do today?" she asked. She had a lot of activities planned, and a bunch of ideas for crafts and hikes and activities, but she also wanted Tade's input. She needed to stay busy, to focus on her job, not how Jack's skin felt under her fingertips. *Stop it.*

"Dunno," Tade said. "Let's go steal an apple from the front desk!"

As they walked out of the Kids Cottage, Jack was standing there.

"Tade, my little man, welcome back," Jack said as Tade jumped into Jack's arms. "Good to see you squirt, I see you two have met."

"Ah, yep, he's my first camper," Dorsey said, unable to control the blush covering her cheeks.

"Jack's a kissy boy. He was Miss Lila's friend, too," Tade said.

"You are a little troublemaker, you know that? To the water with you," Jack said, easily tossing the youngster over his shoulder and heading toward the ocean.

"Save me, Miss Dorsey," Tade yelled, all the while laughing and kicking his legs over Jack's back.

Dorsey jumped into the golf cart eager to rescue her charge and just as happy to be spending time with Jack. He was a natural with the boy, who was now sitting on his shoulders as Dorsey pulled alongside them.

"Hop in, you guys, let's go explore," she said as Jack flipped Tade over his head and placed him on the sand. "Jack, can you come with us?"

She was flirting and she couldn't believe it. She was probably batting her eyelashes, too, she realized, mortified. Fortunately she had her sunglasses on. He was just so hot.

"I'd love to," he said, sliding Tade into the front seat next to her as Dorsey's heart thudded in her chest. "But unfortunately I have to go back to the pool. Hey Dorsey, I'd really like to see you later, though?"

"Ah, sure, of course, me too," she said. Sounding just like a sixth grader. What had happened to her?

"I'll find you," Jack said with a wink before turning to walk back to the pool.

"Me too, me too, kissy kissy," Tade teased Dorsey as she drove around to the back of the inn, the ocean side, where the sun danced and sparkled on the calm surface of the sound. The calm stillness of the ocean was a complete contrast to the crazy longing she was feeling inside.

Dorsey reminded herself to focus on her job and let Tade help her to navigate her crutches across the oyster-and-shell-encrusted cement walkway leading to the back door of the inn, stopping to point out embedded fossils along the way. As they moved past the lawn-bowling court, Dorsey tried to imagine what it would have been like to grow up a hundred years earlier in a huge home at the edge of the ocean, daughter of a cotton farmer. Waited on by slaves.

"You know, back when this was a plantation, we wouldn't be on the island during this time of year," Dorsey explained, reciting Steve's speech that she had heard while she waited with her throbbing foot. "We'd be inland, in the mountains in Asheville or near there. It's malaria season, a dangerous and uncomfortable time to be on the Sea Islands. That was before the invention of air conditioning, and pesticides and malaria pills."

"Yeah, well, the folks who were here year-round then are still here now, you know?" Tade said. "The Gullah people are just outside the gates. Most people here never even see them. But it's really their island."

"Don't tell Steve that," she said. "He likes to think it's his island."

"I know. He was here last summer, too. But he doesn't get it. Indigo Island doesn't belong to him, or the club. It belongs to them. He'll find out," Tade said.

"How do you know so much about the people here?" Dorsey asked.

"I have a friend on the backside. She tells me things. Lila met her." Tade dashed ahead of Dorsey and up the steps to the large porch.

The inn was a replica, a yellow stucco splendor recreated from historic drawings of the original plantation home, once the grandest on the eastern seaboard. Now it was home to an ever-changing horde of tourists like Tade and his parents, who had all begun to look the same to Dorsey since they'd begun arriving throughout the day. White couples. Mid-thirties to late forties, typically from the Midwest or South. Two or three kids, preschool to middle-school aged. They were a type. Mom would play tennis or join Dad at golf. Dorsey didn't know yet how many kids would get stuck in the Kids Club since only Tade had shown up today.

"I think the inn looks like a house made out of butter," Tade said, as Dorsey slowly climbed the brick steps to the veranda, a long, covered porch winding around the first floor like a decorative apron. "Like they painted it with melted butter. I think ghosts live here, too."

"Why would ghosts want to live here? It's way too hot for them," Dorsey said, as Tade held one of the huge mahogany doors open for her.

"Ghosts live where it's not settled. That's where there's room," Tade said, removing his pint-sized sunglasses as the two of them stepped into the air-conditioned lobby.

"This feels good." Goose bumps covered her arms from Tade's ghost speech. She blamed it on the air conditioning. "You just don't realize how hot it is until you come in here, into the air conditioning. Can you imagine before AC? So how long will your parents be gone today?"

"Who cares? All they like is golf, golf, golf," Tade said and dragged the toes of his well-worn tennis shoes across the hard-wood floor as he followed Dorsey to the front desk. "I'd rather just hang out with you anyway."

She smiled. She liked her first camper.

"You two are supposed to be at the Kids Cottage," said Shane Peters from behind the front desk. He was the resort's concierge. Dorsey had never seen him smile and he seemed to have a strong dislike for children.

"We're just on a little field trip, Shane," Dorsey said. "We'll be out of your hair in a minute."

Shane hrumphed and walked away from them, across the lobby to his concierge desk. The coast was clear and Dorsey was about to grab two apples from the bowl on the desk when Paula Ganz appeared behind the front desk.

Paula had been on Indigo Island forever, Dorsey had heard, but still her skin was as pale as paper. She wore reading glasses that gave her the look of a librarian. A terse librarian. Dorsey had yet to see her smile, either.

"Aren't you supposed to be working?"

"Yep. I am. Meet Tade," Dorsey said.

"I know Tade. Son, try not to sneak out of the Kids Club so often this season," Paula said, a stern look crossing her face. "Lila lost several stars because of you."

Dorsey looked over at Tade, and Tade beamed a smile back at her like a little angel. She'd talk to him later about that. She needed to keep any stars she earned.

"Can we have a couple apples for the road?" Dorsey asked, trying to look sweet. "I'm injured." The freckles her mother warned her would return with sun exposure had done just that, adding a certain Raggedy Ann air to her overall appearance.

"One. For the guest. As you know, they have a bunch on sale at the general store—twenty-three, to be exact, if you need more," Paula said, then turned her attention back to the computer screen in front of her. Dorsey knew what she was doing, they'd heard all about it at orientation. Since her promotion to assistant food and beverage manager, Paula didn't make a move without checking the computer. She knew how many apples were consumed each day, which were eaten by guests, which were eaten by employees, and even which were devoured by the horses at the stables. During the morning staff meetings, everyone winced when Paula stood to give her report. Persnickety and detail-oriented, Dorsey's opposite.

Dorsey grabbed two of the shiny red apples and shoved them in the pocket attached to her right crutch before making her way toward the back doors of the inn, Tade following close behind, laughing. When Tade's parents picked him up at four, Dorsey felt they'd already formed a close bond.

The telephone rang in the Kids Cottage just as she was locking up. It was Steve, summoning her to his office. Dorsey wondered if he'd spotted her taking two apples, somehow, or if he knew she had a crush on Jack, or if it had something to do with the pool incident.

Dorsey slowly climbed the winding Gone with the Wind staircase of the inn to the second floor where his office was located, taking her time with the crutches, and when she finally reached the top she realized Steve had been watching her, arms crossed, at the top of the stairs. Steve wore a cardigan sweater, reminding Dorsey of a mean Mr. Rogers. He smelled like the bad cologne he seemed to drench himself in daily.

She followed Steve slowly as they walked past his assistant's desk until they were standing inside his spacious office with grand ocean views. His large mahogany desktop was empty, except for a closed laptop computer. Dorsey wondered if maybe Steve didn't have enough to do.

"Do you know why I love it here?" Steve asked.

"You have a great office and a really tidy desk?" Dorsey said.

"Cute, you're a funny one. No, it's because I can control everything here. It's a small resort, manageable. I like that. That control. We must always give the impression that everything is OK, even when it is not."

"OK," Dorsey said, dropping into one of the matching brown leather chairs facing his imposing desk.

Steve didn't sit. Instead, he paced back and forth behind his desk. "I'm referring of course to the near drowning. We will not speak of that to anyone, especially the guests and the summer staff. Am I clear?"

"Um, Steve, the summer staff saw what happened. The pool hut attendees and at least five guests were all witnesses," she said. He had his air conditioning turned to icebox setting and Dorsey was getting the chills. She hugged herself.

"Ms. Pittman. The rest of the staff has been spoken to already, and will proceed as if this unfortunate event never happened. The child was checked out and released from the hospital and is headed home. Nothing happened. Am I clear?" he asked, leaning forward, both of his small hands on his desk. He'd never appeared more tortoise-like and Dorsey stifled a giggle, despite the edge in his voice.

"Sure, yes, got it. But shouldn't Jack get a star or an award or something? He saved a life," she said, gathering her crutches so she could make an escape, her stomach tightening as she mentioned his name.

"Jack was merely doing his job. Stars are for going above and beyond. Remember, Dorsey," Steve said, finishing his lecture. "Nothing bad ever happens at a Top Club resort. Now go out there and have a great Top Club evening."

Chapter Six

Jack

REBECCA CONFRONTED HIM as he was closing up the pool. "We need to talk," she said, hands on hips, full lips shiny with the sticky gloss Jack remembered from last summer. Why had he been such an idiot? He could sense she was trouble the first time they talked. After Lila left abruptly last summer, he'd been horny and lonely. Rebecca had been willing and waiting for his attention, as easy as grabbing an apple from the front desk. Maybe easier. Just because it was easy, didn't make it right, and he had been sorry he'd ever started anything.

"How was junior year?" Jack asked, attempting polite banter, trying not to clench his jaw and reveal his distaste. He was straightening the lounge chairs, putting them back into the perfect rows the guests would then move and demolish tomorrow. The busy work kept his mind off the near-drowning of this morning, and at the moment, kept him away from Rebecca.

"Fine. I studied abroad second semester. Paris. It was amazing. I messaged you a couple of times, thought I could pay for you to come over, but you didn't answer."

"Look, Rebecca, I told you this last summer. We're over. It was fun. You're a great girl, but we're through. I'm in management now, I can't date summer staff," Jack said, gathering up a big pile of used pool towels and heading toward the pool hut.

"Can't you stop and talk to me like an adult?"

"Sorry, I've had a long day. We don't have anything else to talk about, OK? There's nothing here." Jack tossed the towels into the laundry hamper and locked the pool hut door. When he turned around, she was gone.

Good riddance, he thought, and headed to the inn.

Jack saw Dorsey standing at the top of the grand staircase and stopped in his tracks. She was so gorgeous, so natural, the opposite of Rebecca with all of her makeup and entitlement oozing through. He knew Rebecca only wanted him because she couldn't have him. He knew nobody had told her no before, just like most of the spoiled rich girls working on the summer staff. Dorsey was different. He could sense a deep hole in her heart and a kindness that he wanted to protect. Just seeing her made him smile. He had been cutting through the inn on his way to hit some golf balls on the driving range. He realized she was about to try sliding down the banister, and he watched as she swung her injured foot over the smooth wood of the rail. She'd get in big trouble, he thought, almost laughing out loud at her spunk, but realizing Paula or Shane would not.

"Dorsey, what are you doing?" he asked, dashing up the stairs. "Let me help you."

"Ah, nothing," she answered, blushing as always, and pulling her leg down. "Just finished being scolded by Steve. I'm sick of these crutches so I was going to try sliding down."

"Not your best idea," he said, picking her up in his arms. She felt so good, so small but strong in her own way. He didn't want to let her go. Holding her he felt a surge of electricity shoot through his body and into his heart.

"I'm so sorry I slept through the bonfire," Dorsey whispered. Her breath smelled like mint and her hair smelled like sea air. Her skin was beginning to tan and her freckles seemed to be growing in number.

"Just so you know, I came by at seven and saw you asleep on your couch and knew that was for the best. Tonight I'm stuck in an administrative meeting. I should be out of here before ten. Can I come by?"

"Please," Dorsey whispered back. She had a beautiful smile, white teeth and the reddest lips, just begging to be kissed. And her crazy hair was beautiful. It took everything in his power to not keep her in his arms and stroll out the door into the sunset. *What was wrong with him?*

He shook his head, and settled her on the ground. He ran back up the steps, grabbed her crutches and came back to help her get her footing. Each time he touched her, heat rushed through him, he realized. He hadn't allowed himself to feel this way ever, not with anyone, not since the accident. This was crazy, he thought. This wasn't just lust, it was something more, something deeper.

"Thanks for the lift," Dorsey said, and she was blushing again. "I'm usually not this helpless. Promise." Jack laughed. Almost since they'd met she'd needed his help. The strange thing was he didn't mind at all.

"Do you need help getting back somewhere?" he asked. Her cheeks were incredibly pink. Jack had to resist the urge to kiss her, right then, right there.

"I still have a cart to use until I heal. Thanks again. See you tonight," Dorsey said as she turned and headed toward the front door of the inn.

Jack smiled a genuine smile as he watched her walk away. He couldn't believe the effect she had on him. He sighed and looked up the stairs, and saw Steve staring down at him. Had Steve seen him carrying Dorsey?

"What are you doing, Jack?" Steve asked, descending the stairs, wearing his ridiculous cardigan sweater. Jack realized Steve pictured himself as some type of Southern gentleman. In complete control of his plantation. The man was a freak. Jack took a deep breath.

"Going to hit some balls before the meeting," Jack said,

keeping all emotion out of his voice.

"I keep seeing you and the new girl together, why is that?" Steve said, licking his lips like a lizard.

"I have no idea," Jack said, adding under his breath, "maybe you should find something else to do?"

"What?"

"Nothing," Jack said and turned and walked away.

He could feel Steve's eyes on him as he passed by the front desk, grabbed an apple and headed out the front doors. Outside the air was thick and hot as usual, suffocating, and it felt even more so given he was dressed for golf not half-naked for life-guarding. He'd hit a few balls at the driving range, catch up with his buddy, Tom, who was an assistant pro. Get his mind off Dorsey and back on the game. He was here to get promoted, to get ahead and that was what he intended to do. He couldn't afford to let a strawberry blonde beauty ruin all of that, no matter how much he wanted her. His mom was depending on him. He couldn't give Steve a reason to fire him.

He crossed the wooden bridge that connected the inn to the golf clubhouse. As he walked he stared down into the dark murky water and wondered if he should even go over to Dorsey's cottage after work. Sure, he convinced himself, they could be friends. She was new and seemed lonely. And she was always getting into trouble it seemed. Of course he'd show up. That was the gentlemanly thing to do. And Jack was a gentleman, despite his reputation with the summer staff. That was his past.

Chapter Seven

Dorsey

DORSEY AWOKE TO a tap-tap on her window. She rolled over on her bed and saw the silhouette of Jack's face pressed against the windowpane, the evening breeze blowing his thick hair. She smiled, wondering how long she'd been asleep as she watched him push the window open, and silently climb inside, a big grin on his face. She loved the dimples framing his perfect smile. His dark brown eyes sparkled as he hopped down from the windowsill and closed the window behind him. She wondered how many times he'd made a similar entrance to another woman's cottage, but tried to push the thought away.

"Hey, sorry I'm so late. How's your foot?" he asked, touching the top of her foot tenderly, sending a bolt of electricity through her body.

"It's getting better, thanks," she said. She felt shy, and wrapped her arms around herself. She wore her favorite jeans and a comfortable light green t-shirt and she'd even managed to tame her hair a bit for him. She'd dreamed of this moment, but now that he was here with her she was nervous and hurried to sit up.

"What's wrong?" he asked, reaching out and placing a firm hand on her shoulder, calming her, grounding her. He smelled like sea breeze and fresh cut grass from the golf course. She felt his breath on her hair. And his touch made her stomach flip.

"Nothing, it's... I'm...well, it's been a long time since I've had a man in my bedroom," she said.

"Hey, I'm just here to get to know you. We could go for a walk, but your foot?" Jack said.

"No, this is great," she said, resisting the urge to touch his leg so close to her own. Just the thought of it sent electricity ripping through her again, reaching deep inside, filling her with longing. They stared into each other's eyes and Dorsey's breathing grew shallow. She broke eye contact, looking down at the floor. She felt the bed dip as he sat down beside her.

"So, uh, Jack, tell me about yourself," she said.

"Well, I like pina coladas and I'd love to get caught in the rain," he said, dimples appearing with his white smile. "Seriously, though, I'm the only son of a single mom, who worked really hard to get me here, helped me pay for college, and so I can't mess up this chance. But you really make me want to take the risk."

Dorsey felt her cheeks turn red. "Well, no. That's why we need to, um, you know just be like this," she said, indicating the space between them on the bed. "I understand, I do. Tell me more."

"You're right, I got ahead of myself, it's just you, well, you have that effect on me. I'm from Orlando, Florida. Only surviving child of Patricia Means. My little brother, Bobby, died when he was twelve, and my mom never got over it."

Dorsey watched as Jack's hands kneaded the side of the bed as he spoke about his brother, watched the light drain from his eyes.

"I'm so sorry," she said.

"Thanks, it was a tough time. Guess it still is," he said. "Anyway, after high school I went to UFC and majored in hospitality. I'm going to be a hotel tycoon. I'm going to run this club someday. I love this island; I've been working here for years."

"Sounds like a plan," she said, smiling. The light had come

back into his eyes and he seemed to relax a bit. Finally, he turned toward her.

"Sorry, but I think you're incredibly hot, I feel this over-whelming need to protect you. I'm drawn to you. God, I don't even know if the feeling is mutual." Jack shook his head, as if to clear a thought.

"It's, yes, it is," she managed to say, leaning back against the headboard.

She heard him release a breath. They sat in silence, both lost in thought. About what couldn't be, she supposed. It was sad, but it was apropos of her life.

"Well, OK. Tell me something about you," he said, finally.

"I'm an only child, too, and my mom is single now. She's glad I'm here, moving on, so I guess we have similar stories, in a way," she said, knowing their stories could never be the same. His could never be as horrific, although his brother had died.

"I guess so, although I doubt it," he said. "My younger brother drowned. I've always felt like it was my fault, because I didn't save him. That's why today hit me so hard, I suppose. That boy looked just like Bobby." Dorsey watched as he grabbed the edge of her bedspread again, gripping it tightly with both hands, kneading the soft cotton in his fingers.

"Oh, Jack," Dorsey said, covering his right hand with hers. He was still holding on tight, rocking gently forward and back. "I'm so very sorry."

"I don't talk about it," he said finally, still staring straight ahead. "He was a little older than the boy today. Just playing with his best friend in a crowded public pool. There were three lifeguards on duty but they didn't see him until it was too late. I was asleep. I was supposed to work later that afternoon so I just crashed on my towel under a tree. My mom was at work. I was in charge of him, of Bobby. I've never forgiven myself for falling asleep."

"Jack, it wasn't your fault. You were a kid, too."

"It was a really hot humid day. I woke up to screams and whistles being blown. I sat up fast, too fast, and I was dizzy. I looked around for Bobby, but he wasn't next to me. His towel – it was light yellow – was on the grass next to mine, but it was dry. Our bag of Lays Potato chips was unopened on the grass between us. I stood up and hurried over to the pool in time to see the lifeguard pulling him up onto the pool deck. Bobby was blue."

Jack stopped and dropped his head into his hands. "I don't know why I'm telling you all this. I don't talk about this."

"It's OK, you don't need to say more, not if it hurts too much," she said, wrapping an arm around his shoulders. "I'm so sorry, so very sorry."

Jack turned toward Dorsey and leaned forward, easing his lips onto hers. It was a soft, gentle kiss, and Dorsey's body took over in response, pressing back into him, wanting more, wanting to comfort him, wanting him. His tongue was parting her lips and Dorsey heard herself moan.

Without breaking the kiss, Jack maneuvered Dorsey so they were lying down facing each other. He was so strong, his lips soft but insistent. His hand cupped the back of her head, her hair wrapped around his hand.

"Dorsey," he said, pulling away from the kiss but staring deeply into her eyes. "You're incredible."

Her stomach fluttered, her head spun. This was what being kissed by a real man was like, she realized. Jack wasn't embarrassed to be with her like Chad had been. And it wasn't a pity date like the ones after college. He wanted to be with her. Their connection had been immediate, their embrace as natural as it was exciting. It all felt so good, so right, but it couldn't happen. Not here. Not with Steve as their boss, not with her past. This was all going too fast.

"We can't do this," she said, suddenly, rolling away, turning her back to him.

"What's wrong?" he asked, sounding hurt, placing his hand

on her hip, sending shock waves through her body.

"It's just that we can't jeopardize our jobs, you need yours as much as I need mine, no matter how handsome you are. I'm sorry," she said. She should never have invited him to her bedroom. What was she thinking? She'd been a tease, and she hadn't meant to be. She forced herself to sit up, crossing her legs, trying to deaden the fire building there.

Jack sat up, too, his expression was kind, not angry. He scooped her up and pulled her into his lap. She relaxed into him, into his embrace, even as she wanted him to touch her everywhere, to fill her. She sighed.

"By the way, you're a great kisser," Jack said. "I'm so turned on." Her face flushed as she burrowed into his chest. She could tell he enjoyed making her blush even as she enjoyed every minute of being with him. And she could feel him hard behind her. This was torture, for both of them. "So tell me more about you."

"I'm not into yoga, and I have half a brain," she said, but not finishing the rest of the lyrics even though she could vividly imagine making love in the moonlight on a dune with Jack. Her heart pumped and her stomach clenched.

"You just might be the love that I've looked for," he said, gently lifting her chin, tilting her face up towards his. "It's OK. You can trust me. Talk to me."

She had to choose her words carefully. She never told the whole truth of her past, not to anyone, and she wasn't going to start now, no matter how amazing he was. "My dad, ah, died when I was fourteen. My mom and I never got over it either. I went to Ohio State, majored in early childhood education but never knew what I wanted to do with it. I was a full-time nanny for four years, but I needed a fresh start. I was searching the Internet and found the ad for the Kids Club position and applied. Here I am," she said. "And I haven't had anyone protect or care about me for a very long time." Dorsey couldn't believe she was admitting this to Jack, even as tears welled up in her eyes.

"I'm here for you. I am," Jack said, wrapping his arms around her tightly, his brown eyes dark and sparkling while he used a finger to gently brush a tear away from her cheek. "I know we have to be careful. I've been under Steve's rule since last summer. We can outsmart him, outlast him, too."

Dorsey's teeth bit into her bottom lip as she thought about Jack's implied proposal, unsure if she could stop herself from wanting more. Not sure she should allow herself to trust a man again after what happened with Chad. This could ruin everything she had come here for, even as it felt so good to be with him. But, what about the others?

"From what I hear, you didn't play by the rules last year, either," she said, and felt his hand tighten on her hip. He let out a sigh behind her.

"Last summer, I was summer staff. I was just goofing around. Nothing serious. This year, it's different with the management position. It's different with you."

"What about Rebecca?" she asked, a question that had been pinging around her mind since she spotted them together at orientation. "It seemed like there was more to it than just goofing around. She was really upset after you yelled at her."

"Sorry you had to see that. She's a little crazy, but I promise you, there's nothing there," Jack said, pulling her back into his chest, gently lifting her chin so their eyes locked. "Give me a chance."

"I'll try, I really will," she said, as Jack hugged her tightly. She loved being in his lap, feeling taken care of and protected. The way his arms felt around her, so strong, so grounding. She wanted to believe him, to believe that the most gorgeous guy on the island really did like her, that this deep emotional connection she felt went both ways. Could it be true?

Jack lifted her up and slid them down the headboard until they were lying next to each other on their right sides, his strong arms holding her tight, his body behind her, curled around hers. He held her until they both fell asleep, Dorsey comforted by the sound of Jack's heart.

Chapter Eight

Jack

JACK DIDN'T KNOW what had come over him as he woke up, fully dressed, in Dorsey's room. This had to be a first. He cuddled a girl all night. *What was wrong with him?*

He was surrounded by gorgeous girls, every summer, all summer long, and if he wanted one, had actually been invited to crawl through her window at night, he'd have sex with her. Every one of them, until now. But until now, none of them had made him feel like Dorsey did. Sure, Dorsey was hot, sexy in an all-natural way, and she always seemed to need his help, his care. And he liked that. When they'd kissed he'd felt things stir inside he hadn't felt in a long time, maybe never. He loved the way she blushed every time they flirted, the way her eyes crinkled at the corners when she laughed. There was intense chemistry between them. It had taken every ounce of his willpower to fall asleep next to her. He had already pictured his hands on her breasts, her soft skin in the moonlight. But now, he'd just take it slowly. They had both had trauma in their past, he was sure of it even though she hadn't been forthcoming. He was surprised he'd told her about Bobby. The near-drowning had weakened his typical walls, he supposed.

Or maybe, she had.

He looked over to where she was sleeping peacefully on her side, knees curled up, a faint smile on her face. One arm was tossed lazily in his direction, palm up. Her hair was a wild tangle covering the pillow, illuminated like a halo by the sunlight sneaking in through the slats of the blinds. She looked like an angel.

The sun was up, Jack suddenly realized, reluctantly pulling his attention from Dorsey to the fact he was still in her room. And it was daylight. He climbed carefully out of her bed. He'd need to get out of there before anyone discovered them. Even the cleaning crew reported directly to Steve, he knew. Everybody would and could run straight to Steve, and be rewarded for ratting out fellow employees. That was the type of culture Steve had created, one of tattletales and mistrust. It would be a problem. Steve's world was emotionless and orderly, asexual.

The opposite of everything Jack saw and felt when he looked down again at Dorsey, sleeping soundly. He fought the over-whelming urge to leap back in bed with her, fighting the urge to wake her up with an urgent, hard kiss, fighting the urge to touch her. He backed away, reluctantly, hoping nothing was ruined last night, believing it was just a start.

Jack pushed up the window and climbed out, closing it silently behind him. A quick jog to his cottage in the fresh morning sea air reminded him he needed to focus on his job. He couldn't allow himself to get sidetracked by Dorsey, no matter how much he wanted her. Remember the goal, Jack told himself. He was going to make his mom proud, he was going to see his mom smile again.

Jack was in his lifeguard chair, eyes scanning the crowded swimming pool when Steve appeared next to him.

"Have you seen that little kid, Tade, around?" Steve asked, anger in his voice. "The little bastard seems to have run off again."

"He's a pistol. He's the one who put the blue crabs in the pool last summer, remember?" Jack said, remembering the sight of panicked vacationers mobbing out of the pool. He struggled to swallow a laugh. It had been a funny prank.

"That's him. He's supposed to be in the Kids Cottage, but he's not there. Would you mind looking for him? I'll get another guard to cover for you," Steve said, smiling his fake smile, sun bouncing off his over-sized sunglasses.

"I'm not good at kid finding," Jack said, turning away, scanning the crowded pool.

"It's not really a request, son," Steve said as another lifeguard appeared. "We will have order here on Indigo Island. Get going."

Power play perfected, Steve, Jack thought. Jack dove into the water from the chair, anxious to cool off and to get away from Steve. He swam under water to the other side of the pool, climbed out, grabbed a towel from Sabrina at the pool hut and set out to find the kid.

The first place he'd look would be the Kids Club; maybe Tade had returned in the time it took Steve to summon Jack. Even if the kid wasn't there, he knew Dorsey would be. He smiled at the thought as he pulled on his white polo shirt. Everything led him back to her.

The playground outside the cottage was empty, but as he walked up the steps to the Kids Club, he spotted Dorsey inside. She was dressed in the official uniform, of khaki shorts and a pale blue polo, but she still looked great. And, she had a tennis shoe on her hurt foot, no crutches in sight.

"Hey," Jack said, shaking his wet hair once more before walking into the cottage. "Feels good in here, chilly."

"What are you doing here?" Dorsey said, a huge smile across her face, and of course, the usual blush.

"Me? Why I just wanted to see how the prettiest woman on the island was doing today. Sorry I had to slip out before you woke up," he said. Being this close to her again made him want her, made him remember the kiss from the night before. He fought to control himself. He didn't want to scare her away.

Dorsey walked over to Jack and held his hand. "It was the

first night I can remember having a really good sleep. Thank you," she said.

The door slammed open and Steve appeared, hands on hips, furious. "How the hell do you expect to find Tade here, Jack? I told you he didn't show up at the Kids Club so why would you?"

"I wanted to be sure he still hadn't showed up." *You tool,* he didn't add. "Dorsey and I are going to look for him now. We'll find him. Right, Dorsey?"

"Right, I don't have any campers today," she said, looking confused but soon following along. "Steve, you really should tell Tade's parents to sign him in, follow the rules. If they don't, how can they expect their kid to?"

"They think they own the place. Tade likes you, so just go find the little brat," Steve said. An angry flush rose on his cheeks and his dark brown eyes flashed at her. He'd pushed his glasses up above his eyebrows.

Jack realized the man's eyes were too small for his face but made up for their size with intensity.

"Look, he's a good kid. Just lonely. We'll find him," Dorsey said. She had to walk past Steve to get out of the cottage and as she did he patted her on the butt.

"Go get 'em, tiger," he said. "And Jack, you can go back to the pool. Dorsey has it covered."

Jack felt his neck tense and his hands form fists. He couldn't believe Steve had touched her that way. And he didn't care what Steve said, he'd help Dorsey find Tade, and tell her to stay away from Steve.

Jack caught up to her by the golf cart, climbing into the driver's seat. "Does he do that often? Touch you like that?"

He saw her shudder. "No, that was a first, but it's nothing I can't handle, really," Dorsey answered, but Jack didn't believe her. And he didn't trust Steve. "Let's focus on finding Tade."

Jack didn't say anything, but he knew if he saw Steve touch her like that again, there would be trouble and he'd be the one making it. He reached over and squeezed Dorsey's hand, and she smiled at him.

"He's probably on the backside of the island," Dorsey said, and she directed him down the beach, past the swimming complex and around a bend. A small creek poured into the ocean there, Jack saw as he pulled to a stop in the golf cart. A sign marked the end of the Top Club Plantation and the beginning of the "backside" of the island.

Jack had yet to venture past the creek, and hadn't been off the plantation since he'd arrived this year. The backside belonged to the island's natives, as Steve called them, and it remained a tangle of moss-covered live oak trees, pine trees, dirt roads and mysteries. When he was a kid on vacation on Indigo Island, he'd explored back here, too.

Jack stared into the thick dark woods. "You ok going in there? I can go find him if you'd like to stay here, rest your foot?"

"If Tade wasn't afraid to venture back there, I'm not," Dorsey said, although Jack suspected she sounded braver than she was.

Jack led the way along the sandy bank of the creek into the island. Inland, the heat was stifling. The dense hum of bugs hung in the thick air. No ocean breeze reached here. Dorsey followed closely behind, following Jack and the snaking water, and started calling Tade's name.

"Hey Dorsey!" the boy said, his voice coming from somewhere inside the thick woods.

"Come out here, would you? You promised not to run away. You said you'd be at the Kids Cottage everyday," Dorsey said, putting her hands on her hips but not budging from her spot on the creek bed.

"Come meet my friend," Tade said, suddenly appearing at the edge of the woods, a smile stretched across his face. "She's awesome, she teaches me so much. Oh, hi Jack."

"What could you be learning out here?" Jack said.

"Lots. You'll walk around the world three times in your lifetime. Cool, huh? Come meet her."

"What? Who are you talking about?" Dorsey asked. "Come here right now."

"No, you come with me," Tade said, and disappeared into the woods.

Jack and Dorsey didn't have a choice, so they followed, reluctant but captivated by his excitement. Not only was Jack afraid to lose him, but also he needed to know that his friend was a safe person for a ten-year-old boy to be hanging out with. Jack grabbed Dorsey's hand reflexively. The bolt of electricity shot through him.

"Tade, slow down!" he demanded, worried about Dorsey's foot. He could hear her panting from her sprint through the thick tangle of grass, vines, and pine trees. Finally Tade came to a stop in front of a seemingly deserted tin-roofed shack. The place reminded Jack of the slave cabins he'd seen in the black-and-white etchings in the inn's art gallery. The roof was the color of the inside of a can of soup. The gray wooden walls were covered with tabby—ground oyster shells—and had leaned toward each other over the years and away from the sloped front porch three steps above the ground.

The cabin was stuck in time—in black and white itself, as the pine-tree and live—oak canopy above forced the sunlight to work hard to break through. The front door was a dusty red, and light blue shutters framed two small, steely windows. Jack felt sure if he stepped onto the porch, he'd fall through to the dirt. He had to get Tade and Dorsey back to the plantation, back to the environment where he was in control.

"Come on, Tade," he said, placing an arm protectively on the boy's small shoulders. "Let's get out of here. We really aren't supposed to be out here." Jack noticed the windows on either side of the door, although partially covered by the shutters, were polished clear.

Tade noticed him looking at the shutters. "I love that color blue, don't you? It's called haint blue and it's the color of heaven. The blue keeps the devil away at night. The bad guys are called haints—you get it?" Tade said.

"No, I don't. Let's go," Dorsey said, and started pulling him backward by his arm.

"Hey, Barbara, I brought my friends, Dorsey and Jack, to see you," Tade said.

"Oh honestly, chile, I'm in no shape to be having company," a deep, gravelly yet singsong Southern voice said from inside the shack.

Jack realized whoever lived here had heard what he said about the island. "Oh, please don't come out on our account, ma'am. We've just come to take Tade back before his parents know he's gone. We're sorry to disturb you, ma'am."

"No problem. He's a fine boy. Lonely boy. But a nice boy," the woman said, as the old red door opened a crack. From below the porch, Jack saw the woman's smooth, walnut-colored face. Wisps of cotton-white mingled with her black hair, pulled back tightly into a bun.

Tade shook Jack's arm off his shoulders and Dorsey's hand off his arm, bounded up the stairs, and pushed the door open wide enough to wrap both arms around the thin figure, now revealed. She wore a simple brown cotton dress. The hand that reached out to pat Tade's head was wrinkled and bumpy, with large, dark, age spots. Jack had no idea how old the woman was—she seemed timeless in her sepia surroundings.

"I'll try to come again, Miss Barbara, before I leave," Tade said, backing out of her embrace.

"That would be nice, honey—now you go so's y'all don't get in no trouble," Barbara said. Then smiling kindly down on them, she closed the door.

"Tade, you're not supposed to be on this side of the island," Dorsey said as they made their way out of the moss-draped forest.

Jack was in the lead, Tade behind him and Dorsey in the rear. He imagined black rat snakes under each tree and alligators lunging at them from the marsh. He hated snakes. He was completely on guard and he knew Dorsey's foot must be throbbing.

"Yeah, yeah. Bet you can't catch me," Tade said, breaking into a run at the creek.

"Bet I can," Jack said, catching Dorsey's eye to be sure she was ok. She nodded and Jack took off after Tade, grabbing him as he rounded the bend at the beach and reached the golf cart.

"Can I drive the cart?"

"No. Scooch over. We need to pick up Dorsey. And Tade, don't do this again," Jack said, relieved to be back in civilization. He looked out over the ocean and was surprised to see thickening dark clouds. He didn't know it was supposed to storm. They reached Dorsey as she was limping across the thick sand and she climbed on the cart, Tade between them in the front seat.

"Want to go put some blue crabs in the pool? I did that once and watched all of those sunbathers scream. It was funny!" Tade said as they drove past the pool area.

"That was you?" Dorsey said, shaking her head. "I heard about the prank at a staff meeting. Listen kiddo, I need your help. You're the senior camper around here. You can help me with these new kids, show them all the fun things to do here. Like a second-in-command?"

"Maybe," Tade said. "Didn't you like Barbara's house?"

"She seemed really nice," Jack said, parking in front of the Kids Club cottage.

"When I leave, you have to visit her for me," Tade said. "You do that, and I'll help you with the kids. Deal?"

"OK, sure," Dorsey said.

"As long as I'm with you," Jack added protectively, meeting Dorsey's eyes over Tade's head. He saw her blush. He realized he was completely nuts about her. He didn't want to go back to the pool, he wanted time to stand still. But he had to go. He parked the golf cart and they all climbed out.

"See you later, guys," Jack said as he headed back to the pool and Dorsey and Tade climbed the steps to the Kids Cottage.

Rebecca was waiting for him as he reached the lifeguard chair.

"Say, just for old times why don't you come by after work? I have a couple of your t-shirts I accidentally kept from last summer. You're probably going to want them, right?" She had her hand on his biceps, her fingernails digging into his shirt.

"Could you just bring them to me, please?" he said, using his hand to pry her nails off of his shirt, smiling at her before climbing the ladder to the chair.

"No, I can't," she said tossing her long brunette hair over her shoulder, arms crossed in front of her. "If you want them, you're going to have to come get them." And then she stormed away from him in a huff.

Maybe Rebecca had finally gotten the hint.

Chapter Nine

Dorsey

DORSEY WATCHED JACK walk away with pure lust in her heart. She hoped she'd see him tonight, even though she knew it was against the club policy, against everything she'd wanted when she started her new life here. She knew she couldn't trust a man again, not with her truth. Once he knew the real story, he wouldn't want her anyway. It would be far easier to push him away now, before it went any further. How had he gotten into her heart and mind so quickly? Her stomach clenched as an answer and her face flushed. He was the hottest guy she'd ever been around. Period.

Dorsey looked out from the porch of the Kids Cottage and saw that girl, Rebecca, standing below Jack's lifeguard chair. What were they saying? Were they making plans? Dorsey was stuck, she couldn't leave the Kids Cottage and couldn't find out what was going on from here. Tade was pulling on her arm.

"What?" she said impatiently.

"So should we take the kids to look for Loggerhead Sea Turtle nests?" Tade said, interrupting her thoughts.

"That's a perfect idea," Dorsey said reluctantly taking her eyes off of Jack and Rebecca and following Tade into the Kids Club where they found Steve finger painting with a group of toddlers. "But we may have to wait until the storm passes."

"Thank God," Steve said, hurrying toward the door, wiping

his hands on a paper towel. He had green paint on his cheek, but Dorsey wasn't going to wipe that for him. "You son, need to stop hiding like that."

"I wasn't hiding," Tade said. "I was visiting a friend."

"That's not allowed. Everyone must follow the rules precisely in order for this club to be the best. You are expected to do so, as are your parents. I will be speaking to them, as well," Steve said, spittle at the corner of his mouth.

"They won't listen," Tade said, hands on his hips, taunting the large man in front of him. Dorsey didn't know why he was being so defiant, but she didn't like seeing Steve get so angry at a child.

"They will, son," Steve said, jaw clenching while his tiny eyes darkened with anger. "You all will. Good work, Dorsey." And then he was gone.

Tade and Dorsey sat side by side on the window seat of the Kids Cottage, watching the waves build as the storm approached. The water grew dark brown as the light drained from the sky. The little kids had stopped painting and Dorsey had put on a Disney movie for them to watch. Dorsey heard the sirens blowing, calling all golfers off the course.

"My parents said this is a northeastern fetch," Tade said. "I'm not sure what a fetch is, but if it cools it down here, it's fine with me."

"Me too. When are you leaving?" she said.

"Tomorrow," Tade said.

"Already? Wow, I'll miss you."

A crack of lightning brightened the sky, followed closely by a loud thunderclap that seemed to be directly above the Kids Cottage. All three toddlers began to cry and Dorsey and Tade gathered them together in the center of the room. Dorsey wondered whether Jack would stop in and check on her, since the pool had to be closed during the storm. Or, maybe he had other duties she didn't know about.

Nervous parents began banging in the door of the cottage, collecting their kids and hurrying out before the downpour. Tade, as usual, was the last to be picked up.

"I don't want to go. Dorsey and I have plans," he said to his parents when they eventually appeared.

"Well, you can just have that to look forward to on your next visit. You know we were only here for the long weekend, son. We're back in three weeks," Tade's mom said, hurrying him out the door.

Dorsey was surprised how sad Tade's departure made her. She had started to clean up the Kids Club for the day when the door burst open again. Tade.

"I forgot. I have something for you, something to keep you safe," he said. "Put out your hand."

"It better not be a bug, or I'll get you," Dorsey said.

"OK, open," Tade said.

"What is it?" she asked, rolling a little figurine the size of a wine bottle cork back and forth in her fingers. It was a tiny clay person glazed periwinkle blue with a white base, four pressed buttons up its middle, two arms, and a little face with a pointed hat.

"It's an oogle. Barbara said it'll keep you safe. She gave me two. One for you. You need to keep it in your pocket, and when you go to sleep, put it by your bed." Tade pulled his own small figurine out of his shorts pocket.

"Tade, I love it. Thank you. I'll miss you, but I'll see you in three weeks," Dorsey said, and watched as he ran to the golf cart and his mother drove quickly away.

It was getting eerily dark outside, almost as if night had fallen when it was only four in the afternoon. A crack of thunder boomed above Dorsey's head and she saw a lightning bolt strike on Hilton Head, near the famous red-and-white striped lighthouse. They'd close the pool for sure, she realized, and decided to head there to find Jack, even though it was wrong for her to want to be near him, even though he might have made plans with Rebecca. It was as if an invisible force was pulling her to him. She made it to the pool as the last of the guests were hurrying away in their golf carts.

Jack grinned when he saw her. "Hey beautiful, ready for your first Indigo Island storm?" he said, unzipping his backpack and rummaging through its contents. "Not that it matters. I'm prepared for both of us."

He pulled out what looked like a yellow garbage bag. "Voilà! A rain poncho, straight from Disney World. Present from Mom. Just ignore the big mouse ears and think of me as a bright yellow beacon on a rather miserable day. I have an extra. Want to borrow it?"

He had unconsciously run his fingers through his dark brown hair, and it stood up. When he grinned, a dimple appeared on the left side of his smile. Dorsey hadn't felt this tingle inside for years, maybe never.

The feeling was happiness, she realized. And a really big, teenage-sized crush.

"Give me a poncho, buster, and let's explore this little resort in the rain. It'll be fun. We look like a couple of overgrown ducks," Dorsey said, pulling the yellow tent over her head.

"Hey, wait for Big Bird, would ya," Jack said, hanging the "pool closed" sign.

They walked together in the pouring rain, past cottage after cottage, first the employee row and then the ocean-front guest cottages, which alternated blue, white, and yellow, blue, white, and yellow, until finally they reached the seawall protecting the cottages and the inn from the ravages of the Atlantic storms that would always come.

"You know, this is pretty." Jack yelled to be heard over the crashing waves, pressing wind, and whipping rain. "Good shelling and arrowhead finding tomorrow!"

"I like finding colonial pottery shards. I have started quite a collection—that and my spearhead." She turned to look up at him, and Jack leaned over and gave her a quick kiss, as water ran down both of their faces. Dorsey's knees almost buckled.

"Sorry, couldn't help it," Jack said, smiling. "Let's go near the water."

"Strong currents," Dorsey said, shaking her head.

"Yes, there are. Oh, you mean the water," he teased. "We're not going swimming. We're just walking next to it. Come on. We're already wet. I love the power of the ocean. I'll hold your hand." He jumped from the seawall to the sand a foot below. Reaching up, he held her with ease before lowering her to the sand. It was scary and sexy, all at the same time she realized as her heart thudded in her chest.

"Come on," he yelled, pulling her hand.

The waves thundered, making it impossible to talk. By the water's edge, the wind's strength forced Dorsey to bend her head down to her chest. Her heart was pounding, the angry waves so close, so violent and still building in the normally flat and calm sound, but holding Jack's hand made her feel safe, grounded. At that moment, she realized, Jack seemed to have always been with her, that he always should be. Protecting her, saving her.

Once they had walked far enough out and were walking parallel to the inn, she pulled on his hand, directing him back toward the gazebo and the grand yellow building beyond.

"OK," he said, grinning at her and then lifting her back up onto the seawall before climbing back up himself. Together they ran to the white lattice gazebo, but it offered no protection from the growing storm.

"We need to get to the inn," he yelled, and she nodded. They hurried up the oyster shell path. When Jack noticed her limping, he scooped her into his arms and carried her the rest of the way. They had climbed the steps to the large porch and were about to go inside when he pulled her to the side, into the shadows in the corner of the porch.

"Hey, do you know what these are? I've been meaning to ask every year," he yelled pointing to a long wooden plank suspended on two rocking horse bases.

He's such a kid, like Tade. Always asking questions, she thought, smiling. She was glad she knew the answer, too.

"It's a joggling board. Made in Charleston," Dorsey yelled. "Like this." She sat in the middle of the long, foot-and-a-half-wide board that was inserted into rocking chair rockers on either end. She started joggling by bouncing up and down, and then added a back and forth rock by kicking her legs. "Ta da," she yelled and Jack joined her. Two yellow ducks swaying on the joggling board.

"This is great," he said, wrapping an arm around her waist. "It'd be great to—"

"In Charleston, rumor was that there weren't any virgins inside a house if it had a joggling board outside," Dorsey said, surprising herself; she was suddenly glad the storm made it almost dark so Jack couldn't see her blush.

"I can understand that. Wow, look at the lightning over the ocean," Jack said, mesmerized by the sharp white streaks of light. He pulled Dorsey closer, holding onto her waist as they joggled. She could feel his strong hands on her sides, felt the electricity of his touch to her core.

Dorsey self-consciously pushed her wet hair away from her face and pulled the plastic hood off her head. She hadn't seen her white Keds this muddy in a long time either, she thought with a smile. She hoped her stitches weren't ruined. Her foot felt fine. She looked at Jack and wondered what they could do, should do.

"I'm glad I got to share this storm with you," Jack said. "If I was in the corporate office now, I'd probably be dealing with hundreds of freaked-out guests. Instead, I just had to hang the pool closed sign and find you."

Dorsey smiled. "Actually, I found you, and I'm glad," she answered, leaning into his strong body.

Jack took his arm from her back and stood up in front of her, pulling her to standing, hugging her tightly. "I didn't know how lonely I was until I met you," he said, his hair wet but sexy, eyes dark and shining. "Now look at me. I'm falling for a soaking wet, muddy shoed, strawberry-blonde, adventuresome girl who is acting like she isn't afraid of storms and who knows how to joggle."

"I'm not afraid of the storm, not with you," Dorsey said, her voice catching in her throat. Could this be happening to her? What about their employment contracts? What about Rebecca? Steve? "Jack, I was so lonely before I met you, too. When my last boyfriend, well my only real boyfriend, broke up with me, well, I haven't been able to get past it."

Jack grabbed Dorsey's wet hair and tilted her head up. He leaned forward, covering her lips with his, gently pressing, exploring. Dorsey opened her mouth, gasping, as his kiss moved to her neck and behind her ear. She felt faint, the kisses were making her dizzy. Jack held her tight as another lightning bolt lit up the sky, this one close to the gazebo.

"I'm sorry he hurt you. I won't," Jack said, his voice low and needy.

Dorsey looked into Jack's darkened eyes, wanting to believe him, as the thunderclap shook her to the core. She couldn't trust him, though. She knew what he didn't. He wouldn't want to be with her once he knew her secrets.

"We better get inside," Dorsey said, reluctantly breaking their embrace by pulling him into the lobby of the inn. Vacationers were everywhere, trapped inside by the storm. The bar was hopping, the library was packed, and Shane and Paula seemed beyond stressed by the volume of people in their lobby. Apples were disappearing faster than they could be counted. Dorsey smiled.

"Can you think of anywhere private we can go?" she whispered, stunned by her own boldness.

KAIRA ROUDA

"Yes, I have an idea—come on," he said, and they hurried up the main stairs, past Steve's office, and down a long corridor, Dorey's wet tennis shoes squeaking with every step. "This is the service entrance to the private dining room. I doubt anybody is in here right now."

He was right. Flipping on the lights, Dorsey saw that they were alone in a formal dining room, complete with sparkling crystal chandelier, oil paintings of the former plantation residents, and three huge windows facing the ocean and the storm.

"Sorry about your boyfriend," Jack offered, his eyebrows knit together with concern. "If you ever want to talk about it, I'm here."

"Thanks," she said. "It really is in the past, but for some reason, I can't let go of it. He was embarrassed to be with me, after, after my dad died. He was from a long-standing family in Grandville, and well, my family's scandal made him uncomfortable."

"What a jerk," Jack said, reaching over to hold Dorsey's hand. They sat on the plush wool area rug, trying not to drip too much on the hardwood floor. "What could possibly make somebody act like that? That's when you needed someone by your side. I mean your father's death is a tragedy, not a scandal. I wish I could meet him. I'd punch him."

"No you wouldn't," Dorsey said, rubbing the oogle in her pocket. "The sad thing, for Mom and me, was that we should have seen it coming. First somebody dyed our swimming pool a blood-red color. I came home from school and the pool, it was so creepy."

"Why would anybody do that?" he asked, squeezing her shoulders.

Dorsey didn't answer, she was lost in the past. She shivered.

"Then, they poisoned my dog, Rufus. He was a husky, with bright blue eyes. He was so sweet, so protective of me. He died in our kitchen, in my arms, foaming at the mouth. It was horrible."

Dorsey paused and took a deep breath. She'd never been able to say the words, she never wanted to believe them. "It was all to warn my dad, to force him to stop performing abortions. That was a tiny part of his practice. He was a celebrated Ob/Gyn doctor. He'd delivered everyone in town's babies. But they took it all away. They threatened to kill us, my mom and me, too."

"Oh, my God, Dorsey, I'm so sorry," Jack said pulling her to him in a firm hug as another bolt of lightning lit up the room. With the crack of thunder, the electricity in the room surged, and then went out. One of the portraits on the wall, a Mrs. Stoddard, seemed to be staring down at them, creepily illuminated by each lightning flash, and she wasn't smiling.

"I can't talk about it anymore tonight," she said, stifling a sob. She'd come close to telling Jack the whole story, and if she had, she would've ruined everything.

"I don't even know what to say, you've been through so much. I'm here, if you need to talk, whenever you need to talk."

They sat in silence, holding each other.

"You know, whenever I think my life has been tough and I get all self-absorbed and angry, especially angry, I try to remind myself that others have been through much worse," Jack said. He leaned against the wall in the dark, Dorsey pulled into his lap. "My dad was such a jerk, leaving my mom with two kids to feed and raise. No child support, nothing. No playing catch, no father-son moments."

"That's just as hard, Jack," she said, realizing that even if she only had a dad around until she was fourteen, he was a great dad. "I was lucky. I know. He was a great man."

"That's probably why you're so good with kids. You had role models, a mom and a dad, showing you how to do it," Jack said, and Dorsey felt him growing tense behind her. "I'd be awful with kids, with a family."

"Are you kidding? You're great with Tade," she said, turning to try to see his face in the pitch-black room. She reached up, touching his cheek. "It's not about role models, it's about your heart. You have a good heart, Jack."

"Whatever, but thanks," he said. Dorsey noticed his hands were clenched into fists. She sensed that his anger just below the surface, waiting to explode.

She wondered if his self-doubt and this simmering anger at his dad were what was holding him back. Was this the reason he'd had a string of relationships? Conquests without meaning, without commitment.

"You deserve to have everything you want, Jack," Dorsey said. "A great career, a family, kids."

"Nobody deserves anything. It's luck and fate and hard work, it's how you were raised and what you can overcome," he said, pulling her against him, nuzzling his chin into her shoulder. "I've watched you with the kids. You'll be a great mom someday."

"I hope so. Jack, let's get out of here, I need some dry clothes," she said eventually, chilled from being damp, from the draft in the room. Jack took her hand and led her slowly through the darkened inn until they reached the candlelit main lobby. Once outside, they made the run home through rain so heavy it concealed everything except what was just in front of them.

Jack's cottage was closest, so they stopped there. He handed Dorsey a dry sweatshirt and sweat pants, and gave her privacy to change. Dorsey glanced at her reflection in the mirror and even in the dark could tell how swollen her eyes were from crying. After she'd changed, he joined her in his bedroom, dropping onto one of the two queen-sized beds. The walls, a bright sky-blue with midnight-blue band at the ceiling, were the most colorful thing she had seen all day. With the wind and the rain of the storm, the entire island seemed gray from the ground to the sky.

"Thanks for telling me about your dog," Jack said. He watched Dorsey use the towel in an attempt to dry her long hair.

"I still can't believe this happened to you. Did they catch whoever poisoned your dog?"

"No," Dorsey answered. She felt guilty for not telling him the whole truth, not telling him that it was worse, much worse than poor Rufus. But she couldn't share that, she doubted she ever would.

Jack didn't say anything in response, just nodded.

"So, what do you want to eat?" he finally asked when she bent over and flipped her hair over to dry the underside. "And did I mention you've got great hair."

"I'm glad you like it, because it drives me crazy. It's big, that's for sure, and it takes forever to dry," she answered from her upside-down position.

"I'm making dinner," Jack announced, standing. "Hey, what's this?" he said, picking up the oogle from the bedside table.

"Oh, it's a little bit of protection from Tade and his friend, Barbara. They gave it to me to ward off evil spirits and things. It's kind of like you, in miniature," Dorsey said.

"Cute," Jack said as he put the oogle back and walked back into the living room. He turned on the gas fireplace and the glow lit the room. The armchairs around the fireplace were brown wicker with bright yellow-and-white-checkered cushions. The kitchen table was sturdy maple. The layout was the same as her cottage.

As they sat in front of the fireplace, nibbling crackers and cheese and bologna slices, safe from the wind and the rain outside, Dorsey decided this might be the happiest moment of her life.

"What time are you working tomorrow?" Jack asked, the light of the fire dancing off his face, chiseled angles of perfection. He was gorgeous, Dorsey decided afresh. She was so happy, and felt so safe, she didn't want to think about tomorrow.

She yawned and stretched. The warmth of the fire had relaxed her. She reached over and grabbed Jack's hand. "I have to work at nine, but I'd better head back to my cottage. What if Steve has someone check on me?" She stood up, holding onto the waistband of his sweatpants to keep them from falling down.

"You had to hide out from the storm. Take one of the beds. I'll sleep on the couch. It's late. Promise it will be OK." Jack stood beside Dorsey in front of the fire and grinned. He smelled like rain and soap, and she wanted him to touch her, to carry her to his bedroom, but that would ruin everything. Jack needed this job even more than she did. And how could she ever be sure she wasn't just another notch on his belt.

"Oh, Jack," Dorsey said, wrapping her arms around his neck, feeling the connection zinging between them as their bodies drew close and pulsed with desire. She took a deep breath and took in the scent that was uniquely his. "You know I appreciate your gentlemanliness, I guess. It's just, well, it's what we have to do, right?"

"Ugh," Jack said, pushing her away. "This following the rules is killing me. We've got to figure out a way to be together."

"I'd like that, too," she said quietly, turning to face the fire. After a moment, she turned back to face him, ignoring the need in his eyes, a need she felt just as strongly. "It's still crazy outside, so I'm sure it's OK for me to stay, just this time. And just to be safe, you better sleep on the couch," Dorsey said. She didn't trust either of them with a whole night together anymore. As Jack closed the door to the bedroom, Dorsey climbed under the blankets of one of Jack's queen-sized beds. Once she'd stopped thinking about Jack and focused on improvements she still had planned for the Kids Cottage, sleep was deep and peaceful, without nightmares.

Chapter Ten

Jack

RELUCTANTLY, JACK CLOSED the bedroom door, and leaned against it. He couldn't believe he could feel this way about someone, could let a woman into his heart this quickly. All of those years of trying to fill the hole left by his brother's death and his mom's emotional distance with one-night stands and overachieving at school and work had never come close to making him feel alive again. Nothing had. Not until Dorsey. Now he stood on the other side of the bedroom door from her, alone and with a huge hard-on.

He let out a deep sigh and eyed the couch, his bed for the evening. All day long, before the storm had blown in, he'd sat up in the lifeguard chair and daydreamed about Dorsey. About her laugh, her soft skin, her incredibly wild hair. He couldn't wait to make love to her, but knew if he would ever get the chance, he would need to take it slow. He had all the time in the world this summer, before he began his real job. He would wait as long as she needed him to, no matter how hard it was. Literally. He knew he could manage Steve, he just hadn't exactly figured out how. The bigger issue was to earn Dorsey's trust – a trust so ruined by her first and only serious boyfriend that he had caused her to believe she was unlovable. Jack had news for her – she was the most lovable woman he'd ever known.

Climbing under the blanket and trying to get comfortable on

the couch, Jack thought about how he'd feel if his family were threatened, if his dog were poisoned and killed. That had to be horrible for Dorsey's father. Dads were supposed to be the protectors, they were supposed to be around, to be the strong ones. Not that Jack would know. He'd been the man in the Means' household since he was eight and his dad left them. He was afraid he had too much of his dad inside him to ever be a father. He hoped he would never abandon his own child, but who knows what kind of genetic monster could awaken. So Jack had decided to play it safe. Play the field, focus on his career, take care of his mom. But now, now there was Dorsey.

There was a knock on the door. Jack hurried to open it before Dorsey woke up. Steve.

"Just checking to make sure everybody's accounted for after the storm," he said, standing on the porch, clothes still wet from the lashing rain. Shining his too-bright flashlight into Jack's eyes. "Dorsey isn't in her cottage. Have you seen her?"

"As a matter of fact, I have," Jack said, opening the door wider, pointing to his couch. Steve's light followed. "I'm sleeping on the couch there and she's asleep in my bedroom. I know it's against resort policy, but as a senior staff member, I needed to be there for her. She was freaked out by the storm."

"Damn right it's against resort policy, Jack," Steve said, leaning forward until their faces were inches apart. "You don't want to jeopardize your promotion, now do you, pretty boy? Your momma is so proud of you and all."

"I have an employment contract that you are bound to honor. I could have sued you already, so back off," Jack said, his anger at the boiling point.

"You cashed the check, son, so you're mine," Steve said, tiny eyes threatening. "Everything around here needs to run according to my excellence plan. You fit into that nicely. Good eye candy, good for the morale of the staff. I don't even mind all your one-night stands with the summer staff. But don't mess with my Kids

Cottage girls. You got close to Lila last summer and she left. Now here you are with Dorsey. Do you want to see her go, too?"

Jack stared back at Steve, seeing more to him than he'd ever noticed before. The realization that he was more than just a control freak was beginning to sink in. Steve really believed everything and everyone belonged to him on Indigo Island. He wondered what had happened to Steve in his childhood. Jack shook his head, still angry but disturbed at the insight. He saw Steve suddenly as a boy in middle school – skinny, squeaky voice and the easy target of every bully. But, even so, he didn't have to turn out this way. Jack's eyes widened, absorbing the reality of what Steve had said.

"Did you send Lila away? What did you do to her? You bastard. She loved it here," Jack said, disgust and anger mixing into a powerful adrenaline rush. Lila was a beautiful girl, always happy and smiling. Jack had been close to falling for her, close to opening up to her during their two picnic dates together. But suddenly she was gone. "Don't you dare do or say anything to Dorsey. I saw you touch her at the Kids Cottage," Jack said as Steve rocked back and forth laughing his high-pitched laugh. "I'm going to be watching you, as much as you're watching me."

"No need for that kind of threat, son. Just keep out of little Dorsey's panties, and we won't have a problem," Steve said, shining his flashlight directly into Jack's eyes, blinding him, before turning and walking into the night.

If Jack had been frustrated before, now he was frustrated and pissed. Still blinded by the bright light shone in his eyes, he fumbled his way back to the couch after locking and chaining the door. How dare this guy check on them like they were kids away for summer camp? And what had he done or said to Lila?

Screw him, Jack thought. When he moved into management he'd get his revenge. He'd report Steve and his practices to the heads of Top Club, and Steve would be fired. Until then, Jack knew he just had to outsmart him, and protect the young woman in the next room whom he couldn't stop thinking about.

He settled back onto the couch, adrenaline still pumping through his veins. Less than three months until Steve would be neutralized, but that seemed like an eternity tonight with Dorsey in the next room.

Jack knew he'd have trouble sleeping for more than one reason tonight.

JACK PANICKED WHEN he woke up.

Looking around, he realized he was on his couch. The sun was fairly bright, and a quick check of the clock told him what he suspected. Only half an hour to get to the pool. He opened the door to his bedroom, expecting to see Dorsey asleep, but she was gone. The sweatshirt she'd borrowed the night before was folded on his bed. He picked it up and smelled it, and breathed in her scent.

He ran a hand through his hair, marveled at how simply smelling something she wore could turn him on. It was great to feel the sizzle and spark of instant attraction—and crazy that they hadn't acted upon it. Maybe Dorsey was right. Maybe they were building up to something incredible. *Maybe waiting was worth it?*

Thinking about it made him crazy with desire, so he had to get moving. It was late. He'd find her and see if they could have a real date tonight. Screw Steve. Jack would find a place for them to go where he couldn't snoop around and find them. He had several ideas. He jumped in the shower, changed into his lifeguard uniform and headed to the pool complex. He hoped he'd see Dorsey on his way past the Kids Cottage and sure enough, there she was leaning her bicycle against the seawall.

Her hair glistened in the sunlight, and he smiled as she smiled at the children waiting for her for the beach walk. Then Jack noticed Steve also there. Why was he always around, Jack thought, hurrying toward them close enough to hear Steve.

"Well, here's Miss Pittman, finally. I told you she'd show up, she was scared of the storm last night and had to sleep at a friend's house," Steve said to the children, wrapping his long arm tightly around Dorsey's shoulders as his angry, dark eyes belied the gentle tone of his voice.

"Hey Dorsey, have a great day," Jack said, trying to reassure her that everything was OK. And it was. He'd make it so.

"Hi, kids, you can call me Dorsey," she said, smiling up at Jack and ignoring Steve even as he continued to hold her tightly to him. "Are you ready to find sea treasures? There should be a bunch after that big storm."

"I was scared," said a little girl with perfect Pippi Longstocking hair and freckles. She walked up to Dorsey providing the perfect extraction from Steve. Dorsey dropped to her knees to be eye-level with the child.

"Me, too, honey," Dorsey said to the child. "But everything's all right today. Sunshine and blue skies. Did your parents put sunscreen on you?"

"Yes," answered the kids in unison.

"Miss Pittman, could I speak with you for a moment?" Steve said, extending his small hand out to Dorsey. She stood up by herself. "We'll be right with you, kids. Why don't y'all pick out a bucket and a shovel? There's a big assortment in that white bag over there."

"What is it?" Dorsey asked, concerned by his tone. She shot a look at Jack who stepped closer to them.

"I will overlook the fact that you were not in your cottage last night. I understand you were afraid of the storm? Just don't let that happen again, especially with a male coworker. You know the rules and you know what happens if you break them," he said.

Dorsey nodded as Jack looked on with distaste.

"Well good, now onto more important issues. Both of you

need to know. See the EMT squad up there?" Steve pointed in the direction of the red truck.

"Yeah, I figured they were getting sandwiches at the general store, as usual," Dorsey said.

Jack looked back toward the cottages at the red emergency vehicle and then noticed another squad parked at the edge of the seawall, farther down the beach, near the swimming pool complex. "What's going on?" he asked.

"A boat is missing. Ten people from a water surveying company were caught out in the sound during the storm yesterday. No one has heard from them since five last night. We hope they'll turn up, washed ashore here or over at Tybee Island," Steve said. "Maybe they made it to Hilton Head, but we don't think so."

"Oh, no. Should I cancel the beach walk?" she said. "I don't want the kids to find anything."

"That's what I was thinking. How about we do a sandcastle-building contest instead?" Steve suggested. "Are you all right, Dorsey? You look a little spooked. It's hard sleeping in an unfamiliar place during a storm and all."

"What does that mean?" Jack said, "Why don't you back off, Steve?"

"Why don't you get to work, son," Steve said to Jack, a vein popping in his forehead.

"I slept very well, actually," Dorsey said, and turned to check on the children, who were playing with brightly colored plastic buckets on the sand, leaving the two men facing each other.

"Get to work, Jack," Steve said, his squinty eyes searching Jack's face for a reaction.

"I'm going," Jack said, but stopped on the seawall to watch Dorsey with the kids. And to make sure Steve didn't touch her again. He felt like a guard dog.

"Guess what, kids, we're going to build sandcastles today instead of looking for treasures. Mr. Steve will be back to check on us in an hour, so let's make sure we build some great things to show him. He'll bring prizes."

"I'm sure you all will impress me," Steve said, before he climbed the seawall, stepped into his golf cart, and, thankfully, drove away.

"Look at this shell, Miss Dorsey," said little Pippi, as Jack had mentally nicknamed her.

"That's beautiful. Enjoy looking at it and then toss it back so another sea animal can move in."

"Can I keep this?" asked a little boy of five or six. His out-stretched hand held a very alive sea star. Jack saw Dorsey smile as she watched him examine his treasure.

"The sea star is still alive—see all of its tiny little legs moving? We should go throw him back into the water so he'll live. He probably washed ashore during the storm," Dorsey said. "I'll go with you to toss it back. The rest of you better build fast. Steve will be back before you know it, and I know he has great prizes."

As Jack watched, Dorsey held the little boy's hand and they walked to the ocean. The waves were rougher than usual, still stirred up by the storm.

At the edge of the farthest-reaching waves lay the debris and treasures claimed and then returned by the ocean. Seaweed clumps. Beached and dead horseshoe crabs. Aluminum beer cans. A piece of blue Styrofoam ripped from a boogie board. A large buoy had washed in, along with a brown plastic bag full of trash. Jack was thinking about organizing a beach clean up party. Maybe Dorsey and the kids could help the lifeguards. Team building and all. Steve couldn't object to that. He stretched and stood up on the seawall. He knew he couldn't watch Dorsey all day, even though that was all he wanted to do.

Jack saw Dorsey and the little boy walk toward something lying on the beach. Afraid it might be a dead dolphin, Jack hopped down off the seawall and began jogging toward them, just as Dorsey turned toward him.

"Please help!" she yelled and she'd grabbed the little boy in her arms and was walking quickly toward Jack. As the boy and Dorsey got closer, Jack realized it wasn't a dolphin, but a person. A woman.

And then the smell, like rotten meat, blew toward him as he grabbed Dorsey's arm and helped her hurry toward the seawall. To his horror, the other four children began to run toward them. Jack knew he had to keep them moving away from the body. He could hear the little boy crying and he lifted him into his arms. Dorsey's face was a mask of determination as she trudged quickly through the thick sand beside him.

"Hey kids," she said, arms out, blocking the little herd from going any further toward the body. "Let's turn back around. Listen, we're all going to have a race. First one to the seawall gets all the candy they can fit in their lunch bag. Go!"

"I get candy, too?" asked the small boy still in Jack's arms.

"All you want," she said as the little boy wiggled free from Jack's arms and joined the rest of the kids running up to the seawall. "Jack, do you have a phone?"

"No, but I can run to the pool hut if you're OK here," Jack said.

"I'm fine. I'll keep the kids busy while you call for the emergency squad. I think it's too late for her, though," Dorsey said, shaking her head. "Go!"

Jack was reluctant to leave her there, but knew they needed help. By the time he jogged to the pool, called 9-1-1 and jogged back, Steve was at the scene, shepherding the confused children from the beach back to his cart.

"Mr. Steve has lots of candy for all of you, but it's all back at the inn," Dorsey was saying as she helped clear the children from the beach while emergency sirens sounded in the distance.

"Help's coming," Steve yelled to them. "Stay here. Jack, keep those people back."

"Give them candy," Dorsey said as Steve finally drove away with the children. "Oh, my God, Jack."

Jack pulled her into an embrace. "It's going to be all right." He noticed the crowd forming and gradually moving toward them on the beach. "I've got to stop those people. I'll be right back."

"Shouldn't someone cover up the woman? Give her privacy. That's what they did for Dad. Covered him the way you see on TV," Dorsey said, shaking while she was speaking. Not making any sense. Jack knew she was in shock.

Two paramedics rushed past them toward the woman, followed closely by two more.

"Dorsey, come help me hold back the onlookers," Jack said, and she nodded, following him up to the seawall.

"Things are under control, everybody. Go on back to what you were doing before," Dorsey said with surprising strength.

"What's going on?" asked a woman wearing a large floppy hat and a pink floral dress.

"A body has washed up on the beach," Jack said. "I'd suggest turning away, especially those of you with children."

A murmur went through the crowd as several of the onlookers did turn back. Jack and Dorsey stayed put, blocking the curious ones from coming any further. Jack watched as Dorsey turned to look back at the scene, shaking her head.

"It is very important that if your children saw anything that you talk to them about it," Dorsey explained. "Your children should see your sadness about this shocking discovery. Please don't tell the young children details. It's OK for you to simply say you are sad about the woman who died on the beach today. Spend time with your family today, give your kids a chance to ask questions and to grieve. Togetherness is key, what can you do with your kids to make them feel better. Light a candle, have a moment of silence. Come and see me at the Kids Cottage if you need anything, any advice."

He knew she'd had professional training in childcare, but Jack was still impressed with Dorsey's composure and her insights. Both of them continued to walk toward the crowd, moving them back.

Jack looked behind him and noticed they had covered the body with a sheet and were putting it onto a gurney. Four paramedics were on the scene. As they solemnly walked up the beach with the stretcher between them, the onlookers were silent. Jack looked at Dorsey's face and saw her eyes bulging. She was biting her lower lip and had wrapped her arms tightly around herself. He was worried about her and knew instinctively he needed to get her out of here before she broke down. She'd been so strong, so competent with the kids, making sure they weren't scared or had even realized what had happened. But now, Jack thought, it was time for her to leave.

"Let's go," he said, pulling her by the hand, away from the beach across the lawn to the Kids Cottage. Once they were inside, Jack closed and locked the door.

"Are you OK? What were you saying about your dad? Talk to me, honey," Jack said, taking both of her hands in his, guiding her to the window seat.

"Jack. She's dead." Dorsey began to sob, her body shaking. "She was so swollen. Her skin stretched like a white balloon. We thought she was a dolphin—the underside is white, you know. My dad had those glassy eyes, like the surprise of death was written all over him. I was there, you know? Planting flowers with him in our front yard. I heard the gunshot, then warm liquid sprayed on my arms and face, and my dad dropped to the grass."

"You watched your dad's murder? Oh, Dorsey," Jack said, but before he could hug her or do anything for her she was standing, and sobbing, walking in a circle on the bright blue rug in the center of the room. Jack jumped up, tried to hold her, but she pushed him away.

"I saw the murderer, too," she said, stopping suddenly in the center of the rug, her eyes huge and blank, not seeing him, not seeing anything on the island. Jack pulled her to him.

"Shh, Dorsey. Calm down, breathe," Jack said, holding her tight.

"I'm fine. It's her, she needs you, she needs help, the poor lady on the beach," Dorsey said pointing out the window to where the body had been on the beach. Then suddenly, she dropped to the carpet, her knees buckling before Jack realized what had happened. Jack frantically checked for a pulse and found it.

"Oh, honey," Jack said, his training kicking in. He turned her head to the side and propped her feet up on one of the child-sized bean bags. Jack hurried to the small sink in the corner and ran cold water over a few paper towels, using them to wipe her forehead. He had no idea how long a fainting spell could last, but he would be right here when she awoke.

Her eyes fluttered a few minutes later and she tried to sit up.

"Whoa, not so fast. Just stay right there for a little bit and then we'll sit up," Jack said, jumping into rescue training mode.

"I'm fine," Dorsey said, rolling over onto her side and then slowly sitting up. "See?"

"Well, let's get you home to your cottage and you'll feel a lot better," Jack said, still watching her closely as he helped her to stand.

"Thanks for being here," Dorsey said.

Jack wondered what she remembered, if she knew what she'd told him. For now, he just wanted to get her home. "I wouldn't want to be anywhere else," he said.

Dorsey surprised him, pulling him close and kissing him deeply on the lips, pressing her body into his. He felt himself coming alive, all of his senses fully awakened as if for the first time in his life.

"Don't start something you can't finish," he murmured,

grabbing her bottom with both hands and pulling her into him, into his growing erection.

A loud knock on the cottage door startled them both, as Jack released a loud sigh.

"Who is it?" he demanded loudly.

"Steve, open up."

Dorsey looked scared, her perfect lips caught in a tiny O.

"Hey, it's ok. We didn't do anything wrong," Jack whispered. He broke the embrace and opened the door.

"What's going on here?" Steve demanded.

"Nothing," Dorsey said. "I um, well, I fainted if you have to know and Jack's been making sure I'm OK."

Steve narrowed his eyes, unsure what to believe, Jack knew. Their mistrust was mutual.

"She's just lucky she didn't crack her head open, fell right here on the new rug. That would have been a terrible liability for the club, right?" Jack said smiling at his boss all the while wanting to punch him in the nose for always interrupting them, for always appearing.

"The investigators are going to want to talk to both of you. Who wants to come with me first?" Steve said.

"I will, after I take Dorsey back to her cottage," Jack said.

"I'll drive Dorsey back, son, you go on and talk to the sheriff, OK?"

"I'm fine, Jack," Dorsey said. Jack knew it was an attempt to calm him down. She was right. He'd go talk to the sheriff and then come and find her.

"Fine," Jack said, leaving Dorsey alone with the person he least trusted on the island.

Chapter Eleven

Dorsey

DORSEY STILL WAS embarrassed. She pulled the covers over her face and said, "I never faint, Jack, honest. It's way too Victorian, just not in my demeanor. It was heat stroke, I'm sure of it."

"I'm just glad to see you feeling better," Jack said, a smile on his handsome, worried face. Jack sat on the bed next to Dorsey and kissed her gently on the forehead. He wasn't wearing his typical lifeguard uniform of white polo and red bathing suit. Instead, he wore jeans and a white button down. He looked like a hot businessman on vacation. Her hot businessman. Dorsey's Indigo Island family, all present. She realized that's how she thought of him, as family. How had they grown so close, so fast, she wondered? He was very much inside her heart, even if it wasn't a good idea. Even if it weren't allowed.

"They want to interview you as soon as you're up to it," Jack said, turning serious, his hand brushing a stray hair from her eye.

"How's the little boy?" Dorsey asked, shuddering.

"Fine. He thinks he saw a dead dolphin. I guess you told him that," Jack said. "Good thinking. Really good. You were amazing out there, you kept it all under control. I'm so proud of you. Don't feel embarrassed, please."

"Did you realize it was a body, right away?" she asked. He'd been by her side so quickly, helping with the kids and the other guests.

"No, I thought it was a dolphin, too. But then I saw your face go white and I knew," he said, shaking his head at the memory. "I'm just glad I was there, but even if I hadn't been, you handled it like a pro." She grinned at his words, knowing she'd said too much to him, realizing he was a gentleman for not asking her any questions. She reached for his hand just as Steve appeared in the doorway.

"Dorsey, could I speak with you a moment?" he asked, ridiculous glasses on, inside, as always.

"Of course," Dorsey said, shooting a look at Jack who nodded slightly. He was their boss so of course she had to talk to him.

"Alone?" Steve said.

"Ah, right. I was just leaving, going back to the pool to be the good little cabana boy," Jack said, and kissed Dorsey on the forehead, despite the fact Steve was watching. "I'll be back after my shift. Don't move. She's tired, Steve."

"I know. I won't be long. Now, Dorsey, what exactly did you see?" Steve asked checking over his shoulder to make sure they were alone. He seemed to have stretched out the sleeves on his cardigan—his hands were missing.

"You can sit down, Steve," Dorsey said, pointing to the chair in the corner of her bedroom. Her other bed was, as always, a mess of just-washed but not-folded clothes, kids' craft supplies and her growing pottery collection.

Steve began to pace back and forth in front of her bed. "It's a problem, this woman. The boat that's missing was filled with men. We don't know who this woman is or how she ended up here. The sheriff has called in assistance from Hilton Head," Steve said, sweat glistening on his top lip. "It's not good for any of us, this development. Bad for tourism, bad for Top Club. Believe it or not, I'm looking out for all of us. This is bad."

"It's especially not good for her, whoever she was. Oh, my

God," Dorsey said, shaking her head as she struggled to again erase the image of the woman from her mind. She wished Jack were still sitting beside her.

Steve walked over next to her bed, placing a hand on her head. She could feel the warmth and moisture of his palm and wanted to squirm away. She was trapped. "Well, I've told the police what I know. They'll want to speak with you. I don't think there's any connection here, to our island. I'm thinking whatever happened probably happened over in Hilton Head and she washed up over here. Nothing bad happens on Indigo Island. Poor woman. Let's hope we can put all of this behind us. Quickly, before the tourists are scared away. Feel better," Steve said, using his entire hand to squeeze her head, too tightly.

"Ouch," Dorsey said, pulling her head away from his grasp.

Steve smiled and looked down at her. "So pretty, so loved by all the kids, aren't you?" he said before turning to leave. He stopped in the doorway, pointing a finger towards her. "But, Dorsey? I don't think you are remembering the policy?" His jaw tensed and his long neck jutted towards her.

"I know all the policies, Steve," she said, staring straight into his eyes, unblinking, until he made the thumbs-up sign, turned and walked out the door.

"OH NO," DORSEY said, waking up and noticing how bright the room was. Had she slept all night? "What has happened? What have I missed?"

Jack was shaking his head as he hurried to her bedside. "Nothing, you've missed nothing. The woman is still dead. The place is swarming with cops and investigators. Crime scene tape is everywhere. More ferries are arriving right now with a team of forensic specialists from Savannah. They'll figure out who that woman was and how she got here."

"Good, I hope they do and find her murderer. It's really important to find the person in the first few hours," Dorsey said, staring at the wall, not looking at Jack.

"This isn't just about that poor woman on the beach, is it?" Jack said, his brown eyes hooded with sadness. "Do you need to tell me something, anything else, maybe about the past?"

"Nope," Dorsey said, and yanked the blue cotton blanket up under her chin. "I need to take a shower."

"OK. That's a good idea," Jack said as he stood, stretched, and plopped the newspaper onto the chair. "You know, whatever you need, whenever you want to talk, I'm here for you. I want to help." He leaned over and helped her climb out of bed. "Don't close me out."

"Thanks," she mumbled, numb and confused, but comforted by the caring man who had entered her life just when she had least expected it. Dorsey stumbled out of bed toward the bathroom, trying to wake up. "If you're lucky, you might have the distinct pleasure of seeing me showered and in makeup. Just don't expect anything grand. Come back in an hour. OK?"

"You and makeup? Now won't that be something to see," Jack said with a smile before walking out the front door and pulling it closed behind him.

"I'm in love," Dorsey said aloud to her empty bathroom. She'd let too much slip about her past, but he'd been a gentleman and hadn't pushed her for more. But what about Rebecca? Was he secretly seeing her, too? Maybe there was more to their relationship than Dorsey realized. They'd slept together last summer after all. Fortunately, the image of the dead woman didn't haunt her in the shower unless she closed her eyes. So she didn't. Instead she focused on what it would feel like to have Jack rubbing the soap all over her body. That, she discovered, was a very pleasant thought.

By the time he returned, she had attempted makeup and had almost dried her hair.

"You're really beautiful," he said, handing her a bunch of hot pink bougainvillea he had yanked from one of the bushes outside the cottage.

"Thanks, but those have ants and major thorns," Dorsey said, holding her hands up and not accepting the flowers. "I found out the hard way when I made a bouquet of them for my table, and they had started an indoor colony by the time I came back from work."

"Bummer." Jack retraced his steps out the door—and bumped into Steve, who was about to knock.

"Sorry," Jack said.

"Nice flowers, kid," he said.

"Check for ants. I had a couple on my hand," Jack said, releasing his grip.

"So what are you all doing tonight? Going on a date? Flowers, and Dorsey, don't you look nice," Steve said. Dorsey saw Steve's eyes narrow, his jaw tense as he glared at Jack.

"Of course not, Steve," Dorsey said. "We know that's not allowed. We're just a couple of friends hanging out."

"Just be sure that is all it is," Steve said, and then chuckled in his high-pitched way. "Remember all Top Club policies apply to everyone. Including young rising stars like you two."

"Is that a threat? Tell me, are you going to write us up for this or do we have your permission to hang out?" Jack said to Steve, his hands on his hips. The tension between the two men pumped through the air.

Steve blinked, and smiled. "Just don't want any drama like we have now with Rebecca, you little Casanova, you. You kids have fun, just keep to the rules."

"Let's go," Jack said to Dorsey and they walked past Steve and out into the night.

Chapter Twelve

Jack

HOW DARE HE bring up Rebecca, in front of Dorsey? Jack was trying hard to keep his temper in check but he felt his fists tightening. He had planned a special evening for Dorsey and he needed to focus on that. One day, he'd get his revenge on Steve, he just had to bide his time.

Jack had decided to create a picnic in the grass near the swimming pool complex, his own domain, and he had a perfect spot hidden from view but still a great view of the sunset. Sure, he'd made out here with a couple girls each summer, most annoyingly Rebecca at the end of last season. But he'd never wanted to make a picnic for anyone. He hoped he'd thought of everything: wine, cheese, bread, and apples he'd actually paid for. He had his favorite red blanket, a pillow and a lantern for after the sunset. He knew Dorsey didn't want to be near the beach, not after today. He hadn't been able to be near a swimming pool for a long time after Bobby drowned. But he also knew it was time for her to make some new, good memories on Indigo Island.

"So what do you think?" Jack asked Dorsey as he unfurled the blanket. "Perfect spot, right?"

Dorsey was wearing a simple white sundress and flip flops. Her hair was in a loose braid down her back tied with a white ribbon. Jack thought she'd never looked more beautiful.

"This is perfect, so private. How did you find it? Have you been here before with somebody?" she asked hands on hips, eyes flashing an accusation.

"Nope. Planning a picnic is a first for me," he said, kissing her on the cheek, enjoying the flush in her face. "Have a seat."

Dorsey plunked down and he sat down next to her, pouring a glass of Merlot and then filled his own glass. He lit the lantern and pulled out the cheese and apples. He could smell the floral scent of her shampoo. Her heart-shaped lips glistened with clear gloss. She was a natural beauty, her green eyes glowing in the setting sun, freckles dotting her small nose.

"How did you get the courage to become a lifeguard, after watching what happened to your brother?" she asked, swirling the red liquid in her glass. "I just don't know if I would ever be able to do that."

"I did it for my mom," he said, swallowing hard, remembering his reluctance when she first told him. "Mom signed me up for lifeguard training at the Y the summer after Bobby died. She made me do it."

She put her hand on his shoulder and he relaxed.

"It was the right thing to do. For both of us. The swimming pool is a second home to me now, like the ocean. And my mom didn't have to worry about me in the water, even though she refuses to ever go swimming." He sighed and shook his head. He could only live his life and help her as much as he could.

"How about you? Are you doing okay?" Jack asked her, wrapping his arm around her, pulling her in close to him as they sat side by side, facing the now calm sound. He marveled about how just earlier this afternoon, the waters were furious, the waves huge for such a protected stretch of water. Huge enough to push a body onto shore, one that had been, he'd heard from one of the investigators he'd been chatting with, anchored to the sea floor with a weight. That little bit of information had given Jack the chills and he had yet to share it with Dorsey, and he hoped he wouldn't have to.

"This really is perfect, Jack," Dorsey said, leaning into his side, trusting him to hold her up. She was holding a clump of the blanket in her right hand, holding on tight. "I feel like I need to tell you everything, tell you my story. It was a night sort of like this one."

"Honestly, Dorsey, you don't have to tell me," Jack said, staring up at the stars beginning to dot the sky. Jack could lose himself in the sky, mesmerized by the number and clarity of the stars and planets. Especially the sky here on Indigo Island – it was so different from the city, from anywhere else he'd known. So freeing. The opposite of Orlando and everything fake that city stood for in his mind. Dorsey was the opposite of every woman he'd known. He didn't want to push her into anything.

"I want to tell you," Dorsey said. As Jack looked at her he saw her eyes were glistening, wet with silent tears. "Dad and Mom were so in love, they were actually high school sweethearts. I'm an only child. I got to see it all, even if they were embarrassing sometimes. They were the kind of couple you hoped to be. They had that kind of love. And according to the tradition my father taught me as a little girl, I always wish silently upon a star. I miss him so much," Dorsey said, quickly wiping the back of her hand across each eye, stemming the flow. "He was really handsome. Big brown eyes, like yours."

"I'm so sorry," Jack said. He didn't know what else to say or what else to do. He didn't know exactly what had happened to her dad, just that something terrible had. He realized listening could be the biggest gift he could give her, even though, like most guys, he wanted to fix things, fix it all for her.

High in the sky, a full moon illuminated a path of light across the ocean, seeming to reach out and touch the blanket they shared on the grass. The air was warm and dry for the island, the perfect temperature.

"It was ten years ago now, but it's still so vivid. Especially after today, on the beach. We were gardening, Dad and I. I was kneeling, planting a row of sunflower seeds when it happened. I saw the gunman and he saw me before he turned and ran, surprised there had been a witness. Surprised his act had been seen. My dad, though, lay still on the grass, his blood soaking into our perfect green lawn, splattered on my face and arms. His eyes a blank stare, his mouth frozen in the shape of no."

Jack was at a loss for words, for what to do or say. He wanted to absorb her pain, make it go away but he knew just like with his brother's death, some things are a weight on your heart forever.

"So they caught the killer, right? You saw him?"

Dorsey's sobs grew harder and all Jack could do was hold her close until she'd cried them all out.

"I'm sorry," she said.

"Don't be. Where is your mom now?" Jack asked, gently rocking her in his arms as she leaned against him.

"She's back home in Kentucky," Dorsey said. "It's where she grew up, although I don't know anybody there. But she likes it. She'll never remarry. She'll garden. Raise horses. Dream about Daddy."

"So who takes care of you?" Jack asked. He pushed the hair back out of her face and bent forward to look into her eyes.

"Me? Well, myself, I guess. My old boyfriend, Chad, stuck around for a bit, until I became too embarrassing. My dad's face was on a website hosted by anti-abortion crusaders, a big red X through his face. The local news covered it, and the national news." Dorsey shuddered, dropping her head in her hands. "Since the killer was never found, the story sort of lingers still. Urban, rather, suburban legend."

"You didn't see who did it?" Jack asked.

"I don't want to talk about that, about the day, okay?" Dorsey said quietly, blinking away the memories. "After he died, I had trouble doing things, trouble concentrating. I made it through high school somehow. I waited tables in different restaurants. Made good money. Worked my way through Ohio

State. I was a nanny for a great family and their love helped me pull my life together. But I needed to find myself. I wanted to get whole, start over. Get past my family's tragedy."

Jack cradled Dorsey as they looked out over the water. The sun had set and stars filled the sky. He was aroused and wanted to touch her, to comfort her, to make her feel like she was home and safe now, but didn't know how she'd react. He liked taking care of her, but he wanted more. Much more. Patience wasn't his strong suit. Finally, he said. "Let's go back to my cottage. Have a nightcap. You can spend the night if you'd like—but you don't have to."

"Sure, and Jack, thanks for listening. Nobody here knows the story. Everyone back home thinks they do."

"I'm honored," Jack said, pulling Dorsey up to standing as he wrapped his arms around her.

"We'll see," Dorsey said, tears springing to her eyes. "After this afternoon, I'm beginning to think death likes finding me."

"Nonsense, Dorsey. Come on," Jack said, quickly cleaning up the picnic, blowing out the candle and folding the red blanket. He looked around, making sure they weren't forgetting anything. He thought he saw a figure off in the woods, a man, but no, nothing was out there, he told himself, and hurried Dorsey to the golf cart.

Back inside his cottage, Jack's heart stopped racing. He wondered why he was suddenly so on edge, here, on this island he wanted to call home. It wasn't Dorsey who was making him feel this way. It was Steve, his lurking, his implied threats. His lying, and not following through with his promises. Just one of those characteristics would be enough for Jack to think he was a squirrely guy – all of them together, well…

"Hey, Jack, could you come in, and help me?" Dorsey called from the bedroom, his bedroom.

Jack steeled himself. He knew it would be a favor, like unhooking her necklace or adjusting the thermostat.

Chapter Thirteen

Dorsey

S HE'D MADE A decision, something she hoped she wouldn't regret. It happened during their picnic together. Jack had listened, really listened to her story and hadn't judged. He hadn't been repelled by her past, not like Chad had been. In fact, he'd held her tighter as she told him the story. He'd been there with her on the beach when the poor woman had washed up, and he'd taken care of her when she'd fallen apart and fainted.

Jack had been everything she could imagine in a partner and even though her heart was beating, and her eyes were swollen from all the crying, and even though she could be wrong and he could be everything terrible that Rebecca said he was, she wanted to be with him.

Dorsey pulled open the top drawer of his dresser and found a white muscle shirt. She smiled even as her hands shook. Could she really do this? Be this assertive? She pulled off her sundress and bra and pulled Jack's shirt over her head. The fabric was thin and cool, her nipples responded as if Jack's hands were already on her body and she felt her face flush. Before she lost her nerve she pulled off her underwear, shook the braid out of her hair, checked her reflection in the mirror and called to Jack to come into the bedroom.

Dorsey smiled at Jack's startled reaction. His full lips, his strong jaw and sparkling eyes focusing on her, all of her. She stared at him in response, his handsome face, his caring eyes. She wanted to feel his strong body on top of her, there was no longer any way to stop this. Their attraction was potent, pulsing through the air between them.

"Jack, I'm ready," she said, as he crossed the room, picked her up in his strong arms and carried her to his bed. Dorsey held on tight, running her fingers through his thick hair, breathing in the masculine scent of him, dizzy with his smell and her desire.

He dropped Dorsey on the bed and fell on top of her, his erection pressing against her through his jeans. He grabbed both of her wrists, holding them over her head as he pressed his mouth over Dorsey's, a kiss full of want and need that matched her own. The kiss was hungry, frantic, his tongue thrusting inside her mouth.

Dorsey pulled her arms free and reached for his shirt, pulling on it, wanting to feel his bare skin against her own. Needing to feel it. She heard Jack moan as he realized she wore nothing under his t-shirt as he quickly slipped it over her head. He cupped her breasts, sucking each of her erect nipples. Dorsey moaned, her pelvis pushing against him, her arms reaching to unbutton his jeans. She nuzzled into his neck, breathing him in, dizzy with desire.

"Please, I need to feel you inside me," she said into his ear, her need so powerful, so overwhelming, her heart felt like it would escape her chest. Her fears about getting too close to him raced through her mind even as she told herself to be in the moment, to trust him, even as her body arched with desire. He was what she'd always waited for, who she thought she'd never find. Her eyes opened, to plead with him, just as his gaze locked on hers, his eyes dark and glistening.

"Slow down, we're going to make this count," he said in a deep strong voice as his mouth moved to her sex, his warm tongue sliding deep inside her, as stars swirled through her head and her hips arched into him until she finally let go, exploding, shuddering. Before she could catch her breath or stop the swirls shooting through her brain, his fingers slid into the spot where his tongue had just been. She was on the brink again.

"Oh, Jack, please."

Finally, he stood and undressed. He kept his eyes locked on Dorsey's as he removed his shirt revealing his tanned six-pack that was the talk of the pool. He undid his jeans, slipping them off with his underwear and stood naked, and completely erect. Dorsey realized he was trusting her, too, revealing himself, all of himself to her.

"I hope you know how much you mean to me," he said as he climbed back on the bed, lying beside her, his erection pressing into her side.

She swallowed, wanting to believe him, staring into his gorgeous eyes, seeing the desire and the care there, too. She shuddered as his warm lips sealed over hers and his hand slid across her stomach and down to her sex, a light touch that caused Dorsey to moan and arch. Jack broke the kiss, sliding his lips to her neck. "You smell so good," he whispered. "You're so beautiful."

"Jack, please," Dorsey moaned as her need mounted and he slid two fingers inside her, feeling her wetness, finding the spot. She was more than ready, again, she didn't know if she could wait any longer as she pushed against his hand, needing all of him inside her. He left her writhing on the bed and, she heard him unwrapping a condom.

"Ready, baby," he said as he straddled her. His eyes were dark and focused on her. Slowly he began thrusting, entering her gently, a little at a time and then pushing further inside as Dorsey moaned, wrapping her legs around his perfect torso, her hands grasping his muscled shoulders, pulling him deeper, their eyes still locked on each other.

"You feel so good, just keep coming," Jack said, as he started to drive deeper inside her. Dorsey's head spun as she began to climax again, and she dug her fingernails into his back as he ground into her with a final thrust and they came together.

Afterward, lying naked in Jack's arms while he slept, Dorsey knew she'd never felt this safe, this loved. She hoped this could last, that she meant as much to Jack as he did to her. She'd heard stories of his past summer conquests, of course, as everyone – Steve, Sabrina, Rebecca – had all made it their mission to share those with her. And Dorsey saw how all the other female staffers flirted with him during meetings, how the pool staff swarmed around his lifeguard chair. Even the tourists tried to catch his eye.

But Dorsey had decided to trust him, believe in what he said. For now, that had to be enough. She had to admit if great sex meant they had a deep emotional connection, well, she was certain they'd connected deeply. Her stomach clenched at the thought and she snuggled closer to Jack. And finally, she closed her eyes and instead of death and bodies, she allowed herself to dream of Jack.

THE NEXT MORNING, Dorsey woke up early, rolling out of Jack's arms to hurry back to her own cottage. It was hard to leave him, his arm flung out to his side, his powerful body so peaceful in sleep. His face was so handsome in sleep, worry-free, relaxed. But, for both of them she knew she had to hide their relationship, so she had to get back to her own cottage before Steve found out they'd spent the night together, really spent the night together. It was, Dorsey realized, the most wonderful night of her life. She'd never felt so alive, so loved, so consumed by someone.

She took her time walking back to her cottage, wearing the white sundress and a huge grin. As she walked in the door, the telephone rang. It was Steve's assistant, summoning her to his office to meet with the sheriff. She hopped in the shower, pulled on her uniform and didn't bother trying to dry her hair, making it to Steve's office a half an hour later.

After asking some standard questions, the sheriff asked, "Would you like to add anything else?" He was suntanned a dark brown, and his eyes were kind, with at least twenty different wrinkles fanning out from the edges of each, like a child's drawing of sunbeams. He was peaceful, and as he leaned back in his chair, the fingers of each hand had pointed together, unconsciously mimicking the "Here's the church, here's the steeple" nursery rhyme.

Dorsey watched him, thinking his weathered skin would feel thick to touch.

"We are checking all angles but believe she may be a domestic violence victim from Hilton Head," he said.

"How sad," Steve said, before Dorsey could speak. "That's all you have for her, right? She's got work to do."

That unsatisfying meeting had happened several hours earlier, and Dorsey still felt uneasy. Now, she sat in the sun on the seawall, forcing herself back to the ocean, back to where they found the dead body the day before. It was another beautiful day on Indigo Island, except for the swarm of investigators walking every bit of the beach, combing it for evidence. She had checked in at the Kids Club every few minutes since the scheduled opening time, but she doubted many parents would be apart from their kids today. A chill ran down her spine as she looked at the spot where the body had been.

She was getting sunburned. She pushed on her thigh with her thumb and a white circle appeared. The Calibogue Sound sparkled in the morning sunshine, and the humidity was down. Flowers bloomed everywhere on the well-groomed grounds of the plantation – bright bursts of pink, and orange and yellow, and butterflies swarmed the gazebo, guzzling the pollen from the clusters of flowers decorating its side.

She wondered again how something so horrible could happen in such a beautiful place. Much like her father's murder—

murdered in his own garden next to his child—there was no
reason for it. But hopefully, unlike his unsolved case, they could
find the person responsible for killing the poor woman on the
beach.

After checking in with the Kids Club again, and finding nobody there, as expected, Dorsey made her way back to the beach,
nodding and smiling to investigators along the way. With the air
cooler than it had been for weeks, the walk along the edge of the
sound actually was pleasant. A mild breeze blew across the water
from Hilton Head, carrying the jarring sound of the Jet Skis
circling the waters of that beach, piercing the quiet peace of her
walk. She wondered if Indigo Island would ever suffer the fate of
Jet Skis and what they represented—too much construction, too
many people. She realized that she now preferred it here in this
remote and dangerous place. Hilton Head seemed too crowded,
too busy, too chaotic. Indigo Island seemed suddenly just right.
She smiled at her own realization and knew she also owed a lot of
her happiness here to Jack.

Just thinking about him made her heart beat faster and her
stomach flip. Their night together was everything she had ever
dreamed of. Making love with Jack was not like anything she'd
ever experienced and she hoped she'd experience it again, soon.
She scanned the pool area, but didn't see him. She knew the pool
staff had a meeting every morning. She'd catch up with him on
her way back. She was on a mission.

Just past the plantation's boundaries, she turned northeast to
follow the creek inland to the other side of the island. She
imagined looking for Tade, remembering how long she had
wandered this creek bed before he appeared on the shore above
her. Dorsey rubbed the oogle for luck and kept walking, sensing
that somehow she'd arrive at the right place.

She smelled something wonderful cooking—cornbread or
biscuits maybe? Looking in the direction of the tempting aroma,
she spotted Barbara's tin-roofed shack. At least she hoped she was

in the right place.

Dorsey climbed out of the creek bed, up the small slope to her front yard, and up the three steps to her porch. Her hand shook as she reached out and knocked on the light blue door. "Hello? Miss Barbara? It's Dorsey, Tade's friend. May I come in?" Dorsey said loudly enough that she scared a cardinal, who flew away in blood-red terror.

The door slowly opened and Barbara appeared. "My long pot drew you here?" Barbara asked, inviting Dorsey to follow her into her home with a nod of her head.

"Sorry?" Dorsey said, not understanding.

"The good ol' 'romas. Ya nevah know who gonna drop by," Barbara said.

"Yes! I smelled your cooking!" she exclaimed, finally picking up on the words she was saying. She was speaking English, but the words came together so differently, Dorsey had trouble following. She was, Dorsey realized, speaking the same language as Jim, the bus driver. It was Gullah. Dorsey had given a little talk about it as part of her history walk for vacationers and their kids. It was a mix of African and English the slaves who suffered on this island had created so they could communicate without the masters understanding. A language of survival.

"You're speaking Gullah! It's beautiful," Dorsey said, as Barbara pointed her to a small white wooden chair, one of four surrounding a small wooden table. In the corner, a black pipe stovetop held whatever smelled so divine.

"Gullah? What be dat?" she asked, and before Dorsey could answer, she continued with a smile, sitting down in a chair just like Dorsey's. "I can speak regular English, too, just need to switch my mind, and it's old. Takes a bit. Don't have many comeyahs back here, just my little Tade."

As Barbara smoothed her weathered red apron, Dorsey smiled and said, "Tade's a great little boy. He brought me this oogle, and said it was a present from you."

"Mmmm-hmm," Barbara said.

"I've carried it with me ever since. Thank you. I believe it's protecting me, and helping sort out my new life over there, at the plantation," Dorsey said.

"Eber ting 'n de milk ain' white," Barbara said, nodding her head slowly, reminding Dorsey of Jim, the bus driver, someone else with the same habit.

"I actually really love it here, love the people here, except Steve, I guess. Do you know him?" she asked. Dorsey felt as if she should sit at the older woman's feet, and wondered if she had magical powers or if she was just well connected on the island. Dorsey wondered about all she knew, all she had seen in her lifetime. "Times come a changin,' miss," Barbara said.

"Who is changing? Me?" Dorsey asked, a chill rising in the back of her neck. "Barbara? Who?" she pleaded, when Barbara didn't answer. "I found a dead body, a woman, who washed up on shore."

Barbara folded her hands in her lap. Her eyes twinkled, but she was silent. Standing, she walked over to the pot on the old woodstove, picked up a big metal spoon, and slowly stirred the contents, releasing even more amazing scents. She bent and tossed a piece of wood from the stack into the open belly of the stove, brushed her hands together, and returned to her chair at the table across from Dorsey.

"Chile, keep your oogle with you over deh. Keep your love close, or others will try to break you apart," she said, closing her eyes.

"Barbara?" Dorsey asked. She seemed to have fallen asleep, napping right there in her little wooden chair. *Should I leave her?* Dorsey wondered.

"Go along, chile. Keep your eyes on da sand. Beware of de haints," Barbara said, without opening her eyes.

Dorsey hurried back to the plantation, more scared than ever—but not about being on the backside, where she'd found peace and comfort. More about being on the plantation where the haints were running amok.

As she jogged down the beach, she cut in at the pool area in a blatant attempt to catch a glimpse of Jack lifeguarding. And there he was, tanned and gorgeous, sitting up in the lifeguard chair, the red umbrella tipped to shade him from the intense sun. She couldn't believe he belonged to her. *Keep your love close*, Barbara had said.

Dorsey waved as she jogged by and saw Jack's face light up with his signature smile. She wanted to stop at the pool, to climb up the chair and into his lap but she knew she couldn't.

"See you tonight," she yelled, not caring who heard her, and then headed for the inn, not following Barbara's advice she realized. She needed to keep her love close, keep it secret, that's what Barbara meant. Geesh.

Dorsey realized it was going to be tough to follow the old woman's advice. She was so excited about Jack she wanted to scream it from the top floor of the inn.

Chapter Fourteen

Jack

I T WAS AN hour before sunset, three days since the dead woman had washed ashore on the beach in front of the inn. Jack and Dorsey walked hand in hand along the beach, but not the stretch of sand in front of the inn. Dorsey still didn't want to walk near where the now-identified body of Susan Price, age thirty one, had washed ashore. She'd been a victim of domestic violence, like the sheriff had predicted. Her husband was in custody charged with her murder.

"We shouldn't be holding hands here," Dorsey said. "We need to keep our relationship a secret. Barbara told me that this afternoon."

"You went to the backside, without me?" Jack said, dropping her hand, turning to face her. He couldn't believe she would go there without him. "You promised you wouldn't do that." He stared at her while she dropped her eyes and blushed.

"Ah, I just realized that, well, just now. You were working and it was fine, I just needed someone to talk to, that's all," she said, trying to hold his hand again. "Stop being so worried about everything."

Jack supposed she was right, he realized, as he pulled her into him for a hug. He couldn't be with Dorsey every minute, even though he wanted to be. For the past two days, when they weren't working, it seemed like they were together in bed. It had been the best two days of his life. The sex was incredible, more powerful than anything he'd ever experienced. And it was great having someone to come home to after work, to share a laugh and tell stories about his day at the pool. For so long he'd been focused on achieving, keeping himself walled off from true emotion, just having sex for release. But Dorsey was different. Sure, the sex was great but it was so much more. Like the way her face relaxed after they made love, how the sadness in her eyes would disappear, if only for a little while. He liked knowing he could take her pain away, even for a little while.

Dorsey had been the one who wanted him to show her the island, to help her fall in love with it like he had and so he'd decided to take her to the deserted Southern tip.

They'd driven the golf cart to the end of Top Club's plantation and started their walk again on the beach, heading further south. Jack pointed to a huge home nestled among some live oaks just a bit off the beach. He told Dorsey it belonged to a family from Atlanta named Putnam. She had thought the place was another hotel it was so massive.

"There's even a helipad," Jack said. "Someday, we'll have our own helicopter." He couldn't believe he was talking in 'we', as in a couple. He looked over in time to see her blush.

"I don't think I ever want a helicopter," Dorsey said, leaning into him.

"OK, our own jet then," he teased, leaning over for a quick kiss that suddenly heated up as they pressed against each other. Jack pulled away. "Hey, sexy, we have to keep our focus on the adventure or we'll just end up in bed again."

She laughed, adding to Jack's arousal. He reminded himself he wanted to show Dorsey a magical dolphin encounter he hoped would be recreated while she was with him. "It's a dolphin behavior unique to these waters and it was right here," he said, pointing at the water. "I was looking for the bald eagle, and all of a sudden four dolphins beached themselves a foot away from me, trapping a school of fish on shore between them. Then, just as suddenly, they ate the fish up and wiggled back into the water. Amazing," Jack said. "I could really learn to love it here, live here forever. I want you to feel that, too."

They sat on the warm sand, Dorsey leaning against him, nestled between his legs. Jack dropped his chin on her shoulder. She smelled like coconut and lemon and he felt himself growing hard. Focus on the dolphins, he reminded himself. It didn't help. Jack slipped his hand around her waist, slowly working his way to the waistband of her shorts, unfastening the top button. He slid his hand down inside her shorts. She opened her legs as Jack slid his fingers over her, and she was immediately wet.

She moaned and said, "Ah, Jack," before squirming and playfully pulling his hand away. "We're here to see the dolphins."

"I don't think they're showing up tonight," Jack said, knowing he could give her an orgasm, right here, right now. And she seemed to know it, too. "Relax, and enjoy."

She relaxed against him, her head on his thigh. With one hand he teased her nipples through her shirt as her breath quickened. She spread her legs open and he played with her, sliding his fingers inside her until he hit the sweet spot that caused her to explode, moaning and then collapsing against him, her forehead glistening in sweat. He kissed her on the cheek as he buttoned her shorts.

"My goodness, Mr. Means," she said once her breathing had steadied. She squeezed his hand now resting on her hip. Jack smiled, looking down at her, wondering if she was trying to imagine his dream, wondered if she could picture her life here, with him, on this deserted island.

"You know, I finally love this time of evening again, because of you," she said. "Even when the sky turns the water red, like it's doing now, it doesn't scare me. Not anymore, not when we're together. Well, as long as Steve isn't around."

"Forget Steve,"

They were quiet as the sun dropped into the ocean, the final bow to the day. Seagulls soared past them in search of a meal, otherwise, nothing moved.

"When they put that food coloring in our swimming pool, it turned bright red," she answered, trying to wash the image from her eyes. "It was a warning but my dad didn't take it seriously, didn't even report it to the police. When they poisoned our dog, Rufus, he did report it. Not that it changed anything. Sorry, I don't want to ruin our night."

"You're not ruining anything, Dorsey. Tell me whatever you want to, whenever you want to. I've never wanted to take care of somebody as much as I do you," Jack said. Reaching over to grab his backpack, he said, "close your eyes. I brought a surprise."

He checked to make sure her eyes were shut and popped the champagne cork, scaring several of the egrets from their nests in the tall trees behind them. Dorsey jumped, panicked.

"That sounded like a gun shot," she said, eyes wide with fear, visibly shaking.

"Oh no, sorry, my fault, just champagne," Jack said, handing her a glass, noticing how her hand was shaking. "Here's to us."

Jack watched as she took a big breath, and seemed to calm down.

"Cheers."

They sat side-by-side, leaning against a driftwood log, staring at the now almost dark sky. The crashing waves, soothing and menacing with undertows and cross-currents pulling, pushing. Surging. And sometimes calming, polishing, smoothing over.

"Boy, I'm tipsy," Dorsey said, leaning farther onto Jack after two glasses of bubbly. "You know that rainy night when we talked, really talked? You saved me. I was wallowing in self-pity, really. I needed to move on, let go of the past."

"I'd like to see you this happy all the time," Jack said. "I don't think my dolphin friends are going to make an appearance tonight. Let's head back to the golf cart. I brought my blanket."

When they reached the golf cart, Jack ran up and grabbed his signature red blanket and spread it out on the beach. "Pillows and an extra blanket. At least my iPhone playlist still works."

"You're too much," Dorsey said. Then she fell back onto the pillow Jack had placed behind her.

Stars filled the sky and the wind, blowing the palm fronds, added to the tropical clamor of the evening. After starting some romantic music on his iPhone, Jack unfurled another blanket and crawled under it next to her.

Dorsey smelled so good. She had a powerful effect on him. He stared into her green eyes, touched her perfect lips with his finger. It had been a long time since he'd felt comfortable thinking about a future with a woman. This wasn't a summer fling, he realized. It couldn't be. Jack carefully, slowly pulled down her shorts and massaged her thighs.

"Jack," Dorsey moaned, reaching for his erection. He pushed her hand away, wanting to take care of her first. To always take care of her.

Gently, he unbuttoned her blue denim shirt.

"Beautiful, you're beautiful," Jack said. After he removed her bra, Jack stopped and smiled. With one hand he traced the shapes of her body, from her shoulders across her perfect breasts, over her stomach, and down each gorgeous thigh. Her skin responded to his touch, her nipples firm, her skin was so soft, so smooth and beautiful in the moonlight.

"Perfect," he said.

"What are you waiting for?" She was writhing with need, trying to pull him on top of her.

"Not yet," he answered, and placed his pointer finger on her lips. "Quiet."

Jack rubbed her bottom lip with his finger, as she moaned, and he slid a finger into her mouth, which she sucked expertly. Jack sat up, straddling Dorsey and reached into the cooler.

"You're hot," he said, dripping icy water between her breasts.

She shuddered and gasped as he moved the dripping cube down to her belly button.

"Oh, Jack," she said, "I never want to lose you."

Jack quickly undressed, but he wasn't finished playing with her yet. After kissing her deeply on the lips he moved down her body until she felt him between her legs. Using his hands to grip her hips, Jack pulled her sex into his mouth, using his warm slick tongue to bring her to the brink of orgasm. He knew she'd given herself over to him completely, and he wanted her to have the best night of her life.

Dorsey cried out, writhing and moaning as she climaxed, again, on the beach. Jack moved back up, helping soothe her, kissing her lips and holding her through her shaking. Panting, she begged him to enter her. "Please," she said, reaching for him, desperate for him.

Jack smiled and reached for the condom, sliding it on quickly. With his eyes staring deep into her beautiful green ones, he clasped her wrists above her head and slid inside her, just a bit and then more and more until he was driving into her with a fury and desire beyond what they'd shared before. As Jack pounded harder, Dorsey wrapped her arms and legs around him. Still inside her, he sat up and pulled her onto his lap, his hands on her small waist pumping her up and down on his member, forcing himself deeper and deeper, as they both came together.

After, spooning under the blanket, spent but content, looking up at the stars, Jack decided that the happiest days of his life were just beginning. And a big part of that future was in his arms. The ocean's calm waves made the perfect soothing sound and he loved the smell of the salt spray filling the air. He felt like they were the only two people on the island, and that was fine with him.

"I love you, Dorsey," Jack whispered, surprising himself by speaking the words aloud. He burrowed his face into her wild tangle of hair. It smelled like peaches. He took a deep breath.

What would she say?

"I love you, too," she said, tears welling up before she could stop them. "This night, this all is a dream come true. Can this be real? How can this work?"

"We'll figure it out, together," Jack said, hoping they could, knowing Steve was a problem but no longer caring. Everything would be fine, he'd make sure it was.

Jack didn't know how long they stayed there, but finally, when the beach was completely dark, they packed up. On the ride home, Jack drove the golf cart on the beach instead of on the paved path, surprising the ghost crabs, who jumped out of their holes, one claw raised, to defend themselves from whatever was venturing onto their beach in their time of the evening.

They spent the night at his cottage, and Jack slept a deep, dreamless sleep.

Chapter Fifteen

Dorsey

THE KIDS COTTAGE was hopping. She'd had ten kids, aged four to twelve to entertain today and that was a challenge with the age gap. The group had walked the beach, albeit slowly and then taken a swim at the pool. Unfortunately, Jack wasn't the lifeguard on duty, but she still enjoyed her daydreams about him. Just thinking about him made her insides clench with desire and something much, much more. She'd fallen in love. The day passed quickly and as she was seeing off the last camper, Steve appeared.

"Dorsey, we need to talk," he said, hands on hips, walking past her into the cottage. She hated the way he burst in whenever he wanted to the stance he took, lurking over her, his turtle-like neck never bothered her more than at these moments. She took a deep breath and a step back, bumping into the wall. Did he know something, she wondered. They had been so careful, so sneaky.

"Why, sure, Steve," she said, feeling suddenly small and very alone. And trapped. "You seem upset?"

"It's more like disappointed. In you. Remember when you promised to follow club policy?" He'd pushed his sunglasses up onto his forehead and had placed one hand on either side of her against the wall. Dorsey could smell his stinky cologne as if she'd sprayed it on her own neck.

She quickly ducked and made it out from under his left arm and hurried to the other side of the room. "Yes, I know all the rules," she answered, feeling the blush start on her face despite herself. "I've been the model employee. I got four new stars this week."

"The guests do like you, Dorsey, but you are not making me happy. And that's your problem. You see, I'm the only one who matters, ultimately. I told you not to date a coworker, didn't I?"

Steve had stepped closer to her again. He had taken his glasses off of his head and twirled them in his right hand. Spittle was forming at the corners of his mouth. "But yet, you're fucking the lifeguard, aren't you?"

Dorsey was shocked, and trapped. She didn't know what to say to him. She didn't know whether to deny everything, or to just tell him the truth and beg for mercy. Her heart raced. She looked out the window, praying Jack would appear, would show up and save her or at least tell her what to say.

"Don't lie to me. I know everything that happens here."

He was inches from her, leaning down into her personal space. Dorsey felt herself shaking; she was scared of Steve, but she couldn't speak. But she was in love, and love was always OK, and before she could stop herself she blurted, "Yes, it's true."

"I knew it. Fucker," Steve said, turning his back to her, shaking his head slowly, popping the knuckles of his small right hand.

"Steve, sir, it's my fault. I was lonely. Jack is innocent here. Fire me, transfer me. Or I'll quit."

Steve turned back around and stared at her, his tiny eyes dark. He shook his head, pointing his finger at her. "It stops now. Ends now. You will be summoned to the ethics committee. They will decide your fate. If you don't see him again, they may allow you to stay." Steve shook his head again, putting his glasses back on. He reached out and touched her hair, playing with it in his fingertips before dropping his hand to her shoulder. "You are such a disappointment," he said, before walking out the door.

After he left, Dorsey sat down in one of the child-sized chairs, shaken. She'd made a terrible mistake in confessing the truth to Steve. Barbara had warned her, and she hadn't listened. This was the moment when it mattered, this was when she needed to keep her love close. She felt in her pocket for her oogle but realized she'd left it at home. It would all be OK, she tried to tell herself. Jack didn't need to know about this, Steve would calm down and everything would be fine.

She and Jack just needed to be low-key. They could do that. They would have to now, she realized. And it was all her fault.

Chapter Sixteen

Jack

THREE DAYS LATER, Jack was furious. He was standing in the Kids Cottage holding a note summoning Dorsey to appear for ethics violations in front of the three-person management committee led by Steve. Fortunately the kids had all gone home, so he could yell at Dorsey in private.

"What the hell did you admit to? What did he ask you? And when?" he yelled, "Why didn't you tell me you'd done this?" He was pacing the bright blue carpet and Dorsey, face drained of color, was standing by the door as if she was considering making a run for it. He knew he was yelling, knew he was scaring her but he hadn't been this mad since he could remember. He took a deep breath and tried to calm down.

"It just came out, I swear, Jack," she said, voice quivering. She looked like she was going to cry, but Jack couldn't feel any sympathy. She had ruined everything.

"He walked in here three days ago and asked me point blank if we were having sex. And we are," Dorsey said. She crossed the room reaching out for him, trying to give him a hug to calm him down.

"Don't," he said, brushing past her and continuing to pace back and forth across the bright blue carpet. He knew Dorsey had never seen him this angry, although she could probably tell he had some pent-up anger issues. Usually, he could keep it under control, keep it under the surface. But not this. This ruined everything.

He read the summons again, it had become crumpled as he'd held it in his hands. He stopped walking and tried to calm down. "Look, I don't like it, not at all. I don't even think this is legal. I mean, we had an ethics council in college. But that was for cheating. He works for a large corporation. HR people deal with stuff like this, not tribunals. He's just trying to force one of us to leave. Probably me. I can't believe you didn't tell me this happened." He looked up and Dorsey was sobbing. She had dropped into the window seat.

He had made her cry. He hated himself for that. Dammit. He needed to make a plan, to fix this. He'd have to get to Steve's bosses before Steve could get to them.

He sat down next to Dorsey, and pulled her against him. "Shh, it's going to work out," he said, as she wiped her tears on his shirt. "I've got a plan. But first we have the stupid oyster roast tonight. You still up for helping?"

"Yes," she answered quietly, a catch in her voice from all the tears.

"Ok, stop crying and let's get our game faces on. We can't let him know he got to us, no matter what. So, throw this thing away, or actually I will," he said, ripping up the piece of paper and scrunching it into a tiny ball of waste. "And I'll see you at the pool complex in about an hour. Good?"

Dorsey nodded, and attempted a smile.

"I still love you, even if you spilled the beans," he said, kissing her on the forehead before heading out the door.

Jack headed back to the pool. He was overseeing the oyster roast setup for the evening since it was taking place at the pool complex. Steve had assigned him to the task, explaining it would be like a management position. Jack had said it was more like event-planning, but Steve had insisted. All of the prep work was completed, and Jack saw Dorsey as she walked up the path looking happier than she had an hour ago. He forced a big smile on his face, attempting to hide the worry he still felt deep inside.

"Goody, the two people I've been dying to see," Steve said, coming up behind Jack, putting his arm around Jack's shoulder as Dorsey joined them. Her face had gone white again. "So, how goes life on our fair island, Jack?" he asked, as Jack shook free of his arm. Steve grabbed Dorsey's elbow preventing her from backing away.

"It's fine, thanks," Jack said, trying to keep the anger out of his voice.

Steve pulled Dorsey close to him as he spoke to Jack.

"Jack, my boy, I've given you fair warning. I told you the policy and you signed it when you began working here last year and this year. If you can't keep it in your pants, you know where to get some. Not the summer staff, and not this one," he said, jerking Dorsey's arm. "You are supposed to fuck the tourists. That's who. You did it all last year. But now, you're messing up, star boy. Once Dorsey talks to the committee it'll be one of you who will leave. You can guess who that will be, can't you?" Steve asked, his tongue flicking the sides of his mouth.

"You're all class," Jack said, balling his hands into fists, ready to swing.

Steve grabbed Jack's shoulder: "Hey, boy. Don't act too uppity, you know, because I'm in charge around here. I'm the one who hired you, and I can take it all away. And where are you going to get the money to pay me back, huh?"

Jack knew he should be helping Dorsey as she tried to pull free from Steve's hand on her elbow. But he was stunned. He couldn't believe Steve brought up the money in front of Dorsey. He couldn't believe everything he'd just heard. It was now, officially, war.

"Are you finished, sir?" Jack asked, his jaw clenched, eyes flashing.

"FOR NOW, YEAH, I'm finished," Steve said, finally releasing Dorsey who backed away quickly. "Dorsey, if you're planning on helping out here tonight, you'll need your evening uniform."

"I'll drive you back," Jack said, starting to follow her.

"Oh please, allow me," Steve said, reaching for Dorsey again.

"No, I can run faster. See you in a few," Dorsey said to Jack before she darted off.

Jack still couldn't believe what she'd done. Admitting that they were lovers? To their boss? How could she be so stupid? But it was done. He had to fix it.

Steve smiled at Jack and walked away.

THE OYSTER ROAST was a success, with a country western band and happy tourists two-stepping, wearing the straw cowboy hats supplied by Top Club, most of them drunk, and laughing under the starlit night. Jack kept an eye on Dorsey whenever he could. He liked it when she was behind the bar, he could keep track of her as she helped the overwhelmed bartenders serve beer and wine. Otherwise, she was lost in the crowd of tourists and staff. Meanwhile Jack had been busy. Helping tourists learn to shuck oysters, restocking the bars, even tying bandannas around the necks of little kids who wanted to be cowboys and cowgirls. By the end of the evening, he was exhausted and sticky, covered with beer and oyster sauce and who knew what else.

"Howdy, cowboy. Great shindig!" Dorsey said, wrapping her arms around him from behind as he cleared a plate of oysters. She was warm and smelled like beer. "You need a shower, too. Join me? Come to my cottage tonight? Unless you're still mad at me?" Her arms felt so good around his waist. It had been so nice to not feel alone. But, it was over. He should have known it wouldn't work out. Nothing ever did, not for him.

"Sure," he said, turning around and giving her what he hoped looked like a genuine smile. The stars were bright in the sky and her eyes were impossibly green, her lips red and perfect. Jack looked at her innocent warm smile and didn't have the heart to tell her, couldn't tell her right then that it was over. Had to be over. He couldn't be fired. He had to keep this job because he'd already taken the money. She would have to lie to whatever committee Steve had concocted, say there was nothing between them, and then together they would have to agree that there never would be. It was the only solution he could come up with, even as it broke his heart.

"OK, great. See you soon," she said, giving him a peck on the cheek.

As he watched her walk away, Jack swallowed hard and reminded himself it was the only choice he had. They were over. He would tell her tonight after he finished cleaning up from the oyster roast. He took off the stupid bandanna he had around his neck and threw it to the ground.

"Dammit Dorsey," he said as he dropped his head in his hands.

Chapter Seventeen

Dorsey

THE UPLIGHTS SHINING on the decorative palms in the courtyard in front of the inn made the fronds appear to dance ghoulishly as Dorsey ran by. *I need to stop scaring myself.* She reached into her pocket for the oogle, but she'd left it back at her cottage.

She had to force herself to keep running past Jack's cottage, even though she would have been able to shower there but she needed a change of clothes.

Jack had seemed less angry with her by the end of the oyster roast and she knew a night in bed would be just the kind of release he needed. His temper was fiery, but so was his passion. She'd learn to take the good with the bad. That's what love meant. They would stand up to Steve together and everything would be fine.

She cut through the dark passageway between her cottage and the one next door, and had just caught a glimpse of her porch when she tripped, falling hard on her left hip and shoulder. Her entire left side began to throb as she lay in the wet dirt trying to catch her breath. She imagined all the bugs crawling on the ground and she got the chills. The earth smelled like pine and mold. As she carefully sat up and began to try to stand, someone grabbed her from behind. A gloved hand covered her mouth and a solid arm under her arms lifted her off the ground, holding her tightly against him. She tried to scream, but his hand smashed her mouth, crushing her voice.

In her terror, time stood still. Every step he took, carrying her, played out in her mind as if it took an hour. All she could feel was his solid presence behind her. In front of her was the ocean. She was sure she was going to die, her heart was pounding in her chest. She tried to kick backwards but the man's grip grew tighter and his hand covered her nose and her mouth. She couldn't scream; she couldn't breathe. When she stopped trying to struggle, he uncovered her nose and she sucked in a huge breath of air. Her captor smelled like smoke, or maybe that was her own skin, from the oyster roast.

Sweat trickled down her back and she was getting dizzy from a lack of oxygen. Her side throbbed from where she'd fallen. As if she were a child, the man carried her away from the cottages toward the darkness of the ocean. She could hear the waves pounding against the seawall as he dropped her face down on the grass and pressed her face into the ground. She imagined being found dead—grass, dirt and worms ground into her face, between her teeth.

"Excellence isn't an option, it's an expectation," he whispered. "You will not be warned again. Remember the policies."

His words swirled through her brain individually and collided, breaking into pieces. She needed air but couldn't lift her head. Her nose was filled with dirt, her eyes were streaming tears, and suddenly everything went black.

SPUTTERING AND SPITTING dirt, she sat up. She was alone, soaking wet from the ocean spray cascading over the seawall. It was still night, she realized, slowly remembering what had happened. A chill spread throughout her body. She hoped she could stand up. Her face hurt all over and her left side, especially her hip, was sore and throbbing from when she had landed on it when she fell—or rather, when he had tripped her.

Dorsey wiped her face with her forearm and pushed herself up. Standing up made her head spin, and her left wrist started to throb too. She looked around but couldn't see anything or anyone. When she started to walk toward her cottage, she could feel the blood pumping through her heart. Little sparks of pain shot through her with each step.

One step at a time. One step at a time. When she finally made it to her cottage, she had never felt more relieved. She bolted the door behind her for the first time since she had arrived on Indigo Island.

Leaning against the door, she started shaking so hard she had to slide down to the hardwood floor, where she sat hugging herself, hoping the trembling would stop. She slept somehow, sitting up by the front door, but awoke just as the sun rose and hobbled into her room as she realized with a start, *Jack never came over.*

Her reflection in the bathroom mirror told the story of the attack. She had a bruise on her forehead and a split lip from where her front tooth had been pushed into her lip. Her neck was stiff, but the only marks were fingertip-sized bruises on both sides of her neck below her ears. Her left elbow hurt and her hip was scraped and raw. She worried a little that her wrist was broken, but when she could pick up her toothbrush, she figured it must be fine. Her teeth and gums were covered in dirt and grass. In the back of her mind, something told her she had been attacked by Steve. But was that possible? Was he capable of delivering a warning so fierce, so out of bounds? He'd already had her where he wanted her, didn't he? What more did he want from her?

When she was finished cleaning up, she decided to pull on her uniform meant for cool weather – long pants, long-sleeved shirt, and hobbled back to the bathroom to apply more makeup than she had in her life. Dorsey wondered what a broken rib felt like.

SHE NEEDED TO find Jack. She realized he must be mad about the ethics committee, even though he had seemed better by the end of the oyster roast. He must have been exhausted and fallen asleep at his cottage. It had been their first night apart since they'd gotten serious. She'd tell him she would fix everything. She had decided she'd lie to the committee, of course. Protect him and his career. She could find another Kids Club position, she knew she could. She had learned so much here. She wrapped her arms around herself, knowing that the most important lesson she'd learned so far on Indigo Island was to open herself up to love. And she did love Jack, she knew. She loved him enough to take the blame. From the beach, she scanned the pool for him, but didn't see him.

"Where would you like it, ma'am?" asked the muscle-bound, tanned teenager carrying an umbrella and lounge chair down to the ocean for the mom of one of the little campers in her Kids Club. Fortunately, it was an overcast day so Dorsey could get away with her attire: long khaki uniform pants, long-sleeved button down. She was hot, but fairly well covered up. Her left knee had bled through her pants, but no one had mentioned her lip or her neck. The mom looked around and pointed to a spot. As the campers started building their sandcastles and the mom settled into her lounge chair, Dorsey asked the cabana boy to send Jack down during his break.

"He's sick today," the young man said.

"Sick?" Dorsey said. "Ah, ok, thanks." Jack had never been sick the entire time she'd known him. As soon as her Explorers Club outing was over, she'd go find him in his cottage, bring him some soup if she could manage it. And she'd tell him everything was going to be OK, just like he'd done for her so many times since they'd met.

Fortunately her little explorers were young, five and seven, and there were only two. Slow walkers, perfect for her aching body.

"These are shell sacks, where baby shells grow," Dorsey said, holding up what looked to be snakeskin left behind by a large reptile. It was already hot, trickles of sweat ran down her back between her shoulder blades.

"Ick," said the older of the two girls. Their parents had dressed them in matching bathing suits, hot pink and white striped, with matching pink sunhats. They were like bright little Easter eggs on a field of brown sand and shells.

"Don't say ick. Touch it. Be brave. It's important for girls to know how to take care of themselves," Dorsey said, a reminder to herself more than a lesson for the kids. She had driven the girls in the golf cart to the southern end of the island, near Bloody Point. Now, as they trailed behind her on the beach, she walked toward the spot where she and Jack had made love and her stomach clenched with the memory.

Dorsey knew she had to find Jack, as soon as possible. She realized he'd called in sick because he was mad at her and her big mouth. Why had she told Steve the truth about them, she wondered again. She'd make it right. Take the fall, leave the island and report Steve. She wondered if his fingerprints could be lifted from her neck? She supposed she could ask the sheriff. But no, she didn't need to stir up more trouble for Jack. She needed to fix things. To help him. He owed Steve money somehow and without his job, he'd never be able to pay him back. This was the job of his dreams, the life of his dreams and because of her, it was slipping away. She'd fix it.

"I'm cold. It looks scary over there," said the younger one sitting next to her on the cart.

"That's called the backside of the island. When we round

this point, we're outside the plantation. But don't worry. Some very nice people live in those woods," Dorsey said. "There's a cemetery up on that little hill, too."

"Yeah, and snakes, and alligators, and bugs and ghosts," said the older girl. She stopped. The younger one froze too.

"We want to go back," the younger one said.

"Look, what's that?" the older one said, pointing into the thick woods.

"What? What did you see?" Dorsey asked, walking to stand beside them while looking into the dense trees.

"It was a man. And he didn't have clothes on," said the older one. "I'm scared."

Dorsey followed their gaze, the hair on her neck standing up while a chill ran down her spine. She pulled the two girls close to her. "I don't see anybody, but we'll go." *Oh my gosh, has he followed me here? Is Steve this crazy, this controlling?*

Panicking, she said, "Let's race back to the golf cart. Go." When Dorsey rubbed the oogle in her pocket, she was able to run without pain as she tried to hurry the girls to the cart.

"Hurry, Miss Dorsey, I'm scared. Please hurry," said the little one, sliding close to Dorsey so her sister could sit up front too.

"I don't want to look back that way," the older girl said.

"We'll be back at the Kids Club before you know it." Dorsey pressed the golf cart's pedal to the floor, willing it to go faster and wishing she'd grabbed one without a governor added to keep the cart from going very fast.

Did the girls really see something, or were they just spooked by the end of the island? Little girls don't make their bogeymen naked. They saw something. Instead of heading up to the road that meandered through the desolate pines and live oaks, Dorsey drove them back along the beach. Against the rules, but she was spooked, too.

When they finally arrived, Dorsey hustled the girls into the Kids Club, though she had watched the rearview mirror all the way down the beach and hadn't seen anybody following them. Dorsey's college helper, Suzy, met them on the porch.

"Miss Suzy, these two need a very special lunch with extra French fries," Dorsey said.

"We saw a naked man in the woods," the younger one said.

"Miss Dorsey?" Suzy asked.

"Miss Suzy, I'm headed right now to tell Steve about it. These two think maybe it was a man who's lost and can't find his house or his clothes," Dorsey said, winking at the other woman. "We'll have Sheriff Smith go find him."

"That's a good idea," Miss Suzy said, shooing the girls inside the cottage and giving her a frightened look. "Y'all be sure to tell Mr. Steve right away, Miss Dorsey."

"I will. Bye girls," Dorsey said. Before heading back to the inn, she took a detour, she needed to check on Jack. As she drove past the rows of sunbathers on the beach, Dorsey thought about how intrinsically trusting they all were. Sitting there, drinking what was brought to them, defenseless in their flimsy, bright-colored vacation clothing. And the kids, running back and forth from the water to their parents, building castles.

Maybe the girls saw a wayward golfer, using nature as his re-stroom, she thought. *That's probably all it was.*

She knocked on Jack's cottage door and then walked inside when he didn't answer. His bedroom door was closed but she opened the door quietly, hoping not to wake him if he was sleeping. The shades were pulled, but she could see his gorgeous body outlined in his bed.

Dorsey sat down carefully at the foot of the bed.

"Aaah!" Jack yelled, bounding up, fists drawn.

"Jack, it's me," Dorsey said, jumping backward off the bed, jarring her sore ribs and hip.

"My God, why are you sneaking around?" Jack said, sighing and lying back down.

"Are you still mad at me? Whoa, what's wrong with your

eye?" Dorsey said, standing over him, realizing Jack's left eye was swollen shut.

"Yeah, black eye, concussion, I just need to sleep," Jack said, closing his right eye.

"You're supposed to stay awake, I think? Right? Jack, what happened to you?" Dorsey asked, reaching for his hand. It was cold and damp. He didn't squeeze back.

"The nurse checked me out, gave me some pain meds. I really just need to sleep," Jack said. "I'll be fine once the swelling goes down. No big deal."

"Did somebody attack you, tell you to stay out of their way?"

"Something like that. Didn't even see it coming. I had just sent the rest of the clean-up staff home for the night, had turned out all the lights and bam, someone hit me from behind. The nurse thinks it was some sort of metal pole or spike, maybe what we use to set up the wedding reception tents? Who knows?"

This was all her fault, she realized. She was happy he couldn't see her bruises and he hadn't noticed her lip. She knew she had to leave him alone, let him get over this, get better.

"I'm so sorry, Jack. I'll request a transfer, you'll be fine," Dorsey said, leaning over and kissing his forehead gently.

"Hope it's not too late," he said, rolling over so his back was to her.

She'd ruined everything by confessing her love for Jack to Steve. Tears streaming down her cheeks, Dorsey made her way out the door and back to the golf cart. She knew she had to leave the island, start over again. She would tell Steve she was leaving in the morning. That would save Jack's job and everything would work out fine. Dorsey walked carefully past the front desk— passing by Paula who was flirting with an overweight, bald golfer—and slowly climbed up the stairs.

"Steve is in a meeting, Miss Pittman. Perhaps you could come back later?" his assistant said with an artificial smile once she'd made it up the stairs and to his office door.

"This is important. I'll have to go straight to Sheriff Smith if he's too busy to see me," Dorsey said, slowly turning to leave.

"Just a minute," the assistant said, and then picked up the telephone. "Miss Pittman needs to speak with you."

"Do you have an Advil?" Dorsey asked and Steve's assistant gave her two and a bottle of water before showing her in.

"Now what, Dorsey?" Steve asked. Sheriff Smith was sitting in his conference room. Perfect.

Steve looked like Mr. Rogers with a hangover. Cardigan sweater, white t-shirt, both wrinkled. Even his Top Club nametag was pinned on crooked today.

Could she accuse Steve of attacking her, and Jack? In front of the sheriff? She had no proof. All she could do was keep him around by telling him what the girls saw. "I'm not sure it's anything, but two children and I were on the beach, near the tip of the island at Bloody Point, and the little girls saw a naked man watching us. I didn't see him, but I believe them," she said. "There are a lot of dangerous people on this island, I've found. In fact, I want a transfer, Steve."

"A flasher at Bloody Point?" Sheriff Smith said, slapping his wide leg. "If this doesn't just beat the band."

"But you didn't see anything, right? And a transfer is out of the question for you," Steve sputtered, looking at the sheriff.

"I believe the little girls, and so will their parents. And I deserve a transfer much more than Jack does," she said.

"Great, we'll have to give them their stay for free, and they'll leave the island. This is a disaster," Steve said. "No more bad publicity. And the answer is no."

Dorsey was tired of the double conversation. She wished the sheriff would catch on, but apparently, he never would.

"LIKE I SAID, son, I'm retiring in a month. Nobody's taking my place, least not yet," the sheriff said. "I don't pretend to know what's going on here, not on the front of the island. Didn't used to be this way. Used to be only forty people lived here. Knew 'em all by name. All got along too, black, white, whitish-black, blackish-white. Now, new people. New money. Y'all create plantations, put up fences and expect to divide us, keep out the folks who live here. But we were here first. And now, we ha dat lan' ent wu't."

Dorsey looked at Steve; he looked back at Dorsey and then said, "Miss Pittman hasn't heard Gullah spoken before."

"Actually I have," Dorsey said quietly. "I've been studying it. It's beautiful."

"I agree," the sheriff said. "Steve, have you heard it or just read about it?"

"Well," Steve began and then stopped.

"That's sad, son," the sheriff said. "Gullah is the name of a people and the name of the language spoken by them. It's from the slaves brought here from West Africa and then mixed with English dialects. It's an English creole, and you can only find it spoken on the Sea Islands of Georgia and South Carolina. I picked some up living here, working among these people. You could learn a lot from these people too, if you cared to. It's always wise tuh set tuh de af' de boat. Good day."

After the sheriff left, Dorsey was alone with Steve. She knew without a doubt he was her attacker – and judging from the look in his eyes, he knew that she knew the truth.

"Look, Steve, I'm here to request a transfer. I know I haven't been the model Top Club employee here, but I will be if you will give me a fresh start. Just recommend me to a sister resort. That's all I need and I'll leave here and won't look back," Dorsey said. "Jack has given his heart to this place, this is where he wants to be. Kick me out, OK? You don't need to hurt anyone else to make your point."

"Oh, aren't you cute," Steve said, standing up and walking

to the windows behind his desk. "Everything here is my decision. I decide who stays, who goes. If I want you to stay, you will. Do you understand?"

"No, I don't," she said, tears popping up in the corners of her eyes. She dug her fingernail into her palm to make them stop as she hurried out of his office and down the stairs. Outside, the sun was sliding lower in the sky. Dorsey was sure the bruises were beginning to show through her makeup. Her forehead throbbed and her lip was swollen. The Advil couldn't handle everything that hurt.

She drove the Kids Club golf cart to her cottage, and makeup reapplied, she decided she looked about as good as she could. She didn't know what to do next, where to turn. Jack was mad, her head was pounding, her stomach was growling but when she opened the refrigerator, it was empty. Dorsey glanced at the calendar tacked up in the kitchen and realized, with a start, that Tade would be arriving in the morning. Had it really been three weeks since he'd left? She'd pack her bags, stay one last night, and take the ferry in the morning. Dorsey dropped into the kitchen chair and put her head down on the table.

She had no idea how long she'd been asleep when Jack appeared in her cottage, pulling her into his arms and then kissing her hard on the lips.

"Ahhh," Dorsey cried, before she could stop herself, pulling back and covering her lips with her hands.

"Dorsey, what is wrong? What happened to your lip?" Jack said, concern flooding his beautiful face. His left eye was still swollen shut.

"The little girls and I were flashed at Bloody Point, and like you, somebody jumped me last night and warned me to mind my own business," she said, and then the dam broke and the tears began washing away her carefully applied camouflage.

Jack didn't say anything, just held her tight. After a while, he walked her to the couch and sat beside her until she'd calmed down enough to talk.

"I'm OK, really. Just scared. What's going on in this place, Jack?"

"Tell me what happened to you," Jack said, his jaw tense.

As Dorsey told him the details of the attack, he couldn't sit. He paced back and forth, angry.

"I can't believe I wasn't there for you," he said, shaking his head.

"You were probably knocked out by then. And that was my fault," Dorsey said.

"We're sticking together from now on," Jack said. "And we'll either make it right here, or leave here together. Deal?"

"I'm so sorry, Jack," Dorsey said, dropping her head into her hands, the tears coming again. She didn't tell him she was leaving. She couldn't. But it was the right thing to do.

"It's not your fault," he said, sitting down beside her on the couch.

"Yes, it really is all my fault," Dorsey said hugging him gently.

Chapter Eighteen

Jack

THE NEXT MORNING, they both called in sick and stayed in bed together, laptops open. The problem for him was leaving early meant breaking his contract and he'd owe back the money Steve had advanced him. Jack knew his mom had used the money to pay off her mortgage, it was gone and he couldn't get it back. If he could transfer to another Top Club resort, though, he knew he could figure out a way to work it out. It was the only way now that Dorsey had been attacked. When he saw the bruises on her neck, her swollen lip, well, he had been speechless. Without proof, he couldn't accuse Steve. Not yet. He'd get the proof they needed, somehow.

"How odd," Dorsey said, looking at her computer screen. "The history of this island is so volatile. People through the centuries discover it, try to tame it, try to make it their own, but fail and end up leaving. The only people who have managed to stay have been the former slaves, convicts, all sorts of crazy people."

Jack looked over at Dorsey, using only one eye as his left eye was still mostly closed. The skin around his eye had started to turn exotic colors of purple and blue. He supposed he would now join the ranks of people who fail to make it on Indigo Island, unfortunately. But Dorsey was more important.

"I'm not letting you out of my sight from now on. Understand?" Jack said, running his hand through her hair. Nobody had ever filled the emptiness inside him like she did. Just her touch calmed him, filled him with peace.

Dorsey nodded and nuzzled her head into his shoulder as he squeezed her tight.

"You're so lucky he let you go, that nothing else happened," Jack said, kissing her tenderly. "I'm going to do some research, see what's open at the other Top Club resorts; we'll transfer somewhere together."

"I don't want you to do that for me," she said. "And don't you owe Steve money or something?"

"Well, sort of. But I'm going to figure it out. I'm doing it for us. This is crazy shit going on. We can do better," Jack said, as he rolled out of bed, lost in thought. Jack thought about the other job offers he had turned down, but reminded himself he wouldn't have meet Dorsey if he had taken those paths. Everything would work out fine. He just needed a plan, and a job, so he could take care of his mom. And Dorsey.

By mid-afternoon, he had seven job applications sent out and one interview lined up for the next week. They'd be fine. But he'd miss this place. Indigo Island had his heart, even as Steve was trying to destroy it.

THAT AFTERNOON AFTER work, Tade, Jack and Dorsey sat on a bright blue blanket on the beach, eating turkey sandwiches and drinking water, beer, and wine, respectively.

"Are you guys ready yet?" Tade said, his ten-year-old energy reserves back to full power after his meal.

"OK. This time we're going to beat him," Dorsey said, giving Tade a high five.

"Jack's a kissy boy. We'll beat him," Tade said. Jack grabbed him, hoisted him over his shoulder, and started toward the ocean.

"No, no. You're not a kissy boy. Help, Dorsey!" Tade screamed.

"I'm just a kissy girl," Dorsey said laughing. Jack winked at her, thinking how beautiful she looked in the pale blue sundress she was wearing, her laughter filling his heart. She would be a great mom, he knew.

Times like these, like this evening, when it felt as if they were the only ones on the island, made Jack's spirits soar. He could almost imagine himself as a father, even though he'd had no role model. He almost could forget about Steve and his irrational warnings. Life at this moment became a muted sunset: calm, soft, and happy. But at the same time he knew if they had to leave, they would do it together.

Tade yelled, "Hey, lazy, come on, let's play."

"Oh, all right, but you guys better watch it. I'm feeling powerful tonight," Dorsey said, running to the edge of the surf, carrying the Nerf football. "Go long, Tade."

"WHAT TIME IS it?" Dorsey asked, shooting up straight in bed the next morning.

"Relax, honey," Jack said, hugging her from behind. They were lying in his bed, entwined, after a night of gentle lovemaking. "You're off today, and Tade's parents are actually paying attention to him. I hope. At least for half a day, poor kid. You had a lot of, ah, dreams last night."

"What did I say?" she asked.

"Something about that Chad guy, and your dad, and red. You always talk about the color red," Jack said, stretching. Jack loved how she looked in the morning, her hair a tangled mess, her small body curled up next to him, dressed only in one of his t-shirts. Jack slept in boxers only, and right now, he could pull those off and, well. He rolled onto his side, kissing the tip of her nose. "You're getting better. I mean, you used to cry in your sleep. Now you don't. I think we're making progress."

"What would I do without you?" she asked, snuggling into Jack's side.

"Hey, I've got a lot to be thankful for too," Jack said, breathing in her flowery scent, feeling her warm embrace. "I mean, besides being beat up, I've never been this happy in my whole life. Except that I need to find a new job, and well, I gotta get on that."

"Should I try to fix it, just one more time with Steve?" she asked. At the mention of the jerk's name, Jack realized he needed to focus on getting both of them off the island. No messing around this morning, unfortunately.

"I don't want you around him," he said, stretching and getting out of bed. "We should just plan on leaving. As soon as possible. I'm thinking next week."

Chapter Nineteen

Dorsey

DORSEY NEEDED TO pack, but she was dreading it. Dreading starting over again. Hating the idea that she'd have to leave Jack behind, but knowing it was the right thing to do. This place was his dream, not hers. And she was the one who was ruining it for him.

She hadn't been home to her cottage for two days. She'd been avoiding the inevitable. She had to leave Jack before she ruined his life. The night before during sex she'd almost cried realizing it would be the last time. Somehow she had told herself to treasure every moment instead of dreading today. That's why she'd awoken so suddenly. Today was the day she was giving him up.

She carefully inserted the key into the back door, and turned the lock slowly, pulling the door toward her first, knowing that muted the sound when the lock gave way.

And there sat Tade.

"Geesh, you scared me," she said. "What are you doing here? I thought you were with your parents today?"

"I wanted to be with you," Tade said. "I want to show you the cemetery."

"Creepy," Dorsey said. She'd have to take the little guy. He didn't have anyone else to be with. And she couldn't pack in front of him. "Okay, let's do it. How did you get in my cottage anyway?"

"I have my ways," Tade said grabbing her hand. "Come on!"

Of course, Dorsey didn't want to tell him about the flasher she'd encountered with the girls a week earlier, and nobody else had reported any similar incidents. They'd be fine, and they both carried their oogles.

"If you see a marker with only one name, that was a slave," Tade explained as they walked through the old cemetery, hidden behind sand dunes and among kudzu vines at the end of the island, above Bloody Point beach.

"Sometimes plantation owners would let the house slaves use the family's last name. Most of the time though, that's how it was. Like here," he said, pointing to a weather-beaten, crumbling headstone.

Dorsey squatted down to read, "Dolly Scott—ever submissive" and next to it, "Our Flora." On one tiny stone, she read: "Tribute to Dorinda. Age 19."

"In Charleston, the Gullah tour guide took us to a black cemetery—well, really what used to be the cemetery for city slaves. It had been turned into a parking lot for a church. The old tombstones were stacked against a chain-link fence, kinda in a pile. And on the other side of the fence, there was this house. The people there had used tombstones to make their back patio. They had the barbecue grill sitting on somebody's headstone." Tade looked down. "I wanted to go beat them up."

"That is horrible, this is horrible. It should be protected or have a fence around it or something," Dorsey said, looking at the untended grounds.

"It's way better over here than on the mainland. What else are we doing today?" Tade asked.

Dorsey looked over at the boy and smiled gently. His blue t-shirt made his eyes an even brighter blue. Could she tell him she was leaving? Her eyes filled with tears. No, she couldn't. She couldn't tell either of them.

Dorsey and Tade made their way back to the plantation as the sun was low in the sky. The sky had taken on a gray hue that matched the water, a seamless horizon devoid of color. Storm clouds were building but there was still time to share her last sunset on the island with Jack if she could get Tade to stop collecting arrowheads and hurry. They finally made it to the Kids Cottage to find Tade's mom waiting for them.

"Thank God you're all right," she said to her son, not addressing Dorsey at all.

Dorsey had a feeling Tade hadn't told her where he was going. She'd probably lose a star over this. Well, it didn't matter anymore.

"I'm fine, Mom. See you next time," Tade said, giving Dorsey a high-five.

"Next time, kiddo," she said, keeping her sunglasses on so he wouldn't see the tears.

Dorsey jogged to Jack's cottage and burst through the door.

"Where have you been?" he asked. Jack's eyes flashed. His jaw was clenched and his hands were on his hips.

"Tade wanted to show me the cemetery at Bloody Point," she said, speaking slowly, gently. "We took longer than I expected, but there's still time to see the sunset."

"Nobody knew where you were, you didn't call me, or leave a note at the Kids Cottage. You just vanished," he said.

"Well, he came to my cottage and we left from there. I'm sorry, I didn't even think –"

"You're an adult, Dorsey, you better start thinking. You can't tell your boss you're breaking the rules and you can't go running off with Tade without telling anyone when we have someone, probably our boss, trying to get us fired, or worse," he said. "I think you're spending too much time with Tade, with make believe. It's time you grew up."

"Don't you dare say anything about Tade," Dorsey said, glaring back at Jack. "Are you finished?"

"Yeah, I guess I am," Jack said.

Dorsey turned and walked out the cottage door into the now dark night.

DORSEY PACKED QUICKLY, throwing all of her belongings into the two beat-up suitcases she had arrived with. She'd tell the bus driver to stop by her cottage in the morning on the way to the ferry. She closed and locked her cottage and jogged to the inn. She needed a place to sleep, away from Jack and she figured she could sweet talk the lonely front desk clerk, Sam, into giving her a room.

Dorsey had finally realized she was counting on Jack to save her from her past, just as she had relied on Chad before him. What she needed to learn was how to save herself. That would start now, she told herself.

By the time she reached the inn, she felt like a chill had penetrated her bones even though it was another warm, damp evening and the rain hadn't started to fall yet. The air was thick with moisture. She ached all over, both from what she couldn't explain to Jack and from the profound helplessness that flooded her soul. She'd regain control instead of being controlled by unknown bogeymen hiding in the bushes, first in Ohio and now here, on Indigo Island. She had to, or she'd lose herself.

When she reached the front desk in the otherwise empty and quiet lobby, Sam, the night clerk, nodded in her direction.

"Evening, Dorsey. May I help you?" he asked. He had kind blue eyes with droopy eyelids, perfect for a night clerk. He was tall and lanky, the kind of body that had lots of angles and implicit awkwardness. "You're all wet. From the fog?"

"Uh-huh, I guess," she mumbled, just noticing her clothing clinging to her like a slick piece of cold spaghetti. She shivered.

"You need a change of clothes."

"I'm fine, really."

Sam emerged from behind the counter with a nubby blue wool blanket. "I keep this back here for just this sort of emergency," he said, draping the rough throw around Dorsey's shoulders. "Follow me."

Doing as she was told, she followed Sam through a door and ended up behind the bar of the now-closed members' pub. The dark wood walls and floors were comforting, like a cozy cave where nobody could find her. She climbed into the worn leather barstool seat and felt better already. "I have something that will fix you right up."

Sam pulled a snifter off the hanging glass rack, slid a bottle of brandy off the mirrored shelf of the bar, and poured. He walked to the coffeemaker glowing in the corner of the dark bar, pulled the hot water valve, and filled a teacup with hot water. After adding a tea bag, he placed the steaming cup on the low counter of the backside of the bar, next to Dorsey.

"I'd recommend mixing them together," he said.

She did as she was told, and soon felt the grip of cold and grief release just a little bit. She also saw an image, a memory float by in her mind, of sitting in Barbara's house.

"I need to get back over to the front desk," Sam said, after they had sat for a while in comfortable silence. He smelled faintly of peppermint, and Dorsey liked his company.

"I'll come with you, if it's OK," Dorsey said, standing, this time without shaking legs. "Oh, and I need a reservation for the first ferry to Hilton Head in the morning."

"Sure," Sam said. "You're not leaving for good are you? That's what the last Kids Club gal did. Lila was her name. A real beauty. Never came back."

"I heard about that," she said, wondering again about Jack's relationship with Lila, and about Steve's. "Why did she leave?"

"Um, I don't really know. She was freaked out, though. Spent the whole night with me and then left on the ferry. Nice girl. Kinda looks like you, but she had brown hair."

Dorsey followed Sam back behind the front desk, wondering if there were any other similarities between her and Lila. It didn't matter anymore, she reminded herself. She was going to be gone in the morning. Tears sprang to her eyes, but she brushed them away before he could see them. When Sam excused himself to go gather the ferry departures and checkouts and arrivals for the next day, she slid over to his spot behind the computer. She Googled Lila, but realized she didn't know her last name. *Let it go*, she told herself.

"Sorry it took me so long," Sam said from behind her, making Dorsey jump. "Sorry, didn't mean to scare you."

"Oh, no, it's not you, you've been great. I hope you don't mind, I used the computer," she said, trying to stop her arm from shaking.

"No, course not. I use it all the time to creep on old girl-friends on Facebook. Guess 'cause I don't have anybody to keep up with in real life." Sam blushed. "I mean, you know, my family and friends and stuff are all here, I mean over on Hilton Head and all. That's what I meant."

"Oh, I knew what you meant," Dorsey said reassuringly, understanding the justifications of the lonely all too well. She'd been just like him, until she'd met Jack. She realized, sadly, she'd be just like Sam again now. "Plus, with this kind of job, you work when everybody else is asleep. That's got to be hard."

"Well, there's actually a lot of stuff that goes on at night. More people awake than you'd think, really," Sam said, settling into the chair next to her. "Plus, it's quiet and you can think. I like it, this time of night."

"What do you mean other people are around? I haven't seen anybody," she said.

"Maybe you won't, but believe me, they're there," Sam said, nodding to himself with assurance. "See look, they've been doin' this all week." Sam pointed to two lights glowing on the master console in front of them. "Room 107 and 285. I think it might be love."

"But are they married—I mean to other people?"

"Probably were. I'd say she's seventyish. He's older. They're cute, really. Now, in another twenty minutes, Mr. McCurdy will appear, looking for booze. I'll have to tell him the bar's closed. He'll slip me a twenty, and voilà, the bar will magically open. Just like it did for you," Sam said.

Dorsey realized Sam was really lonely, eager to share his trade secrets with a fellow outcast. She was having trouble keeping her eyes open, even as she listened to his stories. She needed a room, if only to get a few hours of sleep before the ferry.

"So, say, do you have an extra room I could crash in? I need to get some rest before the early boat," she said.

"Sure, let me check the system," Sam said shrugging. He propped his feet, crossed at the ankles, up on the front desk.

Dorsey envisioned Paula fainting at the sight of Sam's big, white, sweaty-boy feet on her front counter, dangerously close to the apples, and it made her smile.

"Oh hi, Mr. McCurdy. Bar's closed," Sam said, snapping to attention, preparing to pocket his twenty-dollar tip. The old man continued on to the bar. "Be right there. Hey, all those things I said—well, those were all our secrets, right?" Sam asked, holding onto the room key as if it were symbolic of their pact.

"Secret. Sure," she agreed. Dorsey walked down the first-floor corridor to the very end, as Sam had instructed. She turned the key and opened the door to a magnificent ocean-front walk-out suite. It was beautiful, and excessive, and just added to the confusion of the evening. She found the huge bathroom, took a long hot shower, and finished by wrapping up in a plush white robe. She fell asleep on top of the covers of the bed, exhausted and broken-hearted.

Chapter Twenty

Jack

JACK COULDN'T FIND Dorsey. She wasn't at her cottage, and she hadn't come to his place. He'd been waiting for hours to apologize, jogging back and forth between their cottages. He'd been so pig-headed, yelling at her for doing her job and babysitting Tade. How could he not support her? And as for Steve, he was an expert at tricking people. She hadn't meant to tell him the truth about their relationship, of course she hadn't. She'd been through so much, with her father and then the body washed up. Of course, she'd freaked out.

But where was she now? Jack looked at his watch. Two a.m. He was back at his own cottage, pacing the living room. And then he had an idea. He'd call an old friend, Lila. Lila was a gorgeous brunette who had worked at the Kids Cottage the summer before and they'd become friends, well, friends with benefits, truth be told. She'd left Indigo suddenly after a run in with Steve.

She'd never even told Jack goodbye.

But he still had her number.

After catching up for a moment and apologizing for the late call, Jack said, "Lila, what happened with you and Steve?"

The woman was silent on the other end of the line, but Jack could hear her breathing.

"I'm not really comfortable talking about it," Lila said. "But,

254

Jack, he's awful. He kept asking me out, sometimes in front of the kids. One night, I was locking up the club, it was late, after a midnight movie night, and he appeared, out of nowhere. He grabbed my wrist and started pulling me behind him. I screamed and luckily, a couple walking on the beach heard me and ran over. Steve sweet-talked them, told them I'd just been spooked. They walked me to the inn."

"Lila, my God," Jack said, his heart racing. "Why didn't you tell me?" What had he done by not listening to Dorsey? They should have left the island a week ago.

"It was the scariest moment of my life. I thought he was going to rape me," Lila said. Jack heard her take a deep breath, and he knew she was crying.

"I'm so sorry, Lila. I had no idea," he said.

"I didn't tell anyone, just my mom and dad. I called them from the inn and they arranged a flight home from Hilton Head the next day. Sam at the front desk gave me a room to sleep in, but I was too scared. I just sat with him, overnight, until the first ferry departed that morning."

After they hung up, Jack called Sheriff Smith. He reported Dorsey's beating, his beating and Lila's incident.

"You need to believe me. Steve is responsible for all of this," Jack said. His heart was pumping.

He heard the man sigh into the telephone. "Son, I only have three more days until retirement."

Jack ran to the inn. Sam sat alone at the front desk, feet propped up, looking bored but quite awake.

"This night is ridiculous. What are you doing here, Jack?" Sam asked.

"Dorsey's here, right? Tell me her room number," Jack said. He knew he was being terse, but he needed to find her.

"She's here, but what if she doesn't want to see you? She's leaving on the first ferry in the morning. Somebody has upset her, she's running. I'm not leading him to her," Sam said.

Jack blew out the breath he'd been holding. "Look man, I'm in love with Dorsey. I'd never hurt her. Steve on the other hand, would, has. Have you seen him around tonight?"

"Ya, he was here, twenty minutes ago."

"Did he ask for Dorsey's room."

"Ya."

"You didn't. Oh my God."

"It's room 120, at the end of the hall. Follow me," Sam said, as he leapt from behind the desk and the two men ran through the lobby and down the hall.

Chapter Twenty-One

Dorsey

D ORSEY AWOKE WITH a hand clamped over her mouth. She was disoriented.

"Shhh, everything is okay," Steve said whispering in her ear. "You were going to leave my island without saying goodbye? I just can't believe that. I can't have that happen again. Lila got away, but you won't."

Dorsey wanted to scream, to bite his hand, anything to get away. This had to be a bad dream. In the moonlit darkness, Steve looked like Uncle Rob, her dad's partner in the practice.

Her dad's murderer. Her memory suddenly jumped to life. Her heart thudded.

Steve was talking again, while pressing his hand so hard over her mouth her teeth were cutting into her lips. "Here's what we're going to do. Since you have a lovely ground-floor suite, we're just going to walk out the sliding doors here and have our special time together."

Dorsey moaned and tried to move out from under him but he yanked her hair hard. He straddled her, pinning the bathrobe she wore to the bed with his knees. She tried to kick him, but he was too heavy to move.

"Stop fighting it, honey. You're going to like this. You don't want another beating, do you?" he asked. His breath was sour, and smelled like whiskey. Dorsey couldn't move, even as he pressed his lips onto hers, trying to force his tongue inside her mouth.

How could she have let him trap her again? She couldn't breathe.

Suddenly the lights turned on in the room and Jack was punching Steve, and Sam was helping her up and hurrying her out of the room.

"Jack," she said as Sam pulled her into the hall.

"He'll be fine, and the sheriff is on the way."

Dorsey nodded and followed Sam into the ice room, where they barricaded the door and huddled together until Jack knocked on the door.

As Dorsey walked out of the closet, and into Jack's open arms, she saw Steve, handcuffed and surrounded by three sheriff's deputies.

Steve stared beady-eyed and scowling at Dorsey until she looked away. The hate was pure, deep, and reciprocated. She wrapped the white robe more tightly around herself as she began to shake.

"We'll get your statement in a little while, miss," Sheriff Smith said. "Get him out of here."

Chapter Twenty-Two

Jack

"I NEED TO tell you the rest of the story," Dorsey said.

It was the second night of their Top Club paid stay at a five-star luxury hotel in Hilton Head. Dorsey sat up in bed, leaning against the headboard. She was wearing a new pair of soft green sweatpants and Jack's oversized white t-shirt. She looked small and a little fragile. Jack wouldn't leave her side, not ever again; he'd told her that as often as he'd told himself. He still felt responsible for Steve getting to Dorsey. If Jack hadn't been angry, if he hadn't turned her away, she never would have spent the night at the inn. He shook his head, automatically clenching his hands into fists at the thought.

Dorsey kept assuring him that it all worked out for a reason. The shock of Steve's attack had brought her father's murderer back to her consciousness. Finally, she had seen that face, the murderer's face, and finally, she could tell Jack the whole story. And he was more than ready to listen, to help her heal. He wanted to pull her into his arms right now, but he knew she wanted to talk. He leaned back against the headboard and listened.

"I was in shock. I never could identify him. I could describe his arm, his black gloved hand but never his face. It was blank. No amount of counseling or hypnosis brought it back to me. For ten years, my dad's killer was on the loose, because of me,"

Dorsey said, finally revealing the shame that had held her back in life. "It was all my fault."

"It wasn't your fault. It was the gunman's, Dorsey," Jack said softly, reaching for her hand.

"That's what everybody said, but I knew. I knew I was the only witness and I had failed my dad. He died in front of me and I couldn't save him, or name his killer. My mom and I had to live in hiding for more than a year after he was killed. The FBI thought the killer might come after me."

"It's all going to be OK now," Jack reminded her. After Steve's arrest Dorsey had insisted on making a statement to Sheriff Smith who had insisted it was his last day and didn't want any more work. But when she told him about her dad, the sheriff was all in. Dorsey's Uncle Rob, her dad's business partner, had been arrested that afternoon.

Dorsey smiled, reaching over and touching his still bruised knuckles.

"It must have felt great punching Steve," Dorsey said for the millionth time. "I wish I could have."

"I know, sweetie," Jack said, kissing her gently on the cheek.

They'd ordered room service again, both of them in need of rest and to be out of the spotlight. The media inquiries had come quickly once word broke of the arrest in the long unsolved murder and the arrest of Steve on Indigo Island.

She popped a French fry in her mouth and smiled. "They told us, for all these years, that my father was murdered because he provided abortions as part of his practice. But now I know it was Uncle Rob. He did it to take over the practice. It's unbelievable. He poisoned Rufus, dyed our swimming pool red, and then finally, one afternoon, shot my dad in our front yard."

Dorsey couldn't hold back the tears, the years of holding her secret inside had taken their toll. Once she started, she couldn't stop. Jack knew with time it would get easier, everything did, especially now that she knew the whole truth.

"I WAS THE only witness and I couldn't provide a description. I blocked it all out, everything about that day, except my dad's face, his eyes," Dorsey said, a shiver running through her. "I'm surprised Rob didn't kill me, too. He wasn't even related, my dad just treated him like a brother. Some brother."

"And your so-called boyfriend?"

"He stuck with me through high school, and college, sort of. I thought we were going to get married. But eventually, my family's shame was too embarrassing."

Jack shook his head. "I remember those looks from people, they gave it to my mom and me, too. Like, don't get too close to those people, they're bad luck. His brother died, stay away. As if tragedy is catching or something. It sucked. Still does."

"It does, but at least I can help bring him to justice now," Dorsey said. "Speaking of that, you beat up Steve pretty good. My hero."

Jack smiled. He was proud he'd broken Steve's jaw, cracked three ribs and gave him a black eye. A little taste of his own medicine. If the police hadn't arrived, Jack was pretty sure he would've killed him.

"I can't wait to get back to Indigo Island. It's our place now. Everything is going to work out just right. I'm in management. You'll get a promotion."

"Maybe," Dorsey said.

After a lot of pushing from Jack, Dorsey finally had agreed to take the ferry over for the day tomorrow, just to see what it felt like to her to be back on Indigo Island. He'd be with her every step of the way, he promised. And he had some surprises he couldn't wait to share. Jack loved Indigo Island and he knew, in time, she would love it again, too.

"Let's get some sleep. Tomorrow is going to be a busy day."

Chapter Twenty-Three

Dorsey

JACK WAS HER hero. Always would be. She could make this journey back for him, because he was with her and had saved her.

He held her tight throughout the forty-five minute ferry ride, even performing a little Leonardo DiCaprio and Kate Winslet move on the bow of the ship and making her laugh. He smelled like security, and home. As they neared the dock, Jack was like a little kid, bursting with excitement, unable to sit down even when the captain scolded him twice. Once the crew had tied up, he pulled her hand and led her up the metal gangway, stopping to look behind him and make sure she was doing okay. She was, as long as she was with him.

"Hop in," Jack said as they debarked, pointing to a four-seat custom golf cart parked at the ferry landing.

"Nice," Dorsey said. "Finally, riding around here in the style to which I'm supposed to become accustomed."

"I'm glad you like it. Check out the glove compartment," Jack said as they zipped through the wilderness of the backside of the island.

She knew he hoped to keep the mood light during her first trip back. Dorsey was trying, too. Her hand barely shook as she pushed the button and the small compartment's door flopped open.

"Oh, very nice box."

"Jeez. Do I have to do everything for you? Take the box out and open it, please," Jack said, feigning impatience, his eyes sparkling.

"Jack?" she said. Now her hands shook. The golf cart hummed. The island beyond the cart was a blur as she fumbled with the white ribbon tied around the signature blue box.

"Tiffany's," she said. "What in the world. Jack, it's beautiful." The platinum band glimmered as two dark blue sapphires hugged the sides of the emerald-cut diamond perched on top of it.

"Now those two blue stones are for protection. Barbara told me to get those. And the diamond, well, that's forever. Will you marry me?" Jack asked, stopping the cart just before the entrance to the plantation, hopping out and bending down on one knee.

"It's gorgeous. I love it," Dorsey said. "And you."

"I'll take that as a yes," Jack said, standing and climbing back into the cart, leaning over to kiss her gently.

Dorsey slipped the sparkling ring onto her left ring finger, and it fit perfectly. She held it up to show Jack and he smiled, as excited as a child. As they cruised into the plantation, Jack asked, "How are you feeling? Scared? OK? Upset?"

"It's nice knowing Steve's not here, that hopefully, he'll be in prison for a long time. I feel safe with you," Dorsey said. "The ocean looks beautiful. My ring is perfect. I'm doing OK."

"Summer is almost over and after that, we'll have this place to ourselves," Jack said.

"That's true. I'll be busy, though. With the trials," Dorsey said, reality washing over her, clouding her face. "I still can't believe Uncle Rob killed my dad for money. My dad would've split the practice, I'm sure of it."

"Are you sure you'll be up to testifying, against him and Steve?"

"Of course, I'm testifying. I finally know. I saw it. I can do it. I'll help make sure both of them get what they deserve. For Dad."

"You're beautiful when you're passionate," Jack said, turning the cart into the inn driveway. "If you'll bear with me, I have one more surprise for you."

Dorsey got the chills as he stopped the cart in front of the inn. Jack noticed, pulling her close.

"This was a bad idea," he said, worry lines crossing his forehead.

Dorsey touched his cheek. "No, I can handle it for a little while," she said as she slowly walked up the steps to the front porch. The last time she had been here she had been attacked. Before that, she had been willing to leave Jack forever to save his future. She could handle anything for Jack, anything for a little while.

"Ah, Dorsey?" Jack said, reaching for her and turning her to face him. "Wait a minute. It's more than a little while, you see, this is what I was thinking. See, Top Club pulled out of Indigo Island. They were planning a big sale, you know, to unload a stigmatized property from their portfolio, and I heard about it. They priced the inn…well, it was a steal, especially if I agreed not to name them in the lawsuit against Steve. I met with the head of Putnam Industries, Richard Putnam and his son, James. You know the people who own that big house at Bloody Point? They love the island as much as I do. And they agreed to buy the plantation – all of it! – if I would run it. I get some equity, too. It's perfect, really."

"You didn't." Her face had drained of all color, she knew. She felt faint, sweaty and looked around for somewhere to sit.

"Honey, it's contingent on you," Jack said, grabbing both of her hands with his, steadying her, calming her thundering heart. "I told them you'd have to agree or the deal was off. First, let's just go inside. Then you can consider it. It's a deal, Dorsey. We could do this for a couple years and then sell our portion. Or, just keep it and live here forever, raise our babies."

Jack leaned forward and kissed Dorsey gently on the lips.

"OK. For you, I'll think about it," Dorsey said quietly, wiping a bead of sweat from her brow. She was shocked how many emotions had hit her standing on this porch. Some so wonderful, some awful. She took Jack's hand, took a deep breath and followed him in the front door of the inn.

"Surprise!" a crowd yelled as they walked into the lobby.

"Hi, Dorsey, welcome home," said Sam. "I'm gonna be your front-desk manager. Cool, huh?"

Paula reached out and handed Dorsey a shiny red apple, with a smile. *What was happening*, she thought, in shock.

"Dorsey, it's a wonderful place. You all will have so much fun with this. I'm Jack's mother, Phyllis, so good to meet you, dear," Jack's mom said, giving Dorsey a squeeze. Now Dorsey knew where Jack got his dimples and his warm smile.

"Contingent?" she said to Jack once his mom left their side to go get a wine.

"I promise. Our moms planned the party, not me," Jack said. "People are really excited about this, but if you aren't, I won't do it. It can just be our engagement party and then we'll head back to the mainland."

"Hi, honey. Surprised?" Dorsey couldn't believe it. It was her mom. "Oh, look at that ring. It's beautiful. Nice choice, Jack." Dorsey's mom looked relaxed and happy, something she hadn't seen in a long time, if ever, since her dad's murder. Maybe they were both healing.

"Mom, you look amazing," Dorsey said, hugging her tight as her mom's green eyes misted.

"Kentucky has been good for me. The horses, the change. It seems you've found the perfect place for you to heal, too," her mom said. "And the perfect guy to help you. He reminds me of your father."

Dorsey smiled and held her mom tighter.

Dorsey saw Barbara and Tade then, together, laughing and smiling in the corner of the lobby. Someone had set up a rocking chair for Barbara.

"Excuse me, Mom," Dorsey said, and ran over to Barbara and Tade, embracing them both in one big hug.

"I've missed you, but now that you guys run this place my parents said we can come back for all the holidays. All the time. And they can golf and I can hang with you," Tade said.

"That'd be great. I'd love it," Dorsey said, and glanced over her shoulder at Jack, chatting excitedly with their moms. He smiled at her. She knew he hoped she would go along with his plan. She looked around at all of the love in the room, and thought of the future, of starting over here with the best man she'd ever met. A man who would love her and protect her. And, who would let her be herself, a man who had already helped her heal.

Barbara reached out and pulled Dorsey close. She whispered, "Must take care of the root for the tree to heal. Keep your love close. Welcome home."

When the party was over and everyone had headed back to their rooms or cottages, Jack walked over to Dorsey and grabbed her hand. "Come here, I want to show you one more thing," he said, a twinkle in his eye. "I've been saving the best surprise for last!"

As the sunset glowed orange and purple out the windows, they held hands and climbed the spiral staircase to the second floor of the inn. Dorsey thought about that night, so long ago, when they'd had their first deep talk sitting on the floor of the private dining room, in the dark. But now, they'd be in charge of the place? It was almost too much.

Jack stopped in front of an impressive set of double doors. "Welcome home," he said, pulling on the doors. "This is all ours now. If you want it to be."

Dorsey walked inside a living room with cream-colored furniture, pale yellow walls, a large fireplace and a direct view across the blooming rose garden, the white gazebo and the sparkling ocean sound beyond. Jack excitedly showed her their full kitchen, the guest bedroom and bath, and then the master suite.

"Oh my goodness, this is beautiful," Dorsey said, overwhelmed and happy, sitting down on the fluffy king bed. The room was painted a pale peach and the bedspread was an exact match, in pale cool silk. The area rug was a thick, white wool. "It's almost too much, too good to be true."

Jack sat down on the bed next to Dorsey. His gaze met hers as he brushed her hair away from her face. As they sat side-by-side at the end of the bed, they faced the ocean a view framed by sliding glass doors that opened to their own private porch. It was the most beautiful bedroom Dorsey had ever seen.

"Dorsey, I know we can make a happy life together. Here, or anywhere we choose. I know you've been through a lot, but it wasn't because of Indigo Island. We found each other here. Steve's gone and can never hurt you again. For that matter, neither can your uncle."

Dorsey looked into Jack's eyes, the happiness she saw there, the pride. She wanted this man, she wanted to have his children, to create an even more successful hotel with him, to create the future of her dreams. Everything was possible now, she realized.

"Yes," Dorsey said, climbing onto Jack, pushing him onto his back on the bed. "Yes, I want you, this life. I love this island."

Jack gently rolled Dorsey onto her back. She knew he was afraid she was too bruised, too hurt to make love. But she wanted him. Needed him. She was healing, would continue to heal. The bruises on her body were nothing as deep as the wounds left from her father's murder, but even that was becoming better now that her memory was restored. Anything was possible now, with Jack by her side.

"Make love to me, please, Jack. It'll be okay. He didn't touch me, not like that, you know that. You saved me, just in time."

Jack let out a deep breath. Dorsey knew it had been hard for him, too, to imagine what might have happened if he hadn't gotten to her in time. What Steve would have done, what he was capable of doing.

He pressed a warm gentle kiss on her lips. His fingertips traced the shape of her face, skimming lightly over the bruises on her cheek and jaw where Steve had clamped his hand over her mouth. Dorsey sighed.

"OK?" he asked.

"Yes, your touch feels so good," Dorsey said, arching her back, pulling at the buttons on her shirt. Jack helped her, and then removed her bra, his fingers traced the edges of her breast, skimmed across her nipples, tracing down to her bruised ribs and abdomen.

"Bastard," he said, his voice deep and angry as he saw her injuries again.

Dorsey grabbed his strong biceps, rubbing his shoulder, assuring him, calming him down. "Jack, it's okay. We'll be okay."

Jack smiled, love and desire and true happiness sparkling in his handsome eyes, he said, "Yes, we will."

Dorsey wrapped her arms around him and knew she was home.

The End

The Trouble with Christmas

An Indigo Island Novella

Kaira Rouda

Dedication

With special thanks to Sinclair Sawhney, Meghan Farrell, Lee Hyatt – the amazing team at Tule Publishing, and my fellow Southern Born authors celebrating A Coastal Christmas *– Kim Boykin, Erika Marks and Tracy Solheim—it's an honor to be with you all. Merry Christmas!*

Note to Readers

Dear Readers,

As with the other books in the Indigo Island series, *The Trouble with Christmas* is set on an island much like Daufuskie Island, South Carolina. In this particular story, food plays a very central role and for inspiration I turned to the fabulous cookbook *Gullah Home Cooking the Daufuskie Way* by Sallie Ann Robinson. Robinson grew up on Daufuskie Island and was one of Pat Conroy's students for the year he spent teaching in the island's one room schoolhouse. His experience was captured in his novel *The Water is Wide*. My character, Sally Ann, is named in her honor.

I hope you'll enjoy your visit to Indigo Island. It's a magical place for the holidays, as is any place where you gather with your loved ones.

May all of your Christmas dreams come true!

Happy Reading! Happy Holidays!

Much love,
Kaira

Chapter One

Lily

LILY EDMONDS GENTLY pulled another soft petal from the white daisy she held in her hand. Only one petal remained, and she looked down at the pile accumulating on the green picnic table on the back deck of her apartment. It was a brisk December day, deceptively cold in Atlanta, but Lily didn't feel the chill.

He loves me not. She tossed the stem to the ground. It had been a week since Bob's phone call shattered her world and undermined all of the confidence Lily had built up in her thirty years on earth. She glanced down at the three-carat, emerald-cut diamond, sparkling on her left finger and again felt a spurt of tears.

"Keep the ring, Lily," Bob had said at the end of the call. "We did have a great time together, and I'll always care about you. I am sorry."

Sorry.

He was sorry?

After spending almost five years together, building a relationship, planning their future, talking about the children they would have, the life they would live, he was, simply, *sorry.*

Once she found out the reason he was dumping her, Lily had been furious. She still was. She had no idea how she would ever get over the betrayal. Her best friend, Avery Putnam, was expecting Lily and Bob to stay with her and her family for the holidays on Indigo Island. Lily knew she should call Avery and tell her, but she couldn't make herself pick up the telephone. Denial was a powerful coping technique, and Lily was guilty of pretending if she didn't tell anyone Bob had broken off their engagement, it might not be real. Pretending had become her life and how she'd been able to go to work at the restaurant each evening, a forced smile painted on her face.

Her routine had saved her. For the past week, at Alfredo's Italian Restaurant in Buckhead, she had focused on her work as a pastry chef, and she continued to be especially proud of her ricotta cheesecake and Tiramisu she'd learned to create during culinary school. She added her own twists to make her confections uniquely hers and a patron favorite at Alfredo's.

Lily swallowed and pushed back tears when she thought about other plans she and Bob had planned after their wedding—buying a building downtown and turning it into a bakery. Gone, she thought in despair. All her dreams were gone, erased by one phone call, and Bob no longer took her calls. Instead, he texted, *What's the point? It's over.*

Lily stood up and stretched her arms to the sky. The backyard of her apartment was as sad in winter as her heart. The grass was brown. The leaves had fallen from the giant oak trees gracing her neighborhood, leaving bare branches beseeching an empty grey sky. Lily had always made it a point to have a sunny floral arrangement in her apartment at all times. Just before Bob's call, she'd purchased two dozen of her favorite white daisies from the flower store on the corner. She hadn't even made a dent in the bunch during her new daily petal-plucking ritual. As she walked inside to get ready for work, Lily stared at the bouquet, resigned. She could pick petals for the rest of the week, but it wouldn't matter what each daisy told her, she would never be able to change his heart.

As always, Alfredo's was packed with hungry diners who were the who's who of Atlanta. For the most part, Lily worked busily at her pastry station, hidden, while the majority of the kitchen and wait staff, mostly male and Italian, bustled around her. Lily often thought she'd been hired fresh out of culinary school due more to her dark, glossy hair and chocolate brown eyes—so large in her small face she sometimes felt like a cartoon character—than she had been recruited for her pastry skills. She definitely could pass for Italian; Lily quickly swept her long hair into a topknot and put a white chef's hat on her head.

Her ingredients were ready to go so she pulled a white apron on to protect her black, long sleeved t-shirt and black pants, her work uniform, which her manager insisted on just in case Lily was ever asked to come to the front of the house to talk to the guests. Luckily, that didn't happen often.

"You never know, bella," Sergio had said when he hired her, with his attempt at a seductive smile. "I would ask to meet you."

She'd been at the restaurant almost three years now, and she might still feel like the shy little girl she'd been when she'd first been engulfed in the sunshine of Avery's friendship so many years ago, but Lily had been able to hold her own with the male employees of Alfredo's. She was all business in the kitchen.

Lily carefully added the finishing touch to a chocolate mousse, squeezing the cone-shaped pastry sleeve in her hand to write *Happy Birthday, James* on the top of the cake.

"Lily, table seven wants you to personally deliver the cake. Go on," Sergio appeared at her side and pulled her chef's hat from her head.

"Oh." She fought the impulse to drag her hat back on and continue to hide. "I'm really not in the mood," she said. "Just have Tony take it over."

"The Putnams insist on having you deliver it. They tell me

you're part of their family? Nice family," Sergio said.

Avery.

Lily huffed out a breath. Her best friend had left her numerous voice mail messages all week, and sent texts Lily hadn't returned because she just couldn't face telling Avery about Bob. That would make her broken engagement real, permanent. No way could she keep the awful news a secret in front of Avery. Lily felt flustered as she pulled her top knot off and allowed her hair to cascade down her back.

She picked up the cake and walked into the small, intimate dining room, determined to find a smile and congratulate James. Then she could flee back to her kitchen and blissful pretending that everything would be okay and she would wake up from the nightmare of Bob's defection. Avery grinned and jumped up to hug Lily the moment she spotted her. Lily managed to shift her stance to protect the cake. Mark, Avery's husband, her brother James, and father Richard all stood politely.

"Hey, Avery, hello everyone," Lily said, forcing a smile. "Happy birthday, James."

"Surprise!" Avery said.

"Lily, dear, so good to see you," Avery's dad said and kissed her cheek as soon as she'd put the cake in front of James.

"You, too, all of you," Lily said, bending to give Avery's mom, Evalyn, a kiss on her cheek.

"How are you, dear? How's Bob? When is the big day? We barely survived Avery's wedding and now, well, I demand to be involved in planning yours," Evalyn said. "You're my second daughter, you know."

Lily swallowed hard and nodded, but no way could she speak.

"You okay?" Avery asked softly as she wrapped Lily in a big hug. "I've been so worried. What is going on? Is it Bob?"

Lily nodded for the third time, purposefully avoiding eye contact with her beautiful blonde friend. Instead, she moved on to give James a hug. Even through her haze of misery, she noticed that for once he didn't have a date. "Happy Birthday, James. Hope you all enjoy the cake. It's so good to see you all. And Merry Christmas, if I don't see you again before then."

"It's only December tenth, Lily, we'll see you before Christmas. You're coming to Indigo remember?" Avery said, hands on hips, watching her closely.

Lily wanted to escape their concerned eyes. "Would you like me to light the candle? Are we singing?"

James grimaced. "No, of course we aren't singing."

Lily remembered his embarrassment at public displays like a birthday cake, and she was thankful. Now she could make her exit.

"Well, enjoy. It's my special chocolate mousse! I've got to get back to the kitchen," she said as cheerfully as she could and bolted back to the kitchen.

Back in the safety of her work space—the comfort of heat, routine chaos, creative mixing, and the smells of garlic and tomato sauce—Lily relaxed a little. She had to tell Avery, she just didn't feel ready to face the concerns, the pity, the questions.

And then, Avery appeared at her station. "Lily, we're all worried about you. What's going on?"

"Nothing," Lily lied, her face flushed with guilt.

"Honestly, Lils, it's not even James's birthday for another week. You should know that."

"I've just been busy at work. You know, we had all those catering jobs over Thanksgiving, just the busy holiday season," Lily said, rolling pastry with her rolling pin, preparing the wafer thin dough her famous Sicilian Cannoli deserved. "You're going to get me in trouble being back here."

If anything, the chefs—all men—appreciated the appearance of the tall, beautiful blonde. Suddenly, they all found a reason to saunter past the pastry station, a miniature white-hatted parade.

"Bull shit. I told Sergio I was coming back here. Are you and

Bob in a fight?" Avery said, blue eyes flashing. "I'm not budging until you tell me the truth. In fact, I want you to come home with me after work. Mark and I drove separately and he's riding home with my parents, leaving our car. So tell me now, or after work. Your choice."

Lily felt the tears well up in her eyes before she could stop them. They rolled down both cheeks, landed on the pastry dough, and ruined the batch, the moisture making the delicate dough too sticky. She'd have to start over.

She was starting over.

"Oh, Avery," she said, hurrying around the stainless steel counter to embrace her friend. "Bob broke our engagement. He said he's in love with someone else. They're getting married this Christmas!" Her voice ended in a wail.

Avery wrapped her arm around Lily and escorted her out the kitchen's back door into the chilly evening. She walked to her car, opened the passenger door and pushed Lily, still wearing her kitchen whites and chef hat, gently inside.

Sobs wracked Lily's body as Avery climbed into the driver's seat.

"He was an asshole, Lils," Avery said, her musical voice for once hard. "I'm sorry, but I couldn't figure out a way to tell you I didn't think he was good for you long term. You only saw one side of him."

"I loved him, Aves," Lily managed.

"I know," Avery rubbed circles on Lily's back. "I know you did. But you deserve much better."

Lily couldn't speak anymore, and Avery seemed at a loss for words, stroking Lily's tangled, damp hair after the chef's hat had fallen off.

"I need to go back in there, finish my shift," Lily gulped.

"You're in no condition," Avery was already taking over like she always did, like Lily had let her take over for years. "I'm texting mom right now to tell Sergio that you're very ill. He'll be fine. Most of the tables are through desert anyway," Avery said.

Lily wondered what she would do without Avery. Only Avery knew how far Lily had come, overcoming the heartbreak of her teens to emerge as a strong, independent woman. Avery had been there every step of the way. In fact, all of the Putnams had been like a second family, even Avery's brothers, Blake, James, and Denton were like siblings to her despite the one time she and James crossed a boundary in the back of his car her senior year in high school. They'd both been drinking, and later had promised each other that it would never happen again.

Lily had imagined that once she and Bob had become engaged, she wouldn't rely on the Putnams' emotional support again. She would get married and start her happy life. Now she was starting over. Alone. Once again, she would need to lean on Avery, maybe even her family. Lily covered her face and tried to stop the stream of tears and Avery drove away from Alfredo's.

"LILY, ARE YOU awake?" Avery asked, pulling Lily from her dreams.

She opened her eyes and smiled wanly at Avery. The whole night came crashing back—crying, confessing that Bob had dumped her for someone else, leaving work. And now she had to face life alone. Again. Lily looked around the guest bedroom at Avery's house, which reminded her of the guest bedroom at the Putnam Estate, the same soothing light pink color scheme. She'd spent many nights at the Putnams' throughout her life, and in almost every case, she'd been there because of an overwhelmingly sad event. Now, she was repeating the pattern, a pathetic guest in Avery and Mark's new home. A chill moved down her spine as she forced herself to ignore the old memories trying to bubble up in her mind. Bob's betrayal was enough to deal with for now. *When did he stop loving me? Why did he stop loving me?*

"It's lunch time," Avery said gently, pulling back the thick silk curtains to reveal a grey, rainy day. "You slept through breakfast."

Lily slowly sat up. "Thanks for bringing me here, Aves."

"I can't believe you didn't call me the minute he broke up with you. The jerk. You know what Mark said about him right?"

"Boring Bob?" Lily repeated, a small smile crossing her face despite herself.

Avery's husband found Bob a boring snob who only wanted to talk about money and social status.

"Yes, well, he has appended the nickname and now it's Boring Bastard Bob. You like it? I do."

Avery plopped down on the end of the queen bed. She wore a simple black cashmere turtleneck and fitted, dark jeans. Her long blonde hair was pulled back in a loose ponytail. Her gorgeous blue eyes were filled with love and concern.

"You have to be sick of my pathetic life," Lily said. "I really thought I was on the road to my future. I really believed he loved me."

"Well, after you went to sleep last night, I did a little snooping," Avery said, her face drawn and sad. "Bob is planning to marry Rebecca Postle. I don't know who set them up, his parents or hers, but it's an arranged marriage of sorts," Avery said.

"How could he possibly agree to marry her when he'd asked me to marry him?" Lily demanded, playing with the diamond ring on her finger. "I know I never was good enough for Bob's family."

"Bob's not good enough for you if, after five years and a proposal, he caves in to his parents' wishes. I mean really? Who does that?" Avery's blue eyes flashed with indignation.

"I don't want to talk about it," Lily fought back a fresh rush of tears. "Or think about it. I can't imagine him, kissing her, making love to her."

"You know what? You need to get angry, and then you need

to realize the Postles have done you a big favor. You are better than that, Lils, you are. Good riddance is all I say. You're keeping the ring right?"

Lily nodded. She hadn't given it too much thought except to toy with idea of returning it so that she could see Bob again, make him explain himself in person, but after Avery's outburst, she realized she needed to stop crying. She did need to stop thinking about Bob in present tense.

"Good. That's a little safety net right there. I know you and Bob had discussed you opening a bakery at one point. That ring could be a nice start to a savings account for that dream."

"I can't think about all of that yet," Lily said. "I don't want to think about anything, but he's still in my dreams. It's like he's haunting me. And it's almost the holidays. This is the trouble with Christmas, and every other major holiday. It's a time for family and love. And once again, I'm alone."

"You have me, and my family. Mom and I are leaving for Indigo Island tomorrow and you're coming, too," Avery said. She excitedly reached for Lily's hand. "It will be the best thing for you to get away and regroup. We'll have fun like when we were kids. You have time to stop your mail, clean out your refrigerator, and pack your clothes. We leave in the helicopter in the morning."

"I can't," Lily finally made a move to get out of the comfy bed so she could face the day and the rest of her life. "I have to work. It's December, the restaurant is crazy busy."

"I told Alfredo you needed time off," Avery said, very sure of herself—like always. "And you do. If you want it, he'll give you your job back when you return. I even helped line up a temporary pastry chef. It's your choice about whether you return after the holidays. I'd rather have you start your own business," Avery said, like it was the most natural thing in the world to arrange her friend's life.

Always so willing to help, Lily thought wryly. To fix her life.

She knew she had to stand on her own, but Lily had to admit it felt good to be taken care of after such a blow.

"You're incredible. You really are. Thank you, Aves," Lily said, her heart lightened a little bit at the thought of a trip to Indigo Island.

The remote Sea Island was like a second home to her. She'd even thought it would be fun to open her bakery there, but Bob had laughed off that idea as unreasonable.

"So let's get started. We won't return until after New Year's. A whole new year and a new start when we get back."

Lily looked down at the diamond ring sparkling on her finger and swallowed a sob. She wasn't quite ready to take it off. And where would she keep it safe, anyway? She took a deep breath and stared out at the grey day. Another new start.

Chapter Two

Lily

S HE FINISHED ZIPPING her suitcase at the same moment the doorbell rang.

"You better be ready, we're all waiting!" Avery yelled through the door.

Lily smiled. What would she do without her best friend? *I'm thirty years old, suddenly single and adrift.* She opened the door and Avery burst inside. *My best friend is my only constant.*

"Wipe that frown off your gorgeous face, immediately," Avery said pulling her into a bear hug.

Avery wore a light blue cashmere sweater, khaki jeans, and ankle boots. She looked chic and ready for an island adventure. Lily looked down at her own outfit – black turtleneck, black jeans, black boots – and sighed. She looked as gloomy as she felt.

"I hope you're ready because the Putnams wait for no one, as you know!"

"I'm all set, but are you sure Sergio is okay with this?" Lily said, imagining her boss and all of his Italian temper boiling over at her departure. She needed her job, especially now.

"Yes, I'm positive. It's all worked out," Avery said, with her breezy confidence.

"Okay, I have no idea how you did it, but if Alfredo's can manage without me during the holiday rush, well, they might decide they can manage without me forever."

"Impossible," Avery said and grabbed Lily's suitcase as she pulled her toward the front door. "They're hosting a guest pastry chef from Paris, a guy who just happens to have always wanted to visit America. He's a friend, from when I studied abroad. It worked out perfectly. Under the table, of course."

"You're amazing," Lily said, and pulled her apartment door behind her tightly. "Thank you."

"Anything for my best friend, Lils," Avery said and led her down the walkway to the white limo, with the Putnam orange P emblazed on the door, waiting at the curb. The driver hopped out and helped them inside and then took care of Lily's suitcase.

"It's been forever, John, how are you?" Lily asked.

"Great, same as always, Miss Lily. It's good to see you," John said. "To the airport, then, Miss Avery?"

"Yes, please," Avery said, then turned to Lily. "I'm so excited. This will be like Christmases during high school when you were always with us."

Lily wished she could share Avery's excitement, but she felt empty. It wasn't at all the same, Avery was married and Lily was supposed to be engaged. She forced a smile since she didn't want to bring everyone down this holiday. "Your family has always been so kind to me."

Avery smiled, accepting Lily, as always, just the way she was. The limo pulled into the private airplane section of the airport and up to the Putnams' white helicopter, sporting the orange script Putnam P on the side. Seeing the copter, Lily did feel a small burst of excitement.

"See, you're smiling, Lils," Avery said as they climb out onto the tarmac. Mrs. Putnam emerged from another car and the three women walked to the helicopter. "My dad is coming over this afternoon. It's a girls' flight now."

"Hello, Avery. Lily." Evalyn kissed both girls on the cheek. She smoothed her sleek gray cashmere dress down her slim body. "Let's get going, shall we?"

And at her command, everyone strapped in, and the helicopter took flight. As they neared the island, Lily felt her shoulders begin to relax. She had been visiting Indigo Island with the Putnams for years, but she never realized until today just how much the island calmed her. She took a deep breath and looked over at Avery, who was smiling out the window.

Lily remembered the December of her freshman year in high school when her dad had packed his bags and said goodbye, telling her he'd found his soul mate and was moving to Chicago to be with her. "But what about me and mom?" Lily had asked, too stunned to be able to comprehend that he really intended to leave them forever.

"I'll always love you, Lily, but I need to live a genuine life," her dad had said, patting her on the head like a dog. And then he'd left. Lily had barely seen him since. Her mom had fallen apart, unable to pull herself out of the alcoholism his sudden exit triggered after their twenty-two year marriage.

And now more than fifteen Decembers later, another man has abruptly left, breaking his promise to her. She was cursed. A tear worked its way down her cheek before she could stop it.

"Hey, no more tears. We're about to land at the most magical island of healing ever," Avery said patting Lily's hand.

Lily smiled.

"You get your own room now! I *have* to share with Mark," Avery joked as they hurried to the waiting golf cart. Lily smiled at the things the Putnams took for granted. The wealth, the happiness, the golf carts that matched their helicopters, and their private jets. But even as much as Avery took all the symbols of her wealth for granted, she was a true and wonderful friend. The best friend Lily could hope for.

Evalyn Putnam walked ahead of the younger women, up the steps to the front door of the Putnam Plantation, a replica of an antebellum Southern plantation that formerly occupied just this spot on Indigo Island. Every time Lily visited, she imagined what it must have been like here before air conditioning and running water, before all the comforts she took for granted. As Evalyn reached the wrap-around porch, she smiled and said, "It's so good to be here, isn't it? Take a deep breath, girls. Ahhh."

Lily smiled, trying to shake off her negative thoughts so she'd be a better guest. Avery rushed past her mom up the stairs to the wide front porch. A huge wreath made from large branches of local pine trees decorated the front door. Garland had been wrapped around the banister of the long porch. White twinkle lights have been threaded through the branches, held in place by cheerful red ribbon. The front porch lights were decorated with the same bold red ribbons, standing out against the white wood of the home. A fresh evergreen wreath adorned every window, held in place by a thick red velvet ribbon. Everything was, as always, perfect.

"Well, do you girls feel the chill in the air?" Evalyn asked as her housekeeper pulled open the front door. "Hope you have a fire going, Millie."

"Yes, in the library and in the family room, Ms. Putnam. Welcome home," Millie said, stepping out of the way.

"Oh, Mom, who decorated the tree?" Avery asked in a voice that made her sound as if she were a small child.

"Millie handled it, since I wasn't sure who would be here when and I wanted the tree up when I arrived. Isn't it gorgeous?"

The tree was massive, easily fifteen feet tall, towering over the Putnams' grand foyer. The entire room was filled with the smell of fresh pine. The tree was decorated with white lights, and the only accent color was red. Huge silver and white ornaments glistened and danced under the light from the tree and the large crystal chandelier was suspended just above the shining, silver star topping the tree. The scale of everything in the room reminded Lily of a grand hotel lobby. And this was only one of the Putnam's homes.

Behind the tree, the bannister of the circular stairway that led up to the second floor was decorated, like the outside deck, with garland, white lights and red ribbon.

"It's gorgeous," Lily said to Evalyn.

Avery had lost interest in the tree and had walked into the library to the right of the foyer.

"Avery is making sure I didn't decorate the library tree," Evalyn said to Lily with a knowing smile. "I didn't, of course. I'll leave that one to you girls."

Avery walked back to where Evalyn and Lily stood admiring the tree. She kissed her mother on the cheek. "Thanks mom. I was worried you'd let someone else decorate the family tree."

"You know I wouldn't, dear," Evalyn said. "Lily, you are in the blue room at the end of the hall. Perhaps you'd like to unpack. Lunch will be served in about an hour, in the kitchen since it's just the three of us."

"Thank you, both, so much. I'm so happy to be here," Lily said and realized it was true.

She followed Avery up the grand staircase, grateful her friend had realized that if Lily had been left alone to dwell on her heartbreak, she would have felt far worse.

"James will be here this afternoon," Avery said as they reached the top of the stairs. "I'm surprised. Usually he doesn't come play family until the last minute. He's almost as bad as Blake used to be."

"Oh great. When do Mark and Denton and Blake get into town?" Lily followed Avery into her bedroom.

Avery's room faced the ocean and had been redone since Lily had last visited. Instead of the two queen beds, there now was a king bed covered with an impossibly fluffy white comforter. The floors, as in all the bedrooms, were hardwood, softened by thick white wool rugs. Two overstuffed white chairs framed the window and the sparkling ocean view.

"This room is gorgeous," Lily said.

The bedside tables were each decorated with matching three-foot tall Christmas trees, with shiny red ball ornaments—the only color in the room. A fresh pine wreath tied with a bright red velvet bow hung from the top of the mirror over the long mahogany dresser.

Avery walked into the passageway that separated the room from the full bath and slid open the mirrored closet doors, inspecting the clothes hanging inside.

"It's always so much fun to see what I left here. Sometimes I leave things here on purpose, just so something will seem new and fresh. Like this sweater—oh, and these sweat pants. I love these," she said, pulling out a pair of gray sweats and hugging them tight. "Mark doesn't like me in sweats so I'll have to wear them all day today."

The staff had unpacked Avery's suitcases and her toiletries were assembled on the white marble countertop in the large bathroom. Avery pulled off her jeans and pulled on her sweats. "That's better," she said. "Let's go get you settled and into some sweats. We have a tree to decorate!"

Chapter Three

Cole

COLE STANTON THOUGHT the chill in the air felt great as he stretched for his morning jog. Compared to the summer months when he'd been sure he'd given himself heat stroke a couple of times, this was the perfect weather for a run. Since he'd moved here a few months ago to start a new life, Cole was now in the best shape of his life, as long as no one looked too closely at his hands, covered with cuts and blisters, and the hair on his right arm had been singed off as well as his eyebrows in a freak flash over fire two days ago. If Sally Ann hadn't been there with a fire extinguisher, the entire restaurant would have been consumed in flames.

He ran along the flat, firm sand at the edge of the ocean, enjoying the views over to Hilton Head, and along the south to the tip of the island, a development called Bloody Point after the notorious battles that had taken place centuries before. In the far distance, he could see Tybee Island, another Sea Island that, like Hilton Head, was connected to the mainland by a bridge ages ago.

What a difference a bridge would make for the restaurant. He stopped at a tangled pile of driftwood that blocked the rest of the beach. A bridge would bring in more diners, which the restaurant desperately needed, but it would also ruin the seclusion and peace of the island, a place his grandmother introduced him to when he was a child. He needed to find an answer to the dwindling profits. As he jogged back home, his mood dark, not improved by the quick five-mile run. For the first time in his life, Cole had failed. His embarrassment still rankled. As the new owner of Marshside Mama's restaurant, he'd overpromised and under delivered on his first major holiday, Thanksgiving. What had he been thinking? He didn't know the restaurant industry, nor did he know the island that well, but he had jumped in anyway, investing in Sally Ann's Marshside Mama's with a lot of ideas fueled by arrogance and enthusiasm and not a lot of knowledge or foresight.

What the hell had happened to his brain? He'd been determined to improve people's lives, not destroy them. His jaw hurt because he's been clenching it so often, but as he ran past the Putnam Plantation, he had a whole different hurt. Christmas had arrived. The porch glowed with white lights, wrapped in garland and cheery red ribbon bows. Christmas. The trouble with Christmas? It was a family holiday, but his family was far away. His parents had begged him to come home to New England for the holidays but he couldn't leave Sally Ann with the mess he had created. So he'd promised his mom he'd make it next year. She hadn't been happy, and he felt even worse.

Cole imagined his family's home in Lincoln, elaborately decorated for Christmas with colorful lights, a tree filled with the handmade ornaments Cole and his brother had made through elementary school. His mom's spiced apple cider always simmered on the stove, filling the house with the scents of family and the holidays. He imagined the snow was already blanketing the ground, and his mom would have a roaring fire in the fireplace. And he was here. Alone.

HE SHOOK HIS head and pushed the sadness away. He'd chosen

to change, to move far away and start over. He decided that after the lunch rush, he'd head to the General Store to find a few Christmas decorations. That would get him in the spirit.

Lily

AFTER LUNCH, AND decorating the library tree together—with Avery explaining the meaning and significance of almost every ornament they unwrapped—Lily suggested they bake Christmas cookies. It was the least she could do to thank the Putnams for their hospitality.

A quick survey of the kitchen pantry revealed all of the ingredients she needed, except sprinkles.

"We can't have Christmas cookies without sprinkles," Avery announced.

"Sure we can," Lily said. "We can make gingerbread boys and girls, even a gingerbread house. That would be fun."

"I need sprinkles, and gumdrops, and those shiny round metal thingamabobs, otherwise, it's just not the same," Avery said. "They'll have some at the General Store. If not, we'll go beg for some from the inn. James and dad own it now somehow, did I tell you that?"

"Something about a sex scandal with the general manager."

"I don't think it was that lurid," Avery laughed. "But two employees there, a couple, are now managing it, and Dad and James agreed to buy it from the corporation that owned it so they could keep it true to the island and its history. I guess it has been going well because I haven't heard James complain at all about it," Avery said. "Speaking of James," she said with studied casualness, which made Lily's ears perk up. "Do you still think he's cute?"

"How about I go round up the decorating supplies?" Lily

said, ignoring Avery's question. "I know your mom wanted your help with the guest list for a dinner or something."

"You're right, she did ask," Avery said. "You still think James is cute, don't you?"

Lily shook her head and laughed. "Your matchmaking skills are not your best attribute and neither is subtlety, but yes, James is cute." She put air quotes around the word. "All your brothers are super cute but so not going to happen."

"I know," Avery sighed. "But I still have this dream of having you as a sister."

"I can be your sister without having to take on your brother," Lilly said. "My fiancé just dumped me. Give me some recovery time."

Lily was surprised that she could even joke about Bob. The island really was magic, but the tears were never far away, and looking for cookie sprinkles would be a welcome distraction.

Avery sighed and smiled. "I know. Ignore me. Take the golf cart out front. Charge whatever you find to our bill."

Lily was happy to escape. She didn't bother to change out of her sweats and instead hopped into the golf cart and drove to the General Store. The drive led her along the edge of the forest, by the golf course and past the large Melrose Inn, another replica of an original plantation, but now it was a successful resort and owned by the Putnams. The inn had been trimmed in red and white lights and huge concrete urns were filled with red poinsettias lining the porch and entrance.

From some deep recess of her mind, Lily remembered her ninth grade project about the "painted leaf" flowers, named after Charlestonian Joel Roberts Poinsett, the first ambassador to Mexico, who in 1828 carried home clippings of the plant to the Lowcountry. Her project partner had been Avery, of course.

Lily laughed and smiled at the blessing of long-time friendship, memories to last a lifetime. Lily pulled the cart up to the front of the General Store, a bright blue wooden cottage with butter yellow shutters. She hurried up the ramp to the entrance. Just as she pushed the door, a man pulled on it to come out and Lily lost her balance, tumbling into him. Strong arms steadied her and Lily looked into the face of the most handsome man she had ever seen. He smiled.

"Sorry," he said, still holding her. His hands wrapped around her arms like an electric band that warmed her all the way to her bones, and there was no way she could tear her riveted gaze from his mesmerizing blue eyes. A jolt of heat zipped throughout her body and lodged deep in her core.

"You okay?" he asked.

Lily didn't want to act like a teenager, but her brain wouldn't function. Her body couldn't move. It was like she'd been here before. Here with this man and his indigo gaze, melting her bones and turning her blood to honey.

"Did I hurt you?" Now he looked concerned, and his hands smoothed up and down her arms.

"I'm fine, my fault," she said, noticing her voice sounded husky. What was her deal? Had she lost her mind? What about Bob, the man she'd wanted to marry, have children with, build a life with?

"Sure you're okay? I think I shook you up."

If he only knew the half of it. Lily wondered what he'd say if she told him, no, she was not fine. She was an idiot.

She smiled and nodded. Truly an idiot.

"Fine," she said. "I wasn't looking."

Missing seeing this man would be a tragedy no woman should have to endure.

"No, I'm afraid I wasn't paying attention and almost flattened you. Deep in thought, none of it good," he laughed. "I'm Cole Stanton, and I'm not typically this clumsy."

"Lily Edmonds, and I typically stumble into at least one man every day."

She nearly clapped her hand over her mouth. Was she flirting? Was she heartbroken?

"So I'm the quota for today. Good to know, Lily Edmonds. It's early." He looked at his watch. "You'll have to be very careful for the rest of the day."

He was flirting back! Lily checked. No ring. And he was hot. Hotter than Brad Pitt. Self-consciously, she spun her ring around so the diamond pressed into her palm, reminding her of everything she no longer had. Why had she flirted? She hated men. She was done with men.

"Maybe go home, draw the shutters."

"Or I could walk through the door again," she said more boldly than she'd ever been in her life. Avery would faint. She would think Lily's personality had been transplanted by aliens.

"I'm willing," he said easily, but he didn't let go of her arm, and Lily could feel his fingers like a pulse through her body.

"So, Lily, are you living on the island or just visiting?"

Cole didn't have a drawl. He definitely sounded like a Northerner. It took every ounce of nerve she had to continue making eye contact with his bright blue gaze. Her heart thudded and her palms were clammy. He finally released her arm and she felt herself sway. He was making her dizzy just standing there. She'd need to go home and drink something much harder than a sweet tea. She remembered he'd asked her a question.

"Just visiting, staying with my best friend Avery Putnam, at the Putnam Plantation," Lily managed, crossing her arms in front of her to try to calm herself down. She thought she saw him wince when she mentioned the Putnam name, but she wasn't sure. "How about you?" she asked, totally horrified to realize she'd batted her lashes like a real Southern Belle. *Am I a cartoon character?*

"Actually, I moved here from Boston in April. Quit my job, sold everything, and I'm starting over right here on the island," Cole said and added "I bought a house, it's on the eighteenth hole, a few miles north of the Putnam's place. That's the enormous white house with all the Christmas decorations out, right?"

"That's the place," she said, laughing a bit. "It is a bit opulent, but Avery's family is really amazing, very down to earth people."

Cole looked a bit skeptical, but his face was so open and friendly she found herself liking him even more, and relaxing a little in his company.

"Mr. and Mrs. Putnam are very generous and entertain friends often. They need a big house because their entire family is often there. Plus, they have corporate events and parties at the house or at the inn." She paused, realizing she sounded defensive. Why should she care what he thought? "Every weekend night they invite friends for cocktails. Why don't you join us?" Lily said before she could stop herself.

"You sure that would be okay?"

"Sure. On the weekends there's a standing seven p.m. cocktail hour," Lily said. "They've had it since we were kids. Friends from the island drop in, have a drink, chat, and sometimes stay for dinner or split up and go out to dinner other places, you know, homes or restaurants on the island."

He straightened up and looked at her a little more intensely.

"Every weekend?"

"When they're in residence, which is a lot. Evalyn says it's a way to keep in touch with friends and the kids of their friends."

"I'd really love that," he sounded so sincere, that Lily had to bite back a sigh.

How could she be so attracted to a stranger? She just got dumped by Bob. The love of her life.

"It will give me a taste of the life I've left behind."

"What…?" Lily began, but was caught by the shadow that crossed his face.

"What can I bring?" Cole quickly interrupted, focusing so intently on her Lily lost her train of thought and just stared.

"Just yourself," she finally managed to drag some words out of her brain. "We're well-stocked at the Putnam's, well, except for sprinkles. I wanted to make a big batch of Christmas cookies but my friend Avery said I just can't do that without sprinkles, and gum drops, and silver dragees, or as Avery calls them, those shiny silver ball thingies."

Cole laughed. "I know, cookies need to have sprinkles, for sure."

"They really don't," Lily said, her hands on her hips. "And they don't need silver beads either. I'm a pastry chef with a degree from the Institute of Culinary Education in New York. This is my area, but there is no arguing with Avery, never was."

Cole laughed and his blue eyes seemed to swallow her up. Lily felt a definite blush washing over her face and neck. *Get over it. You are thirty not fourteen.*

"Well if you're here to look for decorations, you're out of luck. They don't have cookie decorations, just the good ol' slice n' bake cookie dough with the embedded reindeer face," Cole says. "No home decorations either, I'm afraid."

"Guess it's gingerbread men with icing after all," Lily said, daring to look up at Cole's perfect chin, his sculpted cheekbones, his thick blonde hair.

"We have some sprinkles at the restaurant. I can bring them tonight, if you can wait," Cole says.

"What restaurant? Over at the inn?" Lily asked.

"No. Marshside Mama's. The best place on the island," Cole said smiling until he noticed her confusion. "You've never heard of it?"

"Nope," Lily noticed the sadness in his incredible blue eyes. "Is it new?"

"No, it's been around for two generations,"

"Oh," Lily felt bad. She'd been coming to Indigo Island for years. "Probably Avery's heard of it."

She apparently didn't sound confident.

"Damn, I need to figure this out," he said. "It's my restaurant and I seem to have done a poor job of getting the word out, beyond day-trippers and the backside residents."

He ran his fingers through his thick hair. Lily felt his frustration, but her heart lurched, practically sang. *He's in the same business as I am. He owns a restaurant. What's wrong with me?*

"Are you a chef, too?" Lily asked.

"No, I'm the business partner. I'm in charge of advertising and trying to make a profit. Obviously, I've done a bad job," he said.

"Well, come over tonight and tell the Putnams all about it. Once they know about something, it's hard to keep it a secret," Lily said with a smile and swished her ponytail behind her back. "And, any sprinkles you can spare, we'll take."

"Sounds like a plan. I need to head back to the restaurant," Cole said as he headed down the stairs. "You want to come see it? Try a bowl of gumbo? You could follow me over in your cart and meet Sally Ann, my partner."

Lily's heart skipped a beat before she could answer. She did need sprinkles. "Sure, that sounds great," she answered.

"It's a straight line to the backside of the island. You shouldn't have any trouble getting there," Cole said, pushing his hair off his face with his hand.

"I've been to Indigo a bunch, but never to the backside," Lily said climbing into the golf cart.

"It's a treat," Cole said, hopping into his own cart and pulling out in front of her. As Lily followed behind him, the ocean at her back, the cart path twisted through the moss-covered oak trees that looked like something out of a nightmare, with a mist beginning to fill the air. Past the gates of the Melrose Plantation, the forest turned thick and eerie in the afternoon light. The weather was chilly, mid-forties Lily guessed, and misting. And she followed a stranger to the backside of the island for sprinkles. What had she gotten herself into? She was acting out of character. Then she remembered her promise to herself. No more hiding, relying on Avery. She was going to rescue herself instead of letting others do it. And yes, she also remembered Cole's amazing smile and devouring gaze. She quickly texted Avery about her sprinkles, quest, and restaurant detour, but did not mention Cole.

Lily watched as Cole pulled up to a tin-roofed cottage with a hand-painted sign proclaiming Marshside Mama's. Beyond the parking lot, a dock jutted out into the salt water marsh which looked impossibly still and eerie, a sepia scene. Lily shivered as she turned off the golf cart and pocketed the key.

"Welcome to Marshside Mama's," Cole said offering his hand to help her out of the cart. As they touched, the strange current zipped through her. "This is what I decided to purchase, along with my own cottage, when I moved to the island. I had a very convincing Realtor. She saw a sucker."

"Oh, no, it's charming, really," Lily said, noticing the colorfully painted walls visible through the front windows.

"I didn't know anything about restaurants or food service. I thought I could help Sally Ann, the real owner. It's been in her family for two generations until her nephew ran off with all her savings, as well as the restaurant's profits last year. She was headed to foreclosure on her house and the restaurant, and that is the only source of income for her entire family."

"Did you know her?" Lily asked, saddened by the story.

She sensed something dark chase across his face.

"No, not exactly," he said slowly. "But she needed help. I'm afraid I've been the opposite in my life before this," Cole said. "Oh, you're freezing, let's get inside."

Lily was shivering, but she hardly noticed as her mind turned over the problem of the restaurant. Why wasn't it successful? Why did Cole help a stranger? She followed him inside and was immediately charmed by the plastic chairs and simple wood tables, the colorful artwork on the pink and green walls, the tropical feel of the place. She rubbed her hands together, warming up.

"It's cute," she noted. "Very island themed."

"Sally Ann is probably in the kitchen," Cole said and pushed through a swinging door.

Lily smiled at his profile, his strong cleft chin, his thick, curly blonde hair. *He's gorgeous.* She followed him inside the kitchen. She came face to face with the woman who must be Sally Ann.

"Oh, hi," Lily said, embarrassed. Cooks didn't often welcome strangers in their kitchens, and she of all people should have thought of that.

Sally Ann turned and Lily felt the woman's dark brown eyes sizing her up, her large face remaining a mask until she turned her attention back to a large iron pot she's stirring at the stove. The kitchen smelled like garlic and corn and spicy sausage.

"Hey, Sally Ann. This is Lily. She's a chef visiting the island, and I thought you two would enjoy meeting," Cole says, clearly uncomfortable around the woman.

"Hello," Lily said, walking over to the pot and taking a deep breath. "This smells heavenly. Jambalaya?"

Sally Ann turned her attention to Lily, and Lily felt a silent assessment wash over her. "No child. Conch soup with smoked neck bone."

"I haven't had conch soup in so long. May I try it?" Lily asked, and Sally Ann nodded and dipped a spoon into the steaming pot, and held it for Lily. "That's really good. It tastes like conch chowder but with more of a punch. I would love to learn how to make that."

"Mmm, hmm," Sally Ann said, turning her attention back to the pot. "What kind of cooking do you do?"

"I'm a pastry chef back home, but I enjoy all types," Lily said.

"Good, cause we need the help," Sally Ann said.

"Help with what?" Lily asked.

"You bring her here but didn't tell her what you've done?"

Lily turned in time to see Cole pale.

"That's not why I brought her here," he said.

The look Sally Ann leveled at him would have been hilarious if Cole hadn't been so obviously uncomfortable.

"No?" Sally Ann looks Lily up and down and then stares at Cole, hand on her hip. Then she draws out a long "Ooooooooh. I see."

Cole shifted his weight and looked about to speak but said nothing.

"Thought you were all about focusing on business," Sally Ann said to the soup pot.

Lily felt her cheeks flare and silently cursed her revealing face. It was as if Sally Ann had read her mind, maybe Cole's mind, too.

"Yes, tell me about your business. Your business problem," she said quickly.

Sally Ann turned back to the steaming soup pot, and Lily could swear she caught a glimpse of a smile.

She felt like she'd been set up, like there was a secret everyone knew but her.

"Nothing you need to worry about," Cole said.

Sally Ann snorted.

"Let me get you those sprinkles," Cole stepped away and paced randomly around the kitchen, his hand jerked through his hair.

Lily looked back at Sally Ann, who was definitely smiling. She winked at Lily and tilted her head. Lily followed with her eyes and saw a box of baking supplies on a top shelf in a plaid box.

"You are bad," Lily whispered. She reached up and retrieved the box. "Cole, just tell me your problem." She said louder, not enjoying seeing him suffer as obviously Sally Ann did.

"I thought we had a great opportunity to reach out to all

these families staying at different plantations here during the holidays. To spread the word about the restaurant and deliver them a great meal, right to their door. Thanksgiving and Christmas. It was a mistake, clearly," Cole said, his shoulders slumping.

"Why was it a mistake?" Lily asked, thinking it sounded like a great plan. "I'm sure people loved the traditional Indigo Island Thanksgiving, didn't they?"

"We didn't much celebrate Thanksgiving over here," Sally Ann said, her arm stirring the pot more quickly. "So whatever he had me make wasn't authentic to anything." Sally Ann had dropped the wooden spoon and stepped away from the pot, picking up an iron skillet filled with a couple of grouper filets.

"Her famous grouper sandwich," Cole said, pointing to the pan.

"Christmas is gonna be the same thing," Sally Ann said, rolling her eyes. "But you're the boss. Just tell me what to do." She turned her back to them to light the stove to fry the fish.

Lily was stunned. There was huge tension between the two of them, but she sensed they both meant well. She has an odd sense of being a referee on a cooking show. It's like they both needed a good yelling at by Gordon Ramsey then a group hug. She looked at Sally's Ann's stiff back and Cole's obvious discomfort.

There was a mystery here. And a challenge. Those were two things that could definitely take her mind off her troubles, as well as give her something useful to do over the next few weeks. The trouble with Christmas was that it was a time for families, and Lily didn't have one. She no longer even had her fiancé, and with Avery married and Blake engaged to Samantha, she was going to be odd woman out more than usual. But before she jumped into anything, she needed to think.

"Cole, I have to get back to the Putnams. Sally Ann, your cooking is fabulous. Thank you for the taste," she said and walked away from the angry head chef to the swinging door.

"Oh, sprinkles," she rifled through the box and found some green and red sprinkles, but no silver balls.

Lily pushed through the swinging door and waited in the empty dining room. She loved restaurants, the challenge of providing good food, the right timing, a good atmosphere, and that something special, the floor presence that made a place feel more like a welcoming home.

"Got the sprinkles? Great." He looked relieved to be out of the kitchen. His face gained color and he smiled, although he still looked embarrassed. "Listen, I'm really sorry about that in there. I really just brought you here to show you the restaurant and give you sprinkles. I didn't…"

"I know. No foul," Lily smiled. "But, really, you've made me think. You know, I might be able to help. I'm not doing anything except baking cookies and decorating trees. And that second task is complete."

"Really?" Cole asked and again pushed his hair back from his forehead, a move Lily recognized as a stress reflex.

"Really," Lily said. "Let's talk more tonight at the Putnam's. Is the timing alright for you or is it the middle of your dinner rush?"

"There isn't much of a rush these days, and Sally Ann prefers her daughter at the host stand over me these days," Cole said. "Cocktails at seven sounds wonderful. Let me give you a coat for the return drive. I can get it back from you tonight."

Lily watched him open the closet behind the host stand and pull out a black puffy down jacket. He held it out for her and she shrugged inside it. It was big, but cozy and smelled like Cole. *Stop it.* She tried to control her heartbeat.

"Thanks so much. I love this place," Lily said, and she meant it. "I will see you tonight."

"Count on it," Cole said and walked her to the golf cart. He watched her until she drove around the bend of the road and into the forest.

Chapter Four

A S SHE PULLED up to the Putnams', Avery barreled down the front porch stairs, barely waiting for her golf cart to stop before she squealed.

"You met somebody!"

"Shhhh," Lily said. "What are you talking about? I just got sprinkles. See?" She held them up.

Lily pulled her out of the golf cart.

"Oh, my God. He's perfect. Single. Beyond handsome. And in the restaurant business!" she said.

"Are you psychic or a spy?" Lily demanded. "Where are you getting all this info?" She followed her excited friend up the stairs and into the grand foyer.

"When you didn't come back home in forever, I drove over to the General Store and asked a few questions. I wonder if he would be better for you, in the long run, than James. You know how wrapped up in work my oldest brother is."

"Avery, Bob just broke off our engagement. I'm not ready to date anyone," she said. "And I don't want to date James. I may never date again."

Avery waved that pronouncement off as if it were a fly.

"You never know when you're going to meet the one," Avery said. "So did you feel anything? Sparks? Fireworks?"

Lily stared at her best friend, embarrassed and amused. Avery was a mind reader.

"More sparks than James?"

"I love James as a brother, Avery," Lily faced her friend. "We kissed once in high school and we both realized we were wrong for each other. Neither of us wants to repeat that mistake."

"I don't know if neither of you does," Avery said softly. "But still, James has no time for fun and is not at all interested in starting a family anytime soon, so as much as I'd like to have you as a real sister, I want your happiness most, so I could settle for this new guy."

"That guy's name is Cole and you haven't even met him," Lily said, "And I was engaged a week ago. Nobody jumps back in the dating scene so soon."

Avery cocked her hip and raised her brows.

"Well, I don't anyway," Lily shrugged out of Cole's jacket and hung it up, hoping Avery wouldn't notice. Still she had to laugh at her friend enthusiasm and optimism, which was always contagious.

"I hear he's gorgeous, looks like Brad Pitt but better. Donny, the clerk at the General Store, said he bought the Smith cottage and lives in the place all by himself. No family, no wife, and that he also bought something called Marshside Mama's but someone named Sally actually runs it."

Lily smiled. "Sally Ann, actually. And I was just at the restaurant getting your sprinkles."

Lily walked with the sprinkles into the kitchen.

Avery, right behind her, squealed again. "So it's true. I hear you two were blocking the door to the store, flirting up a storm."

"There were no storms brewing," she said.

"Not what I heard. I want to meet him."

"You can tonight. I invited him for cocktails. I hope that's okay. I know your mom always…"

"Perfect," Avery squeezed her arm. "Smart girl, Miss-I'll-Never-Date-Again. See, I knew you were interested in him."

"I'm not," Lily didn't dare meet Avery's intense stare. "Well, I am, but it's more his culinary dilemma than him."

Avery rolled her eyes and shook her head. "Right," she mouthed.

Lily's cheeks reddened. Avery knew her too well. "Okay. He is amazing looking."

"Really like Brad Pitt?"

"Better."

Avery sighed. "I knew dragging you here would perk you up."

"Avery, I just got dumped. I'm not ready to date anyone, and who moves to Indigo Island alone, at his age? There must be something wrong with him."

"Or very, very right," Avery said. "You've always wanted to live on the island full time. You even talked to Bob about opening your bakery here."

Lily frowned. Avery might feel like it would be easy for her to jump back into the dating pool, but Lily still felt shattered. Something must be wrong with her. Her dad had left her and her mom for another woman. Bob had left her for another woman. Lily lined up the sprinkles on the counter barely seeing them through the sheen of tears.

"Let's go to the inn and see if Jack is around. He's the new manager. He'll probably be able to tell us all about Cole. Besides, you didn't bring any of those shiny silver balls," Avery said. "The inn will have sprinkles and balls. That way, we don't need to use up all of your new boyfriend's supplies."

"He's not my boyfriend," Lily denied, but spoke to Avery's back.

"Just planning ahead," she said. "You know me, I'm a planner."

∿

AVERY PARKED THE golf cart along the edge of the drive, in what was clearly marked "no parking".

"Come on," she said and hopped out. Lily smiled. Her friend acted like she owned the place. Probably because she did, Lily reminded herself. As they climbed the stairs to the inn, Lily was enchanted by the lights wrapped around the hand railing, and the pots overflowing with poinsettias hung with shiny red balls. Her heart felt lighter. She felt happy, not just because of the Christmas decorations. It was being with Avery. It was meeting Cole. It was feeling as if someday she would be herself again, not always a lonely, grieving person.

Inside, the inn had been decorated in an explosion of sparkling silver and gold. Large, shiny gold bows decorated the massive grand staircase, while smaller silver and gold bows adorned the check-in desk and the concierge desk. The smell of eucalyptus filled the air, blending with the fresh pine. The center of the large lobby was filled with a twelve foot, live pine tree, decorated with white lights and silver and gold ornaments and balls. A gold angel with a golden trumpet graced the top of the tree.

A group of kids ran past them, followed by a pretty young woman with strawberry blonde hair and a freckled face. She was laughing and holding hands with the youngest of the kids.

"Hey, Dorsey!" Avery said.

"Hey, Avery! When did you get here?" she asked and picked the toddler up in her arms.

"Just today. Meet my friend, Lily. Dorsey is head of the Kids' Club for the inn. Looks like you have a bumper crop of kiddos," Avery said as they watched the children cross the lobby, headed toward the back doors and the Kids' Club.

"We do. It has been an amazing season. We've been booked from the beginning of November. We're so blessed to have your dad and brother helping with everything," Dorsey said, as the toddler in her arms tucked his head onto her shoulder and started sucking his thumb.

"They can't speak highly enough about you two," Avery

said.

"Dorsey, come on," a blonde-haired boy of about ten called from across the lobby.

"Tade, I'm coming," Dorsey said. "I've got to go. Sorry."

"No worries. Is Jack around?" Avery asked.

"He's probably having his food service meeting about now. In the kitchen. You know your way. Nice meeting you, Lily," Dorsey said and then she kissed Avery on the cheek and hurried out toward the back doors of the inn, where the kids waited.

Lily followed Avery down the long hallway of guest rooms past the ballroom and into an unmarked swinging door. Suddenly, they were inside a commercial kitchen and Lily felt right at home. "Now this is a kitchen," Lily said admiring the gleaming stainless steel countertops and the industrial appliances.

"Wonder where everybody is?" Avery asked and pushed through another set of doors where instantly, they were at the front of a meeting with more than two-dozen sets of eyes focused on them. "Oops."

"Avery?" Jack said and quickly gave her a hug.

"Sorry to interrupt, we'll come back later," Avery said as a murmur swept through the crowd. Lily was frozen in embarrassment. They'd suddenly appeared in front of the entire kitchen and wait staff of the inn.

"Everyone, this is Avery Putnam, of the Putnam family and her friend?"

"Lily," Avery said and smiled widely at the assembled crowd.

"Thank you for dropping by," Jack said, continuing to talk as if their appearance had been expected. "You'll see Avery and her family here a lot over the holidays and you should be thankful every time you see them. This is the family that saved the Melrose Inn from foreclosure when Top Club pulled out, making your employment possible."

As a round of applause burst from the audience, Avery kissed Jack on the cheek and pulled Lily behind her back into the kitchen. "We'll find sprinkles later," she said.

And Lily realized for once, Avery was embarrassed, too. On the drive back to the Putnams, Avery pointed out Cole's house to Lily. It was huge, too large for just one man to live in. It was white with black shutters just like the Putnams, with big windows overlooking the golf course and the sound.

But, unlike the Putnams, Cole's house didn't look ready for the holidays.

"Do you guys have any extra Christmas decorations?" Lily asked, suddenly wanting to share the holiday spirit that was lifting her out of her sorrow.

"I'm sure we do. Mom changes themes all the time, you know. Remember her awful purple and white years?"

Lily winced and nodded. Definitely, she remembered that phase.

Clouds had blown in and there was a bigger chill in the air. It was almost time to drop the plastic flaps of the golf cart and turn on the heater. Lily hugged herself.

"What are you thinking? A little surprise decorating for the second most eligible bachelor on the island?"

Lily smiled. "Exactly. Every other house along here has at least a wreath. He must be sad when he comes home."

"We can't have that, now, can we," Avery said as a light mist began to fall.

Cole

WHY WAS IT the friendly, beautiful girls were always taken, he thought as he drove his golf cart home from the restaurant? The clouds had begun to spit rain, and he was wondering why he'd agreed to go to have cocktails with a bunch of happy, wealthy couples. Those were the type of people he'd left behind when he'd left Boston, the type of people who ruined other people's lives. People like him when he worked and lived in Boston. Only difference here was the Southern accents.

So why was he going? The girl was taken. Still, it was good for business, he reminded himself. Old habits died hard and while Marshside Mama's wasn't Wall Street, the beautiful brunette chef hadn't even heard of the place. That was a problem, especially since Lily has been coming to the island with the Putnams for years.

Cole knew the family owned a large part of the island, and he would love to find a way to partner with them for his future project, which he hoped would finally give meaning to his life and make amends for his years of focusing on money, not people, for becoming someone he didn't want to be. Cole had come to Indigo Island lost, but trying to help Sally Ann had also given him a new idea. He now wanted to start the island's first food bank to help out the hungry people he had met on the backside of the island. He had a lot of ideas, but no one to share them with besides Sally Ann, who firmly suggested he should stick to getting the restaurant out of the Christmas trouble he has created. Meeting the Putnams might be a great chance to start working on both concerns.

He slowed his cart so he could look at the mist rising off the water. It was so beautiful and peaceful here. He thought about tonight, but realized he was more fired up to see Lily again, her perfect pink lips, shy smile, dark shiny hair tumbling around her shoulders, and her melting brown eyes, than he was discussing business. He still remembered the floral fragrance of her hair teasing his senses.

Taken. He reminded himself of the enormous rock on her finger. He sped up his cart again. *Focus on business, not a woman.*

He needed to erase his sins of the past until he thought of enjoying himself. He didn't really think he was worthy of a woman's affection, not after what he and his company had done.

It was safer to stay single right now. Besides, his younger brother was married with twin boys, which kept his mom from nagging him too often. Taking a deep breath, he pulled up to his house and tried to shake off the problems of his restaurant. It had been slow this evening, only one turn of the dining room. Meanwhile, Sally Ann grumbled about the lack of storage space in the kitchen, now that she had some of the supplies for Christmas coming in. She needed to start prepping, but she was out of space, she'd told him on his way out the door. Being at the restaurant was supposed to fill him with a sense of purpose and renewal. Instead it magnified his failures.

All in all, he wasn't in the mood for a party, but he could have a cocktail. And he certainly welcomed the excuse to escape Sally Ann's judging eyes. He had excused himself, promising her he was meeting with the most important people on the island, which was not a lie. He took the stairs two at a time and hoped that a steaming hot shower would lead to an attitude adjustment.

As the warm water hit his tension-filled shoulders, Cole smiled at the thought that at least he would see Lily again. After toweling off, he surveyed his small wardrobe with chagrin and for the first time wished he hadn't donated all his designer suits and clothes to charity, but it had been part of his atonement, and he wasn't going back, so khakis and navy blue button down it was. This was now as good as it could get.

COLE HADN'T BEEN this close to the Putnam Plantation before. It was even bigger than it appeared from the beach. There was an entire wing he couldn't see during his morning jogs. The beauty of the Christmas decorations was overwhelming. Wreaths, garlands, ribbons, lights—name it and they'd decorated with it, he realized, and he was just on the front porch. He dropped the large brass knocker and appreciated the loud metallic thud but with a house so large he wondered whether anyone inside could hear it.

Just then, the huge black door swung open and Avery Putnam introduced herself and welcomed him inside. She was a beautiful woman. Cole was surprised by her simple black sheath dress and minimum of make-up. He would have expected a rich, recently married society woman to scream more money than understated elegance.

"Cole, so glad you could make it," she said and led him into a foyer that boasted the largest live pine tree he has ever seen inside a private home. It was decorated as if it were appearing in a movie. Perfection.

"Sure, um, I forgot to bring wine but I did find some more green sprinkles," he said and reached into his pocket, taken aback by how socially awkward he felt. "It's all we had. No silver beads. I'm going to go over to Savannah for supplies tomorrow, I'll get you whatever you need."

"Forget the sprinkles. We're just so glad you're here," she said, a warm smile lighting her face. "Lily's been my best friend since first grade!"

"Ah, that's great," Cole said, feeling his palms sweating just being in this wealth infused environment, which brought back painful memories. Probably, he should have followed his instincts and stayed home tonight.

"Avery? Is Cole here?"

Lily appeared in the foyer standing next to the huge Christmas tree. To Cole, she looked like an angel. She was wearing a soft white sweater with a rounded neckline that hinted at the swell of her breasts. Her black skirt was fitted and hugged her shape and suddenly it was hard to breathe. He forced his eyes north, but even her dark hair, flowing in waves over her shoulders, begged to be touched. Her brown eyes sparkled in the light from the tree and her cheeks were flushed. Cole swallowed hard, words caught in his throat. Lily was the embodiment of every feminine fantasy he had as a kid and as a man, and she was so off limits it hurt.

"Hey, Lils, just showing Cole the other tree," Avery said, laughing. "The real tree is in the library, that's the one the two of us decorated."

"There is more than one tree?" Cole asked, smiling at Lily until she blushed and looked down. *She's so shy, so beautiful.*

"Actually, we have four live, decorated trees, this one, the one in the library, one in the corner of the dining room and one in the master bedroom," Avery threaded her arm through Cole's and then through Lily's. "My mom's a Christmas nut!"

Avery escorted them into a glorious room. It was paneled in dark wood and lined with a bookshelf on one wall and a full bar on another. A large fireplace with a roaring fire popped and hissed, pouring warmth and light into the room. The brick mantel was decorated, of course, with huge red bows at each end and fresh garland stretched across the length of it. Candles glowed on the coffee table. The scene was so warm and comfortable that Cole's heart ached for home even though he was the one who left and settled here in an attempt to remake his life and his work.

"James, meet Cole Stanton. Cole, this is my oldest brother James," Avery said as the two men shook hands. Cole noticed James held the shake a minute longer than necessary, and squeezed tighter than most firm shakes. *Is he warning me off?* Cole wondered. Maybe James was protecting his sister or Lily? It occurred to him then that maybe James and Lily were engaged. His heart settled in his stomach although he knew he shouldn't care.

"Nice to meet you," James said, finally freeing his hand.

Cole saw the tree Lily and Avery had decorated and added, "You're right. This tree is even more beautiful."

Avery beamed. "And this is Jessica, James's date," Avery added.

Lily was not engaged to James. Cole silently rejoiced and quickly shook Jessica's hand. She had the largest breasts Cole had ever seen. They appeared to strain against the top of her tight red shirt. She smiled, and Cole managed to return the gesture.

"What can I get you to drink?" James asked.

"Whatever you're having," Cole said, amenably as he caught Lily's eye.

James walked to the bar to get Cole's drink and Avery disappeared. It was just him and Lily, and some incredible currents that ran between them. Cole wondered if she could feel the tension also, even as he mentally kicked himself for being so stupid. She might not be engaged to James, but she was engaged. *Taken.*

"Show me your favorite ornament," he said, a lame attempt at conversation.

"Oh, um, since they're not really mine, I don't have a favorite. I just had fun helping Aves," she answered, her long eyelashes masked her gorgeous brown eyes. Cole could almost imagine touching her face as he breathed in the scent of her perfume.

James handed him his drink and moved in between him and Lily.

"James, can you and Jessica help me in the kitchen?" Avery said, "We'll be back in a few minutes. Have a seat you two."

James narrowed his eyes at Cole, but escorted his sister and Jessica from the room.

Lily walked over to the oversized leather chairs and perched on the edge of one. Cole sat down in the chair next to hers. He noticed with a start that she was not wearing the engagement ring. He wasn't sure what that meant, but he couldn't help by feel a smile start inside.

"Tell me why you bought a restaurant," Lily said the light from the fireplace danced across her face and highlighted the golden flecks in her brown eyes.

"Well, it's sort of a long story."

"I have time," Lily said, smiling softly, encouraging him.

"I purchased it to help Sally Ann," he said slowly, wishing he could explain it to her so that it made sense. Even his family hadn't really understood his sense of guilt and responsibility. "She was in trouble, thanks to her nephew's embezzlement. I thought I could make a difference. I thought I had business savvy. In my previous life, I was an investment banker, living a lot like this," Cole said, sweeping his arms to encompass the grand library and all its opulence. "But I ruined so many lives simply caring about the bottom line."

"You worked too hard?" She asked.

"Definitely."

"But how could you possibly ruin lives by working hard to help grow people's investments?" She asked softly.

He took a deep drink and stared into the fire.

"I did."

The silence stretched between them, but instead of being uncomfortable, he felt himself relaxing. She had such a soothing presence. So kind. He could change her sympathetic expression in a few words.

"Cole," she gently touched his thigh.

He felt her all the way to his bones although she clearly wasn't flirting. Her beautiful face was soft with sympathy. "I can tell something is really bothering you. You should share it with someone you trust. Do you have family close?"

His eyes closed. She was so kind, so pure. He shouldn't even be on the same piece of furniture with her.

"I caused a man's suicide," Cole said harshly and stood up. He finished off his drink, crossed the room to the bar and poured himself another. "He was a husband and a father." Cole walked to the fireplace, feeling the warmth on his face. He wished he could burn the shame from his heart.

"One of the investments went badly?" She asked.

He could feel her next to him then, joining him by the fire, her small hand on his arm. He didn't dare look down into her warm eyes.

"Worse than that," he said. "It was a chain of events. Some I'd put in motion. Others I didn't know about. Still, I was his advisor. Someone I'd gone to school with was in charge of the hedge fund. I trusted him, but I hadn't really checked too closely."

"Cole, I don't have a degree in finance, but even I know that investments carry risks."

"His wife came to see me, told me what I had done. Destroyed him, left her and the kids destitute. All I could do was write her a check, tell her I was sorry."

Lily stood in front of him. She took his drink and put in down. Then she placed both of her hands over his empty ones. Her eyes held a hint of tears.

"You didn't deliberately bankrupt that man."

"But..."

She shook her head and gripped his hands harder. She was stronger than she looked, he thought, but he could barely think. He felt like he was falling into her, drowning in the heated warmth of her intense gaze.

"People are responsible for their decisions and actions," she said. "You don't have all the facts about his suicide," she said.

"But..."

"I, too, don't have the whole story," she said, "But I do know that if you came to the island to start over, you should start over."

"If only it could be that easy."

"You have to keep trying, but you definitely have to stop punishing yourself."

"I have been doing just that," he said. "Once I heard her story, I knew our company had hurt more than just this family. I couldn't stomach it anymore. So I quit. Left everything I knew and had and came here." Cole shook his head and smiled ruefully. "When I had lunch at Marshside Mama's with my Realtor and heard Sally Ann's story, about how she was about to lose everything, her business, home, and her family would be destitute with no income, I thought if I could help her it would somehow..." He broke off, realizing his actions probably made as little sense to Lily as they had to Sally Ann, although she'd been grateful he had paid off enough of the restaurant's debts that it could still function.

"My family definitely thinks I've lost my mind."

As well as his friends and former coworkers.

"You have to live with your conscience, not them."

He laughed a little bitterly, but for the first time in months he felt human again. He felt a bit more like himself.

"I've totally interfered with the way Sally Ann's ran her restaurant for years."

Lily picked up his drink, handed it to him and led him back to the couch.

"So tell me what's wrong with your restaurant."

"I thought the restaurant would be my new start. I'd get it on track and then start a food bank. There's more hunger on the island than you'd think. With basic needs satisfied on the backside, I'd start getting businesses and families on the island onboard to build a Boys and Girls Club using my money and community funds to construct it and the restaurant profits to help operate it," Cole said. "But I'm afraid there won't be a club anytime soon at this rate."

"Why? What's happened?" Lily said. She turned to him, her full attention on his face, worry across hers.

"I messed up," Cole said, and couldn't believe he was admitting something he just confessed to himself. "I talked Sally Ann into offering catered Thanksgiving and Christmas meals, hoping to attract a new following to the restaurant."

"That's what she was referring to earlier and I thought it was a wonderful idea," Lily said, tucking a strand of her shiny brown hair behind her ear.

"It's not, if you don't have the capacity," he said. "We don't. We don't have the staff, the storage, the freezer space, or the team to deliver the meals. Thanksgiving was a disaster, with more than half of our orders arriving late in the evening, hours past our guaranteed delivery time. Sally Ann didn't speak to me for a week."

Cole noticed a flicker of something cross Lily's face, something he couldn't read but wanted to.

He smiled. "Sally Ann and her husband Otis have five kids, a love of this island, and a way of doing things that is way better than anything I've figured out. They would be better off without me, I'd bet."

Cole took a deep breath. He couldn't believe he'd just shared all of that with Lily.

"You've already taken the orders for Christmas?" Lily asked, a small smile played at the corners of her mouth. "Can't you just refund the money?"

"No, we took it, used it to fund the Thanksgiving purchases. Dozens of the turkeys went bad before Sally Ann could fix them when one of our freezers died. That's the trouble with Christmas. We have to follow through this time or Marshside Mama's hope of growing, surviving even, is over." Cole shook his head. He hated the sound of failure coming from his mouth. He took a gulp of his cocktail.

Lily stood up. "I can help, if you would like. Everything you want to do is good and needed here on the island. But you're not a chef. I am. And I'm here on the island, on my own, doing nothing through Christmas," her voice briefly faltered, but then she continued. "Perhaps I could come up with a scalable, Lowcountry Christmas dinner that will be both delicious and cost-effective and appropriate for your kitchen,"

Cole watched her eyes light up and caught his breath. She was animated. The sadness he'd sensed inside her was replaced by excitement.

He wasn't sure what Sally Ann would think—and he wasn't even sure what Lily was proposing. He knew chefs were protective of their kitchens, but he did know he was open to help if it meant the restaurant would continue to operate. Also, he would be able to see Lily. The fact she wasn't wearing the ring now threw him a little. She didn't seem like someone who would tease him or cheat on a fiancé, yet she'd worn a ring earlier today but not tonight. Should he ask?

Cole felt so attracted to her. Not just her body or her face but how kind she was. He had to fight the urge to kiss her incredibly full lips.

"I'll do some research tonight and we can meet in the morning, what do you think?" "Okay." He had to drag his mind back to the present.

Then she smiled and walked over to the Christmas tree that twinkled in the corner of the room. "Actually, I do have a favorite ornament on this tree. This one."

Cole walked over to the tree and bent to get a look at what Lily pointed to. He saw two white birds, facing each other inside a handcrafted frame made from glued together Popsicle sticks.

"It's mine. I made it when Avery and I were in third grade together. Back when I thought dreams came true," Lily said and Cole saw that her eyes were a bit misty.

He smoothed his hand down her incredibly soft hair and then pulled her in for a quick hug.

"They do come true," he whispered.

"Lily, it's dinner time," James announced from the door of the library, startling them apart.

Cole watched as Lily brushed the tears away from under her eyes then she turned and smiled at James. "Of course. Are you staying for dinner?" she asked Cole.

"No, thank you," he said, although James's sudden tension almost made him want to say yes. "But let's meet tomorrow.

Why don't you come to my house for breakfast tomorrow, nine a.m."

Lily nodded.

"I've really enjoyed this," he said, barely managing to restrain from touching her again. "Please do tell Avery thank you for having me. Nice spending time with you both," he said, trying to force a smile from guard-dog James.

And before the tension could become any thicker, he left the room and showed himself out. The cold air snapped him out of the ridiculous frenzy of the past moments, and he took a deep breath, exhaled and watched his breath dissipate in the night air. Slowly, he walked down the front steps of the elegantly decorated Putnam Plantation and to the darkness of his golf cart.

What just happened? He wondered as he turned the key in the ignition and, blissfully, the cart responded, and he drove away into the night.

Chapter Five

Lily

A VERY APPEARED IN the foyer just as Cole closed the front door behind him.

"James, did you kick him out?" she asked, hands on hips, mouth an angry line.

"Don't be melodramatic, Avery. He left on his own accord, right Lily?"

"Yes, he had other plans, Aves," Lily said quickly. She hated being in the middle of Putnam family fights. She tried to be Switzerland whenever possible, much to Avery's chagrin.

"James was sent in here to invite him to eat with us," Avery said, glaring at James.

"Well, he had to go. Strange fellow. Just can't get a read on him," James said. "I'm famished though, is dinner ready?"

Avery eyed her brother and shot a Lily a look. She shrugged.

"Yes, it's ready. Millie has put everything out, buffet style. Since it's just the four of us and mom. Jessica has already helped herself. Rude."

"Whatever, Avery," James said and headed past them toward the kitchen.

"Coming, Lily?" Avery asked.

Lily would have preferred to stay in the glow of the library Christmas tree and remember the warmth of Cole's embrace, the smell of him, mingled with the Christmas candles and pine. It was strange. She didn't know much about him, yet, only that his former career had left him ashamed and committed to helping others. But that seemed enough right now. After this afternoon and evening, she felt close to him and his goal of improving himself and his small piece of the world.

"Of course," she said and followed Avery into the kitchen.

JAMES AND JESSICA excused themselves after dinner, claiming James had an early morning meeting at the inn. Lily thought it odd James and his date appeared on Indigo Island so soon, but she had forgotten this retreat was now tied to the Putnams' business. Avery's husband Mark and the rest of the Putnam men were back in Atlanta at work. They weren't arriving until tomorrow. Denton and Blake would probably bring dates for Christmas, too. Everyone would be a couple, except for her. That was the trouble with Christmas. There were just too many expectations and not enough sprinkles of magic when someone needed them.

"You two are adorable together," Avery said as soon as they were alone and clearing the table.

"We are not a two," Lily said quickly, but she was embarrassed that her voice seemed to lack conviction because Avery smiled.

Lily began to wrap up the leftovers from their casual meal, which had been a gourmet feast of exotic cheese, charcuterie, fresh field greens, and crisp French bread along with local delicacies.

"Earth to Lily," Avery said, and Lily snapped out of her daydream, hoping Avery hadn't been talking too long. "You like him," Avery accused.

"Yes, he's nice," Lily said trying not to blush. "But I was thinking. Cole has a problem, and I'll bet you can help me figure out how to help."

"You love a good problem, especially when it looks like him, don't you?" Avery teased her while wrapping the leftover shrimp cocktail with a big sheet of aluminum foil.

"I do when it's a culinary problem," Lily said and explained what Cole had told her about his restaurant.

"You two have so much in common," Avery said, dumping the cocktail sauce into a glass container, spilling half of it on the granite counter top. "I think I should let you two solve it together. Plus, I know nothing about the restaurant business, except for how to make a reservation, am I right?"

Lily smiled at her friend. "But that's why I need your input," she said, pouring the remaining kale salad into a bigger glass bowl and sealing the lid. "We need to know what people like you want from an authentic Lowcountry restaurant for Christmas."

"We?" Avery repeated. "He works fast. Bob who?"

"Avery, this is business," Lily said. "But yes, I thought staying busy would help me not think about Bob marrying someone else this Christmas only a few weeks after dumping me."

"I know," Avery said softly. "I shouldn't tease, but Cole is a hottie. And a culinary hottie at that. What could be better?"

"Avery, stop, I'm serious. I'm helping him with his business, that's all. He's not even a chef," Lily said, too embarrassed to look Avery in the face as she was certain she was blushing.

"Okay, honestly, I'd love a meal from a more simple time. A meal with homemade Christmas cookies with sprinkles for desert," she said, laughing.

"Honestly? Isn't that too, well, unsophisticated for the people who have second and third homes on Indigo Island?" Lily said and carried the stemware to the kitchen island.

"No, I don't think so. We come here for a simple pace, to a more peaceful place. But then, being creatures of habit, we import the same foods, the same drinks, the same—well—everything. We aren't really experiencing the island, are we?

We're simply making it a reflection of home," Avery said, stacking the dishes in the sink.

Lily couldn't love her best friend any more if she tried. "You are brilliant," she said and hugged Avery hard. "You are so right. Let the inn serve traditional Christmas dinner. Let all of the homeowners who want to make their own Christmas hams and turkeys—either with their staff or on their own—gasp," Lily said with a wink. "Do just that. Marshside Mama's is going to give them a different experience."

"And just what experience will that be?" Avery asked.

"Well, I think I need to take you on a field trip to the restaurant before I can answer that. Let's do that after my meeting in the morning."

At Avery's questioning look, Lily felt her face flush, and she wished she'd kept her breakfast with Cole a secret, at least until it was over.

"You have a date?"

"It's a meeting to discuss the menu," Lily said and began to put the dishes into the dishwasher.

"You're seeing him tomorrow," Avery grinned and kicked off her shoes. She turned out the kitchen light. "That's a date."

Lily was grateful for the dark so Avery didn't see her bright red face.

"Don't read anything into it, Aves. We're discussing a menu," she helped Avery blow out all the Christmas candles.

"I'm not reading anything into it, until you do," Avery said. "I think we've got all the lights, you need to get a good night's beauty rest. Race you up the stairs."

And just as they had done for years, they raced each other to the top. And this time, Lily actually won.

Chapter Six

Cole

W HAT WAS I *thinking?* Cole asked himself for the millionth time. He was a bachelor, living in a huge house somebody else had decorated for their family. He had a Sub Zero refrigerator that was absolutely empty except for coffee and half a bottle of orange juice. He ate every meal at the restaurant, or, on days off, at the inn. He had a few power bars in the pantry if his blood sugar dropped too low after a workout.

He looked at the clock on the wall. It was eight a.m. Lily, if she showed up, would be here in an hour. In a panic, he called over to the inn for room service. He ordered two plantation breakfasts—two eggs over easy, toast, hash browns, a bowl of fruit, and sausage. He added a large pot of coffee and two fresh squeezed orange juices. When the woman taking his order asked for his room number, he told her to deliver it to the members' club. And, he promised an extra big tip if she got it there in twenty minutes or less.

Hanging up, Cole raced outside, hopped onto his golf cart and pressed the pedal to the floor, thankful he had plugged the cart in the night before. He still remembered the way Lily made him feel, the warmth that had spread throughout his body just by being near her. He arrived at the Melrose Inn, but realized he'd been in such a rush he hadn't worn a coat. He hadn't noticed the temperature had dipped below freezing on this gray morning.

Cole didn't feel any chill as he ran up the inn stairs two at a time and bounded into the lobby. Paula, the front desk clerk, eyed him curiously, but he shot her his most innocent smile, and he crossed the lobby, passed the Christmas tree, and walked into the Member's Club. It reminded him of the Putnams' library, dark wood paneling, walls of bookshelves, and a large fireplace.

Cole sat in one of the brown leather wingback chairs and stared out the large windows, across the winter brown rose garden to the white gazebo and the ocean beyond. It was hard to tell where the sky ended and the sea began; it was that type of gray, drizzly, cold morning.

"Mr. Stanton?" a young woman pushing a cart full of room service domed dishes asked.

"Yes, that's me. Thank you so much for getting this all prepared so quickly. I need to load it all into my golf cart. I'll of course bring all the dishes back. Should I pull around back? Yes, that would be better. Why don't you roll on over to that door over there, and I'll be right back," Cole said, knowing he was overwhelming the young woman whose name tag read *Sarah, Georgia.* Cole assumed her name was Sarah and she was from Georgia but it struck him as odd suddenly. Perhaps because he was in a panic.

She stared at him. "You aren't dining here?"

"Look, Sarah Georgia, I'm in a bit of a rush. I'm going to hand you my club card, here you go, and I want you to add a thirty percent tip on the total. Just roll the food over there to the door and I'll be right back," he said and smiled.

He hurried out the way he'd come and maneuvered his golf cart to the ocean side of the inn, parked at the bottom of the stairs, on the oyster encrusted, no carts allowed path, and bounded back up the stairs. He waved at Sarah through the locked glass door.

Sarah turned the knob and reluctantly let him in. She handed him the check, which he signed without reading, stuck his club card in his pocket and said "Let's just start carrying things out. Shouldn't take us more than two trips."

It didn't and soon he drove carefully, so he didn't spill the hand-squeezed juice, back to his cottage. By the time his doorbell rang, Cole had re-plated the meal onto his own dishes, put them in the oven to stay warm, hidden the telltale room service trappings in his laundry room, taken a shower, and shaved. He was, in his mind, perfectly prepared for a relaxing breakfast.

He opened the door. Her smile stole his breath. It was crazy how she did that. Lily was wrapped in a navy blue wool coat, white mittens and hat. Her nose was red with the cold.

"Come on in," he finally said, and she walked inside, oohing and ahhing about how beautiful his home was. The thing was, he didn't have anything to do with the decoration or the planning or any of the little touches that made his house special. He knew this and saw it through her eyes as if for the first time.

Cole was happy to see her ring finger was unadorned again.

"I haven't taken the time to personalize the place," he said, suddenly, wondering why he was confessing to an almost stranger with huge brown eyes with gold flecks in them. She wore a white turtleneck and jeans that fit her perfectly, showing off her amazing body that he needed to stop obsessing about.

"It takes a while to settle in a place. This was a big move for you," Lily said, her sincerity making him feel better.

"I should at least have a photo of my mom and dad," Cole said, "And my brother and his wife and twins. Anyway, let's go into the kitchen. I hope you're hungry?"

"Famished," she says, smiling as she follows him into the kitchen. "Smells great. What did you make?"

"Oh, it's nothing, have a seat," Cole said. As he pulled the eggs out of the oven he realized the yolks were cooked through. The sausage looked like jerky and forget about the potatoes. He didn't know what to do.

"Hey, what's wrong?" Lily asked. "Oops," she smiled when

she looked at the plates. "It's hard to keep cooked foods warm. But don't worry. I can fix this!"

And as Cole watched, Lily did just that. She grabbed both plates from the oven with a potholder Cole didn't know he owned and hadn't ever used. She dumped the contents of both plates into a skillet she'd pulled from below the oven.

"Butter?" she asked.

Cole shook his head.

"I'll use olive oil," she said, grabbing the bottle he thought was just decoration on the kitchen island. Cole took a seat at the island. He liked to watch her cook. He liked having her in his home.

He liked her. Period.

"Okay, I think I've salvaged everything," Lily said as she re-plated their meal. "What kind of sausage is this? It's great!" She added, popping a piece in her mouth.

Cole smiled, knowing he should confess, but he'd made such a poor showing last night telling her about how he'd screwed up so many of the Thanksgiving orders that he was loathe to let Lily know he not only couldn't cook, that he didn't even have food in his fridge.

"It's an Indigo Island specialty. We serve it at the restaurant," he said, hoping she'd leave it at that.

"Pork, chicken?"

"Pork," he said, taking the plate she handed to him and following her to the kitchen table.

"It's chicken and sage," Lily said and sat across from him just as the clouds outside started to break up and shoot shafts of light through his windows, lighting her up.

"You had someone cook breakfast for us, didn't you?"

"You busted me," he admitted. "I know. I'm a restaurant owner without the slightest idea how to keep a meal warm. Pathetic."

Lily laughed and took a sip of her coffee. Despite the rough start, Cole enjoyed his meal and her company, but he was torn. He wanted to address the ring, or the relationship the ring implied, but he'd just met Lily. Still, he couldn't get past it.

"I hope I'm not being too forward, but I noticed an engagement ring on your ring finger yesterday and last night it was gone. And I, well, it's not there today either. Did you just forget to put it on or is there a chance you aren't engaged?" Cole said. He felt ridiculous, almost desperate to make his hopes crystal clear.

"I was engaged, for three months, to a man named Bob. We dated for almost five years," Lily said softly.

She slumped a little in her seat, and her face shuttered. Cole was afraid he'd ruined everything. He reached across the table and covered her hand with his. Her hand was so soft, so small. She didn't pull away. Instead, she looked up at him with impossibly sad eyes. He never wanted to see her that sad ever again. He had no idea what this Bob guy had done to her, but he felt Bob definitely needed to be decked.

"I'm sorry he hurt you," Cole said. He needed to hold her, and that was all he thought as he stood and walked around the table. And Lily rose and fell into his chest, as he wrapped his arms around her small frame. "And I'm sorry I brought it up," he said, chin resting on the top of her head. He smelled her hair, clean and flowery, and his heart beat faster in his chest.

"Avery said all along he was a snob and a jerk. I didn't listen. I guess I just thought it was all real," Lily said and pulled her head back from his chest to lock eyes with him. "He's marrying somebody else, on Christmas day."

"This Christmas?" Cole asked, stunned.

"Yes," Lily said and buried her face in his shirt again.

"Good riddance," he said. "His loss. You don't need someone like that in your life."

Lily's tears dampened his chest, but she laughed a little. "Are you for real?" she asked.

He reached down and swept the tear off her cheek with his thumb then placed his finger beneath her chin and tilted her head back for a soft kiss. He meant to pull back, but when her lips parted, he instinctively pressed harder. She felt so right in his arms, so yielding, and she smelled wonderful. His arousal increased with Lily's gasp, but reluctantly, he broke off the kiss and pulled her into a tight hug, his heart thudded in his chest. "I'm very real," he said, wishing he hadn't become so instantly and intensely aroused. He wasn't a teenager anymore, but Lily did something to him, yet now was definitely not the time. She'd just broken up with her fiancé, and he had a restaurant to try and run.

"Great breakfast," Lily said and pulled away. "Let's do the dishes and talk about your Christmas catering mess."

Lily stacked their empty plates and carried them to the sink, Cole followed with their glasses and coffee mugs. He was glad that she no longer seemed sad. Instead, her cheeks were flushed and her eyes sparkled. As Lily loaded the dishwasher, she said, "I take it those white boards in the dining room are your plans for the Christmas meal?"

"Yup. I thought I'd use the same system as Thanksgiving, since that was such as success," Cole said and heard her laugh.

She finished putting the dishes into the dishwasher, washed her hands, and walked across the kitchen into the dining room. Cole followed closely behind, enjoying every moment in her presence, but Lily had switched to business mode, he noted, wishing he could get his brain out of the bedroom and back into the kitchen.

"This is your problem right here," she stared at his white boards. "This menu is way too ambitious. The ingredients are too sophisticated, and well, all wrong for your restaurant and Indigo Island, not to mention too high in calories," she said. "I've been thinking about the menu all night, and you definitely want to offer something completely different from what the inn is offering."

Cole had been thinking about something all last night, too, only his obsession was standing in his dining room, proposing a solution to his troubles, and he had to get his head in the game.

"What do you mean?"

"Why are you guys even delivering soup? The She Crab Soup is cream based, hard to reheat let alone keep at the right temperature. It's more highbrowed Charleston, than casual Indigo Island," she added, wiping it off the board.

"Turkey, gravy, stuffing, sweet potatoes. Isn't that exactly what you delivered at Thanksgiving?" she asked and Cole nodded, embarrassed and feeling helpless. "Did Sally Ann plan this menu or did you, based on your New England memories?"

"Sally Ann's planned nothing and I don't blame her. She's mad at me because I got us into this mess. She's teaching me a lesson and just saying it's all up to me. I'm at my wit's end," Cole said, his jaw clenched.

"I'm sure the feeling is mutual."

Cole watched as Lily erased the rest of his planned Christmas menu. She grabbed the black marker and wrote:

Marshside Mama's Christmas Feast
Authentic Lowcountry comfort and cheer
delivered right to your door
Indigo Crab Patties
Ol' fashioned pot pie available in three choices:
Vegetable, Chicken, and Pot Roast.
Smokin' Joe's Butter Beans
Indigo Island Cucumber and Tomato salad
Homemade Christmas Cookies with Sprinkles and Glazes

"What do you think?" Lily said, a grin on her face.

"Sounds good," Cole said slowly. "But how does this save time and kitchen space? Still looks like a lot of work. And what are butter beans?"

"They're an Indigo Island staple. They're similar to lima beans," Lily answered, concentrating on the board. "I think this is very doable. Sally Ann and I can make the side dishes and the Christmas cookies a week ahead. Same with the pot pie dough. I have a great recipe. Each pie serves six people. You'll call and confirm the holiday orders beginning today. Ask for their pie preference, and we're set."

"We? You really want to help?"

"I really do," she said.

"Well, I love the idea and the menu," he said and had to fight the urge to pull her in for another kiss. The way the sun streamed through the window made her hair shimmer. "Will you help me explain it to Sally Ann?"

"Absolutely! This is what I love," Lily said and clasped her hands together in excitement. Cole couldn't help himself. He leaned forward, placed his hands on either side of her face and drew her closer. Their lips came together, soft at first but then sexy as he deepened the kiss. Soon Cole was dizzy with desire, turned on to his core. Lily moaned softly, but then she stiffened and pulled away.

"Stop. We need to slow down," Lily said and pulled away. She turned her back to him and faced the windows. "This is too fast. I can't feel this, be like this. I was just engaged, I was going to marry Bob. I was so sad that he broke it off, and now, you appear."

"I'm sorry," Cole said, and he was. He couldn't believe he was so out of control, so turned on and prone to act on his impulses. He'd always been much more deliberate. They had only met yesterday.

"Lily, I'm sorry. I'm not usually so pushy. I just—" He broke off not really knowing how he could explain his deep attraction to her when he couldn't even explain it to himself. "I promise, no more messing around, not until you're ready. If you ever are."

Lily turned around to face him. His stomach tensed as he watched her swallow. He remembered the taste of her mouth, the softness of her lips, the smell of her hair. She looked at him and he knew she felt the electricity, but it was too soon, she had been too hurt to trust again. He needed to be patient.

"I would love your help, though."

She burst into her signature smile.

"I'd love to help at the restaurant. Let's go, so I can discuss menu ideas with Sally Ann."

The awkwardness evaporated and they walked out the door.

Lily

COLE PARKED THE golf cart in the back of what Lily could only describe as a charming white cottage with turquoise trim tucked inside a canopy of moss-strewn oaks. The view of the saltwater marsh beyond was breathtaking, the wood-planked dock was empty of boats, the entire scene was eerily still like a painting. Although she had been here before, the second time really was the charm.

Cole led Lily in through the back door and they arrived in Sally Ann's kitchen. Cole made a quick excuse that he had to set up the dining room, which left the two women to size each other up again.

Once Cole exited, Sally Ann smiled and she welcomed Lily with open arms. Literally. Once Lily explained her ideas for an authentic down home Christmas meal, Sally Ann wrapped her in a bear hug, she oohed and ahhed over Lily's Christmas menu suggestions. She seemed excited Lily incorporated some of Sally Ann's signature dishes. Sally Ann instantly understood they could prepare every dish ahead of time.

"You're my savior, you are, honey," she said still grinning. "He's about to kill me with these holiday notions. I have five kids, a husband, and a mother-in-law who all expect me to be cookin' for them on Christmas, not messing around here with what all the fancy people need."

"I'm so glad to be helping. But don't thank me yet, we still have to get all of this prepped, ingredients sourced. If we start today confirming all the orders, we should be able to get started tomorrow," Lily said.

It was eleven in the morning, and Sally Ann quickly hurried to the corner of the kitchen and pulled a white board from behind the sink.

"Here's what we're serving today," she said and pulled out a black marker, much like Lily had done at Cole's house. Lily stood beside her watching Sally Ann fill the board with today's offerings: Fresh Local Shrimp, Warm Artichoke Dip, Lowcountry Gumbo, Shrimp and Andouille Creole, Indigo Island Devil Crab Dinner, and Carolina Seafood Boil; Salad and Bread, family style.

Even though Lily and Cole just finished breakfast, her stomach growled. The air was filled with the scent of pine, the sweet, salty air of the marsh, and the spices being used in Sally Ann's cooking. The windows were screenless and open to the chilly air outside. Three large iron pots simmered on the stove and voices could be heard from the restaurant's seating area just through the swinging door. Lily felt an essence of comfort and ease here in this kitchen, a feeling so different than any restaurant she'd ever stepped inside.

While Sally Ann finished putting prices next to the menu list, Lily peeked through the door and watched Cole. He was on host duty, seating customers with a warm smile and a personal greeting to those he'd come to know. She loved the way he filled a room, the presence he commanded. But he wasn't threatening or stuck up, the way Bob acted all the time. Cole was kind, and his blue eyes sparkled with genuine interest as he chatted with each guest, whether the person was a wealthy vacationer or a simple island worker. He looked up, caught her watching him, and smiled. She ducked back inside the kitchen.

"You're sweet on him," Sally Ann said, coming up behind her. "I suppose he's a good boy, just has no feel for this business. I'm gonna go on and start taking orders. Want to stick around and help back here today?"

"I'd love it," Lily said as Sally Ann pushed out the door, humming a tune Lily didn't recognize. She looked around the simple kitchen and took stock of everything in front of her. She knew she could make her menu ideas work. In the corner, she spotted two large freezers and opened one to see how full it was. Both of them were about half full. Yes, it would all work just fine.

"Hey," Cole said appearing behind her. Just his voice rushed heat to her core. "So what do you think?"

"It's going to work out great," Lily said, and she heard the happiness in her voice. She was in a kitchen, she was needed, and she was standing close to the most handsome man she'd ever met. For the first time, Lily realized she would be able to move beyond the pain caused by Bob someday, and Cole just might be the man to help her on the path to healing.

But I need to take charge of my own life. Not just rely on Avery or others. She thought helping Cole and Sally Ann would be a great start towards self-healing.

"Sally Ann asked me to stay and help with lunch, get a feel for the kitchen. Is that okay? I thought you could start making those phone calls?"

"Yes, great idea," he said. "I'll make the calls out from the front once I get the lunch crowd seated. And, tell me what you charge an hour, I'm paying you for this."

"I might blow your budget," Lily teased. Cole tensed. "Seriously, consider this a donation to the cause. I want you to open that Boys and Girls Club. The island needs a food bank, and a program of picking up prepared, but unserved, restaurant meals from the inn and all the restaurants on the island each night and serving the food to those in need. I want to be a part of it."

"Thank you. That's amazing," Cole said, resting his hand on her shoulder, their eyes locked. She could stare into them for days.

"Hello? A little help out here?" Sally Ann said, shooting eye daggers at Cole, who rushed out to seat customers and help take their orders. Lily laughed and tied on an apron.

The next two hours passed in a haze of frying fish, boiling shrimp, tearing lettuce, and basically, doing whatever Sally Ann instructed. At the end of the lunch rush, once all the pots and pans and dishes are washed and put away, Sally Ann walked up to Lily and wrapped her arm around her waist.

"You know how to cook," Sally Ann said. "You could be a beenyah, you could."

"Thank you, this was wonderful," Lily said, wiping her hands on her borrowed apron. "What's a beenyah?"

"Ah, dat's Gullah for folks born here on the island. We's a dying breed," she said, releasing her hold on Lily and stripping off her bright yellow apron. "Best get on home, before the dinner service. You come back whenever you want. With or without that one."

Sally Ann smiled and left. Lily stripped off her apron. She looked a wreck. Her face had been steamed in boiling water, her tank top, which she fortunately had worn under her turtleneck, was splattered in frying oil, her Converse tennis shoes sported a new cocktail sauce stain at the toe. But she was happy.

Cole stood at the front of the restaurant, the phone pressed to his ear. He didn't see Lily but she could hear his frustration on his side of the conversation.

"Yes, we promise on-time delivery, ma'am, but if you have concerns, then of course you can cancel. Fine, I know you didn't bring your chef, that's why we're here. Yes, I understand this is my last chance, thank you," Cole hung up, "Ahhhh. I hate this groveling shit."

"Welcome to the restaurant business," Lily said and caught him by surprise.

"Whatever. People could be polite at least," he grumbled, his eyes dark and angry.

"I can't imagine people were polite in the investment banking world," Lily said.

Cole laughed, a sharp sound. "No, they weren't. They were ruthless assholes. I was on Wall Street. Everybody's a jerk. Just out for money. I was one of them."

"Well, in the restaurant business, my experience is that once customers are full, they're happy. So we'll turn these folks into raving fans. Don't worry," she said. "Uh, hey, would you mind giving me a ride back to the other side? I'm a mess."

Cole seemed to focus on her then. A smile crossed his face. "You are a mess. You smell like fish," he said. "Come on. I can make the rest of the calls from home."

As they drove back to the other side of the island, they were both quiet, lost in thought. Lily planned the shopping list for the Christmas meal in her head. Every once in a while, she turned and looked at Cole, but he too was deep in his own thoughts. She couldn't believe she'd met him only yesterday. She checked out his handsome profile, his strong arms, his prominent chin. She felt as comfortable as she did with Bob, maybe even more so. Because it was business, they were focusing on the same goal.

Cole parked in front of his cottage and they both did a double take. A wreath hung on his front door and green garland decorated the railing of the outside deck.

"Looks like a Christmas elf has been here?" Cole said. "How did you do this?"

"This isn't me. This is Avery," Lily said, marveling at how wonderful her friend is. "Do you lock your door?"

"Nope," Cole said.

Smiling, they ran up the stairs to the front door. The scene took Lily's breath away. The entry hall table was covered with greenery and punctuated by red and white striped ribbon. The staircase bannister was wrapped with the same red and white striped ribbon, accentuated with a big bow at the balustrade.

In the family room, a live Christmas tree filled the corner, adorned with white lights. Four brown cardboard boxes labeled "ornaments" were stacked next to the tree. Above the fireplace, shiny red and white balls hung from a swooping garland of fresh greens. The house smelled like Christmas, pine, and cinnamon. Lily noticed a set of three candles and leaned in to smell them.

"I don't know what to say," Cole said. She thought he might have tears in his eyes, but he quickly turned away from her.

"Just say thank you. She is just like you. She loves helping others, giving to others," Lily said and felt the urge to hug him, to comfort him even though she'd told him she needed a lot more time. He was so moved by simple acts of kindness, like someone who thought Christmas would pass him by.

Lily lightly touched his back with her hand, and he turned to face her. She reached up and wrapped her arms around his neck as his hands found her waist and pulled her close. He kissed her and instantly it was so intense both jumped back gasping.

"I got carried away again," he said. "Sorry."

"I'm sorry. I started, but I can't... I don't want to..."

"It's okay, honey, it's okay," he said, hugging her back into his warm embrace. "Let's just enjoy this amazing moment together under my first Christmas tree of my new life."

And as they stood together, hugging next to the tree, Lily began to feel like this could be her new life, too.

Finally she stepped away. She needed to go home, shower, talk to Avery, get her bearings.

"Cole, I need to go home, to the Putnams, get cleaned up," she said.

"Can I see you tonight? We could decorate the tree together?" he asked, and then paused, adding, "I'll get the food breakdown together between now and then, a count of the pot pies." He sensed her nervousness, she realized, so he focused on food. "Then tonight, we can go over what supplies you'll need from Savannah."

He had brought up business to relax her, to get her to let down her guard, and she did. "Sure, that sounds great. Call me later."

Chapter Seven

Cole

H E REALLY HATED cold showers but Lily had left him with no other choice. She'd just been dumped by a jerk, but he couldn't help his body's reaction whenever she touched him, no matter how innocently. She needed time, but he wanted her now. For always. That thought came out of nowhere, but it was true nonetheless. He had never felt this strongly about a woman before, there was something about Lily that completed him in some fundamental way he hadn't even known existed. She filled a space in his soul he hadn't realized was empty. Before he'd met her, he hadn't felt like he would ever find somebody to love, somebody to take care of and to treasure.

His timing sucked. He wanted to be in a committed relationship with her, but she was still reeling from her broken engagement. There was nothing he could do. Shouting 'I'm not Bob,' wouldn't cut it. He was reduced to waiting and hoping. Two of his weakest points. He had always been a man of action.

"Look at me getting all romantic," he chided himself. He was getting way ahead of himself and he'd never felt so out of whack before. As he stepped out of the shower and toweled off, he marveled again about the smells and sights of Christmas now filling his house, a house that had been transformed into a home. Avery had even decorated the kitchen table with a candy cane themed centerpiece to match the rest of the décor. Where did she even find all of this holiday cheer, he wondered?

As he pulled on his favorite light blue cashmere sweater and a pair of jeans, he noticed a framed photo of Lily, laughing in front of a decorated Christmas tree. Pure joy Lily. He challenged himself to bring that expression back to her face this Christmas. He hurried downstairs to convert all of his ego-crushing telephone calls into solid orders: Christmas dinner orders that would highlight the special Lowcountry cooking of Marshside Mama's and be delivered on time.

Lily

SHE PARKED THE golf cart in its spot out front, hurried up the stairs to the main door, and into the foyer. She looked around and smiled, the coast still was clear. She raced up the grand staircase, taking the steps two at a time, and made it to the top in record speed. As she turned the corner, she careened into James.

"Oh, sorry," she said. "I hope I didn't get you dirty."

"Lily," James backed away from her as if she were a skunk about to spray him. "What happened? You're a mess.

"Cooking happened, James," she extended both arms out, palms up, imagining that she did probably look and smell a bit feral to him. "This is the look of a person who has been working in the kitchen for a shift."

"Where have you been lending out your talents?" He demanded in an imperial tone that uncomfortably reminded her of Bob.

Lily was suddenly proud of her messiness, her wild hair, her shiny face, and her food-splattered clothes. She was proud of her smell because it represented the new dishes she had learned to prepare, the new experiences she'd had, and the new confidence she'd gained. She now knew there was life after Bob, and she had no intention of going back. She liked where she now was.

Do one thing every day that scares you. Her favorite saying popped into her head. She'd forgotten this Eleanor Roosevelt quote, and maybe forgotten herself, for the past five years.

"Have you been at the inn, in the kitchen? They let you just grub about?"

Lily nearly tossed her hair back and snorted at him.

"I've been on the backside of the island, near the marsh, helping the cook at a fabulous local restaurant called Marshide Mama's," she relished his bewildered look. Of course James had never been there. "You really should try it. It's going to be the hottest, most desirable reservation on the island after the holidays. Mark my words," Lily said, feigning a confidence she'd determined to internalize.

"Oh, so now you're the arbiter of taste on Indigo Island, are you?" James said with a sly smile.

"I am, as a matter of fact," Lily said because she didn't want to spar with him but wanted a shower. "One of my many talents. See you downstairs later."

"Don't forget we have a family dinner tonight," James said and surprised her by reaching out to brush a strand of hair from her face.

"Of course," she said, suddenly feeling uncomfortable around him. The way he stared at her unnerved her. "See you."

He reached over and brushed a strand of hair from her face. A gentle gesture and Lily smiled.

Once inside her room, she kicked off her Converse tennis shoes inside the door and inhaled the fresh salty sea air that streamed inside the room from the open window. Smiling at Cole's jacket hanging in her closet, she hurried into the luxurious bathroom, turned on the shower and waited for the steam to fill the glass enclosure before undressing and stepping in. She reluctantly glanced at herself in the mirror and her jaw dropped. She looked wild—her hair was as curly as it had ever been, her face was smudged with grease, but as she looked at herself more closely, she noticed she looked happy. Free. Lily smiled and hurried into the shower, the hot, strong current washing the dirt and the day away.

Showered, dried, lotioned, and dressed, Lily looked at her reflection in the full-length mirror in the corner of her bedroom. Her fitted white corduroy jeans, a chocolate brown turtle neck, cashmere sweater, and ankle boots made her feel warm, happy and comfortable, but she really needed to stop stalling and talk to Avery.

She texted Avery: "Where are you?"

Avery instantly answered her text: "Library. Tell me EVERYTHING. Now!"

Lily hurried downstairs to the library.

"Avery, you're not going to believe my day," she burst out then blushed. "Mark! Great to see you! When did you get in?"

Thankfully she hadn't blurted out about Cole.

"I came over with Richard," Mark said, smiling kindly like he always did. "So, Avery's jumping with excitement. Tell us your news."

Us. Lily needed to get used to the fact that Avery and Mark were a couple. She was the third wheel.

"Here, Lils," Avery said handing her a glass of champagne. "Tell us all about Cole and the amazing date."

"It wasn't a date," she said automatically while Avery winked.

"By the way, did he like the candy canes?" She toasted Lily with her glass and the third wheel feeling vanished.

"Oh my gosh, he had tears in his eyes when he looked around, Aves, it was amazing what you did," she said, "Cheers and thank you. You really made his Christmas."

"I think I had a lot of help with that task," Avery said.

"Who helped? Your mom?" Lily asked.

Avery rolled her eyes and laughed.

"I mean you, but yes, Mom helped, and we had fun. She said she actually missed her whole candy cane theme and was happy to put it to good use. Nice place he has. You'll be glad to know, I didn't find any hidden photos of girlfriends or any other weirdness," Avery said as Mark came up behind her and wrapped his arms around her.

"You broke in to some stranger's house, and snooped through his belongings?" he shook his head. "Should I be booking us a midnight flight to Mexico to escape the police?"

"The door was wide open," Avery said. Mark laughed, but she ignored him. "I needed to be sure the guy Lily met is good enough. His house definitely needs personalization, but you can help with that, Lils."

"Goodbye Bob," he said affectionately toying with his wife's hair. "You already have our Lily moving in with this man. Does he have a name? Should I go demand what his intentions are?"

Lily sipped her champagne. She knew Mark was teasing, but it made her feel awkward.

"I have a good feeling," Avery said sagely. "So I want to help her out so she can be as happy as I am. God knows, she can't be left to make these decisions on her own,"

"Hey, you were with me when I met Bob, Avery," Lily said defensively.

"The minute I met him I said 'boring'," Mark intoned. "Clearly both of you are worthless. Bring him around Lily. I will pass judgment."

"I picked you," Avery retorted. "So clearly I know what I'm doing."

"But I picked you, so clearly my skills are superior," Avery sighed and melted against him.

"How was your day?" Avery asked, practically purring as Mark lightly stroked down her slim arms.

Lily looked at them. The third wheel feeling was back, but she envied the love they shared. At the same time, she felt blessed. "It was one of the best days of my life," she said, sitting down in one of the huge leather chairs. "I felt so alive. I can really make a difference in Cole's restaurant business for the holidays, I love his business partner Sally Ann, and I love the ideas he has to bring more nutritious food to the poorer families on the back of the island. And then, tonight, I'm going to help Cole decorate his tree with the ornaments you guys brought over. He's so grateful. All in all, it has been amazing."

Avery and Mark exchanged a skeptical look.

"What?" she asked. "You found a dead body in his closet?"

Avery took a deep breath and sat down in the chair next to Lily. "No, silly, not at all. I did have dad's guys do a background check."

"Avery," Lily began.

"I hope you don't mind. He is absolutely who he says he is. Never married. Complete workaholic, successful until last April when he dropped off the radar and ended up on Indigo Island. Dad's people cleared him. I'm not worried about Cole, Lils, I'm worried about you."

"You were just telling me I'd be good at personalizing his house."

"I know. I get carried away, but seriously, Lils, I'm not sure you're ready to be in a relationship."

"I'm not in a relationship," Lily said.

"Lils," Avery said.

Lily saw the genuine concern in Avery's eyes and loved her for it. Avery sucked in her bottom lip, a nervous sign, a sign only her best friend could detect. She leaned forward and hugged Avery.

"I'm not. I mean, yes, he's attractive. And he makes me feel like someday I'll get over Bob, but really, I'm enjoying helping to plan out the Christmas dinner. And I love his restaurant, and Sally Ann, and all the hard work everyone over there does. And I love learning all the new recipes."

"That sounds so racy," Mark said.

"Be serious. I'm worried," Avery said as her lip disappeared.

"Is this about James?" Lily asked. She had to. He was the elephant in the room. Lily looked over her shoulder to make sure the elephant wasn't entering. "You're not still thinking he and I should date, are you?"

"No, not really," Avery said, not sounding certain. Mark laughed. "I know James is a workaholic. He's not ready to settle down or to put in the time necessary to really build a relationship, and until then, he keeps dating bitches like Jessica, but I guess I still harbor a hope that we could be sisters for real. I'm sorry."

"It's okay," Lily said. "But I'm not jumping into anything with Cole. I think he's interested, but I told him I need time."

"Good for you," Avery said.

"But you still look worried."

"I guess it's the trouble with Christmas. It's a big holiday, and Bob's getting married on December 25th, and well, I don't want you to jump at the first guy who shows an interest just because it's a great time to be in love," Avery said.

Lily stood and walked over to the bar to fill her glass. She looked over at the Christmas tree they'd decorated and spotted her ornament. She smiled. "I know, Aves. I know. That's the other problem with the holiday season. If it's real, you tend to doubt it because it seems too cliché, you know?"

Evalyn walked into the room and smiled at Lily. "Hello dear. I hope your new friend enjoyed the decorations at his house. Avery and the crew and I had a hoot putting them up," she said. "Dinner time everyone."

Lily hurried over to hug Evalyn and followed her out of the library. She planned on having a quick meal with the Putnams and then heading to Cole's house. It could actually be the perfect ending to the perfect day. She texted Cole her plans.

He responded back that he would pick her up in his heated

golf cart. She smiled. Even better. She'd bundle up extra warmly in his black coat.

In the formal dining room, the third Christmas tree, sporting a nautical theme with navy and red shiny balls, twinkled in the corner. Lily sat between James, who was seated at the head of the table across from his father, and Mark. Avery was across the table from her. Jessica was sitting across from Evalyn.

"It sure will be great when Denton, Blake, and Samantha get here," Richard said, passing the spinach salad to Avery.

"When do they arrive?" Lily asked. She was anxious to see Denton and to meet Blake's girlfriend, Samantha. Avery liked her so Lily would, too. Nobody could believe Blake was in a relationship that had lasted longer than a few dates.

"Denton will be here on the twenty-first, as soon as he's finished with exams," Evalyn said, a twinkle in her eye flashed for her youngest son. "Blake is harder to pin down, of course. I assume he'll arrive on the twenty-fourth and leave on the twenty-sixth, unless Sam can talk some sense into him."

James smiled and turned his attention to Lily. "So, when is Bob marrying that Postle girl?"

Lily could barely process the question; her brain couldn't believe he'd asked it.

"James," Avery said. "That is inappropriate. Bob is a bastard and we all think so. We don't care what he does or when he does it."

"Avery, language," Evalyn said, "But I agree. Good riddance."

Lily took a moment to absorb Evalyn's kindness.

"I made a mistake, James. I almost married a self-centered narcissist. Thankfully, he found a richer prize. But it still hurts. I still feel shocked, but I'm determined to move on and find someone who can love me for who I am. Someone who can focus on love, instead of business and find happiness, and I hope I can find that someday. Of course, I wish the same for you. Pass the potatoes, please."

The room was silent as James handed the bowl of mashed potatoes to Lily, glaring at her with his steely, navy blue eyes. *If looks could kill.* She realized he'd taken her words more personally than she meant. Or maybe she did want to say that to squash, once and for all, any Putnam matchmaking attempts. Even Jessica, nibbling on a long, red nail, shot her a withering glare.

"James?" She wasn't sure what to say to make amends. "I didn't..." she began.

"So, Richard, have you been out on the course?" Mark jumped to her rescue.

James stood and tossed his napkin onto his plate. "Excuse me."

The entire table was stunned as he quickly walked out of the room. Jessica pushed her chair back and followed behind him, wobbling on her stiletto heels.

"You hit a nerve, Lils," Avery said quietly.

"I'll go talk to him," Evalyn said, beginning to stand up.

"No, please, Evalyn, it's my fault. Let me go speak to him. I've upset him and ruined dinner. I'm sorry," Lily said and hurried out of the room. She saw the front door close as she reached the foyer and rushed to pull it open.

"He wants to be alone," Jessica said, hands on her hips. "I know Avery doesn't like me and thinks my manners suck, but I don't know why she thinks you're such a prize."

Lily ignored her and hurried outside. James stood on the porch, staring out into the blackness of the ocean beyond. It was a starless, chilly night and Lily could see his breath clouds.

"James, I'm sorry," she said, stepping onto the porch and closing the front door. The twinkle lights in the garland gave the porch a peaceful, candlelight like glow.

"Me too," he said, still not facing her. "I didn't mean to bring up the jerk. I'm glad you're free of him."

Lily hugged herself, relieved they would get past this. She

hated tension with any member of Avery's family. She watched James kick the toe of his loafer against the porch railing. Finally, he turned to face her. He shoved his hands into his pants pockets, and he stared down at the floor like a little kid who had been scolded. Lily had never seen him look so humble, so young.

He suddenly looked up and his dark blue eyes stared straight into hers. Lily tensed.

"The trouble is, I was so glad to hear about your broken engagement that I even agreed to celebrate my birthday at that tiny restaurant with my family, when it wasn't even my birthday," he said.

"That was really nice of you. Avery was worried about me, I guess."

"That's the thing. I was worried about you, too," James said, taking a step closer to where Lily stood. "I still am. I, well, now that you aren't engaged I was hoping that we could spend time together, be together."

He exhaled as his words collided in her ears.

"No, James, you don't. Not really. It's just that we've known each other such a long time, and we're both a bit lonely, and the trouble with Christmas is that it makes you feel alone if you aren't in a romantic relationship." She grasped at words, wanting to explain so that he wouldn't be hurt. "That explains Jessica. She's not your type. Not really. You're just in that holiday state of mind where you think you need to be a couple because everybody else is," Lily said quickly, trying to diffuse the seriousness of his statements.

"I care for you Lily, I do. I always have. I still remember that night." He took a step closer and touched her cheek.

She covered his hand with hers.

"James," she whispered. "I care about you, of course I do, but not like that." She searched his eyes, trying to gauge how to proceed. "That night was so long ago. It was an impulse. It wasn't real."

"It felt real to me."

Lily didn't know what to say.

"I was in high school, James. You were just finishing sophomore year in college. That was a long time ago. I think of you like a brother," she said. "I love you because you're Avery's brother. I'll always love you. but not like that."

"Like what?" James said, his voice low, his eyes dark.

"You know," Lily said, dropping his hand. She felt uncomfortable and began to back away. Suddenly James's hands were on her shoulders, pushing her against the side of the house.

"James, stop," she said firmly not wanting things to be bad between them.

"How do you know unless we try?" His lips were a whisper from hers.

She turned her head away.

"James, no," she pushed him away.

"My God, I'm so sorry, Lily. I thought you might feel the same about me. I mean we'd be perfect together."

She shook her head afraid to look him in the eye and see his expression of hurt or anger. Most women never said no to James.

"Lily, I'm so sorry."

"James," she said, wanting him to go, wanting to get away herself, but she had to fix this for Avery. "Let's talk, please."

"We don't need to talk anymore, Lily. I really didn't mean to push it. I thought. I hoped," he stopped again and turned away from her. "I understand. And I'm sorry. Please believe me, it won't happen again."

"I believe you."

James walked down the remaining stairs and into the dark night.

Lily's body began to shake. She didn't want to hurt him, and wasn't even sure why he would think there was a future for them. Had she lead James on somehow? She should go back inside and sit with Avery's family, but she didn't feel ready to face them.

Maybe she should just text Cole to come pick her up.

"Lils, what are you doing out here? Get inside," Avery says, yanking open the front door and spotting her friend in the shadows. "It's cold."

"Coming. Wonder if you could give me a ride to Cole's," Lily said, not making eye contact. Her shivering was making her voice sound weird. She hoped Avery wouldn't comment.

"Sure. Mark and I are going to go to the inn for a drink. We'll drop you on our way. I'm excited to see the candy cane red and white decorations at night," she said, pulling the door closed behind her. "Meet down here in ten minutes?"

"Perfect," Lily said, hurrying up the main staircase to avoid any conversation. She felt Jessica's stare but ignored her.

Once inside her bedroom, she let out a sigh and started to relax. She didn't want to think about what happened with James. It was a misunderstanding, and she'd handled it. It was over. Just like her engagement. She walked over to the large bedroom window. Typically, the stars and moonlight illuminated the ocean beyond, but tonight the landscape was eerily dark. She wondered if maybe she shouldn't visit Cole. She didn't want to lead him on, but she really enjoyed his company, his smile, his kind eyes, his strong arms. All of him.

Her heart rate kicked up just thinking about his kiss earlier. She had told him she needed time, but was that really true? She felt a slow burn deep in her core as she anticipated seeing him, talking to him, touching him that she couldn't remember feeling for Bob, or for any man like this. But how could she trust her feelings? How could she feel so strongly about Cole, even lust after him, when a couple of weeks ago she'd thought she was going to marry Bob? She'd been excited about marrying Bob.

Was she rebounding? She didn't feel like it. Cole was perfect. He felt right. He was smart and dedicated and willing to admit mistakes. He wanted to do good work with his life. And he was so honest with his feelings. Lily realized now that she and Bob had never discussed their hopes and dreams and mistakes like she and Cole already had. She craved emotional closeness but to be honest, she had to admit Cole was hot, hot, hot. She felt like she was going to ignite every time he looked at her. Maybe for once in her life, she should throw caution out the window and just embrace her feelings and her desires. Not be so consumed by fear.

Taking a deep breath, Lily texted: "Still okay to come over? Avery can drop me in 10 min."

Cole responded: "*Hurry.*"

Lily sent back: "*:)*"

Smiling, Lily hurried into the bathroom to freshen up, grabbed her warmest coat from the closet—full-length white wool with a matching white cashmere hat—and her red mittens, her purse, and Cole's coat for an extra layer. As she closed her bedroom door behind her, she said a silent prayer that James wouldn't be in the hallway.

She ran down the hall and paused at the top of the stairs, spotting Avery and Mark waiting—the perfect couple. They held hands and smiled at each other.

"Hey, you look gorgeous," Mark said, finally glancing away from his wife.

Lily laughed. "I'm wearing the exact same thing I had on at dinner, but you'd know that, if you ever looked away from Avery," she said. "You two are the most perfect couple ever, but that isn't news to you," Lily said as she pulled on her coat, hat, and mittens and followed Avery and Mark out the door.

They climbed into the covered golf cart, Mark at the wheel, and zipped off into the dark night.

"Ooooh it's perfect!" Avery exclaimed as they pulled up to Cole's cottage. "Look at the red and white lights, Mark! So fun!"

"You are a Christmas nut just like your mom, Aves," Mark said, parking so he could help Lily out.

"Do you guys want to come in?" she asked, hoping they'd

say no.

"I think we'll let you two have some private time," Avery answered, blowing Lily a kiss, and by the way Avery cuddled up to Mark, Lily thought it would be good for Mark and Avery to have some alone time as well.

Lily smelled cinnamon and some other spice as she knocked on the door.

Cole opened the door. He wore a white t-shirt that hugged the muscles of his shoulders and arms. His jeans fit him perfectly. Lily resisted the urge to hug him. She smiled and he gently tugged her inside, waving at Mark and Avery. The sound of Nat King Cole singing Christmas songs filled the air.

"Hello, beautiful," Cole said and kissed her on the cheek as he helped her take off her coat. His cottage was warm and inviting. Cinnamon candles burned on the table in front of the roaring fireplace. The Christmas tree was lit, waiting its ornaments. The lights throughout the cottage were dimmed, adding to the sense of comfort. "Make yourself at home, Lily."

She walked into the family room and sat on the big white couch in front of the fire. She felt warm, and safe, and as Cole joined her on the sofa, she smelled his clean scent, and stared into his amazing baby blue eyes. She relaxed close to him and Cole raised his hand and tucked her hair behind her ear.

"I missed you," Cole said softly. "We were only apart four hours and twenty minutes, and all I could think about was you and your eyes, and your smile," Cole said.

Lily swallowed. Her turtleneck felt too tight. She pulled at it and wished she'd worn something not quite so prim. Her stomach clenched at the thought.

"We're going to decorate the tree, right?" she said, smiling.

"Later," Cole said, his blue eyes darkening as he ran his hand through his thick blonde hair.

"You wanted to talk about the shopping list for the Christmas meal?" Lily asked, in a conspiratorial whisper.

"Definitely later," Cole said. "I'd really like to talk about us."

Lily was certain her turtleneck would strangle her.

"Us?" she whispered and he nodded, gently tipping her face towards his.

Slowly he lowered his lips to hers. Lily sighed into his mouth and relaxed into him, loving the strength of his body. She walked her fingers up his forearms and pulled him closer to her as he deepened the kiss. *And this, this is perfect, this is Cole.* Lily was dizzy with desire but he broke the kiss.

"You are so beautiful, Lily. So perfect," he said and played with the bottom of her turtleneck. She smiled, stretched both arms into the air, and he pulled off her sweater. The cooler air of the room hit her warm skin, and goose bumps sprung up across her upper body. Cole pushed her gently back onto the sofa, knelt next to her, and softly kissed her stomach. Lily shuddered. His kisses moved up between her breasts to her neck and her forehead, and then finally, to her waiting lips. She moaned as she pulled him against her breasts, and ran her hands around his broad shoulders and down his back.

"Cole, should we slow down?" Lily said, "I don't want to ruin anything, not before Christmas."

"We've only just begun, Lily. You could never ruin anything. I've never wanted anything, anyone more than you," Cole murmured, his blue stare pierced her heart. She felt a fire burning inside, a fire he'd flamed. His lips were on hers again, hungry, his tongue slid inside her mouth as his hand gently brushed her nipple through her bra. Lily moaned and arched so her breasts pushed into his hands. His fingers slid around her back and unhooked her bra.

"Oh, Cole," she said as he pulled her bra off and buried his face between her breasts, moving to suck a nipple until it was firm, and then he kissed his way slowly to the other breast. Lily plunged her hands into his hair. His fingers stroked her nipples and his lips sent shivers throughout her entire body until Lily felt an explosion deep inside. She reached for him, ran her fingers under his shirt and relished his hard stomach. She slid her hand lower, traced the waistband of his jeans before she pressed her palm to the front of the denim, cupping his erection.

Suddenly, he took both of her hands and pulled them to his lips, kissing the top of each before he stood up. He looked down at her, lying half-naked and pulsing with desire.

"What?" she asked. She frowned, and he rubbed her pouting bottom lip with a finger before he sat beside her.

"I want to take it slowly. To make our first time special," he said and hugged her against his strong chest.

She was confused, a little hurt. "You changed your mind?" she asked and burrowed her face in his chest, breathing him in deeply. He was right. It made her want him more.

"No, not at all. I thought I could control myself better, I'm sorry," he said. "I mean it. But I want to make sure you're ready. Because I'm all in."

Lily's insides were still clenching with need, but her heart listened. "That's the most romantic thing anyone has ever said to me," she said, finally lifting her head away from his chest to look Cole in the eyes. She felt so many emotions, but one of them, she recognized, was close to love. As she looked at his strong chin, his caring face, she smiled. He pulled her up off the couch and wrapped her in a tight embrace. The Christmas lights, the Nat King Cole songs, the smells, this man—everything was perfect.

Finally, she'd calmed enough to have some fun. "Well, take off your shirt then," she said, thinking it's only fair she should get to see him topless. He pulled the t-shirt off over his head and she admired every toned muscle he revealed.

"Even?" he said with a laugh.

"No. Not even close. Hand me your shirt," she said. When he tossed it to her, she pulled it on, savoring the smell of him on her body. She tucked his shirt into her jeans, blousing it to hide her still-erect nipples.

"That looks good," he said and brushed her breast with his fingers.

"Hey, no fair," she said, arms folded across her chest.

"Let's get a drink and start decorating the tree, shall we?" He asked.

He laced his fingers through hers and led her into his warmly lit kitchen. The candy cane centerpiece candle glowed and the lights were dimmed.

"Champagne?"

"Please," she said. "You know, it's funny. I know the importance of taking it slow. I do. I was a virgin when I met Bob, can you believe that?"

Cole turned toward her and handed her a flute. "Yes, I can," he said and pulled her close, his strong arm around her waist. "You're special, Lily. You deserve everything you've dreamed of in life. Including a man who will treasure you, and help you make your dreams come true. Cheers!"

"Cheers," she clinked her glass on his, still standing pressed against him in his beautiful kitchen. Lily felt like she should pinch herself. Could he be real? She worried. *Maybe he just didn't want me that way.*

"And you're sure you weren't, um, turned off by me?"

"Honestly, Lily? You're exasperating," he said and kissed her softly on the lips. "You felt my response. Come on. We have some ornament hanging to do."

Cole

COLE WAS PROUD he controlled himself. It was the right thing to do, of course, but man was it hard—pun intended.

He stood on the stepladder and hung red and white ornaments on his Christmas tree at his house, which overlooked the ocean on a remote Sea Island, laughing and singing with the most beautiful woman he'd ever met. He was the happiest he'd been in his life and was determined not to ruin it. He wanted to get to know her, talk to her about the little things, and the big things, the important stuff, and the small stuff. He wanted to hold her close, make her feel special.

Of course, he wanted to have sex. He couldn't believe her body, her perfect breasts, her sweet curves. He could hardly keep his eyes off her, much less his hands. Cole dropped an ornament, and it shattered on the hardwood floor.

"Sorry," he said, because that was the second time he'd done that. Somehow the hooks seemed to slip right out of his fingers.

"No problem. Goodness knows the Putnams have more ornaments than they know what to do with," Lily said, from somewhere under the tree. "I'm just about finished down here. How's the top of the tree?"

"Just about finished," he said, wondering if he could trust himself to keep his hands off of her for the rest of the evening. He wanted to ask her to spend the night. He wanted that, more than anything.

"Great. We need to get the shopping list together. I'd love to go with you to Savannah. I can't believe I've never been there," she said.

"That would be great. I love it over there and you will, too," he said and wondered how this, them, even happened. It was a miracle, he decided, though he stopped believing in those many years ago. Cole felt like he should call his mom and tell her he had finally fallen in love.

"Hey, what's your favorite Christmas movie?" he asked, climbing down the ladder.

"*Love Actually*," she said and kissed him on the cheek. Her fingers played with his abs and Cole groaned. She hadn't let him put on another shirt. He could handle it if she could, but it was getting harder. *Focus.*

"That's my favorite, too," he said. "It's amazing how random love can be." Cole stacked the empty boxes together and folded the ladder. Lily joined him and they admire his tree.

"It is random, and wonderful, when it happens. The tree looks beautiful," Lily said. "We did a great job."

"We did," he agreed. "Let's get the shopping list finished so we can have a little more fun."

"Hmmm," Lily said, and she followed him into the dining room.

Cole had been busy. One whiteboard was covered with the delivery schedule: Name of customer, time of promised delivery and address, grouped in clusters to make it easier. He had created four different clusters, and hoped he'd be able to round up a couple extra drivers.

The next board was filled with ingredients, and he hoped he'd captured everything they would need, but knew Lily could double-check it. He'd made it through the entire call list, and only six out of twenty four orders had cancelled and asked for refunds.

Lily took her time, processing everything he'd written on each board. "Have you been over everything with Sally Ann?" she asked, still staring at the ingredients board, her back to him, hands on her hips, gorgeous shiny hair cascading down her back. Cole couldn't help it; he had to touch her. He walked up behind her and wrapped his arms around her waist, pulling her to him.

"I thought this was work time," she said over her shoulder, and he kissed the top of her head.

"It is, I'm just helping you concentrate," he said and turned her around to face him. He wanted her.

Now.

She touched his cheek with her hand and he felt electricity throughout his body. "You know, I was upset at first, when we stopped. But now, I think it was an amazing decision." She rose up on tiptoes and kissed his lips, a slow, seductive movement.

He bent his head, pressed his lips into hers and heard her sigh.

"Okay, we waited. Done with that," he said, swooping her up. She wrapped her arms around his neck and laughed, her head tipped back. Cole nuzzled her neck.

"Put me down," she said, her joy rang in his ears as he ran upstairs.

"Lily, I can't wait," Cole said, his voice husky and needy. "Can you?"

He thought he could be a gentleman, thought he could control himself. He couldn't. He hadn't prepared upstairs for company. His bed wasn't made; the lighting wasn't set on dimmers. He didn't care. Lily was quiet in his arms, curled into him. Her unique scent filled him, her hair tickled his nose, and her dark eyes seemed to burn through him to his soul.

He reached his bedroom but didn't turn on the lights. He glanced out the windows and the ocean was dark black. The night was a blank canvas, one he intended to fill with memories. He placed Lily on the bed and climbed in beside her. In the darkness, her eyes shimmered.

"Cole, what are we doing?" she said quietly.

"Would it be okay if I made love to you?" he asked, brushing the hair from her face.

"I thought you'd never ask," she said, hooking her hand behind his neck and pulling him to her for a kiss. He moaned as he quickly pulled his shirt off of her. Finally, they were skin to skin. But it wasn't enough. He reached down to unbutton her pants and she helped him, squirming out of them as he pulled them down. He ran his finger down her thigh. Quickly, he peeled off his jeans and underwear. He straddled her, leaned forward, found her lips, and kissed her deeply. Her arms wrapped around his neck.

"Lily, you're beautiful," he said, moving his lips to her soft neck, to her breast, sucking until her nipple was hard, and then he nipped the taut peak.

"Ahh," Lily said, her hips rising up, which shot lightning straight to Cole's groin, his erection firm.

Cole wanted to taste all of her, and moved down her body, his mouth and tongue lapped her stomach as she moaned and moved beneath him. His hands eased her thighs apart as he lapped at her sex, licking and sucking until his tongue found the tight bud and her hips shot up. His hands caught her hips and pressed her more tightly to him, his tongue stroked her clit over and over before delving into her body. She gasped when he plunged a finger inside her and caressed her silken walls.

"Cole," she cried and sat up, grabbing his hair, as she came in his mouth, shuddering as she dropped back down on the bed.

He rolled her on top of him, holding her until she calmed, kissing her forehead and tucking her hair behind her ear.

"Are you okay?"

"Are you serious?"

"Yes."

"That's never happened to me. Ever," she said, another convulsion racking her small body.

"And you liked it?" he asked, smiling as he held her head between his hands, causing her to look at him.

"It was amazing," she said, and her hips begin to move around his erection.

He kept her on top of him, placed his hands on her side and gently moved her up and down, his erection pinned between their stomachs. When he couldn't take it anymore, he rolled to his side, braced himself on his elbows, Lily beneath him. He took a deep breath.

"Will this be special enough for you? Do you know how much I care? I know it has only been two days," he said, staring into her eyes, wanting her to know how much he meant his words, how much she had climbed inside his heart.

"Yes," she said in a whisper, her dark brown eyes unblinking, trusting him, trusting them.

"Good," he answered, kissed her forehead, her nose, and finally, found her lips. He loved every inch of her and longed to know her completely. "I want you, Lily."

She took a deep breath and ran her fingers across his chest and he looked into her eyes.

"Okay?"

She nodded. He leaned over her, his member poised at her entrance then he slowly eased inside, part of the way.

"Ahh," she said, breathing hard, and he stopped, worried. "Go," she said, her hips moved up as he pushed all the way inside her. He held her there, bending to kiss her tenderly, wanting to pump in and out of her, but holding on to the moment, their first time.

"Now!" she demanded, her muscles squeezing around him, urging him on as he began to thrust in and out, deeper and deeper, as she moved beneath him and their bodies became one. She tightened and released around him and then he finally found relief collapsing, shuddering, beside her. Once he caught his breath he hugged her to his side.

"That was amazing," he said, breathing hard.

"He loves me," she murmured as she cuddled into his side and fell asleep.

Yes, he does. Cole smiled and held her tight.

Chapter Eight

Lily

S HE HAD NEVER cooked so much in her life, even in culinary school. She was fairly certain she had ruined every fingernail. Somehow, she had managed to get a sunburn on her face—although it could have been windburn or frostbite—and she was fairly certain she had gained a few pounds thanks to Sally Ann's insistence on trying everything they prepared.

And she was positive she'd never been so happy in her life.

It was December twenty-second, three days until Christmas, and so much had changed. Ever since she had woken up a week ago with the morning sunlight streaming in the window and a heavy arm draped over her shoulder, she had been smiling. It wasn't just the great sex. It wasn't just the fact they'd decorated a Christmas tree together. Nope. It also wasn't only the shared responsibility of saving his restaurant and his reputation, of planning a meal, and strategizing the future of Marshside Mama's. It was much more. It was the way his blue eyes sparkled that first morning when he had brought her coffee in bed. It was the way they'd talked and held each other before either of them made a move to take a shower or start their day.

It was the way he listened to her as if she mattered, as if she were the center of his world. She had never experienced pure attention. And, Cole admitted, he had not been capable of giving it until now. Until he had learned his own business decisions had caused a man to take his own life, until he'd seen the man's widow's eyes. He was a changed man and that was why he'd moved to Indigo Island to heal and to make an impact. Lily knew she had to forgive Bob his social climbing and for breaking their engagement in order to move forward. Cole's ability to forgive himself was a model for her. Instead of being stuck in anger and feeling like a victim, she'd move on to a new life helping others even as she helped herself grow into a true, balanced relationship with a partner who deserved her love and full attention to as well.

At mid-morning, she was working in Cole's kitchen, rolling the dough out for her fifteenth pot pie. She looked out the window at the golf course and the sparkling sound beyond and thought once again that this was the most gorgeous place she'd ever been. Right here, right now was the happiest she'd been. In this kitchen, rolling out dough, all by herself. She realized the trouble with Christmas came when she relied on other people to bring her happiness. Because they couldn't. She had to feel good about herself before she could allow Cole into her heart, allow her heart to trust and feel again. Like everything in life, to truly live, it must start within.

She pushed up the sleeves of Cole's cozy sweatshirt and wiped her hands on her apron. She and Sally Ann had prepared the pie fillings in the restaurant kitchen, along with the rest of the sides. There just wasn't enough room for Lily to finish the pie crusts and the cookies at Marshside Mama's, so she had taken over Cole's cottage kitchen. Avery and Blake's girlfriend, Samantha, were coming over at noon to start making the cookies. She had plenty of sprinkles and silver beads for Avery.

The kitchen smelled like cinnamon from the candles, but also of mint as Lily tried her hand at making the famous island mint tea, served at all the finest Lowcountry plantations during the Christmas holiday. She'd found the recipe when she had been researching the Christmas menu. It was a pleasing mix of green tea and mint, and she was enjoying a steaming cup.

She and James had finally run into each other, two days after the porch incident. She'd been home at the Putnams to change, and he had walked out of his bedroom at the same moment she passed by in the hall.

It had been awkward.

"Hi, James," she had said casually, feeling her face flush. She was a mess anyway, from spending the night at Cole's, wearing one of his sweaters to keep warm for the golf cart ride home. Cole always made sure she had a cozy sweater of his to wear.

"Hey, Lily. I just want to apologize again for my behavior. I'm embarrassed. I had no idea you had a boyfriend. Well, even if you didn't, I was wrong," James had said, his eyes kind and sad.

"I know. Seriously, please don't think about it again. Okay? Apology accepted," she had said, putting her hand on his shoulder. "You're a great guy. Nothing's changed."

James took a deep breath, relief flooding his handsome face. "Thanks, and you're great, too. See you later." And then he had walked away from her down the hall, while she had hurried the other way to her bedroom. Relieved.

She spent nearly every moment at Cole's, but the two of them were always invited to Putnam cocktail parties and dinners. They'd declined for now as they've needed to work. Cole's goal was to get everything prepped and ready by December twenty-third. Lily thought they could do it, even as Sally Ann shook her head no. They'd made a lot of progress.

Cole surprised her, bounding into the kitchen, a huge smile on his face. "Hey, babe, what smells so minty?" he asked, coming up behind her, wrapping his arms around her waist, lightly kissing her behind the ear which sent desire searing through her body.

"Not now, I'm making pie crust," Lily said, leaning against his strong chest, wishing she could turn and melt into him.

"I just stopped by to help and tell you some great news," he said, nuzzling her neck.

"Ah, huh," she closed her eyes and relaxed against him. "What's the great news?" she asked, feeling a little dizzy as his fingers brushed against her breasts.

"You're killing me," he whispered. "You aren't wearing a bra."

"But I am working."

He laughed a little ruefully. "Whatever happened to mixing business with pleasure? I did want you to know our lunch and dinners are fully reserved at the restaurant, now until after New Year's."

"Great," she said, closing her eyes, losing herself in his touch, as his hand ran underneath the apron, at the top of her pants along her panty line. Her stomach clenched. She was breathless. "Cole we can't."

He pulled her away from the counter and turned her around to face him, kissing her deeply, his hand behind her neck. Her flour-covered hands were still at her side until she couldn't take it. Needing to touch him, she wrapped her arms around his waist so flour now covered his black cashmere sweater.

"Well, hello there," Avery said, sauntering into the kitchen, a huge smile on her face. "I would have knocked, but I just thought we were making Christmas cookies. I didn't know a naughty elf had dropped by."

Lily blushed and wiped her hands on her apron as Cole gave Avery a lecherous grin. "Just keeping the help in line," he said as another beautiful blonde walked into the kitchen behind Avery. "Wow, Marshside Mama's staff just keeps growing."

Lily smiled and walked forward.

"You must be Samantha. I've heard so much about you," Lily said.

"Hi, yes, great to meet you Lily, Cole," Samantha said with a smile.

Lily liked Samantha's warm, easy presence immediately. She was happy for Blake. She never thought Blake would take the time for a relationship, much like his brother James. Much like Cole, she realized, smiling at him.

"I hope you're a better baker than Avery?" Lily teased her best friend, "Or this is going to be a disaster."

"Nope, have no idea what I'm doing in the kitchen, but this sounds like fun," Samantha said. "Although I doubt we'll get much done with that one around."

She pointed to Cole who laughed and kissed Lily on the cheek. "True," he said, as Avery walked over and tried to brush the flour off of his shoulders. It was in his hair and on his cheeks.

"You better go upstairs and change before you head back to the restaurant," Avery said laughing.

"Right you are," Cole said. "See you later, ladies. Time to stop procrastinating and start baking."

Once he left, Avery squeezed Lily's shoulders. "You guys are the cutest," she said. "Now, where are my shiny silver ball thingies?"

"You're getting way ahead of yourself, Aves. First, you two need to make the cookie dough. Wash up and I'll show you all the ingredients," Lily said.

"Make?" Samantha said, wide-eyed. "Don't we just slice cookie dough, you know, from one of those frozen rolls?"

Lily smiled at the two of them, even as she had her work cut out for her. She had an idea. "Hey, Aves, is your mom free? Could she and Millie come over?" Lily asked, calculating with four more hands, hands with experience, they might finish by midnight.

"I'll call her. She would love to be included, Millie, too. Oh, and I think Denton's girlfriend arrives this afternoon. Maybe she could help, too? I could call Dorsey, see if she wants to come over after work," Avery answered, reaching for the telephone hanging on the kitchen wall.

"The more the merrier," Lily said. It was crunch time in the kitchen.

Cole

SALLY ANN HUMMED a Christmas spiritual as she filled a heavy iron pot at the sink. He knew it was a spiritual hymn because he had asked. He'd never heard her hum before. He considered it a happy thing, and hoped it held.

In addition to preparing the evening's dinner offerings, Cole and Sally Ann worked together to prepare two huge batches of Smokin' Joe's Butter Beans and the sweet smell filled the kitchen and the dining room. Lima beans, pig's tails—he almost gagged when she tossed those in—ham hocks and smoked pork neck bone were the secret ingredients. Cole wished he didn't know about anything but the beans, but kept a smile on his face during the whole process.

He took a moment to step outside and enjoy the winter sky at dusk, the old oaks and the dock beyond silhouetted against the indigo blue. This month they were finally going to turn a profit. Every meal was fully booked, lunch and dinner, from now until three days after the New Year. It was amazing to feel like the business would go someplace. He walked back into the kitchen, past the humming Sally Ann, and into the packed restaurant. The first seating was well into their main courses, and a line had formed at the host stand again for the next. At the front of the line Carol, his Realtor, the one who talked him into buying this place and her husband waited. They must have boated over from Hilton Head.

"Cole, the place is on fire," she said giving him a big hug. "I keep hearing about it, from the locals and from the tourists over on Hilton Head. You've really turned it around. And it looks so festive for the holidays!" He proudly showed them to their table.

As they settled in, Carol said, "I heard your girlfriend is something, too. Beautiful and a chef?"

Cole knew his eyes lit up with the mention of Lily. "I'm not sure how I got so lucky. But I feel like my life is beginning all over again, and I love it. She's the greatest thing that's ever happened to me. We're eventually going to want to buy a piece of land to build the Boys and Girls Club. Enjoy your meal and Merry Christmas," he said, hurrying back to seat the next guests.

The place did look amazing, thanks to Avery and the Putnams' Christmas storage room. He wondered if their supply of decorations could ever be depleted. Lily and Avery spent Monday decorating. Each of the dining tables were draped with a bright red tablecloth. Inside, the windows were rimmed with white twinkle lights and bright red bows. Outside, the eaves of the cottage twinkled with lights, and each piling of the dock was wrapped with lights and adorned with a big red bow. If they could afford the electricity, Cole might keep the white lights year round. They added the perfect sparkle to the place at night. He laughed. *Did I really just think that?*

Fortunately, Sally Ann's daughter, Kacey, had agreed to help wait tables and assist at the front, seating customers. Sally Ann added Otis to her kitchen staff, freeing Cole up to start meeting with the other restaurant owners on the island about the Second Servings program. Jack, at the inn, jumped on the idea immediately, donating one of the inn's vans to transport the food to the backside of the island every evening once the restaurant at the inn closed. For now, Marshside Mama's was the distribution point and several of Sally Ann's kids worked the distribution shift, their wages paid happily by Cole.

Lily spent most lunches and evenings in the kitchen, learning to cook the Lowcountry staples side by side with Sally Ann, and she also taught Sally Ann some of her favorite pastry recipes. To say that Lily had helped save this place was an understatement. He couldn't believe just three short weeks ago he didn't know her. And now, he couldn't imagine his life without her.

The final happy diners left the restaurant at 10:30, and Cole was relieved to close the door in their wake. It had been a busy night. All the tables were cleared and wiped down, except for the last one, which Cole took care of quickly, putting the glassware and plates into a plastic tub and then turning out the dining room lights.

As he carried the tub into the kitchen, he spotted Sally Ann loading the dishwasher. She looked beat. Even the cheery red apron Lily bought for her couldn't mask the exhaustion.

"Are you okay?" Cole asked, reaching out and touching her arm.

"I'll be fine, you just worry about yourself and making sure we have everything ready to box and package tomorrow. I'm not missing my Christmas at home, no sir," she said, as Otis looked over with a smile.

"I hope Otis does the cooking on the twenty-fifth," Cole said, winking at the older man who was bagging the last of the kitchen waste.

"No sir, I made enough of all this"—she waved her hands towards the beans cooling on the stove—"we're havin' what the fancy folk are having. It's our food anyway," Sally Ann said, pulling the apron off.

"Great idea," Cole said, knowing he'd have Christmas dinner at the Putnams, anything but a laid back, Lowcountry feast, he presumed. "If it's alright with you guys, I'm going to go check on Lily and the pie and cookie crew. I hope they got everything finished."

"They'd better, we're out of time and space," Sally Ann said.

He knew. They had stacks of storage containers and festive to-go boxes ready to sort the meals by family tomorrow. The freezer space had been reconfigured, and a plan was in place. The missing ingredients were all in Lily's hands.

On the drive home, he found himself humming a tune, a Christmas song, and it was beginning to look a lot like Christmas. Even though there wasn't any snow like they had in Boston, lights and cheer were everywhere. Driving past the inn, the bridge over the pond was lit with twinkle lights, as were the palm trees. Huge pots of red poinsettias marched up the stairs to the lobby and a group of happy vacationers burst out of the door.

Cole was envious of their carefree fun. As soon as they got the meals packed up, the delivery schedule firm, he would take Lily to the inn for dinner and dancing. They'd focus on just the two of them, a real date without Marshside Mama's hanging over their heads. He smiled at the thought when he pulled up to his cottage. As he ran up the stairs, he heard quite a few women laughing. Loud Christmas music greeted him when he opened the door. The kitchen was a complete disaster.

The hardwood floors were white, dusted with a layer of flour. The counters and the island were coated with the same white powder, bursts of colorful sprinkles, globs of dough and assorted cookie cutters lay discarded all around. It was as if a Christmas cookie bomb exploded in his kitchen.

"Hi ya, Cole!" Avery yelled from where she stood across the island from him. All the women stopped talking and turned toward him. He saw Evalyn and Millie, Lily with Samantha and another gorgeous blonde he'd never met and Dorsey from the inn. Lily rushed over to him and planted a huge kiss directly on his lips. Her face was smudged with flour, her apron dirty, and her eyes were glassy. He reached for her and smelled brandy.

"Lily, are you drunk?" he asked, laughing as she tried unsuccessfully to straighten his Christmas bow tie—a gift from Avery, or the Putnams' Christmas storage, he wasn't certain. He wrapped an arm around her waist to steady her.

"Nope, just happy, happy. Hey, meet Shelby, she goes with Denton."

Shelby waved from where stood with Samantha.

Lily looked adorable, cheeks flushed and a big smile on her face. He saw Avery hold up a small tumbler of amber liquid and fruit to toast him.

"Glad you all had so much fun and thank you for all the help," he said, and then more softly, "Lily, did you get all of the pie crusts finished and pre-baked? What about the cookies?"

She leaned forward, trying to whisper in his ear, but she missed and touched his chin with her mouth.

"Honey, we got it all done! All of it! And now we're celebrating a little. Want one of these special cocktails? Evalyn made them, and they're great!"

"I think I'll pass," he smiled. "Busy day tomorrow. But, all of you, thank you so much. You've saved Marshside Mama's Christmas!" Cole said, wrapping both arms around Lily, picking her up and kissing her.

"Hey, you two, get a room," Avery said, and then to the others, "Come on, gang. Let's head back to our house and get cleaned up. It's almost midnight! We'll drop you at the inn, Dorsey."

Cole settled Lily against the island, and gave Avery a huge hug. "Can I drive you all home? I don't know how to thank you for all you've done, truly," he said.

Avery turned serious. "Millie is driving, she didn't drink. The only thanks I need is Lily's happiness, and so far, you're doing a great job," she said. "Come on girls!"

The women filed past him, all hugging Lily goodnight. Cole walked behind them and held the door while they climbed into the Putnam golf cart, Millie at the wheel. As they drove off, he closed the door and laughed at the trail of flour they'd left in their wake.

"Sweetheart?" Cole said and walked back into the kitchen.

Lily had pulled out a barstool, and rested her head on her arms amid all the cookie debris. He heard a faint snore, and realized she'd passed out, either from Evalyn's secret drink, or from exhaustion. They'd been going full steam all week. He could feel it, too.

Carefully, he pulled her into his arms. She settled in happily, eyes still closed, breathing deeply. Her dark hair had smudges of flour and a streak of what had to be red icing coated the side of her cheek. He hugged her tightly as he turned out all the lights and carried her upstairs to bed. He placed her on what'd become "her side", the left side, facing the framed photo of Lily, happy at Christmas, that Avery had placed there. Cole hoped he could replace the image with one from this Christmas, one with both of them in it.

After tucking Lily in and kissing her lightly on her cheek, he headed to the bathroom to take a long, hot shower. Tomorrow, everything would come together. All the meals would be prepped and ready for delivery on Christmas Eve day. And Marshside Mama's would be the talk of the Lowcountry.

Chapter Nine

Lily

WAKING UP WITH icing caked on her cheek, fully clothed, had to rank up there with one of the most embarrassing moments of her life. She wasn't precisely sure how she'd made it up to Cole's bedroom, but she had a faint memory of Cole's arms around her. She smiled, looking at the photo of her under the Christmas tree. It was taken at the Putnams years ago, when she was in her early twenties. Before Bob. She allowed herself to think about him for a moment. He was marrying somebody else in two days, and now Lily felt that he had done her the biggest favor. She realized her worth now and what it took to make her happy.

She rolled over to reach for Cole, but his side of the bed was empty. She wondered if she did something, said something, to make him sleep in another room. Panicked, she hopped out of bed, landing on her aching bare feet, and hurried down the hall to check the other three bedrooms. But he wasn't there.

She slowly walked back into the master bedroom and looked out at the sound. It was still and very bright. What time was it, she wondered, realizing in a rush that today was the day they'd assemble all of the meals, and that Sally Ann would be waiting for her piecrusts. She turned on her phone. It was ten a.m. She'd overslept.

Lily hurried into the bathroom, stripped her clothes off and stepped into the shower. She caught a glimpse of herself in the mirror and had to laugh. Her face summed up last night—chaos and laughter. She took a quick shower, skipped make up and dressed casually. She dreaded the mess waiting for her in the kitchen, but when she went downstairs, she was stunned.

The room was spotless. It was as if the cookie caper of last evening never happened. Puzzled, she opened the refrigerator to start pulling out the pies. They were gone. She hurried to the pantry where they'd stored the individually wrapped Christmas cookie orders, labeled by family for delivery. The cookies also were gone.

What is going on?

She grabbed the kitchen phone and dialed Marshside Mama's. Cole answered, his voice made her heart beat faster. "Cole, where's all the food?"

"How'd you sleep?" he asked.

"Sorry about last night," Lily blushed. "I guess I just passed out."

"Don't worry about it. We've all been working so hard. And Evalyn makes a mean Planter's Punch, I hear," Cole said, and she heard the laughter in his voice.

"Um, I don't know how you cleaned the kitchen and hauled all of the food over to the restaurant, without me even waking up, but I'm ready to help," she said. "I feel terrible I'm not there already."

"I have my Christmas elves, too, you know. I left you the golf cart, so come over whenever you want. Don't feel bad, Lils, you've already done so much. You saved Christmas, we all know it," he said. "Sally Ann is nodding in agreement, and she told me to tell you the crusts are perfection."

"I'm so glad she likes them! I'll be right there," she said, hanging up the phone.

Lily pushed the pedal of the golf cart all the way down to the floor, hurrying to get across the island and to be a part of the final packaging of all the catering meals. As she pulled up, she noticed three white vans in the parking lot. She pulled the golf cart around back to the kitchen entrance, parked, and ran inside.

The kitchen was bustling with activity and a bunch of people she'd never seen before all in kitchen whites.

Sally Ann hurried over and gave her a huge hug. "Honey, everything is better than good," she said, releasing Lily and then taking her by the hand. "Cole finally had a good idea and hired us day help. All these folks are from the inn, and they're all in foodservice so they know what they're doing." She led Lily out of the kitchen and into the restaurant. Each of the tables had two or three names written on index cards, and food was being assembled per order.

"Your man has come up with a system," Sally Ann said. "Those ones over there, those three girls, they're each in charge of a family's order, pulling the correct amount of each side, the right flavors of pot pie and the like. Then Cole double checks the order before it's boxed into the cardboard boxes, over there. We should have everything all packed up before the lunch rush."

Lily smiled. It was orderly chaos and it was working. Sally Ann gave her arm a squeeze and headed back into the kitchen. Lily spotted Cole as he came through the front door, his blonde hair a mess, his blue eyes sparkling as he laughed with Denton. She watched them talking together for a moment and then Cole sensed her presence. His head turned her way, their eyes locked. Her stomach clenched as she hurried over and threw her arms around his neck, kissing him on the cheek, before giving Denton a huge hug.

"Hey, Lily," Denton said, "So great to see you. And I like this guy here, way better than boring Bob."

Lily blushed. Avery's youngest brother always treated her like a sister, and he was always blunt. He never liked Bob, and he always told her so. "You were right, D."

Cole wrapped his arm around her shoulder. "We're almost

ready to start delivery. A day ahead of time. Given the Thanks-giving fiasco, all the customers are more than excited to receive their orders today. Those were happy calls."

"I'll bet. What can I do?"

"We have the delivery under control. James, Mark, Denton, Blake, and Richard are all helping, can you believe it? We borrowed four vans from Jack, at the inn," he said, explaining the white vans. "If you could work the front of the house today for lunch, that would be a big help," he said, wrapping an arm around her waist, pulling her close.

"Sure," she said and wished she'd dressed up a little more, her pink fleece not exactly host material, but it would have to do. "Hey. Cole, how on earth did you clean that kitchen?"

He bends down and kisses her softly on the lips. "I wish I could take credit for it. Evalyn said she couldn't live with herself if she didn't send a cleaning crew over. She insisted. Can you believe how quiet they were? She called me this morning, said they'd be there by seven thirty a.m. And they were."

The Putnams are incredible. All of them. "Wow, how are we going to be able to thank them for everything," she said, looking into his bright blue eyes.

"They all keep telling me you're a daughter to them and as long as you're happy, that's all the payback they need," Cole said, shaking his head. "They're amazing. So, how am I doing on paying them back? Are you happy?"

Lily nodded and then folded into his arms for another kiss. She felt his body harden against hers.

"God, you're gorgeous," he whispered. "I hate to leave you even for a second. Let's meet back home this afternoon and have a little celebration."

"See you then," she said, watching him walk away with pure love in her heart.

AFTER THE LUNCH crowd left and the tables were cleared, she cut through the kitchen, and waved goodbye to Sally Ann. She couldn't wait to see Cole. She drove as fast as she could towards the Putnams, hoping she could find Avery home. She did. Avery was in the kitchen with her mom and Shelby, laughing and sipping tea. After saying a quick hello, Lily said, "Avery, could I speak to you upstairs please?"

Avery looked perplexed, but followed Lily out of the kitchen. "What is it?"

"I need something sexy, quick," Lily whispered, pulling Avery up the stairs.

"And you didn't pack anything because you thought you'd be a spinster the rest of your life," Avery said using a thick southern accent. "Poor old Lily, never to have sex again."

"Shhhh," Lily hissed, her face bright red, hurrying into Avery's room.

"You crack me up. You're so puritanical," Avery said, "but that's why I love you. Okay, here are some choices."

Avery pulled open a dresser drawer and started flinging lingerie in Lily's direction. Lily didn't know what she wanted, just that she wanted to surprise Cole. "I don't know, Aves, maybe something Christmassy?"

"Oooh, I like that. Let's go with the candy cane theme of his cottage. Here, this is perfect," she said and handed Lily a ruby red silk camisole and a white lace thong. "Not too slutty, but still sexy."

"Oh, this is perfect. I love it," Lily said and stuffed the items into the pocket of her pink fleece. "Please don't tell anybody, just, don't, okay?"

"Your secret's safe with me," Avery said, and Lily knew her friend fought to keep from laughing. But she didn't care.

"Okay, I'll see you later," Lily said, smiling at Avery before opening the door.

"Have fun, my little sex kitten," Avery yelled after her. Lily blushed bright red, but thankfully, nobody else was in the hall as she ran down to her bedroom to grab some more things.

SHE PROBABLY SHOULD just pack a suitcase and move her things into Cole's cottage, she thought as she carried her things up the stairs. But he hadn't invited her, and she wasn't about to presume. She's grabbed a dress for tonight, her favorite red cocktail dress, which didn't make her think of Bob anymore and all of her makeup. She hoped they'd finally have a chance to celebrate, that maybe, just maybe, he could take the night off from the restaurant. She'd be ready, just in case.

As she walked down the upstairs hallway, she hoped she'd made it home before Cole. Home, she thought, and realized the cottage did feel like home. The white woodwork, the high ceilings, the bright sunny kitchen, the wonderful master bedroom with its oceanfront view—it was out of the pages of a magazine. The scale was much more comfortable to her than the Putnams grand plantation home.

She walked in the bedroom and smiled. "Cole?"

No answer. She hurried into the bathroom and plugged in her curling iron and pulled her makeup out of the bag. She yanked the cami and panties out of her pocket, glad to see they weren't too wrinkled as she undressed and then pulled on her attempt at sexy. She looked in the mirror. *Not bad.*

She added a thin layer of foundation, a brush of mascara and liplossed her lips a red shade. She used the curling iron to add soft waves to her hair, hoping she could accomplish everything before his arrival. She had locked the front door to slow him down, so he'd have to knock to come in, but still, she was nervous. And excited.

She heard the knocker on the door. Her heart thudded. She checked herself one more time in the mirror, unplugged the curling iron, and hurried downstairs. At the last minute, she remembered to look through the peephole in the door. *What if it isn't Cole?*

But it was. She smiled when she saw his confused look staring back through the tiny lens. He wasn't used to locked doors on the island.

She opened the door slowly, standing behind it so he couldn't see her.

"Lily?" he asked, confusion in his voice as he stepped inside.

She closed the door and locked it as he stood staring at her.

"Oh. My. Look at you." He grinned and looked her up and down.

She felt loved and a little bit shy.

"Are those for me?" she asked looking at the bouquet of red roses in his hand.

"Oh, yes, I, yes, honey, you look amazing," he said, holding out the roses with one hand and touching the top of her shoulder with his finger. "And this fits you like a dream," he says, his finger running down the strap of the camisole, and then across her breasts, her nipples instantly responded.

Lily shuddered as Cole took her hand in his. "What do you have in mind?" he asked in a low husky voice.

Lily struggled to keep her breathing even. Her heart pounded in her chest as she stared at his darkened blue eyes.

"Upstairs," she said, trying not to blush, trying to be bold and sexy. She would become the woman who picked her man, instead of having men like Bob select her.

And she picked Cole. "I want to make love to you."

"Oh, Lils," Cole said following behind her, still holding the roses in one hand, her hand in the other.

As she led him upstairs, remembering to sway her hips, she worried. She wished again she'd had a mother who had talked her through things like sex and relationships, but she hadn't. By the time the Putnams became her family, they assumed she knew all of the rules of romance and sex. She didn't feel confident in the bedroom, not at all. Her only experiences had been with Bob. But he hadn't been a patient teacher, nor a considerate lover. She'd discovered the difference with just this little time with Cole. And she wanted to show him how much she appreciated him.

You can do this. You can be assertive in bed. It's not bad. It's good when it's with the man you love.

She pulled him into the bedroom. The curtains were closed but sunlight peeked through in odd streams, adding intriguing light to the otherwise darkened room. Cole put the roses down on the dresser and stood looking at Lily, waiting for her to instruct him further.

Lily reached for him, rubbing her fingers across his sculpted chest, circling each of his nipples and then dropping her hand to his firm stomach, reaching the bottom of his t-shirt. He gasped as she pulled his shirt up and he helped her take it off, tossing it on the floor. Her fingers worked fast, unbuckling his belt and the top of his jeans, unzipping them as she kissed his firm stomach.

Cole moaned and his hands were on her shoulders and then in her hair as she bent to pull his pants down. As he stepped out of his jeans, she quickly pulled his underwear down, releasing him and his already hard shaft. She had never taken a man like this before, but she wanted to with Cole. She knelt before him, sucking and swirling him in her mouth, using her hands to pull him deeper inside.

"Lily, I'm going to—" he cried, trying to pull away, but she held his buttocks tight, as he shuddered and came in her mouth, calling out her name as she tried to swallow it all.

"Honey, that was amazing," he said, still convulsing but helping her up to standing, cupping her chin, tilting her head up so he could stare into her eyes. "Thank you."

She blushed as he picked her up into his arms, holding her tight.

"I know you're in charge, but I would really like to return the favor," he said, kissing her on the forehead as he carried her to their bed, placing her gently against the pillows.

"If you insist," she smiled into his handsome face.

"I do," Cole said and climbed on top of her, straddling her. "I love this top, but it has to go." He pulled at the bottom of the cami and it slid up easily, gliding across her skin, grazing her nipples. Cole lowered his head to her breast, his eyes never leaving hers. Taking one nipple in his mouth he rolled his tongue around it, as Lily arched, pressing into him. "Not yet," he said, biting her nipple, sending an electric current of pleasure and pain soaring to her core. She grabbed his thick hair in both hands.

He moved lower, his mouth making a trail of kisses down her stomach to the line of her white lace panties. Lily was beyond wet, beyond ready, but he stopped. She opened her eyes and looked at him. He stared at her.

"Lily, I love you. I want to spend the rest of my life with you," he said.

"I love you, too, please," she said, pushing into his hand, wanting him inside her.

"Please what?" He kissed the base of her throat, moving back down to her breast, open mouth sucking and then kissing, sending waves of pleasure to her core.

"Make love to me," she said.

"Soon," he answered as he yanked down the lace and plunged his fingers inside her, opening her, expertly finding her center, pushing her closer to the edge. She moaned his name. His mouth worked its way down her body again, caressing her stomach with his lips while his fingers danced inside her until he found the spot that sent her over the edge. She screamed as the orgasm shocked her system. When she finally stopped shaking, she realized Cole spooned her and murmured "It's okay."

"Um," she said as he rolled and pulled her on top of him. She was still shaky but loved the feeling of his chest under her head, his heartbeat in her ear. She felt his erection pushing against her and slowly shifted, positioning him at her entrance.

"Lils," he said as she began moving against him and he arched and pushed inside her, pushing her shoulders up until she sat on him, his shaft in deep, as his hands guided her hips up and down. Lily was dizzy and she clenched, about to come again when he rolled her over onto her back, taking over the rhythm, until they both came together.

Lily opened her eyes but couldn't see a thing. The room was completely dark. She felt Cole beside her and smiled. She couldn't believe all of the things they did together, and just thinking about it made her excited again. She was having trouble recognizing this new sexual person she'd become since she met Cole, but she'd try to get used to it.

She reached over and touched his cheek, and he murmured, "Hi."

"Hi. I'm so hungry. You?" she asked.

"Famished," he said, pulling her into his warm embrace. "Good thing I made a reservation for us at the inn for dinner tonight. And it's in an hour. It's time to celebrate the night before the night before Christmas."

Cole

THE AFTERNOON HAD been mind-blowing. He had been emboldened by her and had tried things he hadn't dreamed of trying with Lily before. And she'd enjoyed it. They'd both enjoyed it.

He showered and changed in one of the bedrooms down the hall. Lily wanted to get dressed and surprise him. She had hoped they would have a date tonight, and he was so glad he had it all arranged. He'd called Jack just a few minutes before and everything was set. It was time to go. He checked himself one final time in the mirror. He wore his only remaining suit from his past life. It was black, and fit perfectly, although he noticed his biceps had gotten bigger since he moved to Indigo Island. Physical labor, he assumed. His tie was, of course, Christmas themed, striped red and white. He matched his cottage décor.

He walked down the hall and knocked on the master bedroom door. "Lily, it's time to go," he said, as she pulled the bedroom door open. His heart pounded in his chest. She looked gorgeous. She wore a tight red cocktail dress that hugged her body in all the right places. Her shiny hair was loose, curled, and flowing over her shoulders. She wore a simple gold and pearl necklace around her neck, and almost no makeup that he could tell.

"What do you think?" she asked, her brown eyes wide, searching his face for approval. Cole realized he hadn't yet spoken.

"You took my breath and my words away," he said, "You look beautiful."

"You look quite handsome yourself," she said, turning to grab her coat off the bed. "Shall we?"

He parked the golf cart in front of the inn and helped her out. They walked up the stairs, enchanted by the poinsettias and the sparkling lights. Inside the lobby, the inn was busy with groups of vacationers admiring the gold and silver tree, or sitting in groups enjoying drinks from the bar. Cole waved to the woman behind the front desk, "Merry Christmas, Paula," he said and he felt Lily squeeze his arm. "What?"

"You're amazing, that's all," she said. As they admired the huge tree, Cole pulled out his cell phone.

"Selfie," he said, aiming the camera at them as Lily started to laugh. "That's what I wanted to see. A joyful Lily, with me. Come on." He would frame this photo, replace the picture next to the bed.

Lily was puzzled as he led her to the grand staircase. "I thought the dining room was down the hall?" she says.

"It is." Cole held her hand and guided her up the stairs. At the top, they turned left and walked down a long hall. He stopped in front of a set of double doors. "We will be dining here," he said and threw open the doors, revealing a formal, private dining room with a long mahogany table, and gold-framed oil paintings lining the walls. The room was lit with candles and the light danced off the paintings and the sparkling glass windows with a view of the white gazebo out on the lawn, lit up and decorated with twinkle lights for the holiday.

Next to the windows, a small table for two had been set, with a white tablecloth, a glowing votive candle, and a single red rose in a crystal vase. Cole helped her shrug off her coat, and settled her into her seat.

"So, come here often?" Cole asked, enjoying the way the light bounced off her hair, her eyes shone. "Are you crying?" Worried, he reached for her hand, covered it with his.

"I'm just so happy," she said, wiping a tear away with her finger. "This is so special. I can't believe you planned this evening."

"And I can't believe you planned this afternoon. Now that was special," Cole said squeezing her hand. "Look, I know we both are amazed by how close we've grown in such a short period of time. I feel like I've known you all my life. I want to be with you for all my life. Lily, will you marry me?"

"What?" she said, looking at him like he was an alien.

Cole stood and walked to her side of the table, knelt on one knee. "I said, will you marry me?" He reached inside his suit coat pocket and pulled out the ring. It wasn't as big and grand as the ring she'd had from Bob, but he really hoped she'd like it. Of course, he got Avery's seal of approval, as well as all the Putnam men.

"This is happening?" she said, dazed. "For real?"

He feared she might faint. He handed her a glass of water from the table.

"Drink this," he said, pulling her into his arms after she'd taken a few sips. "Lily, I want to grow old with you, raise children with you, well, you know, in the right order."

And then he heard it. Her magical laugh. "Yes. Yes, I will marry you."

Cole slid the ring onto her finger and it fit perfectly. It was antique, from an estate sale, handled through the best jeweler in Savannah.

"Well, Lils, do you like the ring? Did I do a good job?" he asked, his arms wrapped around her, holding her tight.

"That's the trouble with Christmas, Cole. It's almost like this is too good to be true," she said, holding her hand out, allowing the ring to sparkle in the candlelight. "I'm afraid I'm dreaming and soon I'm going to wake up in my apartment in Atlanta, all alone, pulling daisy petals."

"It's not a dream," Cole said, wrapping her hair around his hand and tilting her head up for a kiss. "This is the rest of our lives."

"He loves me," she said, her eyes glistening with happiness.

"He always will," he said, meaning every word.

Chapter Ten

Lily

I T WAS CHRISTMAS day, and as she looked around at the smiling faces gathered together in the Putnams' dining room, she saw love and happiness, family and hope.

In the twinkling candles and crystal chandelier light, the dessert course was being assembled on the sideboard. Lily's red velvet and white chocolate layered cheesecake was displayed on a sterling stand, nestled amongst the eucalyptus branches, decorating the table. Avery's sugar cookies—Christmas tree cutouts with white icing, hung with her favorite silver balls, with a Key Lime glaze were arranged on a silver plate. Evalyn and Millie had made sugary peppermint bars, cut into squares and individually cushioned in a bright red cupcake liners. Dorsey and Jack brought gooey brownies from the inn's kitchen. Samantha and Shelby worked together, and made Griscotti—grits plus biscotti. Lily had been skeptical of their choice, but the results, as the crunchy treat melted in her mouth with dried cranberries baked into the mix, had convinced her she was wrong.

Ever since Cole's proposal her life had been a blend of love and festivities. The day after their engagement they had enjoyed a leisurely morning. After getting ready for the lunch shift at the restaurant, they had driven together in the golf cart to Marshside Mama's. Sally Ann's scream scared Otis, who had run into the kitchen from out back, certain she'd chopped off her finger slicing something.

"No, old fool. It's these two. They're getting married," she had said, arms still wrapped tightly around Lily. When she'd finally released her from the crushing hug, Lily had grabbed her own red apron and joined Sally Ann, boiling shrimp for lunch, while Cole headed to the front of the house. By the time lunch was over, enough islanders had heard the news that it seemed the whole island would know.

"We need to go tell the Putnams!" Lily had said, rushing out of the kitchen and pulling Cole away from the reservation list. "They can't hear from anybody but me. I know Avery helped pick out the ring, but still, we need to make it official, and it won't be until I get to tell them!"

By the time they'd bounded up the steps to the Putnam Plantation a thick layer of clouds had covered the sun, the ocean was as gray as the sky. Lily shivered on the front porch as Cole wrapped his arm around her shoulder, pulling her close. "I can't believe I'm actually going to live here, in paradise."

"It is paradise, isn't it? Chilly, but paradise," Cole had said as the door swung open.

"And?" Avery had said, grinning, hurrying them inside. The house smelled like gingerbread and pine and Avery was wearing an apron with a smiling Santa Claus face on it.

Lily grabbed her in a huge embrace. "We're engaged!"

"Yes! Mom, Dad, Mark, Sam, Blake, Denton, James, Shelby, Millie get out here! Oh, and Jessica," she bellowed, as Putnams and girlfriends began to appear from the library, from upstairs, from the kitchen joining them where they stood under the Christmas tree.

Cole had kissed Lily's cheek and took her hand as everyone assembled.

"Avery, dear, what is the commotion all about?" Evalyn had said, hurrying in from the kitchen. "The gingerbread is almost ready and needs to be taken out of the oven."

"Mom. Lily and Cole have an announcement," Avery had said, her eyes sparkling.

Lily had looked up to the top of the stairs where James stood, surveying the scene. She had smiled up at him and he had raised the Stella bottle in his hand in a silent toast.

"We're engaged, everybody. We'll be married this summer, right here on Indigo Island. Thank you all for bringing Lily into my life and for helping me surprise her with the ring. It's only been a short time, but I couldn't ask for a better extended family," Cole had said as Lily wiped the tears from her eyes.

"Well, isn't this great news," Richard had said, offering to open a special wine to celebrate. Lily and Cole had explained they had to go back to the restaurant for Christmas Eve dinner, but they'd be over for Christmas, as planned.

And they were. The meal was spectacular, of course: tomato bisque with blue cheese straws, juicy slices of beef tenderloin with horseradish sauce, sage-crusted pork racks with pear chutney, asparagus with curry dip, mini corn cakes with salmon and fresh dill cream, au gratin potatoes, sweet potato casserole, carrot and cauliflower salad, green beans with hollandaise sauce, and a selection of fine red wines. She tried to save room to try all the desserts. She stood and walked with Cole to the arrangement of Christmas goodies. She was wearing a simple, black velvet A-line dress with short sleeves and black patent pumps. A strand of shiny pearls was around her neck and the only jewelry on her hands was her sparkling engagement ring. Her dark hair was curled in soft waves, shining on her shoulders.

"You look gorgeous, Lils," Cole whispered in her ear.

"I love you so much," she said.

As she helped herself to one of each of the deserts, Lily had a quick flashback to picking petals, alone. She realized with a start Bob's wedding was today. Something so important just a short time ago had happened without Lily giving it a thought. She took a bite of the tip of Avery's Christmas tree cookie, savoring the rich buttery taste, smiling as the silver ball melted in her mouth.

The trouble with Christmas wasn't because of the holiday at all. Christmas was what people made it. It was their choice to focus on the bad things that had happened to them and the people who had hurt them, or choose to focus on the magical, light-filled, sparkling season that promised hope and dreams would come true.

Lily chose happiness.

The End

The Billionaire's Bid

An Indigo Island Romance

Kaira Rouda

Dedication

To Sinclair, Meghan and Lindsey of the Tule Publishing team for making sure this story is the best it can be. Thank you.

And, to you, the reader, thank you for such a warm and wonderful welcome for my very first romance series. Your kindness means the world to me. I hope you enjoy the story!

Chapter One

Aubrey

Wednesday

AUBREY TEMPLETON STOOD up from the conference room table and walked to the nearest window, peering through the slats of the half-closed white plantation shutters. It was another perfect day on Indigo Island. Bright sunshine danced on the ocean beyond the rolling green lawn of the butter-yellow Melrose Inn. Looking the other direction, where the pine trees grew in thick bunches lining the golf cart path, Aubrey saw a young couple snuggling in a huge hammock strung between two strong tree trunks. She smiled as they kissed, and then she turned back to the business at hand.

She was here on this island for business, pure and simple, she reminded herself as she crossed the conference room and took her seat next to her Forest Management Consultant, Dirk Cooley. Her dad's will had been clear: save their land for future generations of Templetons. And that's what she intended to do, she reminded herself, swallowing the lump in her throat.

"Need a glass of water?" Dirk asked and she shook her head. What she needed was for the fifth and final presenter of the day to arrive, she thought, just as James Putnam strolled into the sunny conference room as if he owned the place. To be fair, he did, as Aubrey knew, but still, a little humility would have been appreciated. He was just as cocky as she remembered, she thought, watching his confident gait as he strolled to the presenters' table. He was so arrogant, so damn good-looking and spectacular in bed.

Yes, there was that.

Stop it, she reminded herself, snapping the hair tie on her wrist. She'd dressed carefully today and was wearing her favorite dress, tan, sleeveless and tight fitting. It hugged all of her curves and made each one look good. For shoes, she had pulled on the highest heels she'd dare try to walk in, instantly transforming herself from barely five feet, six inches to almost five feet, nine inches of business power. She'd picked gold jewelry, chunky bangles, several thin necklaces and her mom's ring, for good luck. And even though it was only late April, she had managed the start of a tan since she'd arrived on the island three days before. She looked good with a tan, she knew.

"Good afternoon, everyone," James said as he placed his laptop on the table provided for presenters. Aubrey wondered where the rest of his team was from his logging company, Putnam Industries. It was a huge operation, Aubrey knew. All of the other logging firms had sent at least five representatives. In fact, one company had travelled all the way from China with ten people. But here was James Putnam, alone.

As their eyes locked – his blue and mysterious, hers large and dark brown – she knew he must be remembering their night together in Atlanta a year ago. It had been the best night of lovemaking she'd ever experienced, a one-night stand she couldn't get out of her mind. It had been just after her parents' accident, the start of her year of grief and bad decisions—an unmemorable blur—except for him. They'd had a connection she couldn't forget despite all she'd lost. And now, here he was, standing in front of her in a tailored dark grey suit, a blue tie that matched his eyes, smiling that cocky but somehow sweet smile. She imagined his strong biceps pushing inside the confines of his suit, the arms that had carried her to his bed. She remembered their talk in the early morning as he comforted her through her ever-present tears. But that had been all. She'd never seen or heard from him again until this moment.

And this time she was different. She simply needed closure to her year of grieving and one great night with James was the answer, she'd decided. Then she could move on with her life, clear her family's name and find someone to share the rest of her life with. She knew the stakes were high for her and her family, even as she knew one last romp with James Putnam would get him out of her system for good.

She thought about her family's land, a holding covering almost half of Indigo Island, the verdant forest of green, the freshwater stream cutting through the middle of the property. The Spanish moss hanging from hundred-year Live Oak trees, the signature magnolia tree shading her parents' simple Low Country cottage. There was magic on her family's twenty-five hundred acres of land, and deep roots, her parents always told her, although she'd never taken the time to fully believe it, to live in the moment here. She'd pouted when her parents made her spend holidays and summers here, instead of where "everybody else" was vacationing in Florida. So she'd missed out on loving this place and she was determined to fix that even as she was responsible for preserving it all somehow while trying to pay off the creditors. This was her destiny. She was the only one left. It was up to her to sort it all out. It was up to her to survive, alone.

The lump formed in her throat again, and the familiar tears sprang into her eyes. James started humming. The tune was familiar and yet Aubrey couldn't place it. She wondered if it was one of the songs they'd made love to that night. Was he trying to seduce her already, she thought, as her stomach fluttered. Whatever the song was, the distraction had dried the near-tears and for that she was thankful. She'd had a long day. His was the final presentation.

Sitting beside her, Dirk, her forestry consultant, cracked a smile and said, "Well, aren't you a clever one, Mr. Putnam. Where's your father? The CEO too important to pay us a visit today on little Indigo Island?" Dirk wore a dark green polo shirt that he must have several of, she thought, because that's all she'd ever seen him wear. Also ubiquitous, khaki pants and loafers. His hair was curly and blonde and his green eyes typically were warm and caring. But they weren't now, not when he looked at James, Aubrey noticed.

"This land is your land, this land is my land," James sang, ignoring Dirk's question while smiling at Aubrey, answering her unspoken question about the tune he'd been humming. His dimple on his left cheek, the same dimple she remembered from their night together, was driving her crazy. She needed to focus. On her land. Not on him.

"All set," James said, apparently finished with the power point presentation setup. He crossed the room to where they were seated behind a long rectangular table, to give them a copy of his presentation, she assumed. James held out his hand and Dirk shook it without standing. "To answer your question, Dirk, my dad is ill and addressing his health issues back in Atlanta, a fact most everyone in the industry knows. I'm surprised such an esteemed 'Forestry Consultant' wouldn't know that."

Aubrey watched as the two men stared each other down. The hostility was thick in the room, and Aubrey shifted uncomfortably. Dirk had told her he didn't trust the Putnams, that their bid would be low and the costs of reforestation too high. He'd told her about James' reputation as the billionaire playboy, a pretty boy who was born with a silver spoon in his mouth and no business sense. But Aubrey had insisted on including Putnam Industries in the pitch. She was an Atlanta girl, she believed in family business, and, truth be told, she'd really wanted to see James again. It had become a point of closure for her, to be with him one last time to end her year of mourning. She was counting on his party boy reputation.

And something inside her had wanted him to see her as a businesswoman, a force to be reckoned with, and not just in bed. So, even if James' bid wasn't going to be taken seriously by her and Dirk, she was on this remote Sea Island for a few more nights, with a huge ocean view, king-sized bedroom suite all to herself just a few floors above where they were right now. She remembered what James could do in that type of situation. She'd scheduled his presentation last, hoping he wouldn't fly back to Atlanta tonight.

James was standing in front of Dirk; the only thing separating them was the narrow conference table. He was so close she imagined she could feel his body heat. Aubrey had an urge to reach over and touch the top of his hand as it rested on the tabletop. Fortunately, she was able to cross her arms, quench the urge. She smiled up at him, but James' attention was on the man seated next to her. James' jaw was clenched but he had a smile stretched across his face. Meanwhile, Dirk had leaned back in his chair, crossing his arms. His brow was sweaty. He seemed nervous, Aubrey wondered why.

"I have been named interim CEO of Putnam Industries, a position that will become permanent at the next board meeting." James oozed confidence. "So the CEO of Putnam Industries *is* here, standing right in front of you." James dropped the bound presentation onto the table in front of Dirk. Dirk jumped. "Any other questions about my company or my family's sincere interest in this matter and all matters on Indigo Island, Dirk?"

"Whatever," Dirk said under his breath. Aubrey watched as he bit his left thumbnail and flipped open the presentation, his green eyes darkened.

James turned to Aubrey. "As you may or may not know, Dirk's family and mine go way back. My family's roots dig deep into Indigo Island land and history, and it's an honor to be included in the bidding process, Ms. Templeton. Here's a copy for you," he said, and then gently handed a copy to Aubrey.

As their fingers touched, Aubrey felt electricity surge to her core. She grabbed the presentation from James and flipped it open while holding it up in front of her face, pretending to be reading while actually hiding her blushing face. She could feel his presence, still standing in front of her.

"Oh, please don't read ahead. I know you've had a long day of presentations but not like this one. I want my bid to be a surprise," he said before he walked back to his computer.

She knew he must have felt their connection, too, as soon as their fingers had touched. All of her senses were alive in his presence, as if a whole year apart had evaporated with a simple touch. Of course, their night together was something so magical, so sensually intense, no one could have forgotten it, of that she was certain. Focus, she reminded herself, and turned her attention to the screen in the front of the room.

James

THIS WAS HIS first solo presentation, on a bid he needed to win to impress the board. James felt confident both in his knowledge of the tract in question, and the island in general. He needed to secure this bid to assure his promotion to CEO, and as far as he knew, the only obstacle would be Dirk, who was openly hostile and obviously resented the fact James was even invited into the sealed bidding process in the first place. Somehow, despite Dirk, Putnam Industries had been included, as they should have been, and now it was up to James to land the contract. And once he did, he'd become CEO. It was what his dad wanted, what James of course wanted, but the board wasn't so sure, James knew. His dad's right hand man, Walter, had been with the company for almost forty years. And he'd coveted the CEO title for himself.

"At least for a few years, Rick," Walter had said, pleading his case to James' dad in front of James just two days earlier. It had been an embarrassing meeting, in Rick Putnam's hospital suite, Walter standing on one side of the bed, James on the other, his father a white shadow of himself lying between them.

"I've proven myself to you, for almost forty years. You owe this to me," Walter had said, his balding head shining in the glare of the fluorescent hospital lighting. "You know the board will support my promotion. And I'm sorry, son, but we all agree: with your playboy past and your lack of real executive experience, you just don't have what it takes to run Putnam Industries yet."

James had been about to defend himself, tell the old man he'd been born into the business, and he was ready to lead it when his dad had said, "It's my decision, Walter, and I have selected James. You'll be there by his side to help him out, just like you have me. Now, if you two will excuse me, I need a nap."

It had been an awkward and divisive event. Walter had left the hospital room without a word as James bent to kiss his father's cheek. He hadn't seen the older man since. Walter hadn't showed up at the office the next day. James was certain he had gone into Putnam Industries today, though, because he knew James was out of the office on Indigo Island, on a bid that Walter had refused to assist him with.

But that was fine. James was confident he had this. He was used to relying on himself and had learned to take things one day at a time. He didn't need a team of yes men around him – he'd had too many of those in college and as a young adult. He was the future of Putnam Industries, and he'd prove it, just like his grandfather had when he founded the business. The fact this particular bid was going to a woman who appeared to be a hot debutante from Atlanta and was the second largest landowner on Indigo Island – his home away from home – made him a shoo-in. Not only did he know this island, he knew her type. He'd attracted them like flies to honey, or, he used to, when he was living his former party life. She was one of those women, who wasn't interested in careers and only working until they became a Mrs. to some important Mr. She was a woman, who cared about the season's best parties and fashions. Vapid, gorgeous, easy. Yes, he had known her type, quite intimately.

His playboy past could come in handy, he thought, imagining Walter's expression if he'd ever share that thought. Walter had no imagination or sense of fun. All work, work, work. Although this past year, he'd put more hours in the office than anyone else. While he was proud of changing his life and focusing on his career and building the company, he didn't want to become a Walter in thirty-five years. There had to be a balance, he reminded himself. Eventually he would find a woman he could have fun with and build a life with. A woman who was smart, and fiery, as well as being beautiful, a woman who also was his mental equal, someone who could become his wife. But he wasn't looking now.

He sensed Aubrey Templeton had been checking him out since he'd walked into the room, and she'd blushed when he'd handed her the presentation. That had surprised him. It made her and the bid seem even easier. But he'd changed. He wasn't going to seduce her to win the bid, he wasn't that guy anymore and he wouldn't allow himself to fall back on the old patterns, his old way of living in the world.

It would be so easy to come on to her, ask for a break during the presentation and get her alone, away from Dirk. That was the man he used to be until he'd become sober almost a year ago. The new James would win this bid because he had the best proposal. Dirk was the only obstacle James had worried about. He and Dirk had a long history, none of it pleasant. Which meant the only reason he'd been asked here for a presentation, the only reason Putnam Industries had been given a chance was because Ms. Templeton wanted him here. And her wanting him? Well, that had always worked for James in the past, but he wouldn't go there. Not this time. Not anymore.

James had reached the midpoint of the presentation and believed he was on a roll. Aubrey seemed engaged, even smiling at some of his points. She seemed to especially enjoy the information outlining the island's history from Native Americans, to wealthy plantation owners with slaves, to freed slaves and their Gullah traditions. As he explained the different hard and soft woods native to the island, he thought he noticed tears in her eyes. Good, he thought.

But then, he caught Dirk whispering in her ear, and decided he'd better pause the presentation. "Problem, Dirk?"

"No, not really, it's just that I don't see your environmental certifications on your slides," Dirk said, flipping through the pages of James' presentation, even though he'd asked them not to do so.

James flipped to the page, feeling his first pang of uncertainty.

"An oversight. I can assure you, we are up to date on the highest levels of sustainability and certification. Putnam Industries is one of only three US logging companies that created and adhere to the strictest timber harvesting guidelines," James said, while kicking himself that he had somehow edited out the usual information covering all of this. An oversight, and a stupid one because one of the biggest selling points throughout his presentation would be how to preserve most of her lands' character, even if she was committed to logging it. "We created the notion of thoughtful logging, Ms. Templeton. May I proceed?"

"Yes, please continue," Aubrey said, as she pulled her thick dark hair into a ponytail. "Is anyone else hot? I'm going to pump up the AC a bit if you all don't mind."

"Of course," James said, as he watched her stand up and walk to the wall thermostat. He had to admit, she was gorgeous, with thick dark hair, perfect body and she was wearing a tight-fitting tan dress that hugged her in all the right places. She turned around and they locked eyes. James smiled. Women loved his dimple, he knew, and his smile brought it out. Even if the new James was all business, his dimple was something he couldn't control.

Dirk, on the other hand, rolled his eyes. James knew Dirk would love nothing more than to sabotage any chance James had of securing the logging rights to Aubrey's property. The three Cooley boys and the three Putnam boys had been rivals growing up, with the darkest competition between the oldest, James and Dirk. They'd competed at sports, with women and well, any other manner of one-upmanship possible. That Dirk hadn't been invited into his own family's restaurant chain dynasty hadn't escaped notice in the close-knit society they travelled in. Dirk's temper had flared too often, and in front of the wrong people. His family had forced him out, and he had studied to become, for a reason James hadn't initially understood, a forestry consult-ant. But over the years, James had come to strongly suspect, Dirk's career had everything to do with trying to cut the Putnam family out of any land and forestry deals he could. Ever since he'd hung out his shingle, Dirk had been busy trying to secure business for any other logging company but Putnam Industries.

"Ok, jump back in," Aubrey said, smiling at James as she returned to her seat.

"The bottom line," James wound up with his close. "I've extensively reviewed the forest management plan drawn up by Dirk, and it's completely wrong for Indigo Island, and I believe wrong for your bottom line as well. I think, Ms. Templeton, that Putnam Industries is uniquely in position to manage the timber harvesting as well as to ensure that the land and environment of Indigo Island remain healthy ecologically so that the timber and beauty and health of the forest remain for generations. Instead of merely leasing the logging rights, Putnam Industries would like to offer to purchase the entire tract of land from you. We have been on the land and in the industry for generations, whereas your roots and career are in Atlanta. You'll find the bid and offer on the last page." James smiled.

Kapow, he thought, *I've nailed it.*

Aubrey stared at him open-mouthed. It looked to James like shock.

Another prickle of unease slid down his spine. It was like what he'd said had been completely unexpected. Like he was speaking in another language.

Aubrey dropped her forehead onto her left hand and flipped to the back page of his proposal. She shook her head, and looked up at him.

"This is not what we requested from the bidders," she said, turning to look at Dirk but then silencing him with her left hand as she stood up. "If I had wanted to sell my land, I would have entertained offers. I am appalled that you ignored what we stipulated in the RFP and wasted my time." James saw her face flush. The anger coursing through her was palatable, even from across the room.

"Aubrey, Ms. Templeton, please. I love this island. I love the land and the forests. I could not, with a clear conscience, bid on a clear cut of such pristine lands. Dirk's management plan for your land is a travesty," James said.

She glared at him, arms crossed, the table a barrier between them. He tried to keep his irritation that Dirk would propose what amounted to devastating old grown forest and call it management from letting him lose his temper.

"A travesty?" She echoed. "Did you even read the management plan?" she said, leaning toward him, their faces now only inches apart, her hands clenched in fists by her side. "You must have relied on your staff or something."

"Of course not." James said, feeling more and more that the entire situation was off, and he was beginning to suspect why. "I read every word."

James looked down at Dirk, still seated. The man was smiling and leaning back in his chair. He hadn't missed or misinterpreted anything. He'd been set up, even though he wasn't quite sure how.

"We're finished here, Mr. Putnam," Dirk said, standing. "Come along Aubrey. I told you James Putnam and Putnam Industries would be a waste of time. I'll call the Chinese." He looked back at James, smirking the same idiotic way he had in middle school. "They'll be on a plane tonight. This is over."

James watched with disgust as Dirk escorted Aubrey out of the room, his hand on the small of her back. Neither of them turned around as the door closed behind them, leaving James alone, his carefully prepared presentations both left behind on the table.

It was hard to know what was bothering him the most. The prospect of the Chinese coming in and getting a toehold in the Southern US timber industry? Being set up? The possible clear cut of old growth forest that would have a huge impact on the entire island? The way Dirk had smiled and had his hands all over his client, who clearly had no idea of Dirk's true motives. Over? No way in Hell was this over. He wouldn't give up without a fight.

He gathered up the proposals thoughtfully, weighing his options. He was determined to keep his CEO position. He felt like he owed it to the Island and his heritage as well as his personal goals for his future. He also felt like he owed it to Aubrey. She had no idea who she was dealing with, and he doubted Dirk was only interested in his commission.

Chapter Two

Aubrey

Wednesday Evening

THE SUN WAS setting over Calibogue Sound, the body of water separating Hilton Head Island and Indigo Island, as Aubrey, Dirk and State Senator Hawthorne dined in the upstairs private dining room of The Melrose Inn. The setting was elegant; candles dotted the round table, gold-framed oil paintings of the original plantation owners adorned the walls surrounding them. The service had been impeccable, but Aubrey was bored out of her mind.

"Timber is our state's leading cash crop, Ms. Templeton," the heavyset state senator said as he ordered another scotch on the rocks from the server. "Private owners like yourself control almost seventy-five percent of the land here in South Carolina. You're sitting on a goldmine of land, young lady. Sorry again about your folks, of course. My condolences."

Aubrey forced a smile and then took a sip of her pinot noir, using the wine glass as a prop so she didn't have to talk to him. This disaster of a dinner had been arranged by Dirk, who'd explained the importance of political connections and friendships, especially in this part of South Carolina; no matter who she awarded the logging lease to, she'd need politicians to help pave the way. Dirk had warned that Island neighbors and environmentalists could cause quite a stink, had been the word he'd used.

In turn, Dirk had filled the senator in on the basics of Aubrey's history. Her father's family had owned the 2,500 acres on Indigo Island for four generations, but with her parents' tragic deaths in a car accident a year ago, the land had become hers. The taxes on the land alone were beyond what she could manage on her magazine reporter's salary, even with her recent promotion to Lifestyle Editor. As executor of her parents' estate, she'd been in for a rude shock. Her parents had been living far beyond their means. Her father had taken out a second mortgage on their home, and he still owed a lot of money for her college debts. She'd had no idea that their social lifestyle in Atlanta had been a façade, and that other than their land, the couple held no other assets.

Aubrey touched the gold cross at her neck, a gift from her parents at her college graduation. A gift she now wore everyday since their deaths. She had hoped that she would feel closer to her parents on Indigo Island, perhaps even be able to regain a little of her father's family heritage and make it her own, but the debt made that impossible. When James had suggested selling the land, Aubrey had been shocked, but also angry. She wanted to hold onto it. Keep it in the family, not be the one who lost it, even though she was afraid of that. Dirk's forest management plan and his idea of leasing the timber rights had seemed like the answer to her prayers.

Dirk sat next to her, laughing too hard at each of the senator's jokes, talking too loudly. It was annoying and obvious, at least to Aubrey. She supposed the senator had been at it so long he was immune to suck up, probably lived on it like pelicans slurping up a constant supply of fish. She wasn't certain what they were lobbying the overweight gentleman for, not exactly, but Dirk assured her it was like insurance. Insurance was something she'd wished her dad had kept up, but it was one of the things he'd stopped paying for when the economy turned.

As for Aubrey, she felt like she'd done everything right. She had an approved Forest Management Plan, a Tree Farm Inspection, and now, four bids from certified sustainable logging companies. Dirk was pressing her to accept the Chinese bid, and she supposed he was right. Still, she wished she could go with a local company.

How could James Putnam have botched the bid, she wondered again. She'd seen his reaction, and once her anger had subsided, had realized he had been genuinely surprised and caught off guard. She could only guess he must have confused her management plan with another project he was working on. With his dad so ill, she was sure it was chaotic at the office. But still, it was a shame, because even though Dirk had guaranteed she wouldn't like his offer – and she hadn't, he had been right – she had been looking forward to seeing him again. To hopefully being with him in bed again. He was still as smoking hot as he'd been that night in Atlanta a year ago.

"Aubrey?" Dirk said, leaning toward her. "Do you have an answer for the senator here?" He was prompting her, she realized, but she hadn't heard the question.

"Sorry, must have drifted off for a minute. ADD. What did you ask, sir?" she said as, thankfully, their last course arrived. Vanilla crème brûlée and fresh berries.

"I asked if there was a, what do you all call them these days, a significant other?" the senator asked, his jowls jiggling in the candlelight as he scooped a spoonful of dessert.

"No. I'm focused on my writing career and making the best decisions for my family's land and for my future," she said, meeting his eyes.

"A girl like you must have a bunch of fellas after her," the senator said, playfully.

Aubrey wanted to vomit. Really? He was way more than double her age. She wouldn't play this game, no matter how much she may need a politician in her pocket. She wasn't that type of woman.

"Of course she does, sir, but she's focused, like she said," Dirk said. "Heaven knows she's all business."

Was he drunk? Were they both? Honestly.

"I'm getting tired. I think I'll call it a night," Aubrey said, standing quickly while placing her hand on Dirk's shoulder, pinning him to the chair. "You guys can split my dessert. Dirk, we'll have our recap meeting at nine a.m. so don't stay up too late. Senator, it's been a pleasure," she said, shaking the man's large hand as he struggled to rise out of his seat.

"Pleasure's been all mine, dear," he said, yanking her into a bear hug. His cologne stung her eyes and she pushed away.

Aubrey hurried out of the room, trying to shake off the dinner. She'd handled worse before in her thirty-one years, she thought, taking the grand staircase down to the lobby of the hotel.

"Good evening, Miss Templeton," Jack Means said from behind the front desk of the hotel. He was the general manager of the inn and seemed to be everywhere, all the time. Aubrey wondered if the man ever slept. He was young though, so that probably accounted for his stamina. His cute wife, Dorsey, also was omnipresent at the hotel, usually with a gaggle of guests' children following in her wake.

"Hey, Jack, where's your better half?" Aubrey said, walking over to the desk and plucking a red apple from the silver bowl.

"Dorsey had a huge group at the Kids Cottage today. She's wiped out," Jack said. "Say, Miss Templeton, if you don't mind, could you come with me? I need to show you something, over at the bar."

Aubrey shrugged. "Sure, why not," she said, taking a bite of the apple while following Jack to the cozy bar just past the stairs.

"After you," he said, opening the door to the darkened room. Inside, Aubrey could see one person at the bar, otherwise the place was empty. "Mr. Putnam had the bar shut down for the rest of the night, just so he could have a chance to talk to you alone. He's very sorry about this afternoon."

Before she knew what had happened, Jack had backed out of the room and closed the door, leaving her alone with the shadowy figure in the corner who stood up as she arrived. She started backing up, heading for the door.

"Aubrey, wait, please," James said, crossing the room quickly. His suit coat was off, his dress shirt sleeves rolled up revealing muscular forearms, shirt unbuttoned a few buttons teasing her. His hair was messy, sexy. He was so gorgeous, she thought. "Please, give me a chance to explain."

"There's nothing for you to explain, Mr. Putnam," Aubrey said, but she couldn't leave, couldn't move. In the darkened room, she was intensely aware of just how tall James was, how broad his shoulders were and just how thick his dark blonde hair was. They were standing an arm's length apart. The sexual tension between them was like a thick wire pulling at her core.

She loved sex. She especially had loved sex with this guy, and she was hungry to do it again with him, to experience the mind-blowing pleasure that had helped dim her grief and make her feel alive again. Why should she run away now? Hadn't she hoped to get him alone again? She'd been looking forward to their reunion. Her body was drawn to him, her lips waiting, tingling for his kiss.

"I can't get this afternoon's meeting off my mind. Please, have a seat," he said, his voice low as he pulled out a chair for her. It was a small table for two, tucked into the corner of the empty room. A battery operated candle flickered dimly between them.

"Well, we've got that in common. I've had you on my mind for awhile now," she said, her heart racing as she sat down. In her imagination, James leaned forward, cupped her cheeks in his hands and enveloped her mouth with a hot, wet kiss. The kiss was hungry and needy, firm and sent a rush of heat to her core.

He pulled her closer, putting an arm around her back while the other hand threaded through her hair, cradling the back of her head. . . .

But that's not what happened. Instead, he sat across the table from her, looking puzzled. And then, she realized what was wrong. She could see it in his eyes. She sat up taller in her chair, folding her arms across her chest.

"You don't remember me, do you?" Aubrey asked. Her voice had grown husky, strange to her own ears. Shock and embarrassment bloomed.

"What are you talking about?" he asked.

"Atlanta, a year ago? We met at Whiskey Blue," She said. "It was instant attraction, like tonight," she said.

James' face seemed frozen, tense. She wanted to stop talking, but something drove her on. Disappointment, but also anger. Anger at him, but also at herself for remembering that night. For thinking that it had been special. That she had been special.

"You don't remember."

"I...," James' voice had a catch in it. Guilt shadowed his eyes. "I can't imagine forgetting you."

Aubrey laughed. It sounded brittle in the dim light of the fake candle. Fake, she thought staring hard at the battery operated flame. How appropriate. "The best sex of my life you said. You are an amazing woman, Aubrey, you said. So beautiful."

"Oh, God," he breathed.

"Spare me the fake regret. It probably is hard to keep us all straight."

But to forget me entirely?

Aubrey wanted to slap him. Scream at him. But she didn't want to give him the satisfaction of the drama.

Aubrey looked into his face and saw sadness that mirrored her own.

"Are you sure?" he said, looking into her eyes.

"Definitely," she said flatly.

"I'm sorry," he breathed.

Then he took a deep breath. "Aubrey you are a gorgeous woman. You are intelligent and kind. I feel our connection. I've been trying to fight it all day."

Aubrey crossed her arms and leaned back in her chair, but even she was immune enough to not notice that he looked as confused and upset as he had this afternoon.

"Let me try to explain," he said, looking nervous.

Good. She wanted to watch him squirm. But she also wanted to get out of here. This was humiliating, she thought, getting angrier by the second. He might seem sincere, but he must have a different woman every night. She must have been easy for him to forget. She now knew she was crazy for inviting him here to the island, to the bidding process. What a fool. And now, she looked like a slut.

"Well, this is embarrassing." She sucked in a sharp breath, her body still craving his touch even as her mind took over, beginning to process her humiliation. "For you and me."

She stood up quickly. "It's been a long day. I've got early meetings."

"Aubrey. I'm sorry, about everything. Please. Give me a second chance."

"With this," she said, holding her palms out to indicate herself, "or your lame bid? Forget it." She strode to the door, trying to look assertive and confident, when she felt neither.

"Please, Aubrey, wait. I'm not the same man you met a year ago. I'm not, and I'm truly sorry about what must have happened. I understand that doesn't matter, and that it must seem unforgivable, so don't forgive me."

He moved fast and was now in front of her, forcing her to stop. She stared at the last done button on his shirt, unwilling to look him in the eyes.

"But I am an expert at logging sustainably, and I love this

island. Aubrey, Dirk is not working in your best interests or in the island's best interests. Something's not right. I believe Dirk sabotaged my bid. We have a long history. Very unpleasant. Please."

Her hand reached out to wrap around the doorknob; all she had to do was pull it open, walk away from him and his faulty memory, his stupid dimple and his embarrassing bid of earlier in the day. But she was so drawn to him, like a magnetic force field she couldn't escape. She felt the doorknob turn beneath her hands, and the senator and Dirk entered the room.

"Well, whatcha doing in here, you little beauty? Thought you'd turned in for the night?" the senator said, before he'd noticed James.

"James. I thought you'd be back in Atlanta by now, tail between your legs," Dirk said. "I should have known the billionaire party boy from Atlanta would be the one closing down the bar."

Aubrey took an instinctive step towards James even as Dirk's words sent a jolt of reality through her. James was a party boy, a pretty face who slept with a different woman every night. She'd just been one of many on a list he didn't even remember. She wanted to nurse her humiliation alone, not in front of all of these men, but instinctively she trusted James more than she did the senator or Dirk at the moment. James caught her eye, seeming to ask a question. She looked at the door.

"Good night," James said, holding the door open for Aubrey. "We were just leaving."

"We?" Dirk echoed in surprise, reaching out for Aubrey.

"See you at nine a.m., Dirk," Aubrey said, dodging around him and exiting the room with a sigh of relief.

She hurried to the main staircase. "Thanks for getting me out of there. I'd already ditched them once. Creepy old senator. Not sure what value he brings to anything."

"Dirk's just networking for Dirk. If he can bring you to the table, it makes him look good. That's all," James said. "Aubrey,

I'm sorry about everything. I'd like to try to explain, but you must be tired after such a long day. Can I escort you to your room?"

She smiled at the irony. This was exactly what she'd envisioned, the two of them at the bottom of the grand staircase, about to climb the stairs to her suite. A year later, a full-circle night to remember a catharsis that would allow her to go on with the rest of her life. But he hadn't remembered their first night together, she reminded herself, nor did he seem interested in a second. She was an idiot, basing her escape from a year of grieving on a one-night stand that had happened a year ago. Because even as she stared into his gorgeous blue eyes and wanted him to kiss her, more than anything she'd ever wanted before, she finally realized that whatever weight she'd placed on experiencing his passionate lovemaking again, he shared none of her memories or her feelings.

He hadn't remembered she existed. She took a deep breath, resolved to stay strong. She'd find another path to closure now. "I'll be fine here, thanks, James," she said, climbing the main stairs. "I hope your dad gets better. Take care."

She didn't look back even though every ounce of her being wanted to run back down the stairs and force herself into his arms.

James

JAMES WATCHED HELPLESSLY as Aubrey walked up the stairs. Today had been one of the worst days of his life, he was sure of it. First, he had botched the most important presentation of his career and in the process, he'd managed to upset a beautiful woman whom he'd underestimated in business and forgotten about in bed.

How could he not remember her, he wondered. The physical attraction he'd felt in the conference room, and then again in the bar was palpable, real, like an invisible line was strung tightly between them, a line that had been re-energized by being together in the same room.

Again.

James crossed the lobby and walked outside into the damp, cool April air. His golf cart was parked just outside the inn and he hurried to it, zipping the plastic cover down to provide some protection for the short drive home. As he drove along the golf cart path, he looked to his left and saw Cole and Lily's house, two people who had met on the island and fallen in love. They worked at Cole's restaurant, Marshside Mama's together, and every time James saw them, they looked happier, more in love.

James wasn't certain he'd ever find that. He certainly didn't deserve it yet. Yes, he was determined to turn his life around and had been focused on that task for the past year, giving up drinking, focusing on business instead of pleasure and abstaining from any pursuit of women since he'd so embarrassed himself by chasing after his sister's best friend, Lily.

Still he had a lot of work to do. He'd let himself be tricked by Dirk, and he'd acted like Mr. Pompous, a jerk who'd expected the beautiful young woman, recently an orphan, to throw her land at him just because he walked into the conference room and made a bid. A ridiculous bid according to Aubrey. He had thought by offering to buy the land, at a premium, he'd be doing her a favor. But instead, she'd been insulted. And when he'd tried to recover from his mistake, agreeing to more aggressive cutting of the land, she'd balked. But the Forest Management Plan Dirk had provided with the request for proposals had necessitated clear cutting on eighty percent of the land in order for her to pay outstanding bills. James had read the plan at least ten times. He had it back at the house and would review it again.

But what was worse, at a personal level, was that he hadn't

remembered sleeping with her. The two had instant, electric chemistry. James had felt it the moment he stepped into the conference room, and he could feel it still pulling as he drove home. She'd told him they had met at Whiskey Blue, the rooftop bar at the W in Buckhead. Of course he'd been there, he'd been a regular back in the day.

He'd been wracking his brain to remember anything else about their night together, a night she still remembered, a night she just admitted she had wanted to recreate. He was appalled that he had forgotten her. If that weren't proof enough that he needed to stay sober, he didn't know what would do it. He grit his teeth. She had no way to know that he'd been out of control but had since gotten help. And now he'd discovered another person who needed his apology. He was also certain she'd need his help, but she didn't see it that way. Not yet.

As he climbed the stairs to the large plantation home his parents had built on the site of an original antebellum plantation home, James was reminded to count his blessings. He had an amazing family, a privileged lifestyle and, for the most part, a great job. What he didn't have was anyone to share it all with. That was immediately apparent as he walked into his family's home and was greeted by nothing but silence. James shook off a chill and headed to the library.

He started a fire in the oversized fireplace, grabbed the packet he'd received from Dirk's consulting group, and sat down in the oversized leather chair by the fire. He flipped through the Forest Management Plan, confirming what he'd said in the presentation. If this wasn't the actual plan, then Dirk had created this one just for James, to assure Putnam Industries wouldn't get the business.

James wondered if this had been his tactic in all the bidding wars that Putnam Industries had been involved in with him. They'd never won a bid when Dirk was the consultant, and now he knew why. It was clever, but so wrong. Clearly unprofessional.

KAIRA ROUDA

But this time, Dirk had taken it a step too far. Aubrey Temple-ton's family land abutted the Putnams' land. Anything that she did with her logging rights would dramatically affect not just his land, but the entire island, for decades to come.

Dirk didn't care about this island, its people, or Aubrey for that matter. In fact, he'd most likely steer her toward a company that would ruin the island as they logged, making promises of environmental stewardship they'd ignore as soon as the first loggers set foot on the island's dock. He'd heard Dirk mention the bid from a Chinese company. That filled him with dread. Aubrey might not yet realize but China had quietly become the wood workshop for the world, developing an immense import industry. More than half of all timber being shipped anywhere in the world was destined for China, much of it harvested illegally from developing nations. Chinese loggers had proven themselves unscrupulous. They could not be allowed on Indigo Island.

James tossed the papers aside. He felt angry and restless. He was surprised China was interested in the relatively small forest acreage but perhaps the Chinese company thought that even a minor timber interest on a small sea island would lead to gaining a foothold in the South and lead to more logging deals. He had to turn this tide; gain Aubrey's trust before Dirk could use her lack of knowledge about the market and true forest sustainability against her. He couldn't believe that Dirk could dislike him and his family so much that he'd resort to having a thousand plus acres clear-cut. He had to get to Aubrey before Dirk could close the deal.

Aubrey. Just thinking about her made him feel alive. She had guts and independence. She'd asked him here to sleep with him. Again. Her confidence and willingness to go after what she wanted turned him on. They both felt the heat between them, he knew, and now he also discovered the attraction had a basis in something, in their shared night together. They had history, that molecular bond two people carried who'd connected on a deeper, subconscious, sensual level. It had been more than a one-night stand, he realized, willing himself to remember her from the fog of his partying years. Ms. Aubrey Templeton wasn't just another beautiful face; they'd connected. She meant something to him.

But that was the past. He was a new man, a man who couldn't allow himself the luxury of focusing on her incredible lips, amazing butt and perfect legs. No, he had to focus on business first. That's the reason he was here, that's what made him a Putnam.

Chapter Three

Aubrey

Thursday Morning

IT WAS THREE a.m. The clock glowing next to her on the bedside table taunted her, slowly ticking off the hours until daylight. She knew she wouldn't be sleeping anymore tonight. Her dreams, always vivid and disturbing, had been even more so since she'd arrived on the island two days before. She had assumed it was because she was close to her parents' land, as if a piece of them still remained on earth though they were both now in heaven. She hadn't yet visited the cottage by the stream, too worried about stirring up ghosts and memories, too afraid to go there alone. There were enough things haunting her at night without adding a visit to the now empty and lifeless family cottage.

Even tonight, in her sleep, she'd dreamed she'd heard her mother's voice calling to her, begging her for help just before their family car erupted in flames. She imagined her father's head, bleeding, contorted at the wrong angle, neck broken. Her vivid imagination had held onto every detail the coroner had told her during the autopsy. She was a reporter; details and imagery were her specialty. It was how she brought stories to life. The doctors and later the coroner had been verbose, detailing too much about her parents' suffering, both during the accident and in their fruitless hospital stay, where they lingered in pain and suffering for several weeks before passing. She didn't think she'd ever banish the images from her brain.

Somehow, at work, she'd keep it together, filling her easily distracted mind with facts from the stories she was working on, usually juggling several at a time, because her brain thrived on that. But here, on this beautiful island, she'd had plenty of time to think and to be haunted until yesterday when the presentations had begun and she'd listened to a series of men enthuse about how to maim her land in the most respectful way. Then she'd suffered through the dinner with that lecherous, old senator she hoped she'd never need to ask for a favor. She knew what he'd require in return.

And then there was James. All she could imagine when she first saw him in the darkened bar was another kiss like the one a year ago that had left her dizzy and seeing stars. She'd been breathless, waiting for him to remember their past connection, and when he hadn't, she'd been shocked, then embarrassed, then angry. She'd been glad that he'd stumbled on his presentation. It had made it easy to hold on to her anger, but when she'd seen the confusion and regret in his beautiful blue eyes, she'd felt hesitant. It was as if he really wanted to remember her, as if he really cared. But of course, she reminded herself, if he'd cared, he would have called her a year ago, he would have at least remembered her a year later. She wondered why she was being so principled about things with James. Why she'd decided he could bring her closure, finish her year of grieving and help her on to the rest of her life.

From the moment they had met, something about him had made her want more than just great sex. She hated to admit it, but she had really liked him, had even imagined how fun it would be to date him. She rolled over in bed and thought about getting up, hating how her thoughts kept returning to James. She should be done with him. But they'd talked, connected. He'd been a great listener, once he'd let his cocky business tycoon guard down. Their night together had been special, unlike any other nights she'd spent with a man. She hadn't been very experienced before James, but there had been enough others to now make a comparison.

Since her parents' deaths, she'd been reckless. Sleeping with different men whenever she wanted. She hadn't worried about tomorrow. Of course, she'd insisted on protection, and she was on the pill, but otherwise, she had been carelessly dating, even engaging in one night stands that she found were the best way to get through the painful nights since she'd lost both parents. Everyone had been forgettable except for James. She'd even tried to get his number from friends, but no luck. He was a private, wealthy, protected guy surrounded by a group of loyal partying friends.

She knew now that while she had fantasized about linking up with him again, he'd forgotten her as soon as she'd climbed out of his bed. It served her right. When she returned to Atlanta, after all of this land mess was behind her, she'd focus on finding the right guy, a man she could have taken home to her parents. It was time to move on with her life. Build something together with a man, something like the cottage where she'd vacationed as a child, her mom in the sunny kitchen stirring a pitcher of lemonade, her father on the porch rigging a fishing line for each of them. It had been a happy childhood, visiting this island had been a small but meaningful part of it. But now this place would become her lasting legacy and she would fight for it. She'd hold on and protect it, and someday, she'd get up the nerve to walk inside the cottage again. She had hoped it would be on this visit, but now, with her nightmares and her humiliation with James, she doubted she'd do anything more here than sign the deal with the Chinese or a different group Dirk recommended and grab the next ferry for Hilton Head.

Four a.m.

She climbed out of bed and walked to the window, pulled back the curtain. The moonlight shone on the ocean just beyond the green lawn and white Victorian gazebo. This weekend, she knew from Jack, another wedding would take place in front of the gazebo, the ocean sparkling in celebration behind the young couple. A white runner would stretch out across the grass as guests would be seated in white wooden chairs on either side of the aisle. The only variable to the scenario, besides the weather, was the bride's flower and music selections and the color and style of the bridesmaids' dresses. Once she'd become a teenager, Aubrey and her mom had stopped and watched whenever they'd happened upon a wedding in progress here, smiling at the pageantry and the promises a wedding delivers, no matter your age. Just a couple years ago, Aubrey's own mother had suggested Indigo Island as a beautiful place for her only daughter's wedding and Aubrey had laughed.

"Mother, why would anybody want to travel all the way to some South Carolina Sea Island when we can just use the country club here, like everyone else," Aubrey had said.

"They'd come to a wedding here because Indigo Island is special. Because they'd get to know a little about your roots, about your ties to the land there, dear," her mom had said, her shiny brunette hair tucked behind her ears. She had looked so young, so full of life. "You'll understand someday. Indigo Island is your roots, it's in your blood. It'll be there when you need it, timeless and healing," her mom had said.

Now, staring at the empty gazebo, Aubrey felt the tears rolling down her cheeks. "I need it now, Mom," she whispered. "As much as I need you."

Aubrey touched the pane of glass in front of her before allowing herself a good cry.

Five a.m. The horizon had started to brighten a bit. Her tears spent, Aubrey decided she'd go for a jog to shake off her sleepless night and sorrow. She needed to clear her hear and to be sharp for her nine a.m. meeting with Dirk. She'd be making important decisions today. She flipped on the lights in her bathroom, momentarily blinding herself, her eyes swollen and red from crying. She brushed her teeth and pulled on her workout clothes.

She'd discovered the only other thing that cleared her mind, besides work, was jogging. Actually, full out running was more like it since her parents' accident. Aubrey burst out the back doors of the inn and onto the shell-encrusted pathway leading to the gazebo and the ocean beyond. Making her way to the beach, she breathed in the ocean air and breathed out the negativity of the night. The sun was rising, and the sky was the color of pink cotton candy. She glanced to her right and saw an osprey in its nest. Seagulls and pelicans were at work on their morning meals. The beach was alive with crabs, and even though she was alone and today faced the biggest decision so far in her thirty-one years on earth, she felt at peace.

As she reached the end of the island, the beach curved sharply to the right, towards the marsh side or backside. She came to a stop, resting on a piece of bleached driftwood conveniently moored in the sand. The roots of the once-grand tree now exposed, tipped up in the air for all to see. She imagined the tree feeling embarrassed, exposed. She patted the trunk with her hand. She sat enjoying the sunrise, the calm lapping of the ocean tide until she heard footsteps behind her. She turned while standing, ready to karate chop anybody who threatened her.

It was James. She felt her face blush. How could she have been so stupid imagining their reunion as if he'd been pining away for her this past year? It had been a year of mixed-up thinking and bad behavior, and James was just emblematic of the entire thing, of everything she'd lost. Definitely time to move on.

"I'm not the only one who enjoys a morning jog," he said, the words coming out broken as he caught his breath. He bent forward, hands on his knees, giving Aubrey a moment to revel in his beauty. Because he was a perfect specimen of man, if nothing else, she thought.

"I love jogging, especially early in the morning," Aubrey said, swinging around on the driftwood so she could face him, the smooth grey trunk supporting her and giving her a reason to keep her distance even as every receptor in her body woke up. Stop it, she told her way too overactive libido.

"This is great, actually, better than great, seeing you here," James said, standing up, having recovered his normal breath and speech. "I was going to come over to your room and beg you to see me before your meeting with Dirk. I know you don't owe me anything. I wasn't coming for that, but you're trying to protect your inheritance. I want to protect it, to protect the island. You and I have very similar stakes in this beautiful place."

His eyes were so blue. She felt like she was drowning. And his face was so open and sincere. She felt thrown.

"I'm afraid you are being led astray by Dirk. He and I go way back. I think he is leading you astray for money and to get back at me. It sounds melodramatic probably, but I can show you proof. Please. For both of our families' sakes, for your parents' legacy and for the people of this beautiful island, can we talk?"

Aubrey looked at the roots of the driftwood tree, dead and exposed. She pushed her fingers through her hair, shoving some stray strands into her ponytail holder. And then she looked up, and looked into James' eyes. What she saw was truth. "I don't want to give you the impression that the bid is still open. You, Putnam Industries, aren't in consideration anymore, for anything. Understood?"

"I understand," James said, a faint smile triggering his adorable dimple. In two simple words he'd both acknowledged her hurt, and her need for revenge. *And yet, the smile? What did he know that she didn't? Or was Mr. Business flirting with her?*

"Ok, let's see what you've got then. Where are we going? The inn?" Aubrey said.

"No, my house. Race you there," he said, and took off before

Aubrey had a chance to leap from the driftwood.

"Not fair," she called out putting on a burst of speed so she could catch up, maybe pass him. For the first time in a long time, she found herself smiling.

James

SHE WAS FAST, he realized, struggling to stay ahead of Aubrey as they ran down the beach toward his family home. Every time he looked behind him, she'd gained ground on him. Smart, beautiful, athletic. Perfect. And she'd actually wanted to be with him, until his past excesses had ruined the possibility, he thought wryly. He had just reached the steps leading up to the plantation when Aubrey took the steps two at a time. She laughed.

"That was fun," she said. "I almost caught you."

"I noticed, and I didn't power down at all," James said, noticing how the sweat glistened on her face, the bright red in her cheeks, the light in her dark brown eyes. "I'm still working on getting in shape, but you are already there."

Her breathing was accelerated, but not nearly as much as his. He felt a shaft of sorrow shoot through him thinking of the missed opportunity. Every time he thought he'd come to terms with his years of too much partying and had put them behind him, once more the specter of his lack of discipline rose up to haunt him.

"Nice little place you've got here, Mr. Putnam," she teased. "Just a tiny seaside cottage."

"Yes, well, we Putnams tend to do things big scale. But it does hold all four kids, my parents and a lot of friends." He looked up at the large house. "So many memories here, actually," James said, as he thought back to a few months ago at Christmas time when he'd made a fool of himself propositioning his sister

Avery's friend, Lily. He'd been lonely, and alone as usual, struggling with his recovery due to the holidays. Shortly after, Lily had met Cole and the rest was history. James tried to push away his sense that everyone had someone except for him. Patience, he reminded himself, so not his strong suit.

"Come on in."

James led her up the stairs to the wide front porch and opened the door to the grand entryway, with its impressive swooping stairway. Fresh white flowers – lilies and daisies – filled vases throughout the entryway. Everything sparkled with perfection and home, James thought. He was proud of this house and proud of his family. Soon, he hoped, Aubrey would be, too, proud enough to partner with him in business. He would explain the Putnam history and redeem his family's honor in her eyes so she would trust him with the stewardship of her land, even as he knew that personally, he didn't deserve any second chances.

"This way to the kitchen. We can grab some water, and a light breakfast, while I show you what I've found," he said. He smiled as he watched Aubrey take in the Putnam Plantation.

"James, this is the most beautiful home I've ever seen," she said, following him into the huge, airy kitchen. "The flowers, the furnishings, the glittering chandeliers, the woodwork –" they locked eyes and grinned – "Of course the woodwork would be exceptional."

"Of course," he said, pulling out a barstool for her.

"Do you like eggs? Bacon? Sausage? I have some berries, too," he said, pulling things out of the refrigerator. "Oh, and coffee? Orange juice?"

"Yes, yes, yes," she said, "Let me help you?"

"No, please, this is my treat. For some reason we ran into each other this morning, and I believe it's so we can start over. Breakfast is a great start, don't you think?" he said.

Aubrey didn't say anything but accepted the glass of cold water he handed her and smiled. He decided that was a good sign. "Feel free to look around the house while I get everything ready." James started pulling out pots and pans, glasses and a coffeemaker, all the while trying not to steal glimpses of his gorgeous guest. He no longer mixed business with pleasure, and he still hoped to convince her to trust him with the logging rights and to work with Putnam Industries even though he'd never be able to kiss her beautiful face again.

"This place, I'm speechless. I feel like I'm inside a famous southern hotel, no, better because it's simple elegance. Did your mom design all of this?" Aubrey asked, as she appeared next to him at the stove. The bacon sizzled and popped while his heart thumped at her close presence.

"She did, with the help of her decorator. But she has the vision. Great woman, I hope you'll meet her someday," James said, before he could stop himself. He was a babbling idiot. *Why would she ever want to meet his mother? This was business.*

"That would be great," Aubrey said. To James, she sounded sincere, almost wistful. That's when he remembered what he'd read about her parents' tragic death. He'd spent a lot of time researching Aubrey Templeton last night. She hadn't been a debutante, just a straight-A upper middle class girl growing up in Buckhead, the only child of two adoring parents. And now, she was alone and facing a mountain of debt. Her father had been highly leveraged, with two mortgages on his home, several years of unpaid taxes on the South Carolina holdings. There had been no medical or life insurance, the policies had run out. Aubrey was a magazine writer, and writers, James knew, were notoriously underpaid.

"I'm so sorry about your parents," he said, putting the spatula down on the spoon rest, giving her his full attention. "I didn't realize your full situation until I did some research last night. I'm afraid I came into this presentation half-prepared, and it showed. I didn't understand your family's deep roots on Indigo Island and how much the land means now that your parents are gone."

He saw Aubrey swallow hard, and her eyes had a sheen of tears.

"My cash offer must have seemed callous, yet that was not the spirit of the offer."

"It's been a hard year, culminating in a tough day yesterday," she said. "It would have saved the day a little if you had at least remembered our night together. I still can't believe you don't."

"I can't either," he said, shame washing through him.

He should tell her about those years. His recovery. She deserved that even though it further jeopardized any chance of him changing her mind and letting him help her design a more sustainable logging lease on her land.

"I feel so stupid," she said. "Humiliated."

"No," James denied. "You did nothing wrong. The blame is totally mine. Listen, I...," he broke off. He had to hug her. It was nearly a compulsion, and he gave into it pulling her close as she wrapped her arms around his waist. His heart was thumping, and he was certain she could hear it, feel it, but he didn't care. He could stand here, like this, forever. He had an unbelievable desire to help her, to care for her, to make sure no one hurt her. Like he had, he acknowledged. He wanted to protect her land from Dirk and his revenge-laced business schemes, but this was something more. Well beyond their business together. Except something was burning.

"Shoot," he said, as the kitchen's smoke detectors began to blare.

He switched on the exhaust fan of the stove, crossed the room and opened the doors to the outdoor deck. The alarm quieted, and the air started to clear. Aubrey stood where he'd left her, staring at him a little stunned, he thought. He smiled and shrugged. At least her tears had dried.

"A little comic relief for your morning," James said. He'd tried to impress her once again, and disaster. What else could he mess up in front of this woman, he wondered drily.

"I'll cook the eggs," she said, pulling out a new pan and cracking the eggs with finesse. "Let me guess." Her voice sounded teasing, which lightened his heart. "You gave your chef the day off."

"Actually yes."

She laughed. "Honest."

"Yes," he said sincerely.

She glanced at him sharply, colored a bit and then focused on the eggs.

He could give her that, James decided. Honesty. Honesty about her land and honesty about himself. That might be the only thing he had going for him at this point. He opened his mouth to tell her about his recovery, but she was smiling and humming and looked so cute and perfect in his kitchen that he felt breathless. He'd never had such a domestic thought run through his brain, ever. What was she doing to him? Where was his edge?

"Ok, we're ready. I salvaged a couple sausages from the inferno, too," she said, plating the food and sliding it to him across the island.

As she sat down next to him, steaming pot of coffee helping to change the smell of the room from burned bacon, she said, "When's the last time you've cooked a meal, James?"

"While your presumptions about my cooking prowess are correct, I'd like to point out that at least I made the effort to cook for you. I wasn't successful, but I tried," he said. "That has to count for something?"

"Yes, it was a better effort than yesterday's presentation," she said, and laughed.

"Ouch. That bad?"

"Yes."

James loved the sound of her laughter, and hoped there would be a time it wasn't at his expense. He watched her take a bite of her eggs. Even that was sexy. He shifted in his seat, cursing his overactive libido. Keeping this all business was going to require discipline and acting skill that he was sure he had, but he needed to develop both now.

"Let me show you what I've discovered," he said abruptly, needing to focus on something other than the curve of lips when she smiled. "I realized last night why my presentation was so lame from your point of view." James grabbed his laptop from the kitchen table and popped it open in front of them on the island. "One of the logging companies you heard from yesterday was United Logging, right?"

"Yep. They came in with ten guys. Impressive but also intimidating," Aubrey said taking a sip of her coffee. "The CEO smelled like dead fish, and I'm not kidding. Like he'd been on a fishing boat just before he appeared in the conference room. But anyway, I know they are a big, if smelly, company."

"They are a huge, publicly traded company. That means they have to make public any RFPs – request for proposal – they receive, no matter how small. No offense, but your tract is small for their typical bids," James said.

"No offense taken – yet," she said, smiling but looking intently at the screen.

"I was able to view the RFP they received from Dirk on your behalf and compare it to the RFP I received from Dirk. The Forest Management Plan is completely different. Look," James said, pointing to the two RFPs pulled up on the screen. "The RFP I received says you had decided to clear cut all of your land. A tragedy. It takes eighty years for the land to reforest, or more. I couldn't believe it. That's why I made the offer to buy your land. A desperate person, a heartless person, would choose this type of land lease. I'm so relieved this wasn't your intention."

"It never would be. This is horrible. Why would Dirk do this, give you a different management plan to bid on?" Aubrey said, her face was flushed, much like the look he'd seen on her face when he'd presented his bid to her yesterday.

"Dirk is consumed by some weird family rivalry, but I'm worried he's taken things too far. The Chinese, in my opinion, cannot be trusted, and for that matter, neither can United Logging. I hope your other two bidders are more reputable."

Aubrey was still reading the information on his computer screen, her lips compressed. He pushed his luck more.

"With better sustainable credentials and more local presence, like Putnam Industries," he said.

Aubrey stiffened, and he worried he'd gone too far. She reached into her pocket and pulled out her phone, taking a photo of the screen in front of her. "Thank you. I'll handle Dirk. This is unscrupulous. I trusted him."

James' whole body longed to hold her, to touch her hair, her cheek, feel the warmth of her body. He sat back further in his chair trying to keep his focus on a management plan for her land and forest, not her sex life. With him. How the Hell had he forgotten her, he demanded for the tenth time this morning.

Get over it. He urged himself. Focus. He might have blown it with her romantically, but business was different. Business could be salvaged when there was money and a deal to be had.

"Dirk is unscrupulous, I agree, but contrary to what you might think from our encounter a year ago, I'm not. I'm a changed man, Aubrey. I would like to tell you about it, but right now, here, today, I want to tell you in all honesty that I would be honored to work with you to do what is right for your land. I have roots here too," he said, taking a sip of his coffee. He knew he was pushing it, but this was critical and fortune never favored the timid. "Can I resubmit an updated bid?"

She was silent, staring into her coffee cup. He thought of all the ways he would have pushed his advantage in the past. She was attracted to him still, he knew. He had seduced many women who were initially wary of his reputation. He knew what worked. Instead he held himself still. Kept his body as far from hers as was socially polite so that he couldn't use any sensory or sexual pull at all. He thought about his sober coach and mentor. His counselor. He could practically hear them cheering, and instead of feeling successful, he felt hollow, like he was throwing away the opportunity of a lifetime that had nothing to do with proving his worth to his father, or making CEO.

"Sure," she said slowly. "Why don't you do that? Can you do that this morning? I told the other companies I'd make a decision this morning by...." She glanced at her phone. "Shoot, it's almost ten. I told Dirk I'd meet him at nine to go over the bids one last time. Where did the morning go?" she said and hopped off the barstool and carried her plate and coffee mug to the sink.

"Leave that, I'll handle the dishes," James said and wished their time together could last all day. At least their business relationship was improving, even if their personal attraction would have to be left simmering under the surface. He was grateful to be able to bid again.

"Dishes? Another first?" she said.

He smiled, a genuine smile, not one calculated to attract her. It surprised him, but he loved to be teased by her.

"Let me give you a ride, save you the run back on a full stomach," James said, selfishly hoping to prolong their time together, make one more push for Putnam Industries.

"I've got this. But maybe I could use your help later, after I fire Dirk I mean," she said. "I think I'm going to start all over, hire a new forester. I don't even know if I can believe his soil quality analysis, or the tree farm inspection, can I?" She stopped in the doorway of the kitchen, her jogging shorts and t-shirt hugging her perfect body, silhouetted by the light shining in from the grand foyer.

He wanted to cross the arm's length distance between them, swoop her into his arms and carry her upstairs to his bedroom. He gripped the edge of the table hard as if to hold himself in place and took a deep breath instead.

"I can recommend some other industry people for you to

meet with," he said. "I'd love to take a look at your land and let you know," he said, his heart lightening as a new way to spend time with her emerged, even as he told himself to stop thinking of her that way. "Whatever you need, I'm here. I'll work on the bid and have a new bid for you early this afternoon," James said.

He knew he sounded too eager, which was not a good strategy, but he needed this deal, and he needed to sustain the contact between them, even as he reminded himself over and over that this was just business. Maybe that should be his new mantra, he mocked himself. Where was the aloof party guy he had carefully cultivated all these years? Gone, he thought.

"Thank you," she said, leaning close, quickly kissing him on the cheek, the kiss of a friend. He felt the now familiar stirring inside as he imagined pulling her to him, gently bending to kiss her full lips. But he kept his arms at his sides, hands clenched in fists, fighting off the attraction.

"Anytime," he managed, hoping she didn't look back and see how that small, friendly action had sent his body into a completely inappropriate response.

"I've got to go," she said, hurrying out of the kitchen.

James settled down to rework his bid. He tried to not think about the fact that Aubrey might be out of his life forever. His biggest hope was that she'd reconsider and accept his bid, but that was as far as it could go, he reminded himself. Business. Yes, his new mantra, but definitely not an easy one to embrace.

Chapter Four

Aubrey

Thursday

AUBREY WAS MENTALLY kicking herself. She'd almost allowed herself to be seduced by the same guy she'd vowed to avoid forever. And he hadn't even been trying. She'd seen James in action, and today he had been all business. No charm offensive at all, but still she'd wanted to fall into his arms and tug him upstairs to jump in the first available bed. What is my problem, she thought, as she jogged on the beach heading back toward The Melrose Inn, glowing butter yellow in the bright sunshine. The problem was she was completely electrified when she was in his presence. She was thankful for the information he'd provided about Dirk, but then again, could she really trust a Putnam Industries guy to not sway her away from the Chinese and his biggest US competitor? Did she really want another bid, or did she just want to keep James close?

Because breakfast with him, even with the burned bacon, was the most romantic date she'd ever had. They'd sat side by side, talking about her dreams, her land. He hadn't tried anything physical, no, he was seducing her mind even as her body longed for his touch. And, truth it was working.

Argh, men, she thought. But still, she couldn't shake the feeling of longing from her system. Every place his fingers had touched her skin was tingling still. The brush on her arm as he handed her a cup of coffee, the accidental touch of their finger-tips when they were reviewing the two RFPs. When he had wrapped his arms around her waist to comfort her, her heart had flip-flopped in her chest even as she sobbed, still desperately missing her parents. Their chemistry had been amazing, and even if he couldn't remember, her body still did. Just the simple act of kissing him on the cheek had ignited the spark inside her all over again. Her body was a traitor, uber attracted to James while her mind still didn't trust him, in work or pleasure.

Logically, she knew he had only hugged her in pity, sympathy for her orphan status, and the mess over her land. Or, maybe, he wanted in her pants to get her land? Either way, she'd barely been able to control herself whereas he had seemed very professional and friendly. She'd practically needed a cold shower after the hug, for heaven's sake. What if he had started something? What if he had tried to kiss her, she wondered, would it be just as electrifying as it had been a year ago? She'd never know.

Because even though she was beginning to like James Putnam as a person, she'd never be his partner in the bedroom again. She didn't want to be just another sex partner he couldn't remember because there'd been so many. She'd thought being with him again would bring her full circle and a sense of closure, and really it had, only not in the way she'd imagined. She respected herself too much. She wanted something loving and permanent like what her parents had had. She was tired of dating, of hooking up when the mood took her.

And James Putnam was a hookup kind of guy. Nothing more.

James was like a drug and she just needed to resist. It was the same thing as cigarettes. She had loved smoking in college, loved the taste, the feel, the effects. But she had known she had to quit for her health, and she had. She also knew that even this minute, if she had just one puff, she'd be addicted again. She'd have to go through the horrible quitting process all over again. She couldn't handle it. Just like she couldn't sleep with James and walk away with a smile on her face.

So be it. He forgot me, I will forget about him. Period.

She jogged up the stairs to the inn and through the front door, waving to Jack who was at the front desk and then hurried up the stairs. She took a moment to text Dirk and tell him she'd see him in half an hour. She took a cold shower, dressed in jeans and a white cotton shirt, pulled her wet hair into a ponytail and hurried to find Dirk. He'd texted her back, telling her he was in the library downstairs.

She pushed open the heavy wood door and found Dirk, sitting by the fireplace, in a large leather wingback chair. Sitting across the coffee table from him was one of the representatives of the Chinese company. Both men stood as she walked into the room. Aubrey felt a start of surprise.

"There you are," Dirk said. "You must have had a good night's sleep finally. You remember Mr. Chung?" The other man nodded in her direction as Dirk pulled a chair up to the table for her.

"In your absence, Mr. Chung and I have come up with a mutually beneficial plan for the Templeton Tract," Dirk said, a smile stretched across his face. The smile didn't reach his green eyes, Aubrey noticed. "I know you'll be pleased."

"Yes, you should be very pleased, as are we," Mr. Chung said. "For my company, this will be the first project in the American South. It is important for all of us to do this in the right way, mutually beneficial as Mr. Dirk says."

"I still need to review all of the other bids from yesterday," Aubrey said firmly. "That was the plan for this morning's meeting with Dirk. And while I appreciated your offer, it was the most aggressive logging plan for my tract and I'm not certain that is the direction I'm interested in heading," Aubrey said, smiling tightly at Dirk. "I did not realize you had another meeting scheduled. I need to have a word with you privately. Immediately, Dirk. Please excuse us, Mr. Chung."

Aubrey walked to the other corner of the library, as far as possible from the logger sitting in the chair by the fireplace. "Have you insinuated to Mr. Chung that he has the deal?"

"No, of course not, I need your signature for that," Dirk said. "But he does bring the most cash to the table."

"I'm well aware of his bid. I also know the final signature is mine, but what I'm concerned with are optics. This is my deal, Dirk, not yours, but for some reason it seems Mr. Chung thinks we have a deal and that you were authorized to negotiate it. Does he?" Aubrey said. Her hands were on her hips, her jaw locked in anger.

"Aubrey, I'm just looking out for you. It's a great deal," Dirk said. His smile seemed patronizing to her, his eyes cold, evasive, where as James' had been warm and open and so deeply blue. Just yesterday, she'd been happy Dirk was on her team, but now, she wasn't sure.

"But is it an honest deal?" She demanded. "Explain this," she said, holding up her phone to show him the photo of the computer screen. The screen displayed two very different proposals for her land.

"Oh that's a photo of the two different management plans for your land," Dirk said, not missing a beat.

"I only signed off on one," Aubrey said, searching his eyes for the truth.

"No, you signed both. I have copies. Maybe you don't remember. It's been a long few months," he said, patting her on the shoulder, a gesture he'd been doing since they'd started working together, a gesture that bugged her now. And had he always been this condescending and she'd just come out of her fog of grief enough to realize it? What had she done, she wondered.

"Who else received the clear-cut management plan besides Putnam Industries?" she asked, rolling her shoulder to knock his hand off.

"I only sent that plan to Putnam, just to see what they'd do with it. Obviously, that was a disaster, but a good exercise," Dirk said.

"A good exercise? You wasted my time and James Putnam's time on a bid that I would never approve. And you knew it," Aubrey said. She was furious, and she was having trouble keeping her voice down so that Mr. Chung wouldn't overhear.

One quick glance at the businessman showed him getting restless, clearly aware they were arguing and that the deal he'd thought was done, was anything but.

"It seems Ja…Mr. Putnam's time isn't the only person's time you wasted," she said.

Dirk's gaze sharpened.

"Mr. Cooley, Ms. Templeton. I need to get going now," Mr. Chung said. He'd clearly grown tired of waiting for them by the fire and joined them where they were standing. He may have heard everything and she didn't care. "I left signed copies for you on the table. Simply sign and email a copy to my assistant. We will start next week. Thank you."

Aubrey glared at Dirk. He had negotiated a deal without her permission.

"Thank you, Mr. Chung." She said coolly. "I'm sorry for what must look like my rude behavior but Mr. Cooley should not have asked you here yet. It was premature," Aubrey said. "Please, take your contract with you. I will not be signing anything today. And as of this moment, Dirk is no longer my forestry consultant. Any follow up will be directly from me. Any negotiations will only come from and be with me. Are you both clear?"

Both men looked at her with alarm.

"Leave the papers, Mr. Chung." Dirk stepped in front of her and took Mr. Chung's shoulder, lightly in his as he lead him from the room. His voice lowered. "Ms. Templeton's confused right now. She has never negotiated a business deal. She is unclear about protocol and of course knows nothing about land development or forestry practices. Let me walk you out to the lobby, sir."

They walked out the door together, leaving Aubrey alone in the room. She thought about following them out and showing them both how clearly she understood business negotiations but instead stomped over to the coffee table and picked up the signed contract. How dare they make a plan without her, assuming they would start working her land as early as next week? She looked down at the papers she held in her hand and began tearing. Once she had ripped all of the pages into tiny squares, she felt better. She carried the pile of what was now confetti over to the fireplace and tossed it inside, watching as the ink burned, and Dirk's sneaky deal turned to ash.

Deciding that she'd rather handle any other so called negotiations with Dirk by email, she went back to her hotel room. She needed a new plan and a new forestry manager. She needed someone she could trust to negotiate in good faith, but who? She'd kept her inheritance a secret from her coworkers, who would no doubt tease her about being a southern plantation owner, and then ridicule her for desecrating the family's land through the euphemism of "forest management". This wasn't based on any need to manage a forest, as Mother Nature had done that job quite well since the beginning of time. No, this was for money, plain and simple, and in that respect, she was just as guilty as any other scumbucket who ruined the land, natural resources, for their own greed. I'm a scumbucket landowner, she thought. And Dirk is a scumbucket forester and Mr. Chung, James and the rest of them were scumbucket loggers.

Her heart and head hurt and she felt like crying as she dropped into one of the large leather chairs by the fireplace. She wasn't a scumbucket landowner. She wasn't going to become one, no matter how much she needed the money. She looked around this room, the library of the inn, and remembered sitting on her father's lap as a child, his strong arms around her as he read his newspaper by the fire and she'd fallen asleep for her nap. She had felt so safe, so loved, so warm and secure. She needed to feel that way again, to feel whole, even if she couldn't be held, to feel secure knowing she was in control of her own destiny, her own land.

I am a part of this island, just as my mom had told me.

It was her history. She remembered stories her dad told her of visiting Indigo Island as a child, playing in the stream running past their cottage, fishing with his own grandfather, making forts from Spanish Moss, and climbing the beautiful magnolia tree next to their cottage. Her mother had first visited the island as a newlywed and had fallen in love with it, too. Even before Aubrey was born, her parents had begun making memories here as a couple, sailing the sound in their Hobie Cat, sharing romantic picnics in different special hideaways her dad knew on the land, walking for hours along the beach cementing a relationship that would last until death.

I am a part of this island, which is a community.

And why hadn't she thought about the natives, the islanders whose land bordered hers, they had always been nothing but welcoming to generations of her family. It had been easy for her to think only of herself and what she needed when she was tucked away in her cubicle in Atlanta, or meeting with Dirk and coming up with a plan. But not any longer, not now that she was here, among them. What would they think if she destroyed her land, which was their land: cut down all of the trees, polluted the stream, caused erosion and sedimentation and wrecked the ecosystem with ski trails and access roads?

She pushed herself up out of the comfortable chair and hurried back up the stairs to her room. She grabbed her laptop and did a Google search, discovering that South Carolina was itself worried about the optics of forestry operations, encouraging landowners to "manage the visual quality" because perceptions are important when dealing with an increasingly environmentally aware public. They advised sneaky things like cutting trees – harvests – in irregular shapes to break up the impact, using vegetative screens and buffers in sensitive areas and to locate loading decks out of public view. Aubrey didn't even know what all of these things meant, but she knew her island neighbors wouldn't like it, and that they'd know the truth despite creative screens. There would be environmental damage, for sure, roads cut, sound pollution as the machinery cranked up to kill trees. And the birds and other animals that called them home, where would they go.

And what about the water, the creek that meandered from her land and touched all the others on the island? How could they protect the water quality with all of the destruction of the tree harvest, Aubrey wondered.

I am a part of this island, and I need to find another option, a different solution, a competing type of bid.

As much as she needed the money to pay off the back taxes, she knew she had to find another way. Logging much of her land couldn't be the answer. She stood up and stretched, looking out the window at the beautiful manicured lawns of the inn, the golf course meandering along the coast to her right. The trees had been cleared, she assumed, from this coastline years ago to make way for the course and the homes dotting the edge of it. But beyond that, the island's forests remained thick and untouched. That was one of the reasons tourists visited this place, and tourism was the number one industry on Indigo Island. She had to find the way for her to have a careful development and preservation of the integrity of the island while still paying off her taxes and preserving her inheritance for future generations.

Aubrey stared at the beautiful scenery, so many memories from her childhood visits to Indigo Island playing through her mind. She could almost feel her mother's touch and hear her whispered reassurances. *You know what to do. Listen to what is inside you.* For a moment she imagined she could smell her mother's soft floral scent. She closed her eyes and breathed deeply. Then she roused herself, shaking her head. Another crazy moment in her year of grief. She looked around her hotel room, at the formal, four-poster bed, at the silk curtains and the traditional Southern furnishings around her. She'd always loved the Inn, it's historical formality and the way it blended the island culture with Southern culture. Suddenly she had an idea, and it was so different from what she'd been thinking, that it took her a moment to process.

Energized, Aubrey turned from the window and hurried back to her computer. She did a Google search and spent some time researching. The more she read, the more perfect the solution seemed. But would they be interested? Feeling excited with just a hint of nerves, Aubrey placed the call. She was used to hunting down leads, getting people to talk when they hadn't been planning to. For the first time in a while, she felt comfortable, in her element.

She was transferred around a few times, but soon found herself talking to the one of the most powerful CEOs in the resort development business. He was interested, and he had been planning a golf trip to Hilton Head starting day after tomorrow. He easily agreed to fly down a day early to meet with her. Aubrey hung up feeling dazed. She felt like something right had finally happened in a long string of wrong. The ease of this had to be a sign, she thought optimistically, almost as if her mother were helping her from beyond.

Feeling stronger and more herself than she had felt since her parents' accident, she texted Dirk.

James

JAMES WAS JUST putting the finishing touches on his new bid when his assistant, Agnes, called to tell him that Walter had called an emergency board meeting. He thanked her profusely, called his father's assistant, Agnes' mom, Mrs. Trawley, to learn the details. His father was still too weak from his surgery and follow-up cancer treatments to participate from his hospital bed, so he asked James to handle it.

Even as he placed a call to his pilot and hurried upstairs to get ready, his mind focused on the potential coup brewing in Atlanta. Not being in attendance would weaken his hand since every other board member would be there. They wouldn't realize Walter had intended to keep him in the dark about the meeting. He peeled off his jogging clothes and jumped in the shower. His thoughts divided, first on how to handle the meeting and Walter, who was popular and respected, and then to Aubrey. Even though he had promised himself theirs could only be a business relationship, he couldn't get her out of his head. And it wasn't only sex. It was her sweetness, her vulnerability coupled with her sense of humor and determination to stand her ground. How could he not be fascinated? How could he pass her up?

Stop it, he told himself turning off the tap and briskly drying off. Focus on the bid, not Aubrey. Hopefully, she would give his bid more weight knowing his expertise would be at her disposal. He'd present it to her in person this afternoon. He'd only be off-island for a few hours. Walter might be resentful that he had not been made interim CEO, but James had a good record with the company. True his reputation with women and booze had become a problem, but that was in the past. This past year had been all about focus, drive and recovery. No one could complain about his recent work ethic, and even when he'd been partying, he'd never missed a meeting or a day of work.

As he dressed in his favorite navy suit, he thought of Walter and imagined the shock the older man would have as he walked into the room. The look on Walter's face would be priceless, he thought, the surprise enough to swing attention his way. Briefcase loaded, he drove the golf cart to the helipad and climbed into the waiting white helicopter with the Putnam Industries orange script P logo adorning the doors and relaxed. This was his cocoon, a familiar environment where time stood still and no one could bother him. He took a deep breath and vowed to fix everything. For his father. For his legacy. For Indigo Island. And, if possible, for Aubrey, too.

He nodded to the pilot as they took off, cutting a quick path across the blue sky above the beautiful island before heading inland away from the coast. An hour later, the helicopter touched down on the top of the gleaming skyscraper housing his family's heritage, the company his grandfather had founded. James smiled. He knew he was where he should be, and he knew, as the pilot cut the engine, and he climbed out, Walter would not be pleased to see him.

James's assistant, Agnes, met him at the door, ushering him inside along with his father's assistant. Both women nodded their approval of his arrival and fell in behind him like a small army. They hurried down a flight of stairs to the executive level of the office building a floor lined with dark, thick navy carpet, accented with mahogany baseboards and ceiling beams. The finishes were masculine and in all of them, there was a nod to the lumber company that they were. The boardroom was at the end of the hall. James stopped in front of the tall, dark wood doors as Agnes grabbed one doorknob, Mrs. Trawley the other. James nodded and the women pushed the double doors wide open and James stepped into the room.

The eleven men seated at the large mahogany table all turned to look at him, a mixture of expressions on their faces. Walter, who was standing at the other end of the table from James, simply stared.

"Walter, so nice of you to call," James drawled. "I was in the middle of negotiations with Aubrey Templeton regarding her tract of forest on Indigo Island. So what's the emergency?"

Even though he didn't take his steely-eyed gaze from Walter's he was hyper aware of what everyone else was doing around the table. The fidgeting. The indrawn breaths. He could sense shock and puzzlement as well as curiosity.

They wanted a show, did they?

"You may stay if you want, James," Walter said. "Be seated."

"I prefer to stand."

"I called this emergency meeting."

"You have no authority to do so," James said keeping tight reign on his temper. "I am the acting CEO until my father recovers."

"That's a big assumption, James."

"Assumption? It was my father's request when we both visited him in the hospital."

"He is very ill. There is nothing in writing."

James felt his jaw clench at the blatant disregard of his father's wishes. His father had considered Walter a friend and confidant. He trusted him. If Walter were prepared to betray that trust at the first opportunity, what else did he have planned?

Walter looked smug, and that's what stopped James from speaking quickly. He forced his body to relax.

"You were there with me," he spoke quietly. "You heard what he said."

"I am the glue of this company as these gentlemen all know," Walter answered. "I have been the right-hand man of Rick Putnam and Putnam Industries for forty years. I am the only one qualified to lead us through these troubled times. I submit myself as a candidate to take over the vacant CEO position. We need strong leadership. The industry is changing. We need to adapt," Walter said.

James would have laughed had it not been so serious. Walter was pushing seventy. He was the one who was going to steer the company through a rapidly changing business and ecological climate? Only most of the men on the board were over sixty as well. Best not to insult them.

"I don't think my masters in environment science and MBA in business from Emory as well as my ten years with Putnam Industries exactly screams out of touch with the current business and environmental practices or the company," he said.

"James, you're here because your daddy runs the company," Walter said dismissively. "You can't even land a small deal on your own. You were laughed out of the Templeton bid."

Everything in James stilled. Clicked.

"Does Dirk Cooley have you on speed dial?" he asked. "Does he get some kind of kickback for sending me the wrong business plan for Putnam to bid on?"

Walter flushed with anger or embarrassment. James couldn't tell, but Walter was riled, whereas he was keeping himself cool, body relaxed even. He'd have to grudgingly thank his brother, Blake, who was all about control, control, control. It had annoyed the hell out of him growing up, as well as Blake's control lectures when they'd been adults, and he'd been having fun while Blake had been building an empire, but now self-control worked like a dream.

"You blew that on your own."

"No. Had a breakfast meeting with Aubrey Templeton. Submitting the new bid based on her real plan, not Dirk Cooley's made-up one this afternoon at," he checked his watch. "three p.m. once this emergency board meeting is concluded."

"Of course you had a breakfast meeting," Walter shot back, voice laced with sarcasm. "Everyone knows your reputation as a playboy."

For a moment, James had a vision of himself leaping across the room to grab Walter by his jacket collar. How dare he insult

Aubrey in front of all these men, pillars of Atlanta society. What if they met her in a professional setting? He made sure he looked each man in the eye before he spoke. The silence seemed to pulse, and he let it. He waited to see if anyone would come forward to defend him or at least warn off Walter. No one.

"It's true I had a reputation," he said slowly. "And many of you know that I've been focused on rebuilding my life and my reputation over the past year."

He saw a lot of the men shift uncomfortably, and why not? They all had sons, many of whom had had some trouble. He'd seen a lot of these men drunk at the same places where he'd overindulged.

"But Ms. Templeton is not part of that reputation, so let's keep her where she belongs, in the business column."

Even Walter looked uncomfortable. He was enough of a Southern Gentleman to not want to insult a woman or at least be caught out doing so.

"So you called me to an emergency meeting," he said.

"I didn't call you," Walter said. "I thought you were on vacation."

"Vacation?" he repeated, letting the word hang. "Everyone in the executive office knew where I was and why. The Templeton Tract is a local project. I don't want it going to outsiders. I intend to win it."

He could feel the tension in the room. It fairly hummed through him and everything here. He needed to win this bid more than ever. He needed to prove himself. Separate himself from his father and from his past.

"You as interim CEO is not what my father wants, Walter, and you know it. My father is ill, but I am confident he will get better. He hasn't lost his mind. On the contrary, he is quite focused on the future of this company. And it lies with me. I'm interim CEO and will become CEO at the next regular board meeting," James said, speaking slowly and powerfully, beginning to walk around the table toward the man, now his nemesis. He reminded himself to stay calm, executioner-like, and in control. He practiced the breathing technique he'd learned in recovery. Walter had no idea how far James had come, no idea. "So you are so unsure of your position that you wait until I am out of the office on business to make your move."

"I called this meeting, James, because we have important work to be done here." Walter said.

"As do I," James said. "The Templeton Tract."

"Word is the Chinese got it," Walter said, his beady eyes glaring at James. "An unfortunate development for all of us Southern-based loggers and the US in general. Can't believe you lost the bid to them, son."

Walter's information could only have come from Dirk. Their complicity made sense. They both wanted him out of Putnam Industries.

"I'm not your son. Who I am is Rick Putnam's son, and he has selected me to be CEO, a title I will assume with pride and a promise to honor my family's good name," James said. I haven't lost any bids on Indigo Island. Your inside information is faulty. And as I said earlier, I'm meeting with Ms. Templeton later today. No lease has yet been awarded. I will not stand for this power play, Walter. You know it is directly against my father's wishes. He made it clear to the two of us in his hospital room, and if necessary, he will repeat his decision in front of this very board. Although, I would hate to bother him with that when we all know what is right here," James said. The board members all turned and looked at Walter. Did they see a traitor or something else? They couldn't see him as a leader, could they?

"I don't recall any such pronouncement," Walter said.

"Well, then you are a liar or developing severe memory problems, Walter," James said, standing close enough to the man to smell his aftershave. "And before you put any more stock in anything Dirk Cooley tells you, you should know he's been fired from the project. Information stream dried up I'm afraid."

"You think you have all the answers, all the power, but you don't," Walter said, facing James, struggling to maintain composure. James realized he just needed to push him a little bit more and the board would see "the glue" for what he truly was. He was about to speak when Board President, Reginald Foster, stood up.

"All right, gentlemen," said Foster as he walked in between the two men, his slow southern voice calming as always. James thought Reginald looked like Colonel Sanders and talked like a Civil War Confederate general. "We will table any permanent decision on the CEO position until James lands the Indigo Island deal. Sound good?"

"Sounds perfect to me because he's lost it already, just like he's lost the CEO title," Walter said, and again James could hear a smattering of laughter behind him in the room. He couldn't tell how many of the board members Walter already had lined up against him, but judging by the volume of the laughter, there were at least several, maybe more.

"Walter, you're a snake. I will bring back the Indigo Island deal, and you will be looking for a job. My father would be so disappointed to learn of your conduct," James said, his jaw clenching as the "glue", as Walter called himself, walked away toward a group of board members standing by the doors.

"Oh, my conduct. Listen, Mr. Billionaire Playboy. Isn't that what the gossip columnists call you? I'd say you aren't one to judge conduct," Walter quipped from across the room and then turned his back to James.

James glared at the other man. He realized he didn't need to talk about how he'd changed, how he was sorry for those lost years. They may not believe him anyway. No, he needed to prove it, one day at a time, prove his character was up to the highest standards. And he would.

"I'd say time is of the essence, son. Godspeed," Reginald

said; he spoke quietly as he placed his hand on James' shoulder. "I know you're a changed man, son, and we're proud of you for that. You do, however, carry some baggage. No actions of youth are totally without repercussions. Let's see the new you in action and let that speak for itself. Let's take a break, gentlemen."

James locked eyes with Walter across the room until the older man smirked, and turned away.

"Son, revenge is a dish best served cold," Reginald said as they watched the group surrounding Walter file out of the boardroom first. James noticed some of the rest of the board members nodded his way as they left the room, others would not make eye contact. Those were Walter's supporters.

"Land the deal, make your first solo mark on this company, and there won't be any question about succession. I'll see you, and your father, at the next board meeting. Good day."

James stood in the boardroom as Reginald left. When the thick double doors swung shut and he was finally alone, he allowed himself to breathe. He opened his briefcase and pulled out the laptop, opening the new bid. As far as he knew, he'd already lost the Templeton Tract, which meant he'd lost the CEO title. He longed to talk to his father, whom he'd always been close to. Briefly, he considered heading over to the hospital, but knew he wouldn't. He didn't want to upset him, not in the fragile state he was in. James was a man, he couldn't ask his dad to fix things even if he wasn't sick. Same with his mom, she had enough to take care of with her dad's illness. The best thing he could do for all of them would be to retain control of Putnam Industries, keep a Putnam at the helm, on his own.

As he looked around the impressive boardroom and then walked to the window and looked down at the city below, James felt alone. His friends from his partying days were long gone, and since then, he'd focused so much on work, he didn't have a friend to turn to when he needed one. The best conversation he'd had in a long time was over breakfast this morning with Aubrey.

KAIRA ROUDA

He could call his sister, Avery, but even though her husband was getting involved in the family business now, he wasn't privy to board-level decisions yet. He couldn't involve them. His two brothers wouldn't be much help. Blake had distanced himself, literally and figuratively, from the family business, living in Charlotte and running one of the most successful genetic testing companies in the country, a company he founded. And Denton, the youngest? He'd graduate college in a couple months and join Putnam Industries. There was nothing he could do to help until he was working at the company. And the only way to assure Denton's path to leadership was clear would be to get Walter out of the way. James dropped into the leather seat at the head of the board table and pulled out his laptop. He would email the bid to Aubrey, the best he had to offer and still make a good business deal, and fly back to Indigo Island. That was all he could do for now, although he would be searching for more Sea Island leases to bid on, something he should have been doing when he botched the presentation on Thursday.

After checking the second bid contained all of the company's impressive green certifications, the very thing he'd overlooked before, he pressed send. In his mind, he imagined Aubrey sitting in front of her computer, opening the bid and reading intently. In reality, he knew, she had other bidders to entertain. He gathered up his belongings and shoved them into his briefcase. Using the boardroom telephone, he called Agnes and told her to have the helicopter ready for his return trip. Before walking back up to the helipad, he found Mrs. Trawley at her post outside his father's office. She smiled as he approached.

"I'm glad you were here, James. I heard it went well," she said, her pale blue eyes wise behind her wire-rim glasses. "And no word from the hospital, and that's good news." The woman was like a second mother to him, James realized, although the grey bun topping her head made her appear much older than she was. Her lack of care about appearances was just one of her endearing qualities. She was omnipresent, efficiently handling his dad's life, and their entire family's by extension. Her daughter, Agnes, was just as efficient and equally discreet. So, there were two people on team James, he realized.

"Yes, good news," James said, not sure why he was standing here, what he wanted from the woman. She took off her glasses, placing them on her desk and looked up at James.

"James, your daddy is a fighter. He'll be fine. And so will you. Go on back to the island and get that contract. It's what you're meant to be doing right now. Your daddy has everything he needs," she said.

And with her words, he was free to leave. "Thank you, and you'll –"

"I'll call with any news, here at the office or with your dad," she said, putting her glasses back on and turning her attention to the computer. "Go on."

The helicopter ride back to the island seemed to take forever, anxious as he was to find Aubrey. With all the turmoil of the past twenty-four hours, he'd forgotten to ask for her cell phone. He'd called her room at the inn before takeoff, but she hadn't answered. Back on the island, he climbed the steps to the front porch of the plantation and thought he heard voices coming from inside his home.

He turned the key and saw his brother, Blake, and his girlfriend, Samantha, hugging in the entryway.

"James, what are you doing here?" Blake said, breaking his embrace with Samantha and shaking hands with James.

"Great to see you, James," Samantha said, giving him a big hug. She was a friendly, beautiful girl. Bubbly and blonde. Blake seemed to have finally found the one.

"Mom knew I was coming down, I have a business deal involving the island," James said, shrugging. "She said nobody was using it."

"Same thing she told me. Well, she has a lot on her mind,"

Blake said and the brothers locked eyes. They both shared an intense love of their father, who they refused to believe could succumb to anything like cancer, or even old age. "We just came from the hospital. He doesn't look good."

"I know. I saw him right before I flew here. He could barely stay awake for my visit," James said. "It sucks. But he's going to get through it. Mrs. Trawley is confident. And, she does know everything."

"Yep, he's going to be fine, you guys, I know it, too," Samantha said, wrapping an arm around each brother. "Good thoughts. Only good thoughts."

James tried to smile. Good thoughts wouldn't be possible, not today. He was about to lose part of the island to another logging company, his position at work to a man who referred to himself as the glue, and if that wasn't enough, he'd forgotten making love to the most beautiful, intelligent woman he'd met in a long time. A woman he could, if the business wasn't involved, imagine spending a lot of time with. "Well, you guys have fun, I've got to go to the inn. Some business. The refrigerator is sort of stocked."

"Did you try to cook, James?" Samantha asked, her big blue eyes sparkling. "It smells like burned bacon in here."

"Yep, that was me. Sorry," James said, shoving his briefcase under the entry hall table and shrugging out of his suit coat and his tie. "I'll see you guys later." He walked out the door, knowing he wouldn't be missed by the lovebirds, who didn't even say goodbye.

Back at the inn, James found Jack standing behind the front desk. "Hey, Jack, could you ring Ms. Templeton's room?" he said. He tried to sound casual, as if his entire future didn't rely on her opening the email he'd sent with the second bid.

Jack dialed the phone. "Hi yes, Mr. Putnam would like to speak to you. Okay."

"What did she say?" James said as Jack replaced the receiver, hoping she hadn't told Jack to tell him to go away.

"She'll be right down," Jack said as James let out his breath.

James watched her walk down the stairs; her brown hair bounced on her shoulders and a smile lit her face. She wore simple khaki pants and a white shirt, but she looked like a movie star to James. Focus on business, he reminded himself.

"I'm glad you're here," she said as he met her at the bottom of the stairs.

"Really?"

"Yes, if it would be possible, could you give me a tour of my land? I mean I've been vacationing at the cottage since I was a child, but beyond that, I feel like I don't know the property like I should," she said; her brown eyes sparkled as she spoke and James fought the urge to kiss her, to tell her he'd give her whatever she wanted.

"I have just the way to show you. But what about the Chinese? I heard you'd signed the deal with them?" James said.

"No, Dirk signed the deal, but I killed it. They're mad, but they were negotiating without me, on the side. I walked in on them this morning, in a very compromising position," she said. "I think you're right about Dirk."

"That's one thing I know I'm right about. Dirk is a dirt bag. Did you get a chance to review my second bid?" he asked.

"I did. I thought it was right on the mark, if I go through with the logging rights lease," she said, flipping her ponytail over her shoulder.

James was puzzled. He knew she needed money, and he'd thought she'd settled on a logging lease. What did that mean for him and his bid? He decided he wouldn't push it. "Let's go see your land," James said. He needed to be patient. Dirk had ruined the deal with the Chinese company, and now, Aubrey was relying on his advice. It still seemed possible that there could be a deal signed with Putnam Industries, and he'd get to spend more time with Aubrey, something he'd been longing to do, even though he was determined to keep everything all business.

"Give me a minute to make a call and set a few things up," he said. "Do you have a camera? You'll want to take some photos," he said.

He hoped he could arrange a few things to make her tour special and sending her back to her room was a good distraction. He placed a couple calls while she was gone, and he was happy with the results.

∾

"Where are we headed?" she asked as he drove the golf cart along the winding path by the sea.

"To the helipad," James said. He'd called his pilot and asked for an island flyover. The man was basically on standby, ordered to be at the ready if James needed to get to his father's side, or back to the office in Atlanta. This tour of the island would be a more relaxing trip, for both of them.

"Excuse me?" Aubrey said, her beautiful brown eyes as big as saucers.

"The best way for you to get a feel for the beauty and expanse of the land you own is from the air," James explained. "Then we'll land and explore on the ground."

James loved flying in a helicopter, loved the sensation of no tethers, no restrictions; the freedom was very different from his work-obsessed normal life. He was excited to share the sensation with her.

"I'm afraid of heights. Sort of," Aubrey said as they climbed out of the golf cart.

"Hey James," the pilot said. As always, he wore a white t-shirt with company logo P in orange on his chest. "Ready to go?"

"Yes," James said.

"No," Aubrey said.

Both men turned and looked at Aubrey, who glared at them,

hands on hips. "I was picturing walking, or a golf cart tour, not this," she said, pointing to the helicopter.

"You'll love it, ma'am, give it a try," the pilot said, handing Aubrey a headset.

"Aubrey, trust me," James said, looking deep into her eyes to give her encouragement even as electricity surged through him. He wanted to kiss her, right then, but he knew he couldn't. She was gorgeous, even when she was terrified.

"Ok, I trust you," she said finally. James climbed into the backseat with Aubrey, holding her hand as they took off. He watched as her face turned from fear to excitement. "Look, a pod of dolphins!" She pointed out the window as the pilot dropped the helicopter lower for a closer look.

James had given the pilot a map of her holdings, and placed the same map in between them in the back seat.

"See down there, that's the start of your property. He's going to fly us around the perimeter, and then across the middle where the stream runs, just so you can see it all," James said. He noticed she hadn't pulled her hand free from his, and that was just fine with him. Sitting this close, he could smell the flowery shampoo she'd washed her hair with. She was driving him crazy. How could he have forgotten a night with her? Even with his drinking? He found himself wanting to tell her that his days of drinking were over. That he was in control of his life now. No more fuzzy or missing memories. He'd been clean and sober for almost a year. He'd changed his life for the better.

"I think that's my family's cottage!" she said, pointing out the window again. From this perspective the land below them was almost entirely green, various shades from lime to sage, the trees thick and full. The only breaks in the green were for her family's cottage tucked into a small clearing, sheltered by a grand magnolia tree, and the meandering path of the stream.

"It is. It's marked here on the map," he said. It was a gorgeous piece of land that James knew he could save, knew he had to protect even while he would need to carefully harvest a section of the property to ensure his position as CEO and to provide Aubrey the money she needed to get out from under her family's debt. He'd designated what he considered to be the best area to log, and had marked it on the map in front of them. It was the portion of her land closest to a dock for shipping, far away from the stream to reduce the risk of sedimentation. And it was miles away from her cottage, or any others on the island. They wouldn't need to build roads, or stream crossings, they'd simply pave the one dirt road that served the property now. It was the best choice, perhaps the only choice. He only hoped he had the opportunity to implement his plan.

"See this area I've marked in red, here," he said, pointing to his map. "This is my new proposal as outlined in the bid I sent you earlier today. I've looked at all the factors and this is the best solution. This is the only place we'd harvest. Roughly 250 acres."

"That seems like a waste of time, for a company like yours," Aubrey said.

"No, it's not. Those are old growth hardwoods down there, very valuable, and the leasing fee I can pay you will be enough to clear your debts." he said, "And of course you'll keep the land."

"Hmm, interesting, not at all what Dirk had dreamed up," Aubrey said. He saw shadows in her eyes.

"The important thing is you stopped him, and we have a plan," James said. "Ready to explore the land from the ground?"

"Sure," Aubrey said, as the pilot turned the helicopter towards the marsh on the backside of the island, landing in a dirt parking lot a few moments later.

Once the dust settled, James helped Aubrey unbuckle and they said goodbye to the pilot. "Follow me," James said, taking her hand and pulling her behind him, running for cover to a brightly painted house sitting near a dock. "He won't take off until we're inside."

They burst inside Marshside Mama's Restaurant just as they

heard the pilot start up the rotors again.

"Lily? Cole? Sally Ann? Anybody here?" James called out.

"I don't think it's open," Aubrey said, her eyes sparkling at him.

He hoped she was having fun and not making fun of him as usual.

"I can understand how you might think I'm an idiot, but I do know some things like the owners of this restaurant," James said. The smell of Cajun spices was seeping into his nose and he was craving her Low Country meals. "It is between meals, although Sally Ann will open up for dinner in under an hour."

"Hi hon," said Sally Ann, busting through the swinging door from the kitchen and making her way across the kitchen to wrap James in a bear hug. "Gotcha all set up here. And who is this young lady?"

"Sally Ann, please meet Aubrey Templeton," he said.

"Well, aren't you gorgeous," Sally Ann said taking both of Aubrey's hands in hers. "I've made you all some of my famous gumbo and a side of shrimp and cocktail sauce. Oh, and fresh cornbread. How's that sound, hon?"

"It sounds amazing," Aubrey said, and James loved how her face lit up as she talked to Sally Ann.

"This one is a keeper, young lady. He may not have thought much of himself for awhile there, but he's back and we couldn't be happier, uh huh," Sally Ann said. "Be right back."

Aubrey smiled. "I love this place. I want to eat here every night," she said, looking around at the wooden picnic tables painted in bright pastels, the white paper tablecloths, the red carnations stuck into simple glass vases.

"Wait until you taste her cooking," James said, as Sally Ann returned with their to-go order. "Go on, grab a couple of waters, otherwise you should have everything you need."

James gave Sally Ann a kiss on the cheek, grabbed two cold waters from the ice chest by the door, as Aubrey waved goodbye and they walked outside into the bright afternoon sunshine.

"We're walking the whole tract?" Aubrey asked as they walked into the parking lot. "I think we should find a spot to eat first."

"Patience is a virtue," James said, holding the bag of warm food, his own stomach growling. He realized he hadn't eaten since their shared breakfast. And since then, he'd been to Atlanta and back. "Don't worry, we aren't walking, but I do have a spot picked out for our early dinner. And we're riding those," James said, pointing to two horses, Sunshine and Moonshine, tethered to a tree just beyond the gravel parking lot. "Okay?"

"I love horses, but I've never ridden one," Aubrey said, as she squeezed his arm and gave him a quick kiss on the cheek "Thank you for all these surprises."

Aubrey was patting Sunshine's nose; the brown horse had a white diamond marking, while James fastened their picnic to the black horse called Moonshine. "These were the horses I grew up riding as a kid. Gentle, friendly. Did you ever ride on the island?"

"Afraid not," Aubrey said, "but I've always wanted to ride a horse. My parents both had asthma, so we weren't horse or dog people, unfortunately. But I'm not allergic!"

"I hope not," James said, thinking that could seal his fate, and hers. "A lot of firsts for you today, and with luck, an asthma attack won't be one of them," James said, his dimple visible as a smile lit his face. "Put your foot in the stirrup and I'll help you up."

He watched as Aubrey took a deep breath and walked to Sunshine's side. The horse whipped his tail, and Aubrey jumped back, crashing into James. He steadied her, finding his heart rate and breathing spiked as he felt her warm, curves under his hands and pressed against his body. Whenever their bodies touched, the electricity was crazy.

"You're fine. Sunshine's just welcoming you onboard," James said. "Grab the saddle here," he said, placing her hand on the horn, fighting to keep his voice calm, businesslike. This is business, he reminded himself as he helped lift her up into the saddle. She was stunning, sitting on horseback, the sun streaming over her shoulder, like a painting, like a dream. "Great. You're set."

"This is amazing, and sort of scary. I had no idea how high off the ground you are when you're on top of a horse," she said. "I know that's ridiculous."

"Not at all," James said, climbing onto Moonshine's saddle. "We'll take it slow, follow this trail. You'll follow me, Okay?"

"Okay, cowboy," she said and winked at James. She was killing him, looking gorgeous, riding a horse, and enjoying the land. She was his dream. Business partners, he reminded himself, but even that was far from certain. He had a hard time keeping the worry from clouding his mind and ruining this moment, but he forced himself to focus on this wonderful moment, something else he'd learned in recovery.

They reached the clearing James had mapped out about an hour later. It was part of her property, near the boundary of his clear-cut plan. The old growth hardwoods were magnificent, huge trunks with canopies reaching the sky. James dismounted and secured Aubrey's reins, helping her to the ground, his hands around her waist. He tethered the horses in the shade and pulled out their picnic feast. He felt Aubrey behind him.

"Here, let me help," she said, touching his shoulder, sending heat through his body.

James handed her the basket from Sally Ann as he untied the red blanket from Moonshine's saddle, unfurling it under the shade of the trees. It was a beautiful afternoon, the shadows danced from the leaves above them and the grasses in the clearing swayed in the warm afternoon ocean breeze.

As James spread out the blanket, she said, "I can't believe this is my land. It doesn't seem right, really, for me to own all of this." She pulled out the meals from the basket and handed one of the brown packages to him. The smells were making his stomach dance as he popped the to-go package open and began to eat. He wasn't going to comment on land ownership, his family's tract was even larger.

"It's all about what you do with the land," he said, taking a big drink of water. "That's what matters in the end. Were you a good steward, did you leave the place better, or at least lightly touched? That's what my bid offers. We can work together. I would love to teach you all about this magical place, have you learn all about conservation and preservation."

She looked at him, and he noticed her eyes had lost their sparkle, her jaw was tense. She said, "That's all this is about, right? The land lease, the bid."

He looked into her big brown eyes. He knew he owed her the truth, no matter what it cost him. "That's what it was about, all it was about when I arrived here yesterday," James said. "As you know, I didn't remember our history. All I knew was that this island is part of my heritage, and I needed to save it from Dirk and the clear-cut plan."

"Dirk said you need the deal to keep control of your family's business," she said quietly, dipping a shrimp into Sally Ann's famous cocktail sauce.

"True. As you know, with my dad's illness, he appointed me acting CEO. There are a few folks who don't believe I'm capable of holding the title permanently," he said. "But I am. Aubrey, you should know I'm sober and I have been, for almost a year. The man you met a year ago, is changed. I've matured. I have discipline. I don't mix business and pleasure. If anything, I'm too much business."

He saw her swallow, and when she spoke, her voice was soft. "Your essence hasn't changed," she said. "You were so kind, our night together. The sex was fabulous. But it was more than that. I guess that's why I thought finding you again would help me heal, move on. I think a little part of me actually fell in love with you that night. I know that sounds crazy. And don't worry, I'm over it. I was just lonely." She'd dropped her head and was staring at her hands folded in her lap. One of the horses neighed.

They sat in silence; James wanted to tell her the incredible attraction he felt, but felt that wasn't fair as he couldn't have both. "I'm lonely, too," he said to himself, pulling a blade of grass out of the ground.

Aubrey

HAD HE JUST admitted he was lonely, too, Aubrey wondered. Maybe she just imagined that he said those words, like she'd imagined her mom speaking to her every night. Aubrey's heart beat so fast she thought it would explode from her chest. Here she was, on a romantic picnic with the hot, gorgeous man she'd been dreaming about since they'd hooked up a year ago and all they seemed to do was talk business. What was the likelihood that the playboy party animal she'd had the best sex of her life with was now a reformed prude who only wants to save the land. Sure, he was still hot. And yes, she wanted him more now that he had principles, and it seemed like he was looking for love, too, but not with her because he only wanted her land.

It was about her land. The deal. His career. Not her.

But he's lonely, too.

As if he could gauge her changing mood, James broke into her thoughts. "I guess we should be heading back."

Every fiber of her being wanted him to kiss her, to at least confirm the incredible chemistry they shared. She rubbed the red blanket between her fingers and thought about the fact that she was here, on her family's land, sharing this space and time with the gorgeous man who was literally, the man of her dreams.

She couldn't take it anymore. "James," she said, leaning over him where he was lying on his side. "I can't take this hands-off approach any longer." She heard her breath catch in her throat as she looked down into his dark blue eyes. He pushed his hair back from his forehead, but he hadn't moved. It was if he'd made a vow to himself not to touch her.

"Your rules, Ms. Templeton," he said, his voice low as he sat up beside her.

"No, you're the one who is all business, Mr. Putnam," she said.

"Seems we're at a crossroad," he said, using his hand to push a stray hair out of her face, sending a chill down her spine.

"Are we? I think we may be just two lonely people who need each other," she said, touching the side of his face, the one with the dimple, lightly, feeling the stubble of his beard, the warmth of his skin as she leaned in and kissed him on the lips. She felt James' hand behind her neck as he kissed her back, pressing his lips into hers. He nipped her bottom lip and she heard herself moan as her head became dizzy with desire. She felt her lips part as his tongue pushed inside, exploring, until he pulled away.

"Oh my God, this isn't what I planned, you have to believe me," he said. "I'm so sorry."

Aubrey touched her fingers to her now swollen lips. "I believe you, but I started it," she said. "And I don't know if this is a good idea, but it just seems right."

"You really want to give me a second chance?" he said. He was holding her hand, staring into her eyes. The electricity between them was crazy, she knew he had to feel it, too.

"Last chance," she whispered.

Whatever control he'd had snapped.

James pulled her tightly to him and lowered them both to the blanket, grabbing her hair with one hand, kissing her with an urgency she had never felt before, had never imagined. It was as if he wanted to touch every part of her, take all of her for his own. He rolled her onto her back, and plunged his tongue in her mouth as heat slammed through her body. She opened her mouth wider, welcoming him, her tongue exploring him in return. She heard him moan her name. His kisses moved to her neck, and dropped to her chest, his hand brushing against her breasts.

But she needed to stop them, she had to finish the business first, and then she could trust herself with James, trust that he wanted more than just another meaningless hookup. It took a huge effort to turn away from their kiss.

"What's wrong?" he asked, as he propped himself up on an elbow and smiled down at her, his eyes a dark blue, his dimple teasing her.

"I need to be sure this isn't about the bid," she said.

"I told you, it's not," he said and she saw the smile leave his eyes. "Kissing you is, well, I've never felt like that before."

"Yes, you have. Once before," she said, reaching up and touching his face, as his smile returned. "And as soon as business is over, I'd like to pick up right where we've left off. Okay?"

"Sure, that's the logical approach," he said, shaking his head and then sitting up. He seemed in a daze, the same state she was in. He offered her a hand and helped her up as he stood. "We need to get the horses back before dark, although from the looks of things, we won't make it back to the stable in time. We can ride to my house, stable them there for the night. I can call the owner and let him know."

"Sounds like a plan, cowboy," she said, as she reluctantly helped roll up the blanket and clean up the picnic. She looked around at the pristine land around her, the sun setting through the trees. She could live in this beautiful place, she realized. She could feel the pull of the land, much like her parents must have. Of course, she realized, it didn't hurt that she had the most gorgeous bachelor on the island walking towards her with a dimpled grin on his face, two majestic horses following close behind.

She'd never realized horseback riding could be so sensual, not until James helped her climb back up onto the saddle, sending pangs of desire racing through her body, and not until she spent another half an hour following behind him on the trail, memorizing every muscle in his back, dreaming of a time when his strong arms could embrace her without hesitation. Hoping, someday, that would be possible.

Chapter Five

Aubrey

Thursday Afternoon

THE SUN HAD almost set by the time they reached the Putnam Plantation and the horses were eager to head inside the stable. Aubrey watched as James took care of the huge animals, removing their saddles, giving them water and feed. She loved watching him work, the care he showed for the horses. It was just another side of him that she loved, so different than the pompous playboy she'd thought he was, and hoped he wasn't.

"Okay, let's head inside," he said, closing the door to the stable and leading the way to the main stairs of the house and holding the door open for her. She was shocked by the appearance of a gorgeous blonde in the foyer.

"Oh, hi, I'm Samantha," she said, extending her hand to Aubrey.

"Yes, Sam, this is my friend and business associate, Aubrey Templeton," James said.

"Well, I'm his brother's friend and business associate," Sam said, winking at Aubrey.

"Hey Samantha," James said. "Where's Blake?"

"He went to the general store. Great to meet you Aubrey, come on in and tell me all about yourself," Samantha said, grabbing Aubrey's hand and pulling her toward the library. Aubrey turned and looked at James, begging for help. She wasn't in the mood for girl talk. She needed to get back to the inn, back to business. Surely, he could think of something they needed to do, an excuse to get away. And she was starting to get a little itchy.

"Samantha, I'd love to get to know you but I'm afraid I'm having an allergic reaction to the horses," Aubrey said, making eye contact with James, trying to let him know she was fine.

He didn't seem to notice.

"Oh, no, Aubrey, you need to get straight in the shower. I had a friend who was allergic and he'd break into hives everywhere," James said.

"Oh no. Do you have asthma, too?" Sam said.

"I'll be fine," Aubrey said.

"No, you need to shower and change. We'll be right back down," James said, pulling on Aubrey's arm.

"Ok, cool, I'll be in the kitchen," Sam said, as Aubrey followed James – almost in a jog – up the stairs.

"We must look ridiculous," she said, laughing at the top of the stairs. "I'm fine. I just have the tiniest of itches, but I really do need to go."

"I don't care," James said. "I'd feel better if you were safe about it. Just shower here and I'll take you back to the inn. I'm not going to be responsible for an asthma attack."

"Fine, you're right," she said, realizing she was getting itchier, probably because they were talking about it.

James opened the first door on the left, just at the top of the stairs revealing a room befitting the rest of the Putnam Plantation. A gorgeous bedroom with hardwood floors, a king-sized bed and full ocean views out the windows. The sun was just beginning its setting dance, and the room was bathed in an orange glow. The furnishings were all white, white chairs, white comforter, white thick rugs a stark contrast to the dark hardwood floors. It was a room as beautiful as the rest of the home. Aubrey was enchanted, and her head was spinning. How did she end up here, in this room, with this man.

"Welcome to my sister's bedroom, my friend and business associate. The bathroom is just over there. Help yourself to whatever you need. You guys are probably similar in size. I'll be downstairs and when you're ready, I'll drive you back to the inn," he said.

"And your bedroom?" she said. She wanted him to grab her, pull her to him. They were standing so close if she leaned in just a bit she could start another kiss.

James leaned back, as if he sensed what she was doing. "After our business is concluded I'd be delighted to show you all of my bedroom. In the meantime, I do have quite a shell collection I could let you see. My bedroom is conveniently located across the hall. If you'd like to freshen up, decontaminate yourself so to speak, I'll pull out the best specimens."

"I'd like that," she said, and walked into the luxurious bedroom and closed the door.

James

"YOU GUYS ARE cute together," Samantha said as she caught James sneaking downstairs for water and snacks.

"Hey James, never knew shell collections were a chick magnet," Blake said, standing next to Samantha, his arm around her waist, both of them prepared to give him unmitigated grief. Samantha must have overheard them talking, James realized.

"Look, you two weren't even supposed to be here. It was my house for the week and well…" James said, and flung his hands in the air. He'd been riding horses for hours, he hadn't showered, he was sexually frustrated and not in the mood for teasing, even if it was good natured. "Stop eavesdropping. Okay?"

"Whoa, brother, back down, we're just joking," Blake said.

"She's beautiful, James," Samantha added, nodding her head up and down. "And no relationships are easy. Just ask Blake's assistant, Marlene, about ours. One minute we're great, the next he's sulking in his office about a deal."

Blake shot Sam a look, and that made James smile and relax a bit. "I know. Nobody's perfect. But this week, I've discovered I forgot a woman I should have kept in my life and I'm losing a title I've been preparing for all of my working life. I need to focus, and I need to grab some water," he said, walking past them into the kitchen before they could formulate any other questions or comments.

"You can't allow that," Blake said, blocking the doorway out of the kitchen with his lifeguard buff body.

"What? I'm trying my best to prevent Walter from grabbing the CEO title, and I'm walking a fine line with Aubrey. Unlike you, I don't control my own destiny yet, bro. With Dad's sudden illness, things are in a flux. But I'm confident I'll get on top of things," James said, while selfishly enjoying the double entendre he hadn't meant to say. He'd pulled out a baking sheet and gathered two glasses of ice water, a Kind Bar and a bowl of strawberries. He hoped that would do for a post-ride, almost romantic roll in the pasture snack.

"Odd snack choices. But let's talk after you are finished up there. Maybe I can help. By the way, do you know what this is about?" Blake asked, handing him a red piece of paper. Printed on it in thick black letters was: *Stop Putnam Industries! Say NO to deforestation! Meeting tomorrow, 7 p.m. General Store. Be there.*

"Where'd you get this?" James asked.

"They're all over town, stapled to trees, taped to doors, in people's mailboxes. I am not sure who you pissed off, but they're definitely on a mission to stop you from whatever it is you're doing. When I went to the general store today for supplies, I felt like a leper. Me. A Putnam. We built this island, we support it still today. So whatever it is you're doing, you need to stop,"

Blake said, pushing his hand through his white blonde hair.

"This is Dirk," James said, grabbing the flyer from his brother's hands.

"Dirk Dirk? The Cooley Family's Dirk?" Blake said, chuckling. They all had made fun of Dirk's name growing up.

"Yep. Remember he was kicked out of the family business, and has decided his first love is forest management consulting," James said, heading out of the kitchen carrying the tray. He knew Aubrey must be thirsty and she was probably hungry. Also they'd had a lot of exercise.

"So let me guess. He has made it his goal to mess with Putnam Industries and our clients," Blake said, following him to the stairs. "Okay, well, go take care of your girlfriend and then let's all get together for dinner. You need a plan, brother. The town is up in arms."

"You're right. I do need a plan. And thanks for offering to help," James said. He tapped lightly on the door figuring Aubrey must have found something in his sister's wardrobe. When she pulled it open, he was speechless.

Aubrey was dressed in Avery's jeans and a white cashmere sweater. Her hair was clean and still damp, shining in contrast to the sweater. He knew she didn't wear much makeup, but she glowed.

"Hi," she said, seeming to blush as he carried the baking sheet full of random snacks into the room.

"You look beautiful, Aubrey. Are you feeling okay?" he said, placing the tray on Avery's bed, made with the same white linens as his own. "Do you like strawberries?"

"Love them, and yes, all the itchiness is gone," she said, and she plucked one of the strawberries from the bowl and popped it in her mouth. Everything in him wanted to follow that with a tender kiss; the thought of that made his heart beat out of turn. He handed her a glass of water and picked up his own as they both took a drink in unison, watching each other all the while.

"Can we sit for a minute," James said, pointing to the two white, overstuffed chairs facing the ocean. "I need to be sure I apologize, it's part of the program." He took a deep breath as she settled into the chair next to him. "I used to party every night, and I mean every night. I thought I was entitled to it, that I was working hard during the day so that justified it. I don't doubt you when you say we were together, and I thank God that we found each other again, but I honestly have no memory of that first time. But I promise you this, as long as I live, I'll never forget this afternoon, spending time with you on this gorgeous island, laughing, riding horses, getting to know each other. So again, I'm sorry. I hope you'll forgive me."

Aubrey smiled, a tear in the corner of each eye. "You're forgiven. And I was drunk that night, too. If we have another chance, well," she said, blushing and looking at her hands. "Well, it will be better. It's better sober, it's more real, more vivid. Anyway," she said, clearing her throat. "I've got to get back to the inn."

"Looks like I have some business there, too," James said, handing her the flyer from his back pocket.

"Dirk," she said, shaking her head.

"I'm assuming he's no longer in your employ?" he said.

"Of course not. I fired him as soon as I could. How can he do something like this?" Aubrey asked, holding the paper, rereading its incendiary message.

"Anybody can accuse anyone else of anything. We just need to get the facts out about what's happening to your land. If you have decided to work with me, then we stand together and take on all of these folks at the meeting," James said. He turned away from her, shoving both of his hands into the back pockets of his jeans. He didn't want to see her face when she crushed his chance to become CEO by telling him he didn't win the bid.

"I haven't quite decided that part. I need some more time. I have one more presentation tomorrow," she said, and his heart dropped. He thought she understood how much he cared about both her, and her land yet he hadn't persuaded her at all. Suddenly, he needed out of the room, needed space away from her. He turned toward the door, pulling it open. "James, wait. I can explain."

James felt the life rush out of his body, his hopes and dreams with it, all because of a stupid twenty-five hundred acre tract of land. He imagined Walter, the toast of the next board meeting, referring to him as son and assuring him his time would come, just not now. *James, you're just not ready. James, you have a sordid past. James, I want you, I trust you, but you couldn't even land a tiny lease on a tiny Sea Island.*

"I'll see you downstairs. I need to talk with my brother," James said, and walked out of the room without looking back.

Chapter Six

Aubrey

Thursday Evening

S HE'D FELT THE light leave the room as soon as James walked out of the door. His actions proved the land was more important to him than their relationship, something she'd guessed but didn't want to believe, especially after the picnic today. Not after the romantic kiss they had shared, a kiss that promised much more. He'd even apologized for the past, and he'd looked so sincere.

But the truth was hard to hide, and ultimately, when the contract came up he couldn't meet her eyes. If he had, she would have seen that the land contract had been the reason he'd wanted to sleep with her. And she had almost fallen for it. She would have to try to learn to accept that and move on. Fortunately, plan B for business arrived on the early ferry. She had no idea what plan B for love would be.

She understood James was disappointed that she hadn't given him the land management contract after all the time he spent with her today, showing her the possibilities for her tract and how to save most of it from logging. But she still had one more meeting before she could award it to anyone. Even him. And she couldn't tell him about that meeting because she'd agreed to sign an NDA – non-disclosure agreement – before the firm would even set foot on the island. She'd signed it, and they'd agreed to her quick timetable, arriving by private jet in Hilton Head first thing tomorrow morning, and then taking a private ferry to meet her at the inn conference room at nine a.m. sharp. From all of her research, she decided this could be the best answer to save her family's land. But she couldn't share any of this with James.

The man joining her in the morning was a billionaire who had created the most successful eco-friendly resorts in the world, and he was looking for a Sea Island destination. As Aubrey skimmed his website this morning she read all the words she wanted to read. Zero carbon footprint, pristine surroundings, low-impact build-outs, no-visit zones for guests to preserve sensitive lands. She could save her family's cottage, lease land to this hotel developer who would try not to cut any trees and if he did, would use them for construction of the property, the way it was supposed to be. No harvesting, just using local resources. It could be a win-win. He'd even taken his call, his voice warm and friendly on the telephone. Everything could work out.

Except for James. She knew he wanted this deal for Putnam Industries, although she sensed it was more about preservation of the island. If that were the case, he'd understand. If he truly respected her, and her holdings, he'd see this could be a brilliant solution. If he was all about himself, well, he wouldn't like it, not at all. And all the love she felt for him would be misplaced, as it had been before.

Aubrey looked around James' sister's gorgeous bedroom and knew she should be going back to the inn. She couldn't tell James anything more about her meeting in the morning, and he was convinced it was another logging company.

As she made her way down the grand staircase she inhaled the sweet smell of lilies in the vases lining the entry hall. She heard James and his brother talking in the library, and smelled the thick smoke from a fire in the fireplace. And as warm and as welcoming as the home was, as happy as she had been when she'd kissed James on the red blanket just a few hours earlier, she knew now the night was ruined. She couldn't tell him about her plans for the morning. She knew the best thing for both of them would be for her to go home. She looked both ways to make sure nobody was in the foyer, bolted for the door and headed out into the dark night.

James

"CAN'T WE JUST make up another bid you're about to land?" Samantha asked. She was curled up on Blake's lap.

"No, this is different. It's the biggest piece of land to ever become available on Indigo Island. Of course the Putnams would try to control it, bid on it. And how dare anyone believe we could do anything but the right thing for this place. We saved The Melrose Inn, for God's sake. It would be out of business if Dad and I hadn't stepped in," James said, continuing to pace back and forth in front of the fire. "And now, one man can turn them all against us?"

"To be fair, you don't know how many are against us," Blake said. "But it's disconcerting nonetheless. I'd say you tell them you'll put a halt on any harvesting until the community can have its say. Buy her out if you have to, but – and as you know this is the reason I left the logging business – don't cut any trees down. Do you know how magnificent her live oaks are?"

James stopped pacing and glared at his brother. "I'm intimately aware of how gorgeous her live oaks are, as well as her loblolly pines and her magnolia, if you're curious. The problem is she won't sell to me. She's convinced the land is her roots. She's right, the land has been in her family for generations. The problem was she picked the wrong consultant. She's been twisted by Dirk, and now I think, although she won't tell me, that she has another suitor flying in tomorrow, probably another unscrupulous logger. I didn't know there would be so much interest over a small tract on this tiny sea island, but there is. China was here, on Indigo Island and they almost got the deal. Maybe it's North Korea?"

Blake smiled and Samantha chuckled. "I think you're being too hard on her. It's all new, right? She needs to feel in control, not bullied. Sounds like all you and that Dirk creep have done is tell her what to do," Samantha said. "Who's hungry? Go get your girlfriend and let's go eat dinner. I'll talk some sense into her."

"Good plan," Blake said. "Let's eat at the inn, we can talk to some friends there, try to take the pulse of the island before the rally."

"I'll go get Aubrey. Hopefully she'll be up to eating with us," James said, taking the stairs two at a time and hurrying to Avery's door. He hoped she wasn't angry again. He'd only left the room because he didn't want her to see the disappointment in his eyes. She was free to award the bid to whomever she wanted, but he couldn't hide his emotions, especially not from her.

The door to Avery's room was open, but the room was empty. "Aubrey?" he said. He walked across the hall and checked his bedroom, but no Aubrey. He realized, just then, he still didn't have her cell phone number. He walked to the top of the stairs, and looked down at Samantha and Blake who waited for him at the bottom in the entryway.

"You two go on. I'm staying home. She's gone," he said.

"No, you're not," Blake said. "I need you to come to town. We need to hear together what people are saying. With or without Aubrey, we're defending the Putnam name and in the process, screwing over Dirk, and his new friend, Walter. Got it?"

"It's too late, Blake," James said, appreciating his brother's support. "I'm almost certain she's giving the lease to someone else, that's why she left."

"You don't know that," Blake said.

James realized he wasn't certain of much of anything at the

moment. "True," he said and made his way down the stairs.

"That's better, mister," Samantha said as he reached the bottom. "I can't believe she didn't say goodbye."

"Me either, Sam," James said as they walked out into the chilly night. "Hey, I just realized I need to return a picnic basket to Marshside Mama's."

"I'll drive Sally Ann's basket back in the morning. I have a delivery coming on the eight a.m. ferry," Blake said.

"I can take it back tomorrow. I have to return two horses to Pete's stables."

"What's up with you?" Blake asked, looking at his brother as they climbed into the golf cart. "Why do you have Pete's horses here?"

"I had a plan, to show Aubrey the island and woo her with my business prowess. But I think I've been had," James said, climbing in back so Samantha could sit up front next to Blake.

Samantha turned around in the golf cart, giving him that pity look and said, "What is going on?"

"Aubrey insisted Dirk include Putnam Industries in the RFP because we'd hooked up before in Atlanta. She's a Buckhead native," James said, "Aubrey didn't know Dirk despised our family and that he would send me a phony Forest Management Plan to base my proposal on. So my bid was completely opposite of what she expected, and what every other logger presented. I thought the forestry plan was a disaster so I offered to buy the tract, which really pissed her off."

"I bet," Blake said softly.

"And when we hooked up, I was in my out-of-control period. I didn't even remember her or her ties to the island. Perfect, right?"

"Still, she was happy to see your shell collection this afternoon, I'd say," Sam said, with a wink.

"We had a great afternoon together, spent a lot of time on her land," James said, looking out into the dark forest to avoid eye contact. "I really enjoy being with her, but I think she's still out for revenge because I don't remember her."

Samantha looked at him sympathetically., but Blake frowned. "So this time she used you for sex, and she's trying to ruin our family's reputation on the island? What a girl," Blake said. "You sure know how to pick them."

"Blake," Sam said softly.

He made a face. "Let's take the horses back tonight," Blake said. "Pete's pretty protective about them, and I could use the exercise to clear my head. This situation with the company and now people on the Island thinking we're clear cutting is pissing me off."

"You," James said. That was a massive understatement as far as he was concerned.

They parked and James hopped out to open the old barn door. Blake joined him as they saddled the horses.

"Want to ride Sunshine, for old times' sake?" James said, holding the reins to the brown horse out to his brother.

"This is becoming the weirdest night," Blake said, and then said to Sam, "Are you all right getting to the inn from here?"

"Sure, you all go on. I'll get us a table. I'll let the restaurant hostess know to be on the lookout for two hot cowboys and to send them my way. Giddey-up, y'all," Sam said as Blake leaned over and kissed her. James looked away.

Blake and Sunshine were galloping and James and Moonshine were in hot pursuit. The horses were so anxious to get to the barn, James was sure they couldn't have reined them in regardless. The stable manager, Mr. Pete, was waiting for them, sitting in a rocking chair under the single light of the barn's main entrance, his dark face shadowed by his cowboy hat.

"About time," he said, as the men dismounted and the horses made gleeful snorts, relieved to be home. "Did ya'all think you could just keep 'em out as long as you like, son? 'Cause you're a Putnam? Things don't work that way around here."

"I left a message for you," James said, knowing that he was still in the wrong, yet the level of hostility was something far beyond what he'd expected. They'd known Pete since they were all kids, taken riding lessons beginning as toddlers. Pete knew James would take care of the horses. What was going on, he wondered, until he saw the red flyer posted above Pete's head, tacked to the door of the barn.

"I apologize. The horses, as you can see, are fine and well taken care of," James said.

"No thanks to you. Putting them in a strange barn instead of bringing them home. It's just not right."

Everybody knew everybody's business on this island, James thought. "Right. Well, here they are, safe and sound."

Pete scoffed, but slowly rose from the rocking chair and took the horses' reins in his old, gnarled hands.

"Mr. Pete, you should take down that flyer. It's a lie," Blake said. "Putnam Industries has no plans to clear-cut harvest Putnam land holdings or the Templeton Tract. We don't even own the Templeton land, nor were we awarded the bid. Hell, we don't know what logger she will pick. Picket Aubrey Templeton, will you? We are a family of environmentalists, we have invested heavily in preserving this island. You know that. My dad bought you this barn," Blake added, his anger rising with the strength of each statement. James put a hand on his shoulder to calm him.

"Your daddy is a good man and I pray for him to have a speedy recovery, we all do. As for your generation, all I see are spoiled kids in helicopters flying through the air and driving around like they own the place," Pete said, continuing to walk the horses into the stable. "Money can't buy respect, boys, nor can it buy silence. The root doctors will take care of this. Night."

"What the heck?" James said, as he kicked the ground. "Root doctors? Are they bringing out the mystics to fight us, too?"

"You have created a mess. The whole island hates us." Blake yanked the flyer off the barn and shoved it into James' hand.

"What are you going to do about it?"

James held the red paper in his hands. "I'm going to that meeting," James said. "I have honesty on my side. Dirk only has hate and lies."

"We need to go find Sam," Blake said. "I hope she isn't getting this kind of treatment from everyone."

The brothers took off in a jog, hurrying toward the inn, arriving at the circular driveway only to see their golf cart covered in the red flyers. In large letters someone had scrawled: "Enjoy dinner with the rest of the tourists."

"Unbelievable." James began ripping off the flyers and balling them up. The tape pulled up some of the paint. "Unbelievable. We've been here for generations. We've done so much for this island and many of the residents and for them to turn on us like this for nothing but venomous innuendo."

Blake's jaw was clenched as they both hurried up the steps. He barked a laugh when James dumped the torn flyers in the recycle bin.

"We're not total environmental sinners," Blake noted drily.

"The irony of all these flyers wasn't lost on me," James said tensely, pushing open the door with more force than necessary.

Jack Means was behind the front desk, and he looked up startled at their abrupt entry.

"Hey, guys. What's going on?" he asked, holding up a fist full of red flyers. "Everyone's in an uproar and I know it can't be true what they're saying."

James took a deep breath, feeling that at least somebody was on their side.

"Have you seen Samantha? I need to make sure she's Okay," Blake said.

"She's fine. She's upstairs in the dining room, chatting with Dorsey, waiting for you," Jack said, and James felt Blake relax a bit beside him.

"Don't worry, James, I'm not allowing any of these to be

brought inside the Melrose Inn. The Putnams supported me when I needed it most and I'm here for you all, you just tell me what you need," Jack said.

Jack owed his livelihood to James and his dad, who bought the Inn and had named him manager after the last management company pulled out. It was nice to have a friend, but they'd need a lot more than just him on their side.

"Thanks, man. Let's go eat," Blake said, shaking Jack's hand and heading up the stairs to the dining room.

"Right," James said, considering all of his options as they climbed the grand stairway. He wanted to talk to Aubrey; she was probably in her room just down the hall right this moment, but she'd left his house without a goodbye. He needed to move on, make another plan. He'd search the bid boards for another logging project in the Sea Islands and land the contract. He'd move on from Aubrey, a woman he'd forgotten once, but he knew he'd never forget again. But before he left the island, he'd make sure the Putnam image was restored.

As they joined Samantha and Jack's wife, Dorsey, at the table, James felt like the rest of the tables of diners were staring at them. That had to be his imagination, he told himself. Dorsey jumped up, kissed each of the Putnam men on the cheek and then excused herself, leaving the three of them alone at the table.

"Nice of her to keep you company," Blake said, stroking Samantha's cheek. "I got worried about you. Our reception tonight has been unfriendly."

"I'm sorry, honey," Sam said, and then looked at James. "You look horrible. Just withdraw your bid. Find another piece of land, and the board will be happy. Problem solved. Have some She Crab soup. It's really the best. Sorry I didn't save any, but you all should order some."

James tried to smile, tried to imagine if remaking his life, salvaging his career and somehow managing to create a relationship with Aubrey could all be accomplished by a delicious bowl of soup. He wasn't really clear who he would withdraw the bid from. The gorgeous woman who snuck away after their romantic picnic, or the forestry consultant who had screwed him over in the first place. Despite what Aubrey said, Dirk might still be working with her. She didn't trust him, and he was no longer sure he could trust her.

James locked eyes with Blake. "What if she is the opposite of what she seemed? What if this whole thing has been to set me up?" James said.

"Why would she?" Sam asked. Her pretty blue eyes sparkled in the candlelight, and James realized just how happy his brother was, and how lucky.

"What if she is an environmentalist who wanted to trap Putnam Industries into the plan I presented, to make us look terrible to the island?"

"Well, yes, that's all happened," Blake said. "But you said she needs money."

"Maybe a wealthy environmentalist is paying her off, helping her set this all up," James said.

"That sounds paranoid to me," Sam said. "I think you two just need to talk. I didn't meet her for long, but she seemed really into you. I could tell from her eyes. I don't know why she snuck out tonight, but there's got to be a better answer than she's a secret environmentalist double agent spy. Right?"

James looked at the menu, trying to decide what to order when his stomach was as tense as his jaw. A headache was working its way up the back of his neck. "I don't know, Sam," he said. "Whatever she is or isn't, I need to move on and I will. For all of our sakes."

Chapter Seven

Aubrey

Friday Morning

AUBREY SAT DOWN in the inn's dining room, feeling more confident in herself and her future. She'd received several angry texts from Dirk that she'd ignored. He claimed James was a liar, untrustworthy. James may not have strong feelings for her, but she knew his feelings about the island, its people and the forested land were true. If only she could be as confident that he wanted her as much as her land.

As Aubrey stared out at the ocean, she felt a shadow over her shoulder. "I'll have two eggs, over easy and sourdough toast. Black coffee."

As she looked up to hand the waiter her menu, she looked into the eyes of James' brother, Blake.

"Oh, sorry, I thought you were my waiter," she said, feeling the blush spread across her face as Blake took the seat across from her.

"May I take your order, miss?" her waiter asked, and she repeated her order. "Sir?" the waiter asked Blake.

"Coffee. Black. Thanks," he said to the waiter, and then resumed staring at her, his big blue eyes intense.

She watched as he pulled a crumpled piece of red paper out from his pants pocket, pressing it flat with his hand. From his other pocket he pulled out a small leather packet, placing it on the table next to the flyer.

"Is this you?" he said. His voice deep, his eyes squinting.

"No, what are these?" she asked as he pushed the leather pouch closer to her. She picked it up and peeked inside. All she saw was a tangle of hair, human hair, and it smelled awful, like urine. She pushed it back his way, pinching her nose with her fingers.

"That pouch was left on our golf cart last night. We think it's a sign we've been 'fixed' as the natives call it. Someone ordered a root doctor to put a curse on my family." Blake said, his eyes flashed bright blue and she saw his square jaw clench. He was so much like James, just a bit blonder.

"Surely you don't think I would 'fix' you," she said, using air quotes around the word. It was absurd, she couldn't believe a grown man, an educated man who owned a huge company would even ask her such a ridiculous question.

"Is this you?" he said, pushing the red flyer to her.

"Blake, what the Hell are you doing?" James came up to the table, his jaw tense. Aubrey wished her heart hadn't leaped in joy. He looked so handsome.

Blake shrugged. "You weren't going to confront her. We need to know."

She found herself trapped by James' beautiful gaze.

"No. We need to go to the meeting. Explain the situation."

Blake made a rude sound and stood up. Aubrey forced herself to look away from James, focus on the red flyer.

It read: "**Stop Putnam Industries from killing our trees, ruining our island. Rally tonight. 6 p.m. Bring everyone.**"

She looked up and shook her head. "No, this was not me." She looked back at the red paper and in fine type it read, "**The Putnam and Templeton Tracts together comprise more than half of Indigo Island. Logging of these beautiful lands will destroy this special island for generations. ~ The Save Southern Trees Society**"

"Obviously I didn't do this," she said slowly. "But maybe

Dirk is part of this. He's been harassing me by text and phone. He thinks I've awarded the bid to your brother, so he's extracting revenge, trying to block the deal," she said, looking directly into James' eyes, wanting him to know that even if they didn't have a future, she hadn't tried to hurt him. "The contract is still open. You have to believe me."

"It's your land," James said. "Your decision."

Blake tossed the flyer and pouch aside.

"There may be another way," Aubrey said. "I want to look at all my options." She wasn't going to be bullied, not by any man, and definitely not by a Putnam.

"Like what?" Blake demanded. "In the meantime, our family's name is ruined."

"That's not my fault," she said.

The waiter appeared with her plate but she'd lost her appetite.

"Blake. Leave her alone," James said sharply.

"I have another meeting," Aubrey said, wondering why she could just walk away and leave Blake frustrated and James angry, although the fact that he was defending her filled her with a warmth she shouldn't be feeling.

She took another sip of coffee to steady her nerves. She looked at her watch.

"You will have to wait for my decision, James."

He shook his head. "I meant what I said yesterday, Aubrey."

"What?" His eyes were so intensely blue that she found it hard to breathe.

"Yesterday wasn't just about the land or the bid." He held his hands up as if in surrender. "I withdraw the bid."

"What? Unbelievable." Blake shook his head and walked off, muttering a curse under his breath.

"But...." She couldn't continue. What did he mean? What did that mean for them?

"Just go to your meeting. Get the best deal for you. Move on with your life."

She wanted to throw herself in his arms, but wasn't sure of her reception. He looked so alone. Pale. Almost ill, but he smiled. "We can talk later if you want."

"I...," Aubrey took a step forward, but he shook his head. "I'll go to the rally, James. I will fix this. I'll explain to everyone on the island that our families are not connected in any way beyond our adjoining land holdings." She ignored her breakfast and hurried out of the room and rushed down the stairs, making it into the conference room just a little after nine.

The group from Eco Resorts International had already arrived and were busy setting up for their presentation. All four of the men looked up and smiled. "Welcome," they said in unison, and Aubrey began to relax as she shook off her unexpected encounter with Blake and her confusion over James. His defense of her made her think he cared, but then he'd withdrawn his bid. Did that mean he wanted her to think his feelings for her were genuine or that he just wanted to be finished with any contact with her.

Focus, she reminded herself.

She took a deep breath and smiled. The mood in the room was opposite of what Dirk had set up in the meetings he'd hosted for her. He had arranged the room formally, while she had instructed the inn staff to arrange the seats in a circle, a round table facilitating conversation and cooperation, she knew.

"Mr. Davinci, thank you, all of you for coming on such short notice," Aubrey said, crossing the room and shaking his hand. He looked Italian like his name implied, a handsome man with slick dark hair, a fine-featured chiseled face and narrow, slim build. He wore a perfect fitting dark navy suit. Aubrey was impressed.

"A pleasure, Ms. Templeton. Meet my team: Marco, Sid, and Dominic. We're excited to begin. Please, have a seat," he said, pulling out a chair with a flourish.

"Our vision for your property involves just a small corner of your land, a mere 350 acres, leaving the rest in its natural state for you to enjoy now, and your children to enjoy someday," he said. "You will not even know the hotel is there, unless of course you'd like to indulge in spa services."

Aubrey sighed, hoping this wasn't all too good to be true.

Marco stood and presented the quick facts of the project: solar panels would power the hotel, heat generated from air conditioning would be recaptured and used to warm water, non-toxic and organic paints and furnishings would be used throughout the property, composting, rainwater recycling, local employment opportunities with potential for career advancement and mobility within other hotels in their chain, and so many more features that Aubrey stopped writing and couldn't stop smiling. The hotel would be built on pilings, typical in the Low Country, allowing natural water flow to continue across the land. Instead of harvesting any of her trees, they recommended sourcing the highest-grade, tree farm certified lumber for construction.

"We've heard of the famous restaurant on the island, Marshside Mama's," one of the men, she thought it was Marco, said. "We would like her to consider partnering with us, teaching us the authentic cooking of the Sea Islands."

Aubrey hoped Sally Ann would be thrilled at the opportunity. As she listened to the presentation, and looked over the sketches they'd drawn up of what it could look like, she dreamed of being able to show it to her parents. They'd be so proud. Surprisingly, the other person she wanted to share it with was James.

"We will be sure the resort, as with all of our other properties, will be LEED Gold certified and Eco-Certified, Advanced Tourism, the highest designation. It will be the first of its kind in the American South," Mr. Davinci said, his enthusiasm contagious. "Part of the land we'd like to purchase, or lease, from you will be designated learning lands where guests can take a journey back in time, learn about Gullah culture, the healing properties of certain plants, and the importance of the animals and plants found here. Imagine guided bird walks, star gazing perhaps. So wonderful."

Aubrey sat back and placed her palms on the table. "Mr. Davinci, I'm so glad we found each other. I love everything you've described. And while I know any development has an impact, I believe you've discovered a way to leave a very soft footprint."

"That we have, Ms. Templeton. And now, I am assuming you'd like an offer?" he asked, his eyes twinkling as he pulled an envelope from his breast pocket.

"That would be great," Aubrey said, realizing her palms had begun to sweat. All of this must be too good to be true. She held the sealed envelope Mr. Davinci handed her as all the men stood.

"We will give you some time, alone, to contemplate the offer. We will return in say, an hour?"

"Thank you," she said, as each of the men bowed and walked out the door. Once it had shut behind them, Aubrey opened the envelope and couldn't believe what she saw. She sprang out of her chair. "Oh my God, oh my God! This is it! This will work. Why did I listen to Dirk in the first place. This is it!"

"Oh, sorry to interrupt, I was just refreshing water," Jack said, half in, half out of the door. "I thought you were all on break. I'm sorry Ms. Templeton."

"Call me Aubrey. And I'm sorry for screaming in here by myself. You heard that didn't you?" she said, and knew he had as his face flushed bright red. "I just got the best news I've had in a long time, Jack. I'm going to build a luxury eco-resort on the backside of the island, on my property. It will have zero environmental impact. Isn't this great?"

"Yes, great," Jack said, putting the pitcher of water down on the table, and taking a moment to look at the renderings. "This is really cool. You'll be a competitor, you know."

"Oh, my gosh, I hadn't even considered that," Aubrey said. Why did she keep stepping on people's toes on this island?

"No, it's okay. I've always heard more choice is good for both of us. Look, Burger King always put a store on the corner across from McDonald's. It must work," he said smiling. "Anyway, you've got to tell the Putnams and get them out of this mess with the locals. It's ugly."

Her stomach twisted at the mention of James. She never intended to hurt him. She'd come to this place to find her roots, to get closure on her grief and to reconnect with James. It seemed like everything had worked out for her, but not for him. She wanted to fix the mess she'd brought on the Putnams by hiring Dirk.

"I will talk to James," she said. "But first I have to finish this meeting and clarify a few more points, zip this document off to my lawyer and then, I'm going to fix this Putnam mess. Promise. I need your confidentiality though, please. This has to be kept a secret, it's important," she said. She glanced at her watch. It was almost two in the afternoon. She was running out of time.

"Of course. You have my word as a worthy competitor," he said, picking up the pitcher and filling the water glasses. When he'd finished, he looked straight at her. "Do help Mr. Putnam. He's a great guy."

"I know," she said reaching for her cell phone. "Say, do you have his cell number?"

James

TYPICALLY, A JOG on the beach helped to relax him, but today as he sat on the top step of his family's porch, that had had red flyers stapled onto the exquisite wood railing, he felt just as tense as when he'd started the run.

He was lucky Blake was here. Usually he wanted to do everything on his own, but having Blake and Samantha helped him deal with the stress of his father's illness, withdrawing his bid and the anger of the locals, and made him realize how great his family was. He didn't feel so alone.

He believed Aubrey. He knew she might still resent that he hadn't remembered her. And he accepted that he had made it seem like he was as interested in the land as he was in her, but he didn't think she would deliberately try to damage his family's reputation or put a "fix" on them. No, that seemed far more like Dirk. James was just stunned that the locals had turned against his family so quickly after all his family had done for the island and the people calling it home. He was glad his mother and father didn't have to experience this.

He wished Aubrey had called him after her meeting. She had no reason to, he knew, still he missed her. She made him feel alive, not so serious or business focused. He had enjoyed their afternoon together. He'd loved talking with her, the way she teased him. She was funny, smart and beautiful.

"What are you doing out here?" Blake said, through the front screen door. "Somebody's going to drive by in a golf cart and take a photo of you looking like you're about to cry surrounded by a sea of red flyers. Tear those down and get inside."

James stood up. "I'm not about to cry, and you sound paranoid."

"You should be paranoid, dude, somebody, maybe more than one somebody, is out to get you," Blake said, holding the door open and James walked inside, heading for the kitchen, with Blake on his heels. Blake had a point, James thought. Earlier this morning, he'd called the president of the board, Reginald, telling him Putnam Industries did not get the land lease on Indigo Island.

"Have you broken the news to your dad?" Reginald had

asked.

"No sir," James had said. "He had surgery today, sir."

"I'm sorry to hear that, son," Reginald said. "Walter's still set on taking over as CEO, and he has support, many of us don't believe that such an important decision should hinge on one deal, even if it is in your home territory. Who did get it?"

"Not sure she's going to log at all," James said slowly. "She mentioned something about other options."

"I'll keep this news confidential for now. Maybe you can round up a project you can win the bid on in the meantime. Some good news from any South Carolina Sea Island would sure make most of the board vote tip your way."

"I understand, sir. Thank you," James had said, hanging up but still not sure if he'd hold onto his title, certain that if he had to do much more groveling, he wouldn't be able to hold onto his pride.

"We have to strategize about the rally. Did you call Dirk?" Blake asked, following James into the kitchen.

"Yep, no answer, coward," James said, filling a glass with water.

"I called the Save Southern Trees Society and was informed the person I needed to speak with would be here, on the ground she called it, by five thirty this evening, just in time for the rally," Blake said. "I had a lot of other plans for this weekend, I hope you know."

"You and Sam seem really close, is she the one?" James asked as he pulled the flyers off the porch. He paused then looked up as a sudden realization hit. "You were going to propose this weekend and then I showed up. That's it, right?" James watched his brother's cheeks turn pink in response. "God, I'm messing everything up. I'm sorry. After tonight's rally, I'll head back to Atlanta. You can have the house to yourselves for the rest of the weekend."

Blake smiled, and said, "Sam likes seeing you, and we're still having fun even if everyone on the island hates us and wants to put a 'fix' on us."

"Hey guys," Sam said, breezing into the kitchen and wrapping her arms around Blake. "What's up?"

"Things are great. Right now, the whole island hates me and so does the first woman I've been interested in for a long time. The board will probably make Walter CEO this week. My father's got cancer. What's new with you?" James spoke in a super cheerful voice that made Sam laugh despite the fact that he was serious, but not taking himself too seriously.

"Laugh or cry, I guess." Sam smiled.

"His life is pathetic, really," Blake said, squeezing Sam tight. "We're going on a walk to the point and then I'd suggest we all head to the Indigo Island General Store. Get there and find the Save Southern Trees Society representative and plead our case. Maybe we can even stop the rally?"

"Wishful thinking, little brother," James said. "You two lovebirds have fun. I'm taking a shower."

After his shower, James was dressed before he noticed a missed call. It was from an unknown Atlanta number, and he hoped it wasn't the hospital calling about his dad. There was no voicemail message and so he called the number back. He was about to hang up when the voicemail picked up: "You've reached Aubrey Templeton. Leave a message." James didn't know what to say, couldn't believe she'd called him. "Hey, it's James. Call me back."

He was standing in his bedroom, where he had imagined a very different scenario with Aubrey, not her sneaking away without explanation or goodbye and possibly setting up a public skewering of his family. Instead he'd pictured staring into her beautiful eyes as he slowly undressed her and…. James shook his head. He needed to stop daydreaming about impossible romances and start saving his family's reputation. As he hustled downstairs, Sam and Blake were waiting for him.

"I think these turned out great, you?" Blake said, handing him a flyer. "Printed on white recycled paper with recycled green ink. Take that, Dirk."

James laughed and read: "*The Putnam family is responsible for the largest private preserve of green space on Indigo Island. The family owns The Melrose Inn, Pete's Barn and Stables, The Putnam Plantation and is an active participant in preserving all of the beautiful parts of Indigo Island. When asked, we've always come to the support of this island and its residents. We consider ourselves your neighbors and friends. We don't know how these rumors started, but we will not be logging our land, nor will we log the Templeton Tract. Thank you.*"

"Straight to the point, right? I like it," Samantha said.

"You wrote it, that's why you like it, and I like how you carefully dodged the fact we were in the bidding process to log the Templeton land," Blake said, teasing.

"That's my marketing background at work," she said.

"It's perfect. Do we get to tack these and stick these and staple these everywhere to litter the island?" James said. "I'm kidding. Thanks you guys. I'm ready to handle Dirk and whoever else he's dug up."

"The three musketeers against the mob," Sam said as she turned toward the door, Blake following behind.

"No, please, you guys stay here. Enjoy your vacation. I'm the one who started this mess and I'm the one who needs to finish it. I insist," James said, looking at both of them, but then nodding to Blake. He'd decided. He needed to face this to get his mojo back. James had shoved the leather pouch they'd found on the golf cart in his pocket. He would try to discover its meaning, too.

"Good luck. Call me if you need me and I'll be there," Blake said, as the brothers gave each other a quick hug and James walked out the door.

Chapter Eight

Aubrey

Friday Evening

AUBREY HAD DRESSED carefully, dark jeans, a black turtleneck sweater, boots and her favorite black spring coat. She wanted her look to say understated elegance. She wanted her attire to help her apologize to the people of this special island. Especially the one person whose deeply hurt blue eyes she couldn't get out of her mind.

Earlier in the day, her attorney had eagerly signed off on Eco Resorts International's proposal and Mr. Davinci had returned to the conference room to find a beaming Aubrey ready to sign the letter of intent. Of course, there would be a land survey and all of the other formalities, but in principle, they had a deal.

"This is wonderful, Ms. Templeton. We will make you proud, and you'll never know we're there," Mr. Davinci had said.

"Unless I need an organic spa service," Aubrey had said. "I have one small request. When you source the sustainable lumber to build the resort, will you please purchase it from Putnam Industries. The Putnam family owns much of this island, and is a big supporter of the people and the land here. It would mean a lot to me."

"Despite these ludicrous red papers I've seen stuck everywhere, I'm well versed in Putnam Industries' leading sustainability certifications. We have considered utilizing their tree farm, certified renewable products to build many of our resorts. I would be happy to use their company here, and if it is a good fit, consider them for future projects," Mr. Davinci had said. "Consider it done. It would be a pleasure to work with them on this resort."

"Thank you!" Aubrey said. This was better than she'd anticipated. "Could you possibly join me, in a half an hour, at the rally and announce our partnership and the selection of Putnam Industries' lumber?" she had said.

Mr. Davinci had looked at his team. "Would you gentlemen be adverse to staying and taking the later ferry back? Give us a chance to dine at Marshside Mama's before we leave."

"Bless you," Aubrey had said. "Please try to be at the General Store by six. We have a lot of angry islanders to set straight."

"We'll be there," he had said, shaking her hand again. "We always strive to keep the peace with each community where we build and work."

And now, it was fifteen minutes until six, and she was ready. She could hear the chanting from the crowd gathered at the General Store as soon as she stepped outside of the inn. She hurried across a white-light-lit charming wooden bridge spanning a pond in order to reach the road where the General Store stood. The store was actually a small cottage much like her family's property, a charming focal point of the island on most days. The night air was thick with the smell of pine and ocean air and as she walked across the sandy ground she saw a young woman, standing on a tree stump, holding a yoga tree pose.

"I can feel this tree's former life, its energy is still here, it's still hurting," she said. The woman's eyes were closed and she faced the dark ocean, but Aubrey felt as if she was speaking to her.

She swallowed and kept walking, passing a hammock strung between two pine trees, a favorite daytime relaxation spot Aubrey knew as she'd watched vacationers lounging in it during breaks from her meetings. Tonight, the hammock was occupied by a young couple, holding hands. Aubrey smiled at them and the young man said, "We're taking a forest bath."

Well, then, she thought, appreciating their hippie vibes and still wondering where all these people had come from. She realized many of them had come over on the ferry, non-islanders here to save the trees. The number of people at the rally was shocking. There was a crowd six deep standing on the sandy ground in front of the store – at least fifty she guessed – and they were all looking toward the General Store's front porch, looking up facing a young man who stood on the porch behind a podium. He was lit with a spotlight from the back and his features were distorted by shadows. But his words weren't.

"The Putnams are the one percent. Together, we're stronger," he said, and the crowd repeated it. Aubrey felt the energy of the crowd, the anger in their faces, the outrage of betrayal. They had only heard one side of the story, she knew. Did the speaker know the truth? Who was he, Aubrey wondered.

And where was Dirk? She scanned the crowd, looking for his tight curly blonde hair, finally spotting him, on the porch to the left of the young man in the spotlight. Dirk had his arms crossed and a tight smile as he scanned the crowd.

"Save our trees, and the ecosystem of Indigo Island," the man, probably the representative from a Southern chapter of an ecological group called out, working to whip the crowd into an enthusiastic chant.

This could get out of hand, Aubrey thought with a stab of dismay.

"We can stop the one percenters like the Putnams and the Templetons," he said into the microphone.

As if, Aubrey rolled her eyes at the thought of her being a one percenter. And even if she were, they had no right to judge without all the facts.

"Hold on," she called out, trying to be heard over all the

restless talking and the man with the mic. "You don't even know what you're talking about."

A few people turned to look at her. The man with the mic kept talking, but Aubrey heard a few people mutter as she was recognized. "It's her. It's her," she heard as the buzz of recognition passed from person to person.

She felt nervous, but she took a deep breath. She belonged here too.

"You have your facts all wrong," she said. She began to try to move through the crowd so she could get to the makeshift stage and the mic. Some let her pass. Others seemed determined to block her way.

"Excuse me," she said several times. "I want to tell all of you what's really happening with my land."

She heard a few jeers, but rather than deter her, she just felt more empowered. Just as she was about to step up onto the porch of the General Store, she was elbowed hard in the stomach by a man in a dark brown coat. She couldn't tell if it had been deliberate or accidental, but the breath was knocked from her, and she doubled over.

"Aubrey." Strong hands caught her waist. "Are you hurt?"

James. She instantly felt safer, filled with warmth, but she couldn't answer.

"Here, let me help you," he said, and she could feel his lips at her temple. Instantly electricity jolted through her. "This is insane, follow me. Just let me get you out of this crowd."

"No," she finally gulped in a breath. "I want to explain. I have to."

James looked concerned, and very hesitant. She could tell he was thinking about just picking her up and getting her to safety. Unable to stop herself, she reached out and ran her thumb along his cheekbone. He was so beautiful. She loved the way he looked at her, as if she were precious, special. Why had she doubted him so long?

"Trust me," she said. "I got this."

He still looked worried, but he lifted her up to the porch but then stepped beside her almost like a bouncer.

"Oh, now it's a merger of a whole other kind," she heard Dirk sneer behind her.

She ignored him. James didn't, but she caught his hand and held firm. This crowd was hostile enough without adding an ancient family feud into the mix. She took the microphone trying to convey more ease and confidence than she felt.

"My name is Aubrey Templeton, and I belong here," she said. "I have deep roots here like many of you, like the Putnams."

She turned to James and their eyes caught. She felt a sense of warmth and happiness and belonging steal over her. Why had she felt so disconnected? Her home was here. Had always been here. He interlaced their fingers. His other hand rested on the small of her back. He smiled at her, and she smiled back. She felt supported, and she realized that he had been helping her, supporting her, all along, no matter what she chose to do with her land.

"My family has owned land here since before the Civil War. Unfortunately, even though I spent many vacations here, I never took the time to understand this special place until my parents both passed, and I came home to try to reconnect with my life and my roots. I had felt myself to be a city girl, but after spending time here again, I realize that my roots are here."

The crowd was quiet now. James gave her fingers a reassuring squeeze.

"Unfortunately due to finances and taxes and my parents' estate, I needed to do something with the land in order to be able to hold on to it for future generations."

She saw heads nod. They understood debt. They understood taxes. They understood family duty and loss.

"I did consider logging some timber on the land and hired Dirk Cooley, a professional forest management consultant, to design a plan for my land that was sustainable and as green as possible. Dirk calls himself a forestry consultant but he's not about conservation he's all about cash and connections. He almost talked me into signing a deal that would have seen my family's beautiful lands clear-cut by a Chinese company."

The crowd was silent as Aubrey continued. "I didn't sign the deal."

She heard a smattering of applause, but the crowd still looked confused. "Of course I asked Putnam Industries to bid as they are a local company with deep roots here."

Now people started to look down, around, away from her.

"James Putnam explained to me the plan Mr. Cooley had drawn would destroy the land. He offered to help me design a new plan. He even withdrew his bid so that we could come up with something that would be the best for the land, for the island and for me."

Out of the corner of her eye, she could see Dirk shift and look uncomfortable. The spokesman from the Save Southern Trees Society was looking from Dirk to Aubrey almost as if he were watching a tennis match.

"I had trusted Mr. Cooley to ensure the preservation of my land and the island, but he had a different agenda, one that involved a lot more money than I needed as well as evening a score."

She glared at Dirk, then turned back to the crowd. The representative from the Save Southern Trees Society now looked seriously perturbed. His gaze continued to shift nervously from Aubrey to Dirk.

"I do want to let you all know that The Templeton Tract is not going to be actively logged."

At first there was silence, and then cheers and clapping rang out.

"Will you sign a pledge to this effect? Both of you?" the representative from the Save Southern Trees Society asked.

"I have no intention of ever logging our land," James said facing the crowd with a poise and confidence Aubrey envied. "And I have spent the week actively trying to ensure that the Templeton tracts stays as pristine as possible."

But in his eyes, she could see the question.

"But I did need to pay off back taxes," Aubrey said, "And I finally have my answer. The Melrose Inn gave me the idea. The wonderful, historic inn that the Putnam family saved and now owns. Mr Davinci, could you join me up here?"

Aubrey nibbled her bottom lip as Mr. Davinci began to speak. She could see the curiosity in James' eyes. She hoped he would agree with her decision and see that in her own way she had been trying to support him as much as he had been trying to support her.

"Eco Resorts International is the leading developer of environmentally low-impact hotels in the world," Mr. Davinci said. "We will use only a fraction of the Templeton Tract and our construction impact will be minimal. Speaking of construction, we will only utilize certified tree-farmed lumber, with the highest rating and we will purchase it from the most eco-friendly lumber company in the nation, Putnam Industries."

Aubrey felt James startle next to her. She couldn't hide her grin as he mouthed 'Thank you.'

"No, thank you," she said. "For helping me understand the heritage here, my place in it and for pushing me to think things through."

Mr. Davinci wrapped up his short speech by thanking the crowd for their passion for the environment and told them that within a few months there would be renderings of the planned resort up on display at the general store.

As the crowd began to clear out, James gently turned Aubrey to face him. One hand lightly cupped her cheek.

"You made a wonderful decision for your land and for the island," he said softly. "A resort will create many full time jobs as well as bring more tourists to the island, which will help many people here."

She nodded, unable to look away.

"Walter and his team have been trying to make inroads with Eco Resorts as a supplier for years," he shook his head. "A bit ironic. I wish I'd had something to do with it, but I'm not going to complain."

"You had something to do with it," she said teasingly, and he laughed. The sound tickled down her spine. "I wasn't sure how you'd feel," she said a little nervously, not completely sure where they stood, but wanting it very much to be together. "I thought you might be angry. Still think I'd been leading you on."

He smiled. "That was business. This," he said, lightly tracing her cheekbone with his thumb. "This is pleasure."

He bent forward, pressing his lips against hers in a slow, passionate kiss and she felt herself responding, melting into him and softening her lips under the pressure of his. She sighed against his mouth.

"Um, sorry to interrupt," a hesitant voice spoke up behind them. "And well, sorry about all of this," the Save Southern Trees Society organizer said. "This has never happened before, getting such wrong information. This is not how we operate. I'm Josh, a regional organizer, and this never happens. I apologize."

"I appreciate what you do for the planet." Aubrey tried to settle her breathing. It was shocking what James could do to her body with just one small very public and very interrupted kiss.

"But you should get your facts straight," James said, his hand now on Aubrey's waist.

Josh nodded, his face serious. "I usually do. This just came at us so fast. I didn't have time to do all the usual research. I had the impression there was already a strong movement here with the flyers and the rally time and place set. I just grabbed the first flight I could get and hopped on the ferry."

"Dirk Cooley," Aubrey said.

James looked around, wondering where he'd gone.

"Probably ran away, planning his next childish, feudal, destroy the Putnams scheme," he said, but his voice lacked its usual force because Aubrey stood on tip toes and pressed a series of kisses along his jaw.

"We'll see him coming next time," Aubrey said.

"I don't want to see him at all." James voice ended in a groan as she pressed her body against his and let her fingers tangled in his hair.

"Can we get out of here?"

"Definitely." She kissed him. "So, happy now?" she said.

"Almost," he said. "You are all I've thought about since our picnic. Why did you sneak away? Was that revenge for me not remembering our first time?"

Aubrey was shocked. He thought she'd used that afternoon to get revenge for a year ago, because he didn't remember her? "You think I'm that kind of person?" She stepped away from him. "Really?"

She shook her head, hurt seeping in when she didn't want it to. Whatever this thing was between them, just never seemed to be right.

"Aubrey, wait, please." James took a quick, involuntary step forward. "I don't want to lose you again. Talk to me. Explain. Don't run away."

His male scent made her feel dizzy, but his words hit home. She had been running away long before she'd met him. Running from her roots, from her grief, from intimacy. If she wanted to build a life worth living, she had to stop running. She had to make a stand.

"We don't know each other very well, James," she said softly. "But I'd like to."

Her pulse raced as he stared into her eyes and then dropped his gaze to her lips, and then back to her eyes. "I want that too. I need you in my life. I've never felt that before, but I know it's true." As chills spread through her body he slid his hand up her arm and to the nape of her neck, pulling her forward, gently brushing his lips against hers.

Her body came alive remembering him, now and a year ago, how perfect they were together, how wonderful it could be. How it felt so right when he was by her side, holding her hand. She wrapped her arms around his waist, pressing into the kiss with an urgency that surprised her. Her lips parted with a moan as she welcomed his warm kiss, her knees went weak with longing and the release of tension she'd been holding since she'd last seen him, feelings she'd been keeping inside for a year.

James broke the kiss, cupping her face in his hands, and said, "Don't ever sneak away from me again."

"I won't. I'll sign a pledge," she said, her head dizzy with desire and happiness. "Now let's go," she said. She wanted to be alone with him.

James

THEY WALKED HAND in hand towards the inn. He felt happy and calm in a way he'd never felt before. He'd always been driven. Driven to be the best, the smartest, the richest. Everything had been a competition, even women. He knew his title as CEO was still a question mark. The deal with Eco Resorts was good. It could be great if it led to a long lasting business relationship, but even that wasn't bothering him the way it would have in the past. He'd always worn his stress like a straight jacket and his year of recovery, rebuilding his life and now Aubrey allowed him to experience life differently.

It was weird to desire her so much, but also to just enjoy walking, holding her hand, seeing the way she kept looking up at the star-dotted sky with such awe. Always before he'd been focused on getting women undressed and in bed. Now he wanted it all with Aubrey. He could imagine how Blake would laugh at him, but maybe not. He'd certainly changed with Samantha.

"Oh," he said.

"What?"

He switched directions back towards the inn.

"Maybe we should grab a snack here first," he said. "I think I've interrupted my brother's plans enough."

"What kind of plans?"

They walked up the stairs of the inn together.

"I think he was trying to propose to Samantha this weekend, and the flyers and the crazy island "Fix" thing threw him off his game. They were going to come here with me tonight, and I told them to stay home. Hopefully he gets it done quickly so when we get there we won't interrupt anything. You think I'm Type A. Blake has me beat by a mile. Sam's relaxed him a ton, but still I don't want to walk in with him on bended knee, although it would be funny years from now after the bruises and broken bones had healed."

"Get it done quickly?" Aubrey said.

"And romantically," James said. "I'm hungry. You?"

"Hungry." She said the word slowly as if tasting it, and James felt his body harden. "Snack it is," she said and stopped and leaned against a pillar on the inn's porch. "Mr. Putnam, is that a code for you propositioning me?"

"Definitely," he said, smiling. "Will it work?"

"Definitely," she said.

He liked that she teased him, didn't take him so seriously. It helped him get a better balance.

"Hey guys." Jack emerged from the front door of the inn. "James, great job out there. You too, Ms. Templeton. You both really turned things around."

"It was all Aubrey." James rubbed his knuckles along her cheekbones, and she smiled up at him.

"I guess the Templeton Tract is good for more than island development." James watched as Aubrey blushed. He wanted to make her blush some more, find out how much of her skin he could make flush with arousal.

"I'd better get back inside," Jack said. "That rally was great for business. Lots of the folks headed into the bar. Oh, before I forget. Barbara wanted me to tell you that you don't have to carry the leather pouch anymore. Do you know what she's talking about?

James looked at Jack. Barbara was the oldest island resident, a Gullah descendant, and a close friend of Jack's.

"This? I found it on our golf cart. It's a curse," James said, holding the pouch in his hand.

"No, it's not. It was from Barbara. It was 'protection' from the 'fix,' and she said you really needed it," Jack said as James and Aubrey looked at each other.

"She was right," James said slowly. "It worked. I'd like to thank her." James was relieved the pouch was a symbol of friendship, not of hate.

"Her son drove her home. You'll have to catch up with her later."

"That should be easy as we have a lot of the island to explore," he said looking deep into Aubrey's eyes. "I want to have another picnic with you," he whispered.

"Is that another code?"

"Yes and no."

"Good night, you," Jack said. "Keep it PG on the porch. I have an inn to manage with a family reputation on the line."

"Gotcha. Actually we are coming in for a bite to eat."

"Code again?" Aubrey whispered in his ear, and he felt his whole body tighten in anticipation.

"You have a dirty mind," he whispered back, licking his tongue along her ear and enjoying her shiver. "I love it."

Chapter Nine

Aubrey

Friday Night

THEY'D CAUGHT A shuttle back to James' house. She'd considered bringing him to her room at the inn, but James had wanted privacy and time with her. She couldn't argue with that, especially the way he had looked at her and whispered that he wanted to "savor her and spend all night watching her come." She hadn't been able to eat after that. She had sipped her wine and toyed with her food while he had water, wishing they were far, far away from the inn's dining room and the people who continued to interrupt their dinner to share a memory of her parents or to congratulate her on choosing to build the eco resort instead of logging her land. She appreciated the feeling of community, but she fairly bounced in her seat with impatience.

James seemed calm, but when he'd brought her bare foot up to his lap to massage her, she'd felt the evidence of his desire.

"How can you eat?" she had demanded.

"I'm hungry. Ready to go?"

"Hours ago," she'd said, and he'd called for the check.

She felt like a teenager sneaking into his house in the dark with a spare key. They saw remnants of a meal of roast chicken and a variety of vegetable dishes. The air was fragrant with spices, and a fire burned low in the grate in the library.

"Hope she said yes," James said. Then he picked her up and

pressed her against the refrigerator, wrapping her legs around his waist. "Now, we can focus on us," he said. His voice had turned husky. She felt her breath catch in her throat and her heart began to beat faster. "I have so many things I want to do with you," he said, pressing his palm in the small of her back, molding their bodies together in a perfect fit, even with clothes on.

"James," she said as goose bumps dotted her skin as he gently pushed the hair back from her face. He slid his finger inside the top of her white button-down shirt, feathering his fingers over her sensitive neck, then slipping them behind her head and pulling her forward, brushing his lips against hers.

Her lips parted, wanting more, all of him and he pressed deeper, a hot sexy kiss that sent waves of longing through her body as she wrapped her arms around him and pulled her against him more tightly. She loved the way she could feel his body so tight against hers. He pressed his knee up between her thighs, his hands on either side of her face locking her in place. She pushed herself into his knee, rubbing against him, needing him, hearing a low moan escape from somewhere inside her.

Suddenly he released the kiss and yanked her shirt up exposing her bra. When he sucked her nipple through the bra, she thought she'd explode, her brain an empty pool of pleasure. Reaching down, she found his belt buckle, letting her fingers glide along the top of his pants, finding fabric and untucking his shirt.

"As good as I remember. I want you, now," she said and heard him moan as he pressed his lips to hers.

James

WE'VE GOT TO get upstairs, his brain said while his body said, let's just do it right here in the kitchen. *Now.* Her hands were in his hair, accentuating the motion of their tongues, a tangle of senses, as he reached behind her and unfastened her bra, pushing it roughly up and out of the way so each hand could fondle her breasts. But something inside, deep and infuriatingly responsible inside him, told him making love on the floor of the kitchen when his brother and presumed fiancée could walk in at any minute could lead to embarrassment for Aubrey. He didn't want her to be uncomfortable with anyone from his family.

With a huge effort, he pulled away from their kiss and brought a finger to her moist and swollen lips.

"What's wrong?" she said, her words coming out staccato with her labored breath.

"Not here, not like this," he said and pulled her shirt down, tucked her hand in his and touched her cheek with his other hand. "Tonight needs to be the start of something special, not another embarrassment or misunderstanding. I want us to take our time. We've got all night."

She nodded and smiled her agreement as he led them out of the kitchen, through the empty foyer – thank God – up the stairs and into his room, closing and locking the door behind them.

Aubrey

SHE HEARD JAMES lock the door and then felt him come up behind her as she stood at the window. The heat between them was so intense, just as it had been a year ago. It was like nothing else she'd ever experienced, before or since. He turned her around gently, pulling her into him, molding her into his body, his large erection pressing into her stomach. She wanted to feel all of him, all over her.

"You're beautiful, Aubrey," he said, spearing her hair through his fingers, tilting her head up so all she could focus on were his eyes flashing dark blue. "How do you want this, how did we do this before? I want it to be the same, but even better."

She'd dreamed of their time together in Atlanta, rough, fast, intense and unlike anything she'd experienced before, but she had no idea how to explain that to him. "Just be you," she said. She heard him exhale as suddenly he released her hair and grabbed the top of her white blouse in both hands, yanking her top open, buttons flying across the room, skittering across the floor, before he whisked off her shirt. Her skin, glorious creamy skin was covered in goose bumps, her nipples erect, pressing against the fabric of her bra.

He dropped to his knees, his hands on her hips. Heat coursed through her as he kissed her stomach before unbuttoning her pants, yanking the zipper down and pulling them down her legs, taking her shoes and socks off in the process.

In a matter of moments, she was standing in James' bedroom, naked except her bra and underwear, and she'd never been so turned on in her life. He still knelt in front of her and she grabbed his thick blonde hair in her hand. His tongue licked her belly button and then the edge of her bikini line. She felt herself sway, but his strong hands on her hips held her tight.

"Are you getting wet?" he asked, more of a demand than a question and she felt liquid flood her panties.

"Yes, oh, please, yes," she said. Her brain was gone, fogged out by extreme sensory input. All she could hear and feel was where his hands touched her, what his voice demanded.

"Please, what, Aubrey?" he said, and she felt his hands grab her butt, his mouth biting the edge of her underwear until she felt him pulling them down, and off. "I want to taste you."

A shiver ran through her body as her stomach tensed. She heard herself moan as James stood up and grabbed her arms, walking her backwards until she was pinned against the wall. He pressed her lips with his, his tongue plunging inside her as he released her arms, moving his attention to her breasts, releasing her bra and finally, moving his attention to her nipples, which he laved with his tongue. Aubrey writhed against the wall, desperate for him to undress, to take her to bed.

"Open your eyes, Aubrey," he commanded, "look at me. I want to watch you come, in the mirror. I want to always remember this as the real first time. Eyes wide open."

He walked her to the full-length mirror leaning against the corner walls of the room. She leaned against him, her breath labored. She wanted to feel his skin on her back, all of him against her.

"I need to undress you," she said, turning and grabbing the sides of his button down just as he had done. She tugged, but couldn't pop the buttons.

He tore off his shirt for her, as they both unbuckled his belt and his pants dropped to the ground. She reached for his boxers, but he grabbed her hand. "Not yet," he said, spinning her around again so her back was to him.

She looked in the mirror, obeying his command and gasped. His eyes, his perfect chest, his magical hands, his lips – she took him all in, and then they locked eyes in the mirror as his hands tweaked her nipples and then moved lower, down her stomach, circling around her lower stomach, driving her mad with sensation.

"Please, touch me," she begged, and as she watched, he delved a finger inside her wet, swollen folds. Her body exploded with sensation as she arched her back, shuddering.

"Open your eyes," he said, "I want you to watch. I want us to remember every minute." He bit her neck while continuing to tease her clit until she wanted him to take her over the edge, rocking her hips against him. But he had her under his control, backing off when he sensed she was about to come.

Everything was a blur, she was in a trance of sexual desire; even the mirror image had grown blurry when he stopped and scooped her up, carrying her over to the impossible fluffy white bed. He dropped her and she felt like she'd landed on a cloud. James was with her, on top of her, moving down her body. He spread her open, his hands pinning her thighs, and she thought she might scream.

"Are you with me, Aubrey?" he teased. "I'm going to fuck you with my tongue." She felt his tongue press inside her, and she gripped his head with her hands, trying to hang on, while he made her feel things she'd never felt before. She started rocking her hips against his face and heard him moan, even as she heard herself scream. She was arching, moving faster, his hands holding her buttocks in the air as she pressed harder until he pushed his finger inside her, hitting the spot deep inside her that caused a convulsion so deep, an orgasm so intense, stars flooded the room and she forgot everything except this moment, this place.

She felt him lying next to her, stroking the hair from her face as she shuddered, her legs quaking and her center gripped in convulsions.

"How did it measure up?" James asked finally, pulling her close, watching her as the orgasm aftermath washed over her. She could feel his strong arms holding her tight, and she could feel his erection pressing into her hip.

"Oh, it will do," she said, weakly lifting her head for a kiss.

"You taste good, Aubrey," he said, sending another shudder through her.

"That was amazing, really, I think though we have something else to address," she said, reaching for his erection, grabbing it in her hand as she heard him suck in a swift breath. She stroked him as he began moving against her hand. "Condom?"

"Drawer, next to my bed," he murmured as she released his shaft and scooted over to the bedside table, opening the top drawer and discovering a virtual array of condom choices.

"Really?"

"My mom stocks all the bedrooms. Pick one, hurry," he said, as Aubrey tipped her imaginary hat to his mom. They were all meant for enhancing her pleasure, or so they read. She didn't think James needed any help where that was concerned. She rolled the condom on him, as he watched with approving darkened blue eyes.

"Now what?" she teased.

"This," he said, as he kissed her roughly and then, grabbed her butt, pulled her down the bed toward him as he sank into her. Slowly, at first, giving her time to adjust to his size, her still sensitive nerve endings on high alert made her stomach clench as her breasts surged tilting her head back on the bed. He gently placed each of her ankles on his shoulders, wrapping her legs around his neck as he began thrusting, grabbing her nipples and pinching, as he pushed deep inside.

"You feel great," he said, slowing his moves but somehow going deeper inside her, pressing on her stomach until she felt herself about to come. She dug her nails into his side, unable to stop the soft pants that escaped her lips. So close, she bucked against him as he slammed into her once more, and then it came, the tidal wave from deep inside her, as she heard herself moan. But it wasn't over, with each thrust James' cock extended the pleasure, filling her.

And he was still watching her, urging her to lock eyes with him, to be one.

"I want to make you scream, Aubrey, come all over me," he said, as she did, crying out while white light, unbelievable sparks shot through her body, shattering her in bliss. Aubrey wanted to make him come, too, and she slid her hand down, reaching for where they were joined together, encouraging him on until he surged into her once more and his low groan of pleasure filled the room as he came hard and fast. Their bodies were still joined as he fell on top of her, pressing his lips to hers in a sweet kiss before rolling off and lying beside her.

"That was unforgettable," he said, pulling her close to him.

Yes, that was exactly what she had remembered, maybe even better, she thought, as another wave of aftershocks spread through her body.

Chapter Ten

Aubrey

Saturday

AUBREY WOKE UP with her head resting on James' shoulder, her arm draped across his broad, bare chest. She didn't even know what time it was, but it had to be late morning as the sun was high in the sky, pouring through the windows. They'd forgotten to close the shades, of course. She couldn't believe James had the presence of mind to move them upstairs to the privacy of his room. If it had been up to her, she would've been naked in the kitchen and probably, busted by his brother.

Instead she'd enjoyed a night with passionate lovemaking, mind-blowing orgasms – at least four, she'd lost count – with a man who made her laugh, defended her honor, made sure she was comfortable and was amazing in bed. If he woke up and didn't remember their night together, she'd never survive it. Not again.

She felt James stir beneath her, his arm wrapped around her waist.

"Hey," he said, kissing her on the forehead.

"Do you know who I am?" she said, teasing, of course. But still.

"Aubrey, don't be silly. I'm a new man. A man who could never forget you," he said. "What time is it?"

She rolled to her side and looked at the bedside clock.

"Wow, it's ten thirty."

"My board conference call is now," he said, bolting out of bed.

"Call in, from here, I'll go take a shower," she said, handing him his phone. She was amazed he'd remembered to plug it in. Hers was dead.

She watched as he sat back down on the bed and dialed into the meeting. He looked over his shoulder and winked. She decided to stay in bed and cheer him on. He didn't seem to mind.

"Yes, I'm here, sorry I'm a bit late," he said.

Aubrey wasn't sure if it was okay for her to listen in, but he didn't shoo her away, so she plumped the pillow behind her and got comfortable for the show. And it was a show. James was still naked, and he looked sexy as hell as he stood up from the bed and began to prowl the room, clearly listening.

Aubrey imagined a bunch of men all talking at almost the same time, all jockeying for position in the company. James stopped pacing the room then, and locked eyes with her. She could feel her body go liquid with arousal, but she didn't want to distract him, but wow, she could so get used to waking up beside him every morning. Hopefully not with him making a serious business call most of the time.

"Dad, fabulous to hear your voice," he said. Aubrey's heart filled with joy for him. His dad was stronger.

"Yes, we did lose that bid, but so did everyone else. The landowner decided to move in a different direction. She's leasing part of her acreage to Eco Resorts so there is no lumber lease. Since I was on the island, I was able to meet with the CEO of Eco Resorts the night of the announcement and make a pitch to supply the lumber for that project, which was accepted, and I am this morning in the process of drawing up a proposal to work with them on other US based projects and am hoping to get a shot on bidding for the international projects as well. We haven't been able to get our foot in their door, so last night was a welcome opportunity. We have a meeting scheduled for next week." James spoke calmly, easily, as if the news weren't a complete slap in the face to his rival, Walter.

James was quiet for a bit. Then he said, "Thank you." Still more listening. Aubrey felt as if she were on pins and needles. He continued to watch her as he listened on the phone, motioning for her to lower the comforter so that he could see her body. Aubrey blushed, but did so. James' eyes darkened. Aubrey felt moisture between her thighs and her nipples peaked. She had a vision of her taking him into her mouth while he spoke, but was worried about distracting him on such an important call.

"Thank you, Dad. Board members. Yes, I will provide you with the proposal. I'll be working the weekend to get that together. Of course. Have a great weekend."

James ended the call and sauntered back to the bed. She loved when he had his swagger on.

"Well, that was only stretching the truth some." He pressed a kiss to her at the juncture between her thighs. "I won't be working all weekend," he drawled, but Aubrey parted her thighs so that he could press against her.

"Congratulations, Mr. CEO," she said and pulled him on top of her. "Things are looking, and feeling up again."

"Yes, they certainly are," he said as he rocked against her.

"James," she whispered ready for him all over again.

"James, are you in there?" Sam said from the other side of the door. "Are you up?"

"Definitely up," he whispered against Aubrey's lips.

"Are you on the phone? I need to show you something."

He kissed Aubrey's lips, and said, "Hey Sam, give me ten minutes and I'll be down. I need coffee stat."

"Five minutes. Hurry. It's so exciting," she said through the door.

"Okay, five minutes," he said. Aubrey waved her arms, trying to get his attention. She pointed to herself and then the door. He had to tell Sam she was here. "Oh and Aubrey will be down with me."

"Oh, okay. Hi, Aubrey. Don't sneak out this time. I need to show you something, too," Sam said.

"Five minutes is not enough time," James grumbled.

Aubrey laughed and looked around for her clothes.

"Forget five minutes," he pulled Aubrey back to him. "It's not like we don't know what her surprise is."

She kissed him and then wiggled away. "Be nice. She's going to be your new sister-in-law. They are excited, and I know that you want to be a good brother and make them happy."

"I do. After I make you happy."

"You can make me happy afterwards in the shower."

"Deal." But he still stood there naked and watched her get dressed. Aubrey found herself clumsy with the scrutiny, and he had to help her find buttons still attached to her shirt since many of the buttons were now missing, which made him laugh.

"This is silly. I'm doing the opposite of what I want to."

Aubrey went into the bathroom to scrub her face and brush her teeth with her finger and some toothpaste.

"Act surprised," she said.

"Got it," he said.

Sam was waiting at the bottom of the stairs, her left arm extended like a British monarch waiting for her subjects. Aubrey smiled and James rushed down the stairs, grabbed her in a bear hug and said, "Welcome to the family, Sam."

"It's beautiful," Aubrey said grabbing Sam's hand and taking a closer look at the sparkling diamonds. "So unique. Just wonderful."

"If you guys want coffee, come and get it," Blake said from the kitchen. Aubrey dreaded facing him, knowing he blamed her for all of James' problems. She followed James into the room a little reluctantly, but James caught her hand, and pulled her to his side.

"Congrats man," James said to Blake, grabbing him in a hug. "Did you already tell Mom and Dad?"

"I told them a month ago, before Dad's diagnosis. They are so excited."

"Yes, so happy for you both," she said brightly, hoping he didn't say anything caustic.

"Coffee?" Blake said, holding up a steaming white mug.

"Yes," she said, crossing the room and taking the mug as he handed it to her. "Thanks."

"Eco Resorts," he said slowly. "Interesting choice after nearly deforesting a large part of the island," Blake said conversationally.

James bristled beside her, but Aubrey laid her hand on his arm.

"A woman's allowed to change her mind," Aubrey said. "Once she sees all her options. And learns she's been tricked."

"Don't count on me changing mine," Samantha said coming up to Blake, handing James a cup of coffee and wrapping her arms around her fiancé.

"You remind me a bit of Sam," Blake said, smiling at Aubrey. "Spunk and solid roots. I didn't think I would like you, but I do."

"Thanks, Blake, that means a lot, almost as much as this one liking me," Aubrey said as James came up behind her and gave her a squeeze. "My mom always said the two most important things you can give your kids are roots and wings. Indigo Island is a part of it, for all of us. We're blessed with shared roots."

"Do you guys want to go horseback riding with us today?" Sam asked.

"That'd be great," James said, "Aubrey rode a horse for the first time the other day."

"Can we ride my property? I'd love to show it to you all. Maybe we could ride to the cottage," Aubrey said, directing the cottage question to James.

"If Pete has the horses available, I say that's the perfect plan,"
Blake said. "Meet downstairs in thirty minutes."

Aubrey decided, at James' urging, that for this weekend at
least, she'd be an honorary Putnam and take advantage of Avery's
fully stocked closet. James assured her that Avery wouldn't mind
at all. Aubrey hoped she'd meet Avery soon. It was amazing to be
thinking about the future without fear. She was digging herself
out of the mountain of debt her parents' death had left her in.
She was managing to hang on to her legacy on Indigo Island, and
she had fallen deeply in love and was feeling loved back. She
almost wanted to pinch herself.

As she dressed, her mind thought about the future, about
what it would feel like to escape from the mountain of debt and
to actually have some extra cash. Her attorney had told her that
Mr. Davinci's offer had been more than generous, and now, if
she wanted to, she could give up her day job. She wondered if it
was time, if she had the guts to actually quit her job and try her
hand at writing a novel. Sure, she'd finish the cover story piece
she'd promised her editor, but maybe, just maybe it was time to
spread her wings, challenge herself to step into the future she'd
always imagined, even if she never imagined not having her
parents cheering her on.

She pushed away the tears as she looked at herself in the mirror, admiring the perfect fit of the borrowed riding pants. Her
parents would be so happy that she was trying horseback riding,
that she was exploring the island they loved. And she was getting
excited to show James her Indigo Island home, a place an eighth
of the size of his plantation, but equally full of love. She'd need
him by her side to have the courage to walk inside, though, now
that her parents were gone. She couldn't imagine anyone else in
the world she'd rather take that step across the threshold with.
Just thinking about him, her heart gave an extra quick beat. She
wasn't sure she believed in love at first sight, but she was glad
she'd forced a reunion between the two of them, even with all the

hurdles they'd had to overcome on the business side. Their relationship would be worth it, she just knew it.

"You look beautiful," James said as she walked down the stairs wearing Avery's riding pants and fitted top. When she reached the bottom step he pulled her into him, their bodies pressed against each other, sending her into a frenzy of desire.

"Better not get something started you can't finish right now, cowboy," she said, kissing his cheek and pulling away. "We need to go see my cottage. It's an important step for me. She looked into his eyes and knew he understood.

"I'm honored to be taking you there," James said as they walked out the front door, into the sunshine.

Mr. Pete had agreed to bring the four horses over to them. "Least he could do for his ignorance," he'd said. The old man was talking to Blake and Sam as they joined them under the pine trees.

"James, I'm sorry I doubted you," Pete said, shaking James' hand. Aubrey felt sorry for the man. Everyone on the island had believed Dirk's side of the story, especially once the Save Southern Trees Society had fallen for it. And the fact was, she had almost allowed Dirk's scenario to come true, at least on her land.

"I'm Aubrey, sort of the cause of all the confusion," she said, shaking the man's hand.

"Glad it's all fixed," Mr. Pete said. Aubrey saw Blake and James lock eyes over his use of the word "fix". She wasn't a believer in all the voodoo island stuff, but they seemed to be, or at least to know all about it. Probably good to understand it, and appreciate it, she thought, adding it to her mental to-do list of things to learn about Indigo Island. She knew she was almost ready to finish her family's story. She'd been working on it, mulling it over in her head for months. Now that her prayers had been answered, on so many fronts, she could allow herself to be creative again, she thought. But first, it was time to enjoy the island and, hopefully, spend quality time with James.

"Ready?" James said, holding the reins of her horse. They were letting her ride Sunshine again, she noted with a smile, walking up and patting the white diamond between his eyes.

"Absolutely," she said, slipping her foot into the stirrup as James helped her into the saddle. She could pinch herself. This was happiness she could never have imagined just a few days ago.

James

THE TWO OF them sat side-by-side on the edge of the stream, breathing in the fresh smell of pine, sheltered by magnificent live oaks draped in Spanish moss. The horses drank deeply – they'd ridden for hours through the Templeton lands. It was almost time for lunch at Marshside Mama's, but before they joined Sam and Blake there for what would be, James knew, the start of a year of engagement celebrations, he promised Aubrey he'd visit her parents' house with her. It would be the first time she'd been there since they died.

He could tell she was on edge, knees drawn up to her chest. Even though his arm was wrapped around her shoulders, she felt far away.

"You ready?" he said. The cottage was behind them, a traditional Low Country clapboard with "haint" blue shutters and door. The light blue was another Gullah tradition, a color of protection although most non-Gullah chose the color because they liked it. James wondered whether Aubrey's parents knew the island's traditions and presumed they did, even though their daughter seemed less than in tune. He'd change that, he thought, squeezing her tight.

"This really is a beautiful place. It would make a great writer's studio, don't you think?" he said, hoping to paint positive possibilities in her mind before they confronted the memories.

"That would be fabulous, actually. A writer's studio. A place just for me, where I could come and create, maybe even start a novel," she said, releasing her knees from her arms and seeming to relax a little bit. "I mean I wouldn't need the whole place, just maybe the side room, off of the kitchen. My mom used to paint there because the light is so good."

"I bet good light is important for writers, too," he said, kissing her on the cheek. "Ready?"

"Okay, let's do this," she said, accepting his help to stand up. They left the horses by the stream, happily grazing on grasses and climbed the small hill to the cottage. "I love this magnolia tree. I could never imagine cutting it down. That was never part of the lease, I can't believe any of this was."

"She's a beauty, probably at least ninety years old," James said as they walked under the tree to the front porch steps, ignoring the regret in her words, knowing she fully understood that she'd been conned by Dirk. "Do y'all have a caretaker for the property? It looks great."

"We do, a husband and wife who have been caring for the house since I was a baby," she said, pulling aside the doormat and retrieving a key. "Thank goodness I can pay them what they're owed now. I've only paid them half of what they deserved, with all the bills mounting up. But now, everything is settled," she said, hugging herself. "I'm not sure why we even lock the door."

James saw her hand shaking as she tried to insert the key and his heart went out to her, for all she'd lost. His father was recovering. She'd lost both parents in an instant.

"Take a deep breath, honey, I'm here," he said touching her shoulder to help steady her, and watching as she finally was able to insert the key, and turn the knob. He followed her inside. The cottage was warm and bright, opening to a family room with wood floors painted white with minimal furnishings and an open kitchen with a brick fireplace connecting the two rooms.

"This is me," she said, picking up a framed photo of a chubby-cheeked toddler standing on the beach, wearing only a diaper, holding a bright orange shovel.

"You were adorable then, beautiful now," he said, as she replaced the photo and handed him another one. This one showed a teenaged Aubrey, a full mouth of braces, sandwiched between her parents sitting on the front steps of this cottage. He placed the frame back down on the table and turned to see her in front of the fireplace, looking at even more family photos.

"We did have great times here. This is my home, too. My mom always told me when I needed it, I'd feel my roots here. And I do," she said. Tears were rolling down her cheeks and all James could think to do was give her a kiss. He cupped her cheeks in his hands, wiping the tears away, and kissed her lips tenderly until she pulled back. "Thank you, for coming with me. I wouldn't have been able to walk inside without you."

She wrapped her arms around his waist, and pressed her head against his chest, her long dark hair falling down her back in soft waves, the smell of flowers and grass and sunshine. It felt so right. "Thank you for finding me, and for giving me a second chance," he said. "I didn't know what I'd forgotten, what I could have lost by never knowing you."

He knew he would stand here, in this cottage, hugging this woman for as long as she needed him. Time had stopped and this was where he needed to be. This was what love felt like, he realized.

"Aubrey, you asked before, what's next for us. I want to know the answer, too," he said, continuing the hug, surrounded by her past.

"I suppose the only way to find out is to stick together," she said, looking up into his eyes.

James had a feeling this woman, this new start, could mean the end of his loneliness forever. He'd come to the island this time certain he'd win a bid that in reality, he had never wanted.

Instead, in losing, he'd been given a bigger opportunity in business, and in life. A beautiful, amazing woman he'd forgotten had remembered him, had decided finding him, knowing him again, would end her year of mourning.

He hoped he could be the man she deserved. He had changed. He'd been given a second chance. And now, because of her, he felt the start of something big, the roots of a lifelong love.

The End

If you enjoyed the Indio Island series, you will love Kaira Rouda's other stories!

WOMEN'S FICTION
Here, Home, Hope
In the Mirror
A Mother's Day
The Goodbye Year

MYSTERY / SUSPENSE
All the Difference

CONTEMPORARY ROMANCE
The Laguna Beach Series
Laguna Nights
Laguna Heights
Laguna Lights

KINDLE WORLDS
The Remingtons: Spotlight on Love
Dare to Love Series: The Celebrity Dare

NONFICTION
Real You Incorporated: 8 Essentials for Women Entrepreneurs

Available now from your favorite online retailer!

About the Author

Kaira Rouda is a USA Today bestselling, multiple award-winning author of contemporary women's fiction and sexy modern romance novels that sparkle with humor and heart. Her work has won the Indie Excellence Award, USA Book Awards, the Reader's Choice Awards and honorable mention in the Writer's Digest International Book Awards. Her books have been widely reviewed and featured in leading magazines.

Kaira lives in Southern California with her husband and four almost-grown kids, and is at work on her next novel. Connect with her on Twitter, Facebook at Kaira Rouda Books and on her website, KairaRouda.com.

Thank you for reading

Indigo Island

If you enjoyed this book, you can find more from all our great authors at TulePublishing.com, or from your favorite online retailer.

TULE
PUBLISHING

Made in the USA
Charleston, SC
25 November 2015